I0740436

Helen M. Bowen

A Daughter of Cuba

Helen M. Bowen

A Daughter of Cuba

ISBN/EAN: 9783337380670

Printed in Europe, USA, Canada, Australia, Japan

Cover: Foto ©Andreas Hilbeck / pixelio.de

More available books at **www.hansebooks.com**

A Daughter of Cuba

By
Helen M. Bowen.

Chicago and New York:
Rand, McNally & Company,
Publishers.

Copyright, 1896, by the Merriam Company.
Copyright, 1898, by Helen M. Bowen.

To

THAT ONE,

WHOSE COMPANIONSHIP AND READY COMPREHENSION

MAKE BEAUTIFUL MY DAYS,

THIS BOOK

IS

TENDERLY INSCRIBED.

A DAUGHTER OF CUBA.

CHAPTER I.

LITHGOW HAMILTON was moving up Broadway after the fashion of a New Yorker intent on his own affairs, when he found himself wheeled about suddenly by a friendly arm.

"Why, hello, Bertram!" he exclaimed, stopping to exchange salutations.

"You are just the man I want to see," declared Mr. Bertram, with satisfaction. "Demmes tells me that you are going to Cuba."

"Yes," admitted Lithgow Hamilton, believing this to be but one of many congratulations which he had received from those who were forced to remain in the North during the winter which already enveloped the land. "Fortune favors me this year. Jersdan & Lester are sending me down to make better contracts with the coffee planters. Last year's product was below grade. By having a man in the island at this season they hope to secure larger consignments from those plantations that have a reputation for growing the finest qualities."

"You always were a lucky dog," commented Mr. Bertram, with pleasant envy.

Lithgow Hamilton lifted his brows skeptically.

"There might be two opinions about that," he returned; "but I must confess that this trip is exactly to my liking now. We touched at Cuba when I came up from Honduras, but the island is quite unfamiliar. I suppose it was my ability to speak the Spanish language that secured me this opportunity."

"Shall you go into the interior?"

"Certainly; that I shall be forced to do. Not an enviable

task, if what I hear is true. It is declared, however, that travelling in Cuba has this advantage over journeyings in other countries, that one always can catch on the morrow the train which should have gone yesterday."

Mr. Bertram viewed through his pince-nez the stalwart figure in front of him, with its brown hair growing far back on the temples, the alert gray eyes, between the brows of which was a thoughtful line, the mouth not so hidden by its dark mustache as to conceal the fact that its under lip had a habit of being bitten in by the strong upper teeth.

"Ha, ha!" Mr. Bertram laughed amusedly, while he mentally was taking notes as if to convince himself that he had decided on the right man. "Surely there is nothing to complain about in that. Have you any objections to undertaking a little business for me down there—on the side?"

"Legitimate process?" queried Lithgow, smiling.

"Did you ever know me to deal in any other?" demanded Mr. Bertram, drawing a cigar-case from his pocket and offering its contents to Lithgow.

"Well! You are a lawyer," explained Lithgow banteringly. "What is the scheme?"

"It's no scheme; it's a search," corrected Bertram.

"For what?"

"An estate in England is going begging for a master. The heir is believed to be in Cuba."

"Ah, and you wish me to poke about seeking him," Lithgow nodded as he lighted his cigar. "Do you know the island? Every one who goes there is placed under surveillance, especially if he be an American. They suspect you of everything until you can prove how innocent are your intentions; they even have a fashion of not waiting long for explanations, I believe. They clap you into jail; sometimes the only explanation that they deem necessary is a rifle—with you at the small end of it!"

"Yes, yes," assented the lawyer, hastily. "I know all that. That is exactly why I thought, when I heard at the club of your intended departure, that perhaps *you* could do what others who had gone there for the same purpose have found impossible. Your business will be known. You will be hampered by espionage but little. If, in moving through the interior, you should find opportunities for gaining information which would escape other people, it certainly is no affair of Spain."

Lithgow appeared rather doubtful.

"Let me know what I have to do, first," he suggested. "What is the story?"

"It is rather long. Have you the time to listen now? If so, come up to the office."

Lithgow glanced at his watch.

"I can spare twenty minutes," he agreed. "After I hear the kind of work involved I can tell you whether I will attempt it. I should not like to make a failure of it; and of course I would. I never was cut out for a detective."

"There is no reason why you should hesitate," Bertram urged, as they walked in the direction of his office. "All that you really can do is to bear in mind the history which I will recount to you. If anything that might appear to have any connection with it should happen in your way, I would wish you to follow the clue, leaving no stone unturned. We have a detective down there now; he pursues one will-o'-the-wisp after another, but achieves no satisfactory results. Searchers have been sent from England, but nothing has been accomplished. The matter of scouring the States was placed with our firm, thinking that the child might have been brought here. We are convinced, however, that he never left the island. Securing him means a neat sum for us, I can assure you."

Passing through the outer office, he ushered Lithgow into his private room and closed the door. From his desk he drew forth a bundle of documents and a small box, which, when opened, revealed a very peculiar ornament. This he handed to Lithgow for inspection. It was a ring, clumsy in design, half-barbaric. It bore a stone of a rich purple hue.

"This is only a copy of the original," the lawyer explained. "It was intrusted to us by the English solicitors. The original is supposed to be in the possession of—but I must tell you the story:

"About thirty years ago, an English planter stationed in Cuba came into unexpected possession, he being a fourth son, of an estate and title in his mother-country. Immediately, he prepared to sail with his wife and infant. For some reason, there appears to have been hatred or jealousy on the

plantation sufficient to cause one of the black women to ex.
change her baby for that of her mistress without the latter
being aware of the deception until too late to remedy.

"This half-breed, called 'Brown Annizae,' had been the
child's nurse, and had rebelled fiercely when she learned that
she was not to accompany them, a young mulattress having
been chosen in her place.   The mistress, being fond of Annizae, would have relented, but the master peremptorily refused
to allow Annizae, either with or without her child, to leave
the island.   This fact, coming to Annizae's knowledge, fired
her with such a desire for revenge as only the breast of a de-
spised or deserted woman can harbor.   While the preparations
were being completed, she busied herself about her usual duties; for, in a capricious humor, the little heir refused to permit any one but his customary nurse to minister to him.   Owing to this, she was allowed to attend them to the ship, having
her own child with her as well as the one who seemed to divine that soon he was to be separated from her.   When she
was rowed back to land she bore one wrapped in her arms,
having succeeded in crooning both of them to sleep before she
left the sailing-vessel.   To the delight of the young mulattress,
the remaining child continued to sleep after Annizae's departure.   With occasional glances in his direction, but with most
of her visual faculty devoted to watching the objects on shore
disappear from view, she spent the time immediately following the embarking.   It was not until it was hours too late that
she discovered that the slumbering child was Annizae's.

"Vainly they implored the captain to put back.   It was
impossible, or at least he deemed it impossible, for him to
comply with their requests.   It was in the slow days of sail-
ing-vessels, and many months elapsed before they were able to
secure any information from Cuba in response to their wild inquiries; then it was only the meagre statement that the woman never had been seen after their departure, and it had been
supposed that, at the last moment, they had concluded to take
her with them.

"Whether the child is alive, or whether she dropped him
over the side of the boat is the question which his parents
spent years in attempting to ascertain.   The mother died after
ten years; but the father, Lord Harberton, kept up the search.
It has degenerated now, principally, into an effort to ascertain .

if the little lost heir met death.   This proven, the next of kin come into possession.   The solicitors in London insist that they must have some proof of the lost heir's death, or that he must be found."

Lithgow was biting his nether lip thoughtfully.   The story interested him.   He turned the ring over curiously and watched the December sunshine bring out the colors of the stone.

"What has this to do with it" he questioned.   "You think that the original is in the possession of whom?   You have left something untold."

"Why, this ring was missed, or the one like it was missed, and, it being the property of the master, it always was supposed that the woman Annizac had stolen it."

"And this ring is all that one has to go on?"   Lithgow shook his brown head dubiously.

"The name, *Annizac;* we have that, and it may be of more importance than it seems.   It is said to be very uncommon."

Lithgow laid the ring down.   He appeared to have made up his mind not to attempt an effort in a field where failure looked to be so certain.   Mr. Bertram began to argue that even if he were not successful the matter would stand just as it did now.   If nothing should be gained, nothing would be lost.

Lithgow looked at his watch.   He arose with an exclamation of surprise.   His twenty minutes had lengthened into thirty.   He picked up the ring again.

"Supposing that I conclude to do what I can, may I take the ring to refresh my memory?" he asked.   "The bizarre object is fascinating.   With it to remind me constantly of my mission, I should be more likely to allow no opportunity to escape me."

"Of course," agreed the lawyer.   "Take it!   If it brings us the heir or any knowledge concerning him, I fancy that neither of us will have to worry about money matters for some time to come.   When do you sail?"

"On the next steamer.   Will it be necessary to see you again?"   Lithgow turned up his coat-collar as he asked the question.   He was anxious to be off.

"No; but you will keep me posted if you learn anything?"   Bertram shook hands warmly.   "You can't know how thankful

I am to you for your readiness to help me. Really, it seemed
to be too good a chance to be lost."

"Oh, yes; I'll keep you apprised of my movements,"
laughed Lithgow, secretly amused that Bertram should cher-
ish hopes that appeared so hopeless. "Write me in charge of
the American consulate. Good-by, if I don't see you again."

"Good-by!" cried Bertram. "Take good care of yourself!
I'll be down to see you off."

Lithgow took a street-car, rode ten blocks, then walked
five. Entering a building that bore no outward evidence of
its being the home of Art's devotees, he directed his way to a
nook reached only by the elevator and the north light. This
had been his prospective destination when he was accosted by
Mr. Bertram. He knocked at the door.

"Come in," said a clear voice hospitably, but the owner of
it did not look around to discern who the individual was that
had accepted her invitation to enter. Intent on the work with
which her hands were engaged, she had no thought for anything else at that moment. Little by little she was building
up with bits of clay the svelte form of a well-known society
woman, who had given her an order for one of the graceful,
minute productions which, in the artistic world, were becoming identified with the name of Beatrice Warrington.

"Working yet?" Lithgow exclaimed, with a tone of gladness. "I was afraid that you had gone home." He advanced
toward her, and stood inspecting her labor critically.

"Oh, it is you, Lithgow!" Beatrice Warrington said, glancing over her shoulder. "I am anxious to satisfy myself in regard to this. What impression does it make upon you? Does
it wear her characteristics?" She moved back to his side and
viewed through discouraged eyes the result of her afternoon's
labor. "I know that it lacks something. What is it?"

He pulled his mustache reflectively. He did not wish to
fall short of her expectations, but he really had no fault to
find with the dainty object before him.

"You know that I am no judge, Bee," he murmured, apologetically. "It looks quite perfect. I recognized it in a second. You might—yes, don't you think that you might give a
trifle more of a tilt to her head? That is one of her manner-
isms, you know."

"Possibly I might," admitted the young sculptress reluctantly. "But this is for her husband's Christmas present, and she held her head very erect to-day, all of her little airs quite gone. Perhaps he is not accustomed to them at home and she wishes to appear natural."

"It may be that this is the aspect she wears when she is making a demand on his bank account," suggested Lithgow.

Beatrice laughed, and began to put her work in proper shape for the night.

With the familiarity of long acquaintance Lithgow moved about the studio, investigating whatever he chose, lifting up the cloths enveloping the several swathed creations that reared themselves spectrally in the gathering twilight.

"You have lots of work on hand, I see," he commented; and Beatrice turned questioningly as she noted his rueful tone.

"More than I can well do," she answered, with enthusiasm. "My star is beginning to creep up. Was it not fortunate that I took advice and followed up my first success in the statuette line? The idea, being novel, wins attention where more pretentious work would pass unnoticed by those on whose caprices my livelihood depends. I really am making a diminutive fortune."

Lithgow seemed intently studying some sketches that were pinned irregularly on the wall. His lip was shut in almost fiercely by his teeth. He turned his eyes from the sketches to her face. His voice was very quiet when he spoke.

"I suppose that you think I ought to congratulate you on your success," he said; "but, instead of being glad, I am sorry—for myself."

Beatrice pushed a chair into position with unnecessary haste, hung up her clay-daubed apron, and took down her hat and jacket.

"How ridiculous!" she exclaimed, with a laugh that tried not to lose its carelessness. "I intend that all of my friends shall rejoice with me. I am not going to be so busy that I shall have to deny myself our old quarrelsome chats, Lithgow."

"Well, let's have one now," he begged, moving toward the Dutch settle which was Beatrice's pride. "It is the last one we shall have for some time, unless——"

"Why?" queried Beatrice. "What has happened?"

"I am going to Cuba!"

"Oh!" Lithgow observed with some satisfaction that there was an unmistakable touch of regret in her voice. "When?"

"On the next steamer." He paused a moment; then asked, softly: "Won't you and the dear mother go with me?"

Beatrice's blue eyes deepened in tint. She drew herself up with a breath of surprise. There was a question expressed emphatically in her attitude, but she said nothing.

Lithgow took one of her hands and drew her persuasively to the settle.

"I love you, Beatrice," he said. "I came up here this time not to quarrel, but to ask you to marry me. We can go to Cuba on our wedding-trip; I thought that you would like it. You can pack a bag and away we will fly;—of course, we would not leave the mother!"

Beatrice looked at him with puzzled eyes. His very quietness showed her his earnestness, but his method of acquainting her with his hopes was, to say the least, astonishingly abrupt.

"It would be a delightful voyage, and mamma would enjoy it intensely; but"—she pulled her fingers from his retaining grasp—"there would be one objection—I am certain that both of us would eventually find it an objection—we would be married!"

"Of course, we would be married," he declared. "Do you mean to say that you——"

"Wouldn't like it?" she supplemented, with a smile. "That is just what we finally would discover, only, you see, it would be too late."

Lithgow viewed her questioningly. The darkening light made her hair appear a warmer gold than usual; her eyes were more blue and more friendly than even they were wont to be.

"Fond as I am of you, Lithgow, I certainly don't think that I am the woman for you to marry," she told him gently.

"There is no other," he said, looking at her with his black-lashed gray eyes full of truth.

"Perhaps not this instant," she smiled, teasingly; "but there have been others, and there yet will be."

"I have told you too much!" he regretted. "But why

have you made me reveal my weaknesses to you? I never would think of confessing to another mortal as I have to you; and you, of all others, are the one I desire should think well of me!"

"That is folly!" she exclaimed. "I never have made you tell me a single thing! How could I?"

"Well, the fact remains that I have talked to you more as I would to a man," he said, retrospectively. "What has made me do it, Heaven only knows!—unless it was that smile of yours, which says——"

"What?" Beatrice lifted her brows curiously.

"I don't know what it says," answered the man, doubtfully, looking at her frank face with keen eyes. "I wish that I did. It has seemed to speak of so much to me, yet little that is tangible. I always go from your presence with a consciousness of being uplifted. The weight of life is less crushing. You make one believe in humanity once more."

"I like such words," Beatrice announced, with candor. "Women value tribute of that nature more than priceless jewels."

"Perhaps—some women do," agreed Lithgow sceptically; "women like you, who rebuild men's faith. We get dreadfully shaken at times."

" *You* should not," blamed Beatrice. "Do you forget those lines?

            "'Happy he
With such a mother! Faith in womankind
Beats with his blood, and trust in all things high
Comes easy to him, and tho' he trip and fall
He shall not blind his soul with clay.'"

Lithgow took her energetic fingers within his own reverently.

"Is it because you have believed that prophecy that you have been so patient with me?" he asked, with humility. "I have wished to make myself think that you—were interested, that you cared for me."

"I do," vowed Beatrice warmly; "but, instead of marrying you, I will tell you what I crave: your sympathy, your belief in my ability to accomplish, the best that you have to offer in the way of friendship."

"You have all those now," he declared. "Are they all that I may give to you, Bee?"

Beatrice Warrington hesitated. The color crept slowly up through her cheeks; her eyes grew almost daring. Lithgow felt that she never had appeared more tempting. People thought her cold, but he knew how tender was her heart, how catholic her wide sympathy.

"You often have confessed to me," she said; "now I will tell *you* something. It is a great secret. Only I and my heart know it. I will love when one comes who can master me. To him I will bow gladly, but his superiority must be real; it must be such that my soul can recognize."

"I fear that you will have to look for the coming of the archangel Michael," he discouraged. "Men are distressingly human. Among them you never will find your superior spiritually, I can tell you. I would have been glad to have mastered you if I had known for what species of a creature you were waiting. Is it too late for me to have another try?"

"I am afraid so," she laughed. "My masterful lord probably never will appear save in stone or bronze. Such a creation I could worship without fear of making it egotistical. I believe what we women long for is not so much equal rights as the opportunity to worship. But we have discovered that man is not worthy of our adoration. See how pitiable a god he is—bowled over by the tiniest temptation!"

"You are severe on us, Bee," he expostulated. "Lots of temptations go by us without touching us."

"But you always go over as easily as a tenpin if the rolling ball hits you," she insisted. "Do I not know? Remember how many peeps you have given me of your various discomfitures!"

"Well, I have been frank with you," smiled Lithgow. "I have not posed for other than I am—a man with grievous faults, but faults that you can eradicate."

"Oh, it is too much to ask a woman to do all the remodelling!" The girl shook her head. "As I told you, she does not wish to go down after her lord; she wishes him to be on such a lofty pinnacle that she must look up to him; it is her nature to desire to be able to do so. Some poor things live happily all their lives under the delusion that the man they reverence is worthy it. I almost envy them. Delusions are nice, if one can stay deluded."

"But one never does," sighed Lithgow. "I have deluded myself with the hope that you cared enough to be willing to give me the help of your hand. You do not know it, perhaps, but a man always has the dream, or the reality, of a woman's hand in his before he climbs very high."

"If one *loves* one can climb on forever, even without the encouragement of the object beloved," declared Beatrice. "Love means progression, a continued striving after 'the flying perfect.'"

"You are talking of etherealizations," he remonstrated. "Such a love is beyond the conception of mortals."

"Because mortals like to play with little tin gods and ginger-bread toys, from which they will not lift their gaze, and they cry to themselves: 'These are real! These are all that exist!'"

"I have raised my eyes from the toys at last, Beatrice," he told her meaningly. "They can attract me no more. If the time ever comes that I can prove this to you, will you listen?"

Something leaped into Beatrice's face that softened it indescribably.

"If the time ever comes," she promised, with perceptible scepticism as to its probable arrival.

He assisted in the laborious task of getting her sleeves into the no less bouffant ones that her jacket boasted. He watched her while she adjusted her hat before an antique mirror which had the appearance of having suffered from the small-pox at some time in its career. He concluded that it would be well to begin the conquering without delay.

"I am going out home with you," he informed her. "It is too late for you to be out alone; besides, the mother will wish to give me a kiss of farewell. Must I not tell her about the delightful trip she might have had as a mother-in-law?"

"Not a breath!" commanded Beatrice tragically, sending a covert smile into the speckled mirror. "It was a preposterous proposition! The idea of asking a woman to start on such a journey with but a moment's notice. What is a week? Why, it takes years for some people to get ready to be married. I don't think I have been half severe enough. I should not be surprised if this is one of your jokes! You always have played jokes on me from babyhood." She pulled down her dotted veil, wriggled her nose to make sure that the dainty gauze was perfectly arranged, and opened the door.

"I am serious more often than you fancy," he told her lightly. "You simply have not got the key to my nature. Just because we have known each other always you believe that you read me like a book."

"Don't I?" she queried.

"You read always in the same place," was his injured reply. "There are other pages."

"And other women's faces are on them."

"Well—you can erase them all if you will."

"I want you to do the erasing," she laughed. "But you never will. I wager—my next work—that you will return from Cuba freshly enamored."

"Of you."

"No, not of me; of some southern beauty or of a northern girl wintering there."

"What is the use of having good intentions when so little faith is placed in them?" demanded Lithgow. "I receive no encouragement from you. Your fancy paints me much blacker than I am. All that I need is a governor. I am like an engine that goes on making numberless revolutions to no purpose. Be my governor, Bee!"

"Too responsible a position," returned the girl. "I don't know what a governor on an engine is. However, you may write me often enough to keep me posted. I can determine from your letters how the affair is progressing."

"What affair?"

"Oh, any affair that happens to be on the tapis."

"Do I reveal myself so? By the way, I must tell you of the odd thing that cropped up to-day. I am commissioned not only to look up coffee estates but to discover the whereabouts of an heir who has been so fortunate as to fall into possession of a title of which he never has heard."

He recounted his meeting with Mr. Bertram and its results. Beatrice listened with the keenest interest.

"Why, it is like a story!" she exclaimed. "You may have great adventures before you! You must rehearse this for mamma's ears. You will dine with us, of course. I will

make the coffee myself—you know my coffee!—and mamma
shall concoct some of those hot tea-cakes that you used to
like. Don't you remember?"

"Remember? The mere mention of them takes me
back——"

"Mercy! Don't tell how far!" she begged. "When I realize how long ago we were children I can feel that a new
wrinkle creeps in at the corner of my frightened eye. You
used to order me around outrageously then."

"Did I?" he questioned, with rather wistful reflection.
"Yet I am mildness itself now. It is well enough to have a
master, but isn't it better to have slaves? If I once possessed
imperious qualities, I suppose that I can conjure them again
to my aid. I will make the effort while I am gone. Prepare
to defend yourself against the attack which will be inaugu-
rated on my return."

"Forewarned——" she said. "You never would do for a
general!"

Lithgow was welcomed by Mrs. Warrington with the
warmth that his dead mother's friend always accorded him.
This household had been a second home to him, and when the
fortune which supported it had flown and the death of Mr.
Warrington followed, Lithgow had proved to the bereaved
woman the help and comfort that a son would have been.

Five days later he was aboard a steamer that pushed its
way out through the Narrows bound for southern seas. His
thoughts were of Beatrice as he leaned over the taffrail and
watched the pilot swing down into the boat below. He was
full of regret that she had chosen not to have the delights of
this voyage. He was man enough to believe that, despite her
seeming indifference, he would win her some day; then, why
not now?

There was a pleasant wintry sharpness in the air when he
embarked, but by the third morning out the atmosphere pulsed
with a warmth that rendered heavy clothing insupportable.

Lithgow sauntered on the deck, past the white boats and
orange-tipped chimneys. He smoked much and read desultorily in a worn little volume which Beatrice had handed him,
with the comment that the sight of it might keep her in his
mind and so enable him to cling to his intentions.

2

Through waters that grew more divinely blue, under skies that throbbed with color, caressed by winds which seemed only the warm, sleepy breath of a sea beating with slumberous emotions, the hours bore him. The gold and sapphire days became longer, the sunsets more gorgeous, until the twilights vanished altogether and darkness dropped with the suddenness peculiar to the far south.

In the wake of the steamer a long plume of phosphorescent light stretched its iridescence to that magic line where sky and whispering waters mingled. The well-known glittering Orion and the Pleiads floated in the heavens, as if they, too, were voyaging and lost in admiration of their southern kindred.

Indolently sunk in his sea-chair, lulled by the narcotic atmosphere that rests in Caribbean waters, Lithgow's thoughts still drifted to Beatrice; but they were very dreamy, disconnected thoughts. It seemed to him that he had been floating thus for many years. His eyes were turned to where the Southern Cross flamed through the purple night. Slowly it was mounting to a height from which, at the hour when night and day become one, it would send its proclamation of supremacy over all the little worlds beneath.

The captain came near and Lithgow, with the *ennui* of an ocean traveller, inquired:

"When shall we be in Havana?"

"In the morning, sir, the ship will be riding in the finest harbor known; it boasts that it can hold the fleets of the world."

"Will it ever hold other fleet than that of Spain?" questioned the American.

"If certain hopeful spirits are to be believed—yes!" answered the captain cautiously. "But it is wiser to reply as the Cubans themselves do: '*Quien sabe?*'"

"The inevitable answer to every question in the lands on which Spain has set her seal!" commented Lithgow. "Who knows?" After a pause he asked: "Is there any disturbance in the island now?"

"It is safe to conjecture that one is just finished or another about to be begun," the captain laughed, with a shake of his broad shoulders. "What Cuba needs is a general such as the States have known. There were such in the last war, the ten-year war, but they had tremendous forces against them. Just at present there is a bandit who is causing the government some trouble. He is daring enough for a leader; but other qualities are requisite. His name is Gonzalo Alarcon. If you go into the interior you must look out for him and his men. He is unscrupulous enough to take you as prisoner and demand ransom."

"I would be much more likely to join them than pay a ransom to secure liberty," declared Lithgow. "I'd like nothing better than to help the Cubans win their freedom!"

"Ssh—" warned the captain, glancing about them. "You must learn better than to utter such expressions in these waters, or you are likely never to return to the States. This Alarcon is no patriot; he simply is a brigand for gain, I suppose. In case there were a war no doubt but what he would join the forces of the rebels; but it is not men like him who make up Cuba's dauntless armies. Her wars have been fought by the flower of the island, youths who died with the word of liberty on their lips. It makes the blood of a Yankee boil when he thinks of the oppression these Cubans endure!"

Lithgow could not but be amused at the vehemence of the man who had but that instant warned him against such utterances. They discussed the Cuban question in guarded tones until the captain pointed upward.

"The Cross begins to bend!" he said. "It is midnight."

The hour being past for which he had waited, Lithgow rose to his feet, stifling a yawn.

"I shall sleep on deck," he returned. "It will be daylight in two or three hours."

But he did not sleep. A curious unrest grew upon him with the coming of the dawn which he watched creep up. The sun followed with the rapidity known to the tropics. It disclosed that they lay outside the harbor.

When the magic waters were entered he stared down delightedly through the transparent emerald fluid. The brilliant tints of the fish frolicking beneath the surface were to be seen as plainly as if they lay throbbing on the marble of Marti's fish market.

The shadow of the grim fortress, the Moro, threw itself far. The shadow of the secrets which it holds, of the thousands who, entering its walls, have never since been heard of, lies heavier on the heart of the people. From its towers hung the red and yellow flag of Spain, blood and gold—typical, indeed, of that avaricious realm.

The red-tiled roofs and many-colored façades of the houses on the west and southwest sides of the bright water began to glisten as the day waxed strong. In the distance rose purpling hilltops crowned with palms and decked with a green fire of foliage that centuries can not quench. Vociferous boys came out in boats. Lithgow tossed coins to the sand below, in order to see the lithe, naked bodies dive through the sapphire waters. He was alert with that expectancy which attends landing on new shores. When the quarantine boat had made its appearance and the officials had rendered a clean bill of health to all passengers, he descended into one of the small craft that swarmed around the steamer. As he did so the book which Beatrice had given him fell from his pocket into the water. Instantly it was fished out and presented to him, some the worse for its mishap. As he regarded it regretfully his glance caught the passage:

"No man can antedate his experience, or guess what faculty or feeling a new object shall unlock, any more than he can draw to-day the face of a person whom he shall see to-morrow for the first time."

A quiver ran over him, tingling every nerve. Wondering what was in the lines to awaken dormant senses in that fashion, he reread them, but the surprising emotion did not return. He thrust the volume back in his pocket. The words were impressed indelibly on his memory, from which they were destined to repeat themselves with deep and deeper meaning during the days that were to come to him on Cuban shores.

CHAPTER II.

THE radiant sunlight of the tropics lay over the emerald stretches of the Cuban cane-fields that comprised Gilbert Palgrave's sugar plantation of *La Sacra Sonrisa*. The swaying tassel-tips at the head of each succulent shaft had yellowed slowly beneath the breathless heat of many such afternoons that drowsed their way toward the west. Ebony workers moved like a colony of ants through the rows, cutting down the slender stalks with machetes that swung with rhythmic regularity. Shapely mulattoes with curiously turbaned heads lent color to the scene as they, amid much chattering, spread out the crushed cane to dry, to serve again in the capacity of *bagazo*, fuel for the voracious maw of the engine that rumbled ponderously in the low, white buildings where the manufacture of sugar went on tirelessly night and day during the four months of the grinding season.

Beyond the rich green of the orange grove gleamed the walls of the dwelling, its austere exterior betraying no hint of the beauty and bloom enclosed in the cloistered court, roofed only with the blue of the sky.

In the most comfortable chair of the *estrada*,—the six rocking-chairs, which, facing each other, form a marked feature of a Cuban drawing-room,—sat the master of the estate, the inevitable cigar between his fingers, a half-amused, half-troubled contraction on his brows. From under lids just lifted from the sleep of the customary afternoon siesta he was watching the restless movement to and fro through the sala of a lithe, girlish figure behind which trailed long, white draperies that were caught up occasionally through her girdle. She was his only child, Raquel, motherless since infancy. He remarked mentally, with a wave of gladness, how like her mother she looked now that she was merging into womanhood: the same dusky, riotous hair, the identical rich color, the same—no, not the same eyes! Beneath Raquel's slumberous lids shone something that had been wholly foreign to her mother. Gilbert Palgrave wondered vaguely whence had come to the child that fire, that fierce intensity which made her such an enigma to him, try though he would to understand her moods.

"*Ay de mi!*" she sighed as she paused in front of a little case of books that showed indubitable signs of much usage. "Was it not sufficient evil to be born a woman without the additional one of being born in Cuba, where nothing ever happens?"

"Except revolutions," completed her father.

"Yes, nothing except revolutions—that fail!" she amended, wheeling herself suddenly face to face with him to demand: "Do you know what I would do, *papa mio*, if I were a man?"

"That is easy enough to prophesy, *mi cara mia*," he responded lightly. "You would follow the customary path trod by Cuban youths. Going abroad to be educated, you would imbibe ideas inimical to tyranny. Incidentally you would squander what little fortune your old English father is trying to keep from the hands of the Spanish Jews. Then you would return to the island to throw yourself into whatever struggle for liberty might then be on the tapis."

With loving impetuosity she clasped him, turning his features up to view them scrutinizingly, after which she kissed his eyes and lips with tender fervor.

"Old!" she cried indignantly. "You are younger now than I am, *papa mio!* I have grown old in nursing impatient longings; but you—are content. You are not all the time fighting against yourself as I am."

"Why do you fight, *nina?*" the father asked curiously.

"*Quien sabe?*" she answered discouragedly with that sphinx-like reply which the Spanish-speaking tongue gives to every troublesome query: "Who knows?" She resumed her impatient march around the spacious room much as a lioness glides with noiseless swing back and forth in the cage. Behind bars the topazolite orbs of imprisoned creatures turn with feverish questions in their depths; and so burned the eyes which looked out from the face of this Cuban señorita shut in by the monotony of cane-fields.

"I only know that I hunger for action," she continued after a pause, during which she seemed to have been making an endeavor to analyze herself. "This stagnant plantation life seems unbearable. I want to live, *papa mio!* I want to make the world know that I am in it. If I were a man I would be the Napoleon for whom Cuba waits. I would have but one thought before me—the liberation of my land from Spanish rule!"

Gilbert Palgrave could not forbear smiling. He was somewhat accustomed to those outbreaks; he had grown to accept them as inseparable from Raquel.

"It is well that the Governor-General is not aware of your anti-Spain proclivities, or I might find myself immured in the Moro, the ingenio confiscated, and you——! What under the sun makes Cuba's liberation of such moment to you, a child who has seen nothing of life?"

"Ah, it is that, it is that!" she cried. "Perhaps it is because I have seen so little of anything that I long for change, work, something that will banish the length of these days that sleep themselves away one into the other until often I fancy that I can imagine what might have been the reflections of an antediluvian toad when he discovered that the cell was forming which, for a thousand years, was to shut him in from the world."

Gilbert Palgrave pushed back his rapidly graying hair as he surveyed her critically, from her rebellious, shadowy tresses to the arch of her instep.

" If the season turns out well and I can manage to pay some of my debts, perhaps Havana will be possible next year," he suggested. " There you will find a field more fascinating than the struggle for Cuban independence. I must not forget that you are no longer my childish comrade, but, instead, a tall beauty who must be presented to society, ride in the Pasco to be stared at, and—marry well." There was a slight flavor of tender sarcasm in his tone, not for his daughter but for the sex whose aim in life is supposed to be so circumscribed. In his own mind he had little doubt that all these vagaries of Raquel's would vanish under the magic spell of Havanese gay life. It was true that she had seen little. Most of her education had been gleaned from the rather heterogeneous collection of books with which he had surrounded himself when he had taken up his abode so far from his native land. Possibly he had made a mistake in not placing her under more feminine influence than the plantation afforded. Old Tia Juana had hardly been equal to the rearing of this half-English nature. These were his reflections as he listened to her passionate reply, flung not at him but at fate.

" That is what is so intensely humiliating about being a woman! Instead of seeking fame or fortune for myself, shoulder to shoulder with others in the race, I must swing in my hammock and eat my heart out with longing to achieve, until that day when one who has won these things for himself will come and offer to share his honors with me, as if I were a mendicant."

The sound of wheels followed her speech. Gilbert Palgrave arose with some alacrity, as if even he found an interruption in the quiet day rather enjoyable.

" It is only old Monsieur Theuriet!" Raquel disappointedly exclaimed, watching the approach of the old-fashioned volante with its silver trimmings, gayly decked horses, and smiling postilion.

"I wonder that he ventures out so boldly minus outriders!" commented the sugar planter, as he went into the court to welcome the owner of the coffee estate of La Buena Esperanza. "The reports are that the highways are watched by banditti of late. Here is the event for which you have prayed, in the shape of a visitor, Raquel. Come and bid him welcome."

Raquel's eyes were very sombre.

"He is so tiresome!" she said, half to herself, in extenuation of her intention to escape the caller. "I suppose that he will stay for supper. I must go and tell Tia Juana."

The clatter of the horses' feet resounded on the tiles at the entrance. The girl listened for a moment to the exchange of salutations between host and guest, undecided whether to obey duty or inclination. When she heard the voices approaching the sala she stepped backward quickly into the adjoining apartment, from which she took her way to the cocina, where the culinary operations of the household went on under the supervision of old Tia Juana, who had been the only mother Raquel ever had known. The sharp, staccato utterances of the women could be heard even above the roar of the mill, as they gossiped and quarrelled over their kitchen labor. Sometimes Raquel sat among them, watching Tia Juana's fingers as she fashioned tempting delicacies, the while recounting grewsome tales that could congeal even adult blood. But to-day she was not in the mood for such entertainment. Instead, she slipped back into the court, now deserted, and rolled herself into the hammock of maguey ropes.

During the blazing noon, great, gorgeous strips of brilliant-hued cloth were stretched across the little quadrangle. Now they hung with lazy, clinging folds down the azure-tinted stucco, lending an oriental effect to the corridor-bordered square filled with heavy bloom which half hid the old fountain where the water splashed and dripped so drowsily that even the lizards hung to the edge, mesmerized by the spell it seemed to exercise over all whose ears caught its cadences. Gossamery vines, which appeared to spring from air and feed on it, created blossoms that hung like butterflies from hair-like stems.

Here, in this spot of calm, Raquel had swung and dreamed

until she felt a kinship with the lizard and his mates, chained by a life of inertia.

"Wake!" she murmured commiseratingly, reaching out to poke a lizard with her slender forefinger until he fell over into the water. "You have not moved from that spot all day. You might as well be dead!"

That brief excitement over, she sought to amuse herself by watching to see which of the gently swaying plumes of the lofty palm that shot its gray Corinthian column up from the centre of the quadrangle would be the first to lose the glint of the rapidly dying day.

"*Santissima!* What exasperation there is in the thought that while I sleep in the few hours before the morrow you will have looked upon all the vast unknown for which I hunger!" she cried, apostrophizing the declining sun. "You will have smiled, as you have done for ages, at your own image in the Nile; and, rising again on the Antilles, you will find me as ignorant, as full of longings as ever, praying for some break in the monotony of my slowly creeping days."

There was an infinitesimal amount of comfort to be derived from commiserating herself as well as the lizard, and she extracted the most possible from it while she idly noted the mellow tints, followed by tender grays and ethereal greens, steal through the sky, the shadow of approaching night sweeping slowly after.

"I should like to know *why* we have to live!" she mused discontentedly. "Why are we placed here without our wish to live out our lives as best we can; then, if we fail to live well, be punished for not overcoming evils that we don't know how to vanquish? Tia Juana says that babies always cry when they find themselves here. I wonder is it because they are disappointed to find themselves within the limitations of a life on this earth?"

A star that gleamed like a ruby came out of the darkening heaven and feigned to dance on the tip of the silent palm up into which she was gazing. This green-crested palm shaft, whose concentric rings revealed its claims to antiquity, was the only confidant to whom she propounded these troublesome queries. To both problems and solutions it gave but sighs. From its vantage of years it could discern that all human questions meet with but one answer—silence.

"Sometimes I think that people who unwillingly have died desire to come back here and live again," she continued. "Who knows but that their wistful spirits steal into the bodies of those just entering upon this existence? Perhaps that is why some men have women's natures, and why some women are torn by fierce, eager souls which long to be again what they were in the previous life! What would a woman do with the soul that was Napoleon's? How it would torment her! How it would turn with loathing from the needle, demanding the sword! How it would storm within her, longing for action, ready to lead an army again over the Alps!"

She put her fingers to her throat as if to free something that fluttered there and choked her.

"I like to fancy that it was Napoleon's spirit that came into the world with me," she whispered to the palm, stretching out one arm to throw it around the trunk as she swung near. She held herself against the tree, her cheek pressed close to the tawny-gray swathing encasing its heart. "How foolish my rebellion must seem to you!" she said to it in sudden self-scorn. "You lift your head up and up unceasingly, conscious there is a constant growth within you which nothing can baffle. You still will toss your plumes when I and my ambitions are but a memory. Yet, king though you are, I am mightier than you; my span of years may be only one thousandth part of yours, but in it I shall know—I must know—the heights and depths, the bliss and bane which are vouchsafed to mortals. You who are immortal are debarred from such experiences, though perhaps you have known them too in some other age— the cycle in which Daphne flourished. Who knows? Is that why your leaves sigh so when I rail at the fate which set me in the cane-fields of sleepy Cuba?"

She had watched the stars creep out and swing their varied censer-lamps across her little patch of sky for so many nights through so many years that she knew where to look for each wanderer in heaven's highway. Though she did not know them by name she had christened them with appellations culled from mythology, and they were viewed as friends, these nightly comers. But there were hours like this when their impassiveness irritated her.

"It is well enough for them to be calm," she thought. "They have seen everything. The world obediently turns her many phases toward them and they are forever in motion themselves. But I—I am nothing. I see nothing. I only know of what I read. I presume it will be my lot to be married and never see beyond the edge of Cuba; never learn any more; never grow wiser; only grow fat and sit in estradas and gossip! *O Madre de Dios! Libra me de mal!*"

She sprang from the hammock to escape the picture her fancy had drawn of her mature years. The sound of her father's earnest voice drew her toward it. Midway in the doorway of the sala she paused, observing M. Theuriet. It seemed to her that he had not changed an iota in all the years during which she had been advancing into womanhood. He always had looked old to her youthful vision. A Frenchman, his nationality would have been patent to any eyes. Years among the Cubans had removed none of the characteristics of his race; if anything, they were intensified. The jet-black appearance of his hair and mustache seemed at variance with the yellow parchment-like skin, but in keeping with the foppish elegance which he ever maintained and which ever was associated in her mind with him. He was gesticulating gently with his graceful, slender fingers. She did not catch his words. Presently her father spoke again:

"If all goes well this year and I meet with no reverses, I may be able to stand firmly on my feet once more; then, I can free myself from the hands of those atrocious usurers, the Catalans. As you know, the expenses of the last two years have been double the profit, owing partly to the cost of the new machinery. However, the principal loss has been due to the increase in the manufacture of beet sugar. You coffee planters don't have such things to worry you."

"Ah, pardon, *mon ami!*" M. Theuriet shook his cigar in a slightly argumentative way at his host. "You forget ze cen-sects! Unseen, can zey not ruin ma centire crop? Cairtainlee! Worse—zey can ruin ze reputation which I hav' won for ma plantaceon as producing ze finest coffee een Cuba! Hav' I told you zat ze New York firm ov Jersdan & Lester are sending a man down here to negotiate wiz me for ze whole output from La Buena Esperanza? *Ma foi!* Hav' I not? I hav' received notice some time ago. Ze man was to sail soon. I expect heem daily now. His societe will be quite a treat for us, will cet not? Zese Americains are often clevair."

Gilbert Palgrave sighed.   He had no particular interest in the possible wit of a man who was coming to buy a crop not his own.   He was blaming the choice which had made him a sugar planter instead of a coffee grower.   M. Theuriet had been steadily waxing richer and he himself had become poorer. Sugar was lower in price with each year.   The plantation now was mortgaged to its fullest extent, and, in addition, he owed ten thousand to the man before him.   He knocked the ashes off the end of his cigar with the tip of his little finger, which had become calloused by reason of being thus continually employed.

"What shall you do if the close of the season finds me a bankrupt, Monsieur?" he asked, placing his cigar again between his lips while he eyed the Frenchman anxiously.   "You know that you would lose your loan completely, for I was able to give you little or no security."

M. Theuriet glanced up at that moment and beheld the vision in the doorway.

Like some revivified creation of the Past, straight as a palm, with the witching grace of a veritable Hebe in face and limb, Raquel stood; one arm, bare but for the drapery that fell from the shoulder, held back the gauze curtain that shut the sala from the court.   In her luminous eyes lay mingled all the fire and all the dreams born of the clime.

After viewing her a moment in silent admiration, M. Theuriet said in a tone which reached only the father's ear:

"You are fortunate enough, *mon ami*, to hav' one possession which I would be glad to tak' as securitee an' len' you een addition twenty times ze amount.   *C'est vrai!*"

Gilbert Palgrave turned wonderingly in the direction indicated by M. Theuriet's glance, as the Frenchman rose to his feet with an alacrity which years had been powerless to impair.   Puzzled, not comprehending the full meaning of his guest's words, Palgrave watched Raquel as she advanced, giving to M. Theuriet the salutation for which he stood waiting. Her face was troubled.   She turned to her father anxiously.

"Is it as bad as you picture, *papa mio?*" she cried distressedly.   "Are we so near bankruptcy and you have not told me? I should have been the first to know."

"No, no, *dulce*," he reassured her; "there is nothing for you to worry about.   I am in a bit of a financial strait, but

M. Theuriet has been kind enough to tide me over what appears to be the worst of it. Bestow your thanks upon him. He has done us great service."

"What can I say to him that you have not already said in gratitude?" she exclaimed, all of her old dislike for the man vanishing before this proof that he had been obliging to her father. "I am certain that we never can repay him in full measure. One can pay pesos, but not kindness."

"I intend to," announced Gilbert Palgrave, with grave decision, "though I caution him that it may be some time before I am able. However, we will hope for the best. 'It's a long lane that has no turning!'"

Raquel bent her dark head until her lovely face was in front of her father's. Compelling his eyes to look into her disturbed ones, she said pleadingly:

"You must let me help you pay these debts, *papa mio*. There is nothing I would not do to help you."

"I know, dear; I know," smiled Palgrave, patting her cheek with loving fingers. "But what is there that you could do?"

"Oh, I don't know!" she breathed hopelessly. "In Cuba a woman can do nothing. Now, if we were in your country I could work at many things. All there seems to be here is cane cutting—and the blacks do that far better than I could." She smiled a trifle at the thought of attempting such labor, but the shadow did not lift from her countenance.

M. Theuriet was contemplating her with his sharp, black eyes. Once he opened his thin lips to speak, then closed them again tightly.

"So the only thing that you really can do is to make me happy," Palgrave added convincingly. "And, the way you can succeed is to be happy yourself. When I think that you are irked and discontented, I feel that I have failed in my life work."

"Ah, I never will be selfish again," she told him contritely. "I never will complain more, yet—I would work for you, papa, if only I might. I could be happier so. I am too idle. I only dream."

"Sometimes, mademoiselle, an opportunitee comes before one is prepared," suggested M. Theuriet with a peculiar intentness in his gaze. "You are full of hope; you may help him mor' zan he fancies. Who knows?"

Raquel threw out her hands with a wearied gesture. What was the use of hoping when she knew so well what each day would bring? Nothing new had been brought for years. Her sanguine nature was becoming morbid.

"Who knows anything here in Cuba, except that Spain crushes us more cruelly every year?" she returned, stepping out of the long window, which, guiltless of glass, opened its iron-barred jalousies outward.

"That is her pet grievance," explained her father amusedly. "I can't imagine what good she hopes to accomplish by nourishing it; but it is true she has little to occupy her time. Perhaps she should have been placed in a convent; however, I could not have spared her."

"Pardon, but I could suggest a remedee," remarked the Frenchman. "At some future day I will tell you what eet ees, eef you choose. *Non;* to me eet appears not necessaire, now. Your words hav' mad' her content for ze time at least. You, she idolizes. To mak' you feel joy she would deny herself; ees eet not so? *Oui, oui, mon ami!* Zat ces as eet should be! Eet ees filial lov'. Eet should be encouraged."

It was growing late. With the suddenness peculiar to the West Indies, darkness was opening great, wide eyes over the slumberous Caribbean and its coral isles. The deep blue of the vault overhead was becoming lit with immense stars which hung so near that it seemed as if it would be an easy thing to accomplish the Spanish saying, "*Tomar el cielo con las manos,*" to take the sky with one's hands. Between the boughs which met overhead she caught glimpses of these planets, and walked with her head tilted backward, her hands clasped behind her, until she reached the river.

A tiny boat-house, built of rich Indian woods, floored with cool tiles, and covered with flowering vines, had been erected so that it projected over the stream. Tied to one of the tree boles supporting the thatched roof of maguey was a canoe which long ago had been fashioned into suitable shape for her. She stepped down into the boat and pushed out. Hedged in by cane the river wound its tortuous way through the plantation, past the plantain grove and the negro quarters, on its way to join larger streams that drifted to the sea. During the rainy season it often became swollen to the size of a torrent; but now it purled along quietly, caressing the sides of the canoe in a friendly manner as Raquel propelled her craft indolently.

The rhythmic chant of the workers at the mills reached her ears; a mournful melody which lost by distance its harshness, being blended with the dull crunching of the cane and the hum of the engine. She could distinguish the cries of the negroes at the cauldrons: "*A-a-b'la! A-a-b'la! E-c-cha candela!*" The sound rose above the barbaric chorus of the gangs at work filling the troughs with cane and carting away the crushed strips to spread out as bagazo.

Half occupied in listening to these rude melodies, familiar though they were, she failed to notice that the canoe had left the middle of the river and was drifting leisurely toward the other bank. Suddenly its gentle motion ceased. Glancing backward in surprise, thinking that the boat had run ashore, she found her face in close proximity to the rough, bearded one of a man who stood waist-deep in the water, holding the sides of the canoe.

Uncertain at first that it was not a creature concocted by her fearful fancy, she made only a frantic effort to push the craft from his reach; then a terrorized cry rose to her lips, but it was crushed back by a heavy hand. The paddle was wrenched from her grasp by another figure which loomed up on the other side of her. The two men dragged the boat ashore. Here they were surrounded by other shadowy forms that stole out of the cane, seeming to the frightened girl to gloat over her capture.

They spoke in whispers. Now and then they indulged in subdued laughs at her desperate struggles to free herself. They bound her limbs. They tied a thick bandage over her mouth. She was powerless.

"*Caramba!* It is a small tiger that we have snared!" commented one as, in spite of her wild resistance, he took her in his arms and made his way into the safety of the cane.

"*Es verdad!*" admitted the others admiringly. "Alarcon will welcome this capture, even though it be a woman. She has the courage of a man!"

The stars shone on. The water became still. The palm in the court whispered to itself uneasily. Gilbert Palgrave offered M. Theuriet another cigar.

CHAPTER III.

AN entire army might hide within the green fastnesses of the enormous stretches of cane covering a Cuban sugar plantation.

It was with no fear of discovery that the brigands had tethered their horses therein. Mounting their animals, the party sped into what seemed a rustling sea of shadows.

Raquel struggled vigorously, and found herself but held the more firmly.

"*Madre de Jesu!* She is a little fighter!" the one who bore her cried to the man next behind him.

They rode swiftly but stealthily. The tassels of the cane above their heads waved and nodded in rhythm with the melody the blade leaves made, clashing against each other in a mimic war.

But Raquel heard nothing of the music of the whispering, swaying cane forest through whose aisles she was borne. That she was at the mercy of one of the lawless bands of refugees who made their rendezvous in the mountainous district she knew for a certainty. She had caught the sound of a name which had power to strike terror to every timid heart. To be in the grasp of Gonzalo Alarcon's men was held to be enough to curdle the blood of the most courageous of captives. Her horror was intense to the point of agony. She knew that her father would beggar himself before he would fail to raise any sum that they might demand; but her memory brought to mind frightful atrocities which she knew often were perpetrated upon such unfortunate victims as herself whose ransom might be delayed. The recollection of these marrow-freezing tales which she had heard recounted in the cocina by the black women, who no doubt had embellished the stories to please their imaginations, filled every step of the journey with inconceivable dread.

When the cavalcade left the protection of the cane and began an upward ascent Raquel's hope died within her. She fought her captor with renewed energy, which, however, was of little avail considering that she was pinioned and unable to utter a sound. His laugh of amusement stirred her with impotent fury that exhausted her without effecting her escape.

The hushed march went on.

At last they struck the edge of the forest, which, mantling the hills in a tangled mass of green as impregnable as the Chinese wall to one not initiated, offers retreats more secure than buttressed fortresses.

The men divided. Two of them went in front of the one who carried Raquel across his high saddle. The others brought up the rear.

A vivid flash cut the darkness for an instant, followed by a second flash; then a steady light. The foremost riders bore aloft tapers of brown wax which cast faint gleams ahead into the labyrinth of Briarean arms that seemed to call a voiceless halt to the invaders.

As they pushed on up the precipitous cliffs of green, turned black beneath the alchemic touch of night, long, clinging vines wound themselves about the adventurous ones daring to pierce the mysteries of tropical jungles. Cool leaves swept with lingering caress over the colorless face of the girl prisoner. Sharp weapons in the hands of the horsemen cut right and left through the green growth which formed so dense a barrier at every step of the way.

"*Diablo!* If we had gone back by the other route we would not have had to carve our way through," grumbled the second brigand with dissatisfaction.

"*Basta,* José!" exclaimed the one who appeared to act as leader. "Art thou a nine-lived cat that thou couldst afford to run the risk of having a bullet put through thy skin? Thou dost hate exertion more than thou dost value anything, even the pesetas which this night's work will bring us."

"As God wills!" shrugged José, with what seemed curious irrelevancy. "But I have two eyes, and thou dost pull wool over thine when thou hopest this labor will net us a centavo, Manuel."

"*Porqué?*" demanded Manuel, clasping his burden a trifle more securely. "Don Gilberto Palgrave is a rich man; is that not true? Of course! And he will pay royally. If he does not we will know how to make him." He felt Raquel shiver apprehensively in his arms.

"That is as it may be," agreed José, "but is that saying

3

that *we* will get any of it? To where did the Molinos ransom go? Answer me that if thou knowest! *I* had none of it!"

"It would all have gone down thy throat if thou hadst had it," laughed Manuel, appealing to the others to know if his words were not the words of a truth-speaker.

For a few moments there was a prospect of a drawn battle between Manuel, the temporary leader, and José, the insubordinate, but the danger was averted by the quick intervention of the other members of the raiding party. José went on in moody silence.

Hour after hour passed. Still they kept the slow tread through the tortuous forest ways, which were filled with the heavy fragrance of the marvellous bloom which hung around and above them veiled in the darkness. A silence which seemed filled with the respiration of countless forms of vegetable life palpitated about them. But the men were familiar with it. To Raquel alone did it feel oppressive, ominous.

Just as the first golden shaft of dawn fell upon the forest, penetrating dimly through the dense, green darkness of tropical luxuriance, the band halted and dismounted.

Raquel was unbound.

Bruised by the thongs, cramped by the uncomfortable position in which she had been held so long, the girl was forced to close her teeth upon her lip to keep a little cry from escaping her as she drew herself to her full stature. All of the endurance and resolution of her nature came into play. She was determined that they should discover neither fear nor suffering in her demeanor.

A peculiar call was given by the leader of the band.

Pushing through what appeared to be an impenetrable thicket, Raquel and her captors faced a group of half-clad men who, springing up at the sight of the returning party, crowded around them, crying excitedly:

"*Qué fortuna ?*"

"Good fortune!" replied the marauders triumphantly, falling back to reveal the trembling but defiant girl in their midst. "See for yourselves! Is it not so—no?"

"*Dios !*" ejaculated one of the members of the camp admiringly. "Go summon Alarcon!" he added to a youth at his elbow; but the youth did not move to obey the bidding. Fascinatedly his lustrous eyes dwelt on Raquel's pale face, in which the terror was apparent in spite of her effort to hide it.

"*Vaya*, Zuñega!" ordered the man again. "Go on! Hast thou not seen a woman before? One would think her a fer-de-lance by the way thou dost stare at her!"

The long, black eyes of the boy flashed and his thin nostrils expanded with the quick gasp one sometimes gives on awakening. He turned and moved swiftly toward the surrounding masses of undergrowth.

Raquel had heard the words. From the row of peering faces in front of her the eyes of the youth had looked upon her with none of the expression that the countenances of his companions wore. She read in his surprised gaze something that she took to be pity, and, snatching at even this faint hope, she watched his graceful body swinging as lightly as a panther across the space of the clearing. His wavy, blue-black hair tossed with his rapid movements; his gold-tinted physique was perfectly molded. He seemed a reincarnated faun as he darted into the mysterious alleys of the forest. Anxiously she waited his reappearing. He came in company with a stalwart figure that strode toward the group with the imperiousness of a commander. She knew that she looked upon the most dreaded man among the mountain bandits. With eyes rendered keen by fear she studied him as he approached.

Instead of the monster she had anticipated she beheld an imposing man, but one in whose face lurked none of the hideous cruelty she had supposed was inseparable from his daily countenance. Had she met him anywhere save in the depths of this forest surrounded by his sworn followers she would have set him down as a courtier of exceptional manners. His glance was austere, his air masterful; clad in the habiliments of some former captive, he was as far removed from what she had expected as a man well could be. She was conscious that her courage revived in a wonderful degree. Her utter lack of knowledge of the world was responsible for her belief that scoundrelism and a gentlemanly air of breeding are incompatible. That she had less to fear than she had thought, his first words seemed to prove. After his deep glance at her, a glance that she felt had reached through and beyond her, he demanded with evident dissatisfaction:

"Is this as much as you men are capable of—after all this

waiting? Where is the game you meant to bag? We have no time to waste with small captures, and above all—with women."

"But, Comandante, her father is Palgrave, the sugar planter," explained Manuel, the leader of the capturing party. "She will bring a heavy ransom. Old Theuriet escaped us, and while we watched for him this muchacha slipped right into our hands. It seemed a shame not to take her. We can capture the Frenchman another time."

"Bah! Who can tell of to-morrow?" returned Alarcon. "You have been watching him for weeks. He would have been worth taking. He is an old coward, fond of luxury and life. He would have given half his estate for escape from Gonzalo Alarcon. This señorita will be more trouble than gain."

"She is all that he has. He will pay any sum for her," declared Manuel. "You will find that my words are true, *señor mio!*"

Manuel's assertion caused Raquel to forget both timidity and exhaustion.

"He is not telling you the truth, Señor Alarcon," she cried excitedly. "My father is not able to pay even a small ransom. The ingenio is mortgaged now to its fullest extent. He can get no more money from the Catalans, and he has had to borrow from old Monsieur Theuriet to pay interest on the mortgage. He fears that he can not pull through this year, señor, —how then can he pay one centavo for ransom? Your eyes are not cruel, Señor Alarcon; surely you would not wish to make him a pauper! Would you harm one who would fight for Cuba if need be?"

Gonzalo Alarcon's stern eyes dilated. He fell back a step involuntarily.

"Is your father against Spain?" he demanded, with surprise. For a man to dare to take such a stand in Cuba would be suicide almost. It was small wonder that the guerrilla chief viewed her with amazement.

"No, señor; but I am!"

Standing there in the midst of these mountain men, her long, white draperies loosened by her struggles, her dusky hair dishevelled, she looked so fragile and so tender that the almost imperceptible smile which crossed Alarcon's face was permissible. He bowed low before her.

"I am glad that there is one soul in Cuba fearless enough to assert itself," he said admiringly. "Consider Gonzalo Alarcon and his men your slaves."

"Were I a man, as Our Holy Mother of Sorrows knows I would I were, I would not allow you to send for ransom," she went on passionately. "I would join your band; I would urge you not to fight for petty spoil but for Cuba's freedom. With such a grand issue at stake how can you spend your time in wrenching ransom from innocent captives? Though I am a woman I yearn to be doing the work that you might do—if you would. I would never rest. I would devote my all to the hope of liberty for the island. You, in whose hands lies the power to aid your country, content yourself with an ignoble occupation, robbing your fellow-men of liberty and fortune."

Gonzalo Alarcon motioned his men away. He folded his arms across his breast and regarded her with a gaze that narrowed and deepened as he listened to her words. He never had encountered a captive of similar dauntlessness. She interested him.

"*Bueno y santo!*" he said with an assumption of submission. "You would urge me to throw myself and men into the struggle for what never will come to Cuba—liberty! How do you know, *señorita mia*, but that is what we are doing? Do you suppose that we proclaim our plans from the house-tops?"

Raquel hesitated. The man's manner puzzled her. She was amazed at her own temerity in addressing him as she had, and more amazed at his reception of her words. She looked at him questioningly, wondering how it was that this gentle brigand had acquired so unenviable a reputation throughout the island.

"But you are said to be merciless and mercenary," she told him slowly. "You can not have the interest of Cuba at heart when you seize her people and hold them for ransom that they cannot afford to give without impoverishing themselves. I never have heard that you were suspected of cherishing revolutionary intentions. You are known simply as Alarcon, the brigand, not the patriot."

The man's face flushed darkly under its coat of bronze. This being called to account by a prisoner was a novel experience to a man who wielded such power as the brigand leader did; but its very unusualness made it attractive to him.

"No; you never have heard and you never will hear of one tenth of the brave souls who have given and will give their lives for the vain hope of Cuban emancipation," he said.   "You count that giving your father's all would be forfeiting too much for the cause.   The men who follow me have done more; their lives are Cuba's."

He watched the effect of his utterance on Raquel.   A swift change went over her face.   For the instant she forgot her perilous position in her delight at finding that the mountain nourished a band of men thrilling with a hope like her own.

"So would I give mine, señor!" she cried.   "I would devote everything to it!"

"Yet you declare that no ransom must be demanded of your father, though you must know that the sum which you bring us will go into the exchequer destined to secure Cuba's liberty.   This is our only way of obtaining supplies for these forest soldiers.   We cannot tax the people as Spain does to feed and pay her army that she sets over Cubans to keep them in subjection.   All we can do is to insist that those whom we take as prisoners shall pay us enough to enable us to add to the fund which eventually is to free the entire island from her tyrant."   Alarcon was an astute student of men—and women as well.   He could anticipate the impression which these sentences would make upon her, and he was not disappointed in his estimate of her character.   She had shown him with her first words where her sympathies lay, and he was far too clever not to keep in the line with them.

"I would not demur if there were none but myself to consider," she declared, with a despairing gesture of her hands. "Gladly would I give my life to carry on the hope to fulfillment; but my father, he cannot raise one peso, señor! I speak the truth.   If the plantation must be forfeited to win my freedom there will be no place for the blacks to go—there even will be no roof to cover our heads.   Be merciful, señor!   It is a poor system to secure Cuba's freedom by making her daughters sacrifice theirs!"

Over the chief's countenance had been creeping a change. Into his eyes had stolen a cunning; the hard lines of his face softened beneath the power of a thought that made him say with the persuasive flattery common to southern tongues:

"And the señorita laments that she is not a man!   What

feminine ignorance!   God knows that there is many a woman's heart in Cuba capable of accomplishing more than its men ever will.   It is a pity that you are not what you so ardently desire to be.   I need such as you would prove.   Believe my words that it was not by my orders that you were seized; but, since you are here, it scarcely would be wise to permit so needed a prize to escape.   We men of the mountains must live; and we also must supply ourselves with ammunition against the day when we shall rise in might to drive the Spaniards from the island.   Those who enter our domains must be ransomed or—"

There was a pause, during which she looked anxiously into his face for a hint of what was coming.   She nerved herself to receive the alternative without flinching.

"—or they must join us."

"But that—I cannot!" she cried, with a little bewildered gasp.

"No?" he queried calmly.   "*Porqué?*"

"Of what use should I be?"   Unmitigated wonderment was in her voice and eyes.

"Have you lived so little that you do not know that often it is the power behind the throne that controls?"   He asked the question with a look that made his eyes soft and powerful.   "Know you so little of the history of man and nations?"

"Know?   How should I know?" demanded she.   Into her face flashed new fears which her resolute spirit could not banish.   There was something in Alarcon's look against which she felt herself fighting blindly.   She realized afresh her helplessness and dependence.   His proffered alternative, instead of showing her the power of woman, revealed to her how completely at his mercy she was.   Here was the seeming opportunity to help Cuba which she had craved, but, rising up in wildest opposition to it, was the love for her father which stormed within her.   The island's future sunk into insignificance before the awful prospect of being separated from him.   All of her courage was gone.   She shivered with apprehension.

Gonzalo Alarcon took a quick step forward.

"You have seen nothing?" questioned he meaningly.   "I can see that you long to live—to conquer.   It has been women like you who have urged men on to achieve great deeds that would have remained undone but for their inspiration.   Women like you make Cuba's freedom possible. In your eyes—deep down—one can read the thirst. I will lead you to victories. Will you follow?"

Raquel's eyes indeed now burned with an odd intensity. She was frightened by those black ones which held hers by a spell which seemed sapping her volition. The scene about her appeared to revolve with lightning rapidity. Only that unfamiliar face with its strange smile stood out before her vision. She was conscious that he still spoke to her.

"I will go for the ransom myself, señorita. Failing to secure that, you are to become one of us—and you shall rule, rule even me, Gonzalo Alarcon."

Raquel's reply was only the frightened quickening of her breath.

How dear the safety and monotonous peace of La Sacra Sonrisa seemed as she realized that, even if ransomed, the walls of the old hacienda could shelter her no more; her ransom would place the plantation in the grasp of strangers. She reeled at the thought and put out her hands vaguely, ignorant that the relief of temporary unconsciousness was coming to her aid.

The chief saw the movement and caught her fingers in his own.

"You are tired, señorita!" he exclaimed, with self-reproach. "Your courage made me forget that you have not the endurance of a man."

But his hold on her was not sufficient to prevent her from slipping downward limply with white face. The strength produced by her momentary courage had vanished. All of the terror and exhaustion which she had suffered now showed in her face. Alarcon drew her forcibly up into his arms for a moment, while he curiously inspected her pale features.

"*Caspita!* What a daring little one she is!" he murmured.

As he placed her on the soft forest carpet, he glanced about him and discovered Zuñega crossing the open space with a saddle on his shoulder.

"*Hola*, Zuñega! Call Annizae!" Alarcon ordered.

As if the entire camp had been watching, the summons was obeyed by each and all. Two women crowded forward eagerly. To the foremost one the chief said authoritatively:

"Take charge of her! She is not to be out of your sight."

The woman, tall and muscular, bent over the outstretched form of Raquel, then glanced up at Alarcon questioningly.

"She is exhausted," explained the chief. "She must have the best of care." The other woman went and peered down over Annizae's shoulder. The indubitable beauty of the girl appeared to excite her. She also glanced up at the chief, but the expression of her eyes was quite different from that which had been given by Annizae.

"Is she to be ransomed?" she demanded in an undertone of Alarcon.

"What is that to you, Faquita?" asked he carelessly.

"What is it not to me?" she retorted.

Alarcon placed one finger under her chin and lifted it teasingly.

"Jealous again?" he inquired. "Does a woman never learn that jealousy is death to love?"

The eyes of Faquita smouldered beneath their heavy lids.

Annizae had picked Raquel up lightly in her strong arms and now carried her through the green network from which the chief had advanced.

Faquita followed her.

Gonzalo Alarcon joined his men, inquiring into the full particulars of the capture.

"It is little gold that we will get from it," he told them, intentionally belittling their success. "M. Theuriet would have been a mine to us."

Here arose a chorus of voices proclaiming how great was the estate called La Sacra Sonrisa, and how indefatigable were the sugar mills.

Alarcon listened in silence for a time, then he said impatiently:

"For all that, Señor Palgrave may not be able to procure sufficient pesos to ransom his daughter; and we shall have another woman in camp."

The men glanced from under their lids significantly at each other. "Who goes for the ransom, Comandante?" queried José, striking his spurs together reflectively as he sat on the felled trunk of one of the forest monarchs.

"Don Gonzalo knows better than to send thee, José," laughed Manuel provokingly. "Thou wouldst sleep and forget thy mission."

"I pray he sends not me," returned José without show of anger. "It is too perilous. Zuñega is most cat-like. He could pin the threats on Señor Palgrave's pillow with ten knives and none would hear him."

"Zuñega is to be placed as guard over the girl," announced Alarcon with decision. "I myself will go for the ransom."

"*Diablo!* Before the threats have been delivered?" exclaimed the men. "Do you forget the price of ten thousand pesos set on your head, Comandante?"

"I forget nothing," answered Alarcon quietly. "If it is possible to secure gold, you know well that I am the one to do it. I will go alone. Twenty of you station yourselves at the Paso del Diablo the night of the morrow. I will summon you from there when I need you."

Despite the evident camaraderie which existed between Gonzalo Alarcon and his men, gathered from many sources, he never failed to make himself obeyed. His was a motley company that required of no man his past. The invincible will of Alarcon ruled.

Preparations were made for his departure. After the camp breakfast with its fragrant coffee had been disposed of, the lithe Cuban horse which always carried the chief was duly caparisoned. In vivid contrast with the general properties of the camp, the gaily embroidered saddle-cloth on which the high-peaked Spanish saddle was placed shone against the sombre background of the forest with something of barbaric splendor. Zuñega stood at the head of the animal, caressing it with the tenderness one bestows on a beloved object.

Alarcon was conferring with Annizae, in whose charge he intended to leave Raquel. At breakfast, in the presence of the camp, he had commissioned Zuñega to act in the capacity of guard, supplementing Annizae's watchful care. Zuñega had received his orders with eyes that gave no evidence of the tremor which shook him at this proof of the faith reposed in him. That the post had been coveted by other members of the camp was shown by the signs of disapproval with which his appointment was accepted, disapproval which quickly was silenced by Alarcon's lightning glance. It did not take a great amount of perception to acquaint them with Alarcon's decision that, failing in securing the ransom, the new acquisition to his band would be a satisfactory one so far as he was concerned, despite his assertion that the feminine element in a guerrilla camp was more trouble than gain.

When Alarcon came to mount he viewed the trappings of his caballo with disfavor. He had them removed and an inconspicuous blanket placed in lieu of the saddle-cloth.

"When the Spanish government is anxious for a man it is well for that man to attract little attention," he remarked grimly, as he swung himself into position on his horse's back.

"*Adios, hombres!*"

"*Adios! Adios! Vaya usted con Dios!*" cried the members of the camp, as he rode off into the emerald wall surrounding them. "God go with you!" And they appeared to see nothing absurd in the hope that the High Ruler of the universe would assist Alarcon in his nefarious design of exacting the impossible from Gilbert Palgrave.

Zuñega watched the moving horseman as far as the green forest veil would permit.

An unanalyzed feeling of exultation was in his heart.

He turned and went with supple step to begin his duties as jailer.

CHAPTER IV.

When Raquel's absence was discovered, the wildest excitement reigned at the ingenio. The devastation which the horses' feet had created in the cane left little doubt to be entertained as to what fate had befallen the beloved one of the plantation.

Frantic with fear, Palgrave got his men together hastily, leaving a few boys and decrepit negroes to watch over the furnace fires. Double affliction was his in this enforced idleness which would fall upon the mill and fields right in the height of the grinding season, when forces should have been kept at work night and day in order to complete the work within the usual four months. He realized fully what this loss of time meant to him and his sugar crop; but there was no alternative. Raquel must be found and wrested from her captors.

M. Theuriet, as anxious as his neighbor, summoned all of the available blacks from his coffee estate, and, at their head, presented himself at La Sacra Sonrisa, subject to the orders of the bereft father.

Leaving the wellnigh deserted plantation lying lonesomely beneath the midnight sky, the two cavalcades followed the course left by the tread of the abductors' horses. Palgrave knew that it would have been wiser to have waited for dawn, but the terrible pressure of Raquel's need would not permit him to delay one second longer than necessity demanded for making preparations to rescue her.

In the edge of the forest the two companies separated, taking different routes in the hope of circumventing the rascals.

The tangles and dense growth of fecund tropical vegetation balked their progress continually. To their untrained eyes the mysterious ways through which they pushed laboriously were misleading in the extreme. What with the darkness of the heavens and the gruesome blackness of this wanton plant luxuriation they finally were forced to pause and wait for day, relaxing none in vigilance lest they might be attacked by some of the dauntless denizens to whom this intricate mountain labyrinth was home. To the tense nerves of Gilbert Palgrave it seemed as if he could hear the winging flight of the precious moments, so oppressively still was nature's vast cathedral. And yet there was a constant murmur of growth in the air. Everything was thrilling with the vitality of a rich life; but there was an odor, warm, damp, which chilled him, as if the wind of destiny had blown to him from off Death's pallid face.

With the first suggestion of sunlight to aid them they took up the interrupted search. As day grew their eyes perceived that overhead hung canopies of vines flung from tree to tree, tapestries of a million hues interwoven.

Through the long hours that followed ere another night shut down, they scoured the forest as well as they were able, unfamiliar as they were with its secrets. Long ago they had lost the trail of the brigands, but still they kept on, hoping against hope. Palgrave trusted that M. Theuriet had been more fortunate than he. The thought that the Frenchman possibly might have stumbled into the proper route secured him against utter discouragement as the fruitless moments crept by.

When the second night stole up shadow-like from the edge of the distant sea, he felt himself no nearer her.

"God in Heaven! What is to be done?" he cried in despair.

Suddenly the sound of voices reached their ears, accompanied by the crash of underbrush. His men threw themselves into an attitude of defence.

"Thank the Lord!" he breathed joyously. "We have run across their path."

But in another instant he caught M. Theuriet's unmistakable pronunciation, which, despite his many years in the country, still retained its distinctive Gallic features.

"*Cuidado, hombres!*" the Frenchman was cautioning the foremost. "Tak' care! We mus' mov' wiz sure steps. To remain zere anozer night will be folly, but too much haste may be disastrous as well."

Gilbert Palgrave knew then with sinking heart how wholly vain had been the effort to wrench Raquel from the hands that held her. Doubtless, for fear of pursuit, the guerrillas had borne her far beyond his most persistent seeking.

He raised his voice and called to M. Theuriet, urging his horse forward as he did so.

As they met, the combined yellow glare of the many candles, each black now being the bearer of one as the darkness deepened, threw the haggard countenance of the father and the sallow, wrinkled visage of the coffee planter into relief against the background of the forest foliage.

Each viewed the other with keen disappointment.

"We must have been moving in circles," said Palgrave, with a hopeless cadence in his speech.

"To my mind, ze most senseeble course to pairsue, now zat all trace of zem we hav' lost, ees to return to ze plantaceon and await——" began M. Theuriet.

"And leave her in the hands of those devils?" cried the father with fierce opposition, though he also was aware that it was useless to wander thus blindly through the mazes of the mountain vegetation.

"*Mais*—but what bettair can we?" questioned the coffee planter anxiously. "Zis expediceon ees useless, *n'est-ce pas?* Cairtainlee we can call for aid in ze shape of ze *guardia civile,* or—"

"Yes, but what may be her fate in the mean time!" interrupted Palgrave wildly. "Do you forget the national trait? I only shall have '*mañana, mañana,*' that everlasting cry of the Spaniard, breathed into my ears—that is all!"

"Pardon, mon ami, you hav' not pairmit me to complet' mon sentence," observed M. Theuriet apologetically. "Ze first move zat ze brigands will be likelee to mak' will be to demand an enormous ransom,—ees eet not so? Pairfectlee. *Bien*, eef zat be forthcoming, well and good! You will hav' Raquelita returned to La Sacra Sonrisa. But eef eet be absent or difficile to appear, you may receiv' occasional remindairs ov her een ze shape ov fractions ov her pairson."

"Satan take your diabolical tongue!" groaned Palgrave distractedly. "Do you desire to drive me mad? Do you think that, during these terrible hours I have not recalled every atrocious violence that I ever heard was committed by them? I mean to find her if it takes the rest of my life, God helping me!"

"But, zay hav' anticipated pairsuit and, wherever zay are, hav' fortified zemselves against attack," M. Theuriet argued. "Are zay not sartain to be well armed? Zare ees but one zing to do."

Gilbert Palgrave's face grew whiter. He knew how impossible that one thing would be. He thrust his spurs recklessly into his horse's sides and plunged rashly down the precipitous path which turned in the direction of the valley. His men followed quickly. After a quarter of an hour he paused and allowed the Frenchman to urge his animal abreast.

"What on earth am I to do, Theuriet?" he asked helplessly. "My hands practically are tied when it comes to the question of raising a ransom. None know better than you how difficult, how fruitless will be the effort to secure gold, situated as I now am. If you recollect, we were discussing my position when she disappeared from the sala."

"I remember," assented Theuriet with a sigh. With Palgrave's confession of utter inability to cope with this serious monetary problem, the Frenchman's face had undergone a subtle change that the shadows of the coming night concealed. "Ov cours' eet will be out ov ze posseebl' for you to furnish much gold quicklee; but for ze sak' ov our long friendsheep an' also for ze sak' ov ze belle mademoiselle who ees dear to me I am more zan willing to advance any sum ov which you may hav' need."

Gilbert Palgrave's countenance turned a purplish tinge. He appeared to reel in his saddle for an instant. The parsimony of M. Theuriet was well known. Not for a moment had Palgrave thought that the Frenchman would propose to place him under additional indebtedness, knowing as Theuriet did the Englishman's inability to give him satisfactory security. The father leaned down and forward, looking into the face of Theuriet with doubting eyes.

"Do my ears play me false?" he demanded sharply. "Do you jest with me?"

"Nevair befor' was I so een earnest," swore M. Theuriet emphatically.

"Have you thought what your offer may bring upon you?" Palgrave asked anxiously. "It may cripple you seriously. It will be long before I can repay you. Have you thought of that?"

"Cairtainlee! I hav' thought of all," replied Theuriet calmly.

Palgrave drew a long breath. He had been almost afraid to ask the Frenchman to reconsider his proposition, yet his sense of fairness would not permit him to accept the generosity of his neighbor without reminding him what a precarious loan it was likely to prove.

"I would rather die than permit you to make such a sacrifice for me," he declared warmly, "but I see nothing else for me to do; my death would be productive of nothing. With life, however, there is a prospect that in a few years I may be able to discharge my indebtedness. Until then your only reward will be in the consciousness of having performed a most noble deed."

"You hav' ze opportunitee ov repaying me at once and also ov cancelling all previous indebtedness eef you but choose to say ze word," returned M. Theuriet. He spoke not quite as calmly now. There was a hint of repression in his voice, but the words themselves were electrical enough to claim the attention of their hearer.

Palgrave looked at him in questioning silence for some moments, during which he was endeavoring to fathom the meaning of the statement. At length he said slowly:

"I do not comprehend."

"Do you not recall, *mon ami*," explained Theuriet, moistening his lips as he spoke, "when we were talking ov securitee I said zat you had one possession which I would be willing to take as securitee and lend you many pesos more?"

"Yes," answered Palgrave cautiously. "It was just as Raquel entered. I intended to ask you, after she went out, to what you referred; but it went out of my mind."

M. Theuriet smiled.

"Zat was ze security to which I referred," he murmured.

"The devil! Have you taken leave of your senses?" Palgrave demanded. "I have not the faintest idea what you mean."

"I mean zis," said M. Theuriet slowly. "I will pay ze ransom and your entire indebtedness—not alone what you owe me, *mon ami*—on ze condition zat when she ees returned to you, you will giv' her to me. She ees ze security which would indemnify me against all losses."

"Give her to you! For what?" The undisguised amazement in the father's tone brought a dull hue of color into M. Theuriet's faded face, but he managed to answer steadily:

"For my wife."

Palgrave jerked his horse to a sudden halt.

"For your wife?" he gasped. "Why, man, you are old enough to be her father!"

"*C'est vrai*," admitted the Frenchman, wincing a trifle beneath the sting in the exclamation of the girl's parent, "but, pardon, I would be more kind to her zan her captors are likelee to be, zink you not so, unless ze ransom arreev' quicklee?"

The teeth of the sugar planter met fiercely through his nether lip.

"Are those your only terms?" he asked bitterly.

"Could you wish bettair, my friend?" replied M. Theuriet, with evident surprise. "Wiz one stroke, you recovair your daughtair an' remov' your largest creditor, besides securing his aid een settling wiz ze Catalans." He lighted a cigar while he spoke, to hide the nervous twitching of his lips. He had had a desire for Raquel ever since he had seen her blooming into womanhood, but he never had dared to hope that such an opportunity as this would be afforded him. He had made his proposition. He felt certain that the fear of the parent for the safety of his child would lead Palgrave to accept it, acting on the maxim: "Of two evils, choose the lesser." Not that he considered himself in the light of an evil, but it was evident that Palgrave did in this connection.

"Not to save myself from the deepest dye of disgrace would I consent to such an agreement," groaned the hard-pressed man to himself, "but to save her from the life that is before her if she is not ransomed—that is different. Anything is better than her present condition." His eyes were burning. He saw no other way by which he might take his loved one from the perils which had become hers.

"Both ov us will zen hav' her," M. Theuriet said suggestively. He spoke as if it already were settled. Perhaps it would be a high price to pay for a bride, but, he consoled himself with the reflection that she was worth it; and besides, he was fond of his neighbor and was not averse to helping him thus in his sore dilemma.

It was a long time before Palgrave uttered a word. They proceeded silently. The night closed in about them. The darkness seemed to throb with its own intensity. Palgrave felt that it stifled him. The tapers in the fingers of the men melted, bent, died down, and were replaced by others that flared fitfully at first, lighting up with feeble glimmer the anaconda-like twistings of the parasitic vines about them.

The minutes dropped away.

Fatigue and depression lay with heavy gloom over the entire number.

It was dawn of the second day before they crept, like a column of ants, out from the shadow of the forest and began to descend to the savannah.

The broad fields stretched wide their undulating surfaces of yellow green cane.

Gilbert Palgrave's heart leaped into his throat and choked him as he looked out over the magical scene. If it were sacrificed to ransom her, to what place could they go? No home would be ready for her. Both of them would be destitute, obliged to accept M. Theuriet's hospitality until they could right themselves and get a fresh start. What would become of the blacks? Some of them had never known other home than this. He turned to the Frenchman abruptly.

"I accept your offer," he said, with the air of one who after a hard struggle, yields to the inevitable, "on this condition:

she shall be allowed to choose. If she is willing to prove her gratitude to you for doing what I am not able to do, I will have nothing to say. But if she shrinks from fulfilling the stipulations she shall not be forced into the union. I will go out as a common laborer rather than——"

"We are agreed," M. Theuriet hastened to say. "I accept your restreection. I zink zat she will not need be forced eento eet. I would desire only her willing acquiescence een ze mattair."

But he knew Raquel's nature well enough to be certain that, learning on what terms her freedom had been purchased, she would remove the debt at any cost.

In the mean time, Gonzalo Alarcon had been forcing his way rapidly through the jungles of interlaced green life gay with magnificent bloom. The path became more formidable the higher he climbed. His fleet animal moved with infinite caution on the verge of precipices that jutted daringly over foaming cascades of a thousand opaline tints, waters that gushed joyously from subterranean sources, the sumideros or caverns that honeycomb the surface of the island. The route which he had chosen was far shorter than the one up which Raquel had been taken. Many hours had not passed before he halted on an eminence which afforded him an excellent view of the ingenio of La Sacra Sonrisa.

Looking down on it from above, only the mass of tree-tops was visible surrounding the house. The palms, alternating with the mangoes and aguacates, rising far beyond them to the height of a hundred feet or more, looked like green plumes as they tossed gently in the breeze, which did not reach down to touch a leaf of the smaller trees. Set in the midst of the bright gold-tinged cane fields, the grove of beautiful foliage resembled nothing so much as an exquisite emerald in a glittering setting.

The absence of life on the plantation convinced him that the male portion of the retinue of blacks had been detailed to search for the missing girl, and he decided to make his way to the hacienda without delay.

He spurred his horse down the precipitous wall of green with a fearlessness that brought him a couple of hours later out upon the unfrequented highway leading to the sugar plantation. None would have thought, judging from his seemingly careless demeanor, that there was a goodly price offered for his person, alive or dead.

At a curve in the road he came suddenly upon two equestrians. His hand instantly was on his weapons, as were theirs.

"Halt!" ordered one of them in English, covering the solitary horseman with a revolver.

Alarcon's horse was drawn up sharply.

"Peace, *amigos*," he returned with the courtesy of the country. "You have the advantage of me, señors. Can I serve you? I place myself at your feet"—the latter declaration being nothing more than a common salutation in all lands where Spanish blood has entered.

Still wary, the two riders approached him.

"*Sí, señor ;* the estate of La Buena Esperanza, the coffee plantation of M. Theuriet, we seek it," explained the one whom Alarcon divined to be a Havanese guide escorting the stranger through the interior. "Will you direct us? There is a fork in the road some distance back. We fear we have taken the wrong turning."

"*Es verdad*," nodded Alarcon in a most friendly manner. "You have done so. I go to the same turning. Will you have the grace to permit me to accompany you?"

"*Con mucho gusto, señor*," answered the first speaker, the one who had been so peremptory with his demand. It was no other than Lithgow, who had succeeded in coming this near the property of the coffee planter to whom he bore letters. His journey through the mysterious land of inland Cuba had been fraught with no adventures worth chronicling. Owing to warnings received in Havana he had been suspicious and on the alert, but to no purpose; and he had indulged in some merriment over the exaggerated reports of the dangers attending an interior trip. Even this encounter, which had had the flavor of possible trouble, quickly resolved itself into an amicable meeting, though, when Alarcon came abreast, the American still deemed it advisable to keep a vigilant eye on this highway acquaintance.

"*El señor es Inglés—no ?*" queried Alarcon smilingly.

"*No ; Americano*," corrected Lithgow, with the briefness of the foreigner.

"Ah, *sí ;* one might have known," commented Alarcon. "None but an American who knows nothing but freedom would be wandering thus alone through this portion of the island. Were you not warned, señor?"

"Times without number," answered Lithgow, adding with a tone of apology: "That was the reason, pardon, señor, why I mistook you for a possible——"

"Guerrilla?" laughed Alarcon, helping him out. "I must appear dangerous; is it so? Believe me, señors, I am pained to have alarmed you. The last thing that a Cuban desires is to frighten away American enterprise from the island."

Lithgow felt his doubts diminishing as to the reputable standing of this gentleman. In his mind he set him down for a planter of note.

"You are the first individual, señor, from whom I have heard such a remark," he said with satisfaction. "It is a strange people down here. They appear determined not to advance. They put obstacles in the way of each proposed improvement."

"Call it not the fault of the people but the fault of the power that governs us," Alarcon answered, glancing at the guide. "How can the tax-ridden populace take that which Spain does not give them? She is not anxious for improvements. She has no desire that the full resources of her rich possession shall become known and draw covetous eyes, least of all those of the mighty republic north of us."

The guide turned a gaze in which was dawning a wondering distrust upon this fearless speaker; for, even with but the forest to hear, it is a bold man that utters such sentences in Cuba. But Alarcon's attention was riveted now on the American. He missed the glance of the Havanese. He went on earnestly:

"Cuba's mines are unworked because the taxes on the exhumed ore are more than the value of the stuff itself. Of its thirty-five million acres, over fifteen million are forests, over seven million are barren, only about three million are devoted to agriculture, here where the ground needs only to be 'tickled with a hoe and it laughs' and brings forth such harvests as no other land knows. Many plantations have lain in waste since the ten-year war. The planters become poorer each year because the taxes eat their profits. Not until Cuba gains her freedom will she be anything but an orange sucked dry. Spain drains her of everything. Spanish soldiers quartered on us, thriving at the island's expense, will some day find themselves pushed into the sea, and before Spain can send others over, Cuba will be able to take possession of herself."

"Such words are not uttered in Havana," the American said significantly.

"No, nor here, señor, save by those who dare," returned Alarcon as significantly.

Lithgow regarded him keenly.

"I am glad to have met you, señor," he told him. "You are the only person I have seen who has not been afraid of something, governor-general, priests, taxes, fever, failure— but you appear to defy such small matters."

Alarcon indulged in a peculiar smile. They had reached the fork in the road. He urged his horse into it, at the same time lifting his sombrero with the ineffable grace of him who boasts of Castilian blood.

"*Gracias, señor,*" he replied, with a gesture of farewell. "A Cuban sometimes rejoices at an opportunity to say what he thinks. *Adios!* You now are on the borders of the estate of M. Theuriet. Two miles will bring you to the hacienda. *Vaya usted con Dios!*"

And each rode his way, unaware that their first was not to be their last meeting.

CHAPTER V.

JUST as night fell, Tia Juana, the present head of the Palgrave household, was summoned to the bolted entrance by a loud and repeated knocking. She thrust a turbaned head out of a safe aperture and took a deliberate survey of the producer of the commotion.

"*Madre de Dios!* Thinkest thou that I will let thee in?" she queried silently. "How knowest I that thou art not the devil himself in disguise?"

The disturbance continued, and she heard the words:

"Open quickly! I have news of the lost señorita."

Tia Juana scrambled hastily from her post of observation and obeyed the mandate of the stranger joyfully, besieging him with questions that elicited but meagre replies.

"The communication is only for Señor Palgrave," he rebuked her with authority. "Where is he?"

"He seeks the señorita in the mountains, *señor mio.* Satan take the black souls of those brigands!" she answered, dropping into the lamentations which prevailed at the ingenio.

Alarcon showed his white teeth in a satisfied smile.

"How long since he went, *mi bonita?*" he asked, giving her a glance of such flattering admiration that the heart of Tia Juana never could have withheld any information that he might have demanded. It was long since the eye of masculinity had accorded her anything but indifference, and she expanded under it as a faded violet will beneath the rains of April.

"A night and a day, *señor mio*—ever since the señorita was stolen. Dios visit the fires of perdition upon the wild riders!"

"Then it is safe to presume that this night will bring his return," commented Alarcon comfortably, preparing to make himself at home.

"God grant it!" breathed the woman. "But he will return only when he brings her; he so swore."

Alarcon shrugged his broad shoulders lightly.

"*Muy bien,*" he said. "Then I must wait. I am as ravenous as a judio. Will your sweet hands have the grace to bring me the best that the hacienda affords?—and wine, too, *querida mia;* a bottle of Don Gilberto's best wine!"

Flushed with the tremor that his endearing words gave her long-quiet heart, Tia Juana hastened into the cocina to do his bidding, imparting to the other women the excitement of her own manner.

While waiting for his orders to be executed, Alarcon looked about him. He was pleased with the scrutiny. He found himself surrounded by an air of comfort to which he had been a stranger these many years. He appropriated Palgrave's cigars. He glanced over the well-filled bookshelves, but therefrom he gained little, as most of the volumes were printed in the English language and Alarcon's education had been acquired in Spain, from which land he had been exiled to Cuba for some early misdemeanor for which exile had been deemed the most suitable punishment.

Completing his examination of the hacienda as far as was

possible, he went out to investigate the estate and measure its resources.

The fires had gone out in the mill, something that never had happened during the sugar season in all the years that the plantation had been in the Englishman's hands. Cold and black the furnaces loomed up, filled with the ashes of dead fires—fires that had made the place appear a veritable Pluto's realm as the lurid light flamed and flickered over the bare, ebony backs of the workers as they passed to and fro, keeping time to the high, weird, monotonous chant of the gangs filling the troughs with cane. For a scene of ceaseless activity none is equal to a sugar plantation during the season, and, by comparison, the spot now looked as if a plague had struck it.

Alarcon knew what a tremendous loss these few days of absolute idleness would mean to the planter, yet he did not think of swerving from his intention of securing ransom from the strained exchequer of Palgrave.

After partaking with appreciation of the meal which Tia Juana and her supernumeraries had concocted, he swung himself in Raquel's hammock, disregarding Tia Juana's plain announcement that it was considered sacred since the disappearance of the young mistress.

With a soul not wholly insensible to the whisperings of the palm's high-lifted crest, he revelled in the temerity that allowed him to eat and sleep beneath the roof from which his men had stolen its chief treasure. His thoughts dwelt on the girl. He could fancy how she had lain thus, idly swinging night after night, shut in so completely from the world.

"No wonder that she longs for work to do, for worlds to win!" he said to himself in the darkness. "If it were not for the gold that I hope to get, she should remain with us: she should know the exhilaration of danger, the wildness of victory. Her frail body shelters the soul of a man hungry to make the world *feel* him, praise him, blame him. And if the gold is not to be had—she *shall* become one of us!"

The sound of the water splashing forlornly in the fountain broke in upon his thoughts. After a time he continued his cogitations:

"At first she might hate me for the loss of all these delights, but some day—she would thank me; for with her bold spirit to urge a man on there would be no limits placed on his possible achievements. On some to-morrow she would look back with shrugs to the uneventful hours spent here, some to-morrow when Cuba might be at her feet and I, Cuba's hero. Stranger things have been. It would be a sweet revenge on old Spain for the indignities she heaped on me as a prisoner. I've a mind to let the girl stir me to action. So far I have been content to levy tribute on Spain's subjects. To raise a force sufficient to drive Spain from the country would be to wreak a grand vengeance on her and her rulers. *Por Dios !* I will do it on some *mañana !* "

He lighted another cigar and indulged in a faint smile at his own expense as he realized that his castles in Spain were towering up with only the blue of the heavens to roof them.

" There is Faquita, however," he reminded himself, with a frown. " One camp could never hold her and her successor. Dust of the saints! Why is it that women will be faithful when one would prefer them otherwise?"

The purple night wore on and away.

Alarcon retained his position in the hammock and slept the sound sleep that tradition accords to the innocent alone.

He did not hear the approaching hoofs which wound their way slowly toward the entrance.

Twice a sharp summons rang out.

When Tia Juana hurried fearfully to the heavily barred door, Alarcon caught her by the arm persuasively.

" Speak not a word of me," he whispered, with a threat in his tender tones, " or I shall know how to silence you."

Bewildered, for she had intended to announce at once his presence, Tia Juana blundered with agitated fingers that slowly undid the chains. Before swinging wide the entrance, she glanced behind her. The stranger was nowhere to be seen.

When Gilbert Palgrave finally secured admittance to the court, the fact that he was not accompanied by Raquel caused such a wail of disappointment to be sent up that for the time Tia Juana completely forgot the unbidden guest.

" Hush!" exclaimed Palgrave peremptorily, to whom this show of grief was intolerable. " No good is to be done by such a commotion. Get me some coffee, Juana, and put the other women to work caring for the men. We are exhausted."

Obediently she served him, watching him the while with anxious eyes. Outside the tired blacks were relating sorrowfully the discouragements which had met the essay to penetrate the forest; but the master told her nothing. A blight seemed to have fallen upon him. He appeared to have aged twenty years.

She looked about her searchingly, wondering where the stranger had concealed himself. She marvelled at such concealment. Why did he not make triumphant declaration that he bore information concerning the señorita? She knew that longer delay to announce his presence would be inexcusable on her part.

"Dear master, Juana has good news," she ventured tremulously, at last.

Gilbert Palgrave looked up at her with a mute question in his worn face. He waited for her to tell it.

"One has come, señor, who brings word of the señorita."

The sugar planter rose to his feet and laid his hand instinctively on the weapon at his belt. He had no doubt what kind of a message had been brought.

"Where is he?" he demanded. His voice was full of menace.

"*Aquí, señor*," came the answer calmly, and, turning, Gilbert Palgrave found himself face to face with the stalwart figure of the man who had had the audacity to sleep within his walls.

"And you are——?" asked the father.

"One who has come to aid you in freeing the señorita." Alarcon's quiet tone was convincing. Palgrave hesitated. This was a little different from what he had expected.

"How?" he questioned, his voice tense and strained with the curb he was keeping upon himself. "By what method?"

"Furnish the ransom that is requested, señor."

"Never!" declared the Englishman, bringing down his hand with force among the dishes which Tia Juana had set before him. "I will have you strung up as a malefactor and all who come after you on the same mission, until your leader will be glad to return my daughter to secure a cessation of hostilities."

"*Muy bien*," bowed Alarcon. "The señor knows best how he values his child, and which is of more importance, the señorita or gold."

Gilbert Palgrave's face quivered.

"We need the gold," Alarcon went on, "and that is why I have dared to present myself before you unattended—to warn you. *We* need the pesos far more than we need the girl; but the chief has become so enamored of her"—here a smile curved his lips a trifle—"that he may refuse even ransom for her. I am here to urge you to immediate action if you hope to have her returned to you. Alarcon knows our need of the ransom, but the danger is that he may let his inclinations get the better of his judgment, and leave us to secure gold from some other source."

Palgrave's already pale face turned ashen in hue.

"My God! *Alarcon!* Is it into his hands that she has fallen? Heaven help us! It is not that I care for the gold; it is the fact that I cannot secure it. The money-lenders have me in their power completely. I cannot raise another medio, even on next year's crop. Think of the position I am in, man, and have pity! I would sell my soul to procure her freedom, but—what can I do? You demand gold—gold I have not."

Gonzalo Alarcon wisely gave no evidence of his identity.

"Yes, señor, we must have gold," he replied. "There is more at stake than you think. Possibly you are in favor of Spanish officials and Spanish soldiers for whom you are taxed so severely; they are the ones who pocket your profits. This money which must redeem your child will go to arm those who are willing to fight for such as you who are crushed by the iron heel of Spain. Cuba must be rid of her oppressors."

The sugar planter thrust out his hands bitterly.

"Yes!" he cried. "Cuba has heard that again and again, and what does it amount to? Defeat, defeat! And then the taxes are piled on anew to pay for Spain's war expenses in conquering us. The planters are the ones who suffer the most lamentably. Look how it was after the last revolt! Even if I could afford it, I should be a fool to furnish funds to equip an army that will make havoc of every estate in the island, my own included."

The chief's shoulders moved with the philosophical shrug of the Cuban. Though he had not the faintest connection with the patriots, even then planning cautiously for a future revolution, Alarcon deemed it wise to pretend that the ransom was to be devoted to the noble cause of liberty. In case of insurrection he and his men would be certain to link themselves with the common cause, but never could he be classed legitimately among those dauntless ones who pour their noble blood so freely forth for the land that they love.

"The revolution will come some day whether you help or not, señor," he observed. "If a portion of the assistance proceeds from you, you and your possessions will be protected."

"But it is impossible!" Palgrave asserted, with despairing accent. "I am at your mercy. I must have my child, but— I have nothing to offer you as purchase-money."

Gonzalo Alarcon looked at him steadily.

"Borrow of M. Theuriet," he suggested. "He has accommodated you before; he may again."

The planter's expression became one of angered astonishment.

"How could you know?" he demanded.

"Our sources of information are extensive," smiled Alarcon, not thinking it necessary to betray that he had learned this from Raquel herself. "M. Theuriet will loan you any amount now, is it not so?"

Gilbert Palgrave realized his bitter position. A convulsion of impotent rage shook him. He saw that his effort to secure her without this sacrifice was of no avail. It was like beating against a stone wall to appeal to the emissary before him. Controlling himself with all the force of a strong will, he summoned Tia Juana, who had withdrawn discreetly on the discovery that she had not been far wrong in her first remarks on Alarcon when she had viewed him from her post of vantage.

"Send Diego for M. Theuriet," ordered the master. "Tell him to make haste. M. Theuriet must come back with him."

On returning from the mountains, M. Theuriet found that those he had left in charge had recognized the American as the guest their master was expecting and had installed him as hospitably as M. Theuriet himself could have done.

The commotion of the early home-comers awakened the entire household, and Lithgow, dressing hastily, descended to the sala to meet his host.

The worn appearance of M. Theuriet and his men and the lamentations of the women told Lithgow how fruitless had been the search, even before M. Theuriet himself acquainted him with the result.

"I grieve zat I was not 'ere to giv' you ze welcome zat has been waiting for you, Mr. Hamilton," Theuriet said when Lithgow presented himself with his credentials. "Doubtless you hav' learned ze cause ov my absence. *Oui?* Ah, eet ees verra sad! You will pardon eef I leav' you while I remov' my fatigue? *Merci!* Consider my house your own."

Lithgow had listened the night before to a most vivid account of the abduction, and, after rehearsing it to Beatrice in a letter which he gave to the guide, had gone to sleep in the unluxurious bed known to tropical countries, feeling that he indeed was in the land of romance and mystery. He scarcely had been able to credit the story as first it was related to him. His host's manner convinced him that it had not been the dream it had seemed to him on awakening.

Thinking it scarcely worth while to go back to bed, he stationed himself in one of the chairs of the estrada to take another nap, if might be, and so wear away the time until the proprietor of the estate should be in a condition to execute business. Despite the tempting, dreamful ease which appeared to hover over the plantation, he contemplated remaining at La Buena Esperanza no longer than was necessary for the proper consummation of the matter he had in hand.

That it would be a halcyon spot in which to spend the rest of his life he had decided after one glance up the cool, perfumed avenue of West Indian trees that led to the white galleries of the mansion which M. Theuriet had had constructed after the style of French architecture.

He had not been able to compose himself to somnolency when the rapid beat of horses' hoofs up the palm-lined avenue broke in upon his thoughts. There was something suggestive of alarm in the sound, and the household was in commotion again.

It was Diego and a companion, bearing Don Gilberto Palgrave's message.

M. Theuriet soon appeared in response to the summons, looking very haggard by the brightness of the day.

A curious elation was in his face.

He approached his guest.

"My neighbor, whose daughtair was taken by zose scoundreals, has sent word for me to return wiz hees messengairs," he explained. "I shall ride over een ze volante, and as such episodes are rare een ze States I zought zat you might enjoy accompanying me. From what I can gathair from Diego a demand has been made for ransom."

"You could not favor me more," Lithgow cried gratefully, preparing with alacrity to avail himself of the opportunity. "When your servants recounted the tale of what had occurred, I found it difficult to believe that such things could take place in this age of the world. I thought that feats of that nature had fallen into disuse. There is hope for the world yet, if romance is not all dead."

"Call you eet 'romance'?" queried M. Theuriet. "We call eet ze horrors of brigandage."

During the drive over to the sugar plantation, M. Theuriet rehearsed the story of Raquel's unfortunate abduction; and the American listened and exclaimed, all the while congratulating himself that it was to be his luck to witness the close of this adventure which had befallen a Cuban maiden.

"Beatrice will regret that she did not come," he thought complacently while the old-fashioned volante was rocked along cumbersomely.

With a word of explanation from his host, Lithgow found himself received with grave cordiality by the bereft father. Being ushered into the sala, he was electrified to behold that he was face to face with his highway acquaintance. His first impression was that the man was, like M. Theuriet, a neighboring planter who had come to the assistance of Palgrave; but there was that latitude in his attire which, contrasted with the simpleness of taste which both planters displayed, suggested a certain freedom from conventional restraint that only an untrammelled existence can give. To the American's questioning gaze Alarcon responded with a smile of grim amusement.

"*Buenas dias, señor*," he saluted, with the pleasant courtesy of the land. "It appears that we are destined to know each other better—no?"

CHAPTER VI.

WHEN Raquel returned to consciousness, she found herself within the shelter of a palm hut fashioned after the simple style of architecture known to the humble montero.

The hazy recollection of the experiences through which she had passed beat in upon her mind with the vagueness of a dream, until, with the entrance of the woman called Faquita, she sprang up with a cry of complete remembrance.

Faquita viewed her with eyes that were not easy to read, and knelt beside her with a utensil filled with hot coffee.

"Drink!" she urged.

Raquel pushed the proffered refreshment aside gently.

"Who are you?" she asked, looking wonderingly into the countenance before her. "Are you another unfortunate captive?"

Faquita shrugged her shoulders and revealed beautiful white teeth in a mocking laugh.

"Perhaps; who knows?" she replied lightly. "Some call me the wife of Alarcon. I am known as 'Faquita.'"

Raquel raised herself on her rude bed and grasped the arm of the speaker tightly, peering into the woman's eyes with trenchant gaze.

"His wife!" she echoed. "He did not——"

"Speak as if he had one?" completed Faquita, with a disagreeable laugh.

"I am so glad!" breathed Raquel, with a sigh of relief. "You will remain with me—no? Oh, *señora mia*, I beg you!"

"No; I may not," returned Faquita. "He has told Annizae to care for you. *Mira!* I have brought you coffee. You must eat; you must drink. You will need your strength if you hope to return to the house of your father."

Thus propelled by the most powerful incentive which could be given her, Raquel drained the dish of the familiar beverage. She had not realized how weak and faint she was from lack of nourishment. She was uncertain whether or not to venture to ask this girl to help her to escape. That had been her first impulse; but the discovery of the creature's relation to the chief made her hesitate. She lay back on the couch and closed her eyes. Her brain was awhirl with the intoxication of the hope which had burst into life at the sight of a companion of her own sex.

Faquita had risen and stood regarding the white face of the prostrate girl narrowly. Almost was there malevolence in her gaze. Raquel lifted her lids again. Something in the interchange of their eyes impelled her to reach out and catch hold of Faquita's hand.

"If the ransom does not come, you will help me?" she whispered.

Faquita bent nearer. Her coal-black orbs, closely set in her gypsy-like face, glistened as she said softly:

"What would you wish?"

"To escape!" Raquel's voice and eyes were eloquent in their pleading.

At that instant the masculine figure of the elder woman appeared in the entrance. She gave an unmistakable exclamation of anger at the sight of Faquita, and snatched the dish from which Raquel had drank the coffee. Into it she looked half suspiciously, glancing from it to Faquita, then to Raquel, with an expression resembling anxiety.

"It would not be well for Gonzalo to see thee here," she said meaningly. "What didst thou bring in this?"

Faquita lifted her shoulders in that inimitable gesture of the Cuban and walked carelessly out of the hut, humming a refrain that revealed that this forest existence was by no means the only one she had known.

Raquel arose and tried to steady herself against the frail walls of the tropical dwelling. The exhaustion and excessive fear which she had undergone the night previous had told seriously on her strength.

"Has the chief gone for ransom?" she questioned anxiously.

"What then?" returned the woman coldly; but she placed food before Raquel and urged her to partake of it. Then she left her charge alone.

Raquel watched for the return of Faquita, but the girl came not. Remembering her suggestion, Raquel endeavored to eat that she might be possessed of all possible endurance whatever should come, but the coarse food was not tempting and she was too sick at soul to do anything but turn over in her mind again and again different methods of escape that suggested themselves.

She crept stealthily toward the entrance, believing that she was not guarded, but as she reached the aperture which served as door she caught the sound of cautious voices.

"She would not dare!" she heard a man say in response to some low words that had proceeded from Annizae.

"*Quien sabe?*" replied the woman, unconvinced. "Alarcon told her not to approach the señorita. She stole past you while I was getting almerzo for the señorita."

"I saw her," said the other voice. "She told me you had sent her with coffee."

"Ah, she lied with that quick tongue of hers!" cried Annizae. "Here is the bowl. What was in it besides coffee? Faquita does nothing like that to help me. She had another motive. What was it?"

The man drew nearer the entrance. Raquel perceived that it was the gold-skinned youth who had been called Zuñega. There was agitation in his tone.

"Faquita would not dare use the juice of the manchineel apple," he declared, "not now, anyway. The señorita may be ransomed. If she is not, then it may be well to watch Faquita; but—she is too cowardly."

Annizae was sombre.

"Think you so?" she queried skeptically. "You men believe anything that wears petticoats. Faquita saw the look on Alarcon's face. She knows that even a ransom may not restore the señorita to her home."

Zuñega's brow contracted.

"I will guard well," he said. "Faquita shall enter no more."

Raquel had crouched on the ground. She now laid her face against the earth to hide the moan that rose to her lips in spite of herself.

The mere name of the deadly manchineel apple curdled her blood for a time; then a curious relief followed on the horror. She understood what lay before her if she were not ransomed, and this discovery of the danger to be apprehended from the quickly aroused jealousy of Faquita revealed to her an avenue of escape of which she felt she would be swift to take advantage. The poison of the manchineel!

Surely she would have no difficulty in obtaining the deadly fruit! She would beg Faquita to procure it. Faquita need fear no usurpation of her power. Perhaps when convinced of this, Faquita would assist her to fly from the camp and Gonzalo Alarcon.

She recalled her boastful words in the sala—how that she would be the Napoleon for whom Cuba waited. Here was the opportunity at hand for her to wield an inspiring influence over one who claimed to have the Cuban cause at heart; but, face to face with the awful sacrifice of self involved, death seemed nobler and infinitely more to be desired.

Fearful that Annizae would find her there, she slipped back to her couch and lay motionless, concocting and rejecting, as impossible, plan after plan.

The taciturn woman came and peered at her often, once even shaking her gently. Upon Raquel opening her eyes inquiringly, she went away satisfied, stationing herself outside the hut.

It seemed to Raquel that she had been in this place for years. Time moved so heavily. In fancy she could hear the dripping of the water in the dear old court. She marvelled that ever she had complained of its monotony. To hear once again the roar and rumble of the mill, all the familiar sounds which had made her life—what would she not give? Love of country, adventure, glory, achievement, sank into nothingness before that imperative longing for the safety of the walls against which she had chafed with the impatience of youth.

Knowing how helpless she was, but feeling that absolute inaction was no longer bearable, she arose again and placed herself by the entrance to watch Zuñega as he split the palm boles into poles, staking them and tying them together with ropes from the majaguay, forming thus a roof and rafters possessing all requisite strength. That he was constructing a hut like the one she was in was very evident. The long stalks encircling the trunk of the palm he utilized by placing them over the framework already built. In this, as well as in thatching the roof with the long plume-stems, the uncommunicative Annizae assisted.

Raquel wished that they would talk as they worked. They were silent. She peered forth into the cathedral-like gloom of the surrounding forest and wondered if ever she could find her way through its mysteries did she succeed in escaping. She fancied that she could hear the vegetation struggling in its battle for supremacy. She strained her hearing to catch the speech that appeared striving to break through the solemn stillness that, by a peculiar anomaly, was pulsing with sound, the murmur of growth, the sigh of decay. Something seemed to be whispering to her with cold, damp breath:

"This which you call *yourself* will be on some to-morrow but a tiny heap of dust of no more consequence than this forest mould in which the feet sink noiselessly. What then? Will the real identity go on living, progressing? What is the meaning of the passion to accomplish something that shakes you? Is it only the selfish desire to make the world aware of your presence before that to-morrow arrives? The chance you have craved has come to you: you turn from it with shudder and dread. You fancied that you had a man's soul within you —but, it is the timorous heart of a child."

"No! It is the miserable fear of a woman's nature," she answered with mental fierceness. "Of a man nothing is required but courage; that will place him anywhere. But a woman may not stand out fearlessly and face the world, not here in Cuba. It is said that she can in other lands. Here, she only can strike through the hands of others."

To escape from herself she turned toward Zuñega. Annizae had disappeared amid the crepusculous gloom of the green aisles for fresh material.

"When is the next uprising to be?" she asked him suddenly.

Zuñega flashed upon her the surprised glance of his great eyes, in the depths of which hid the melancholy one finds in the orbs of those in whose veins flows a trace of Carib blood.

"What uprising, señorita?" he questioned wonderingly.

"That which is to win Cuba her freedom," she replied, astonished to find that explanation was necessary.

Zuñega's marvellously moulded shoulders moved with a suspicion of irresponsibility.

"How should I know anything of that, señorita?" he queried puzzledly.

"Is not my ransom to go for the arming of Gonzalo Alarcon's men and the freedom of Cuba?" demanded Raquel.

"It is not for me to decide, señorita," was the evasive reply, as he bent again to his work.

With swift impulse, Raquel was out of the hut and facing him before he divined her intention.

"You shall tell me," she cried breathlessly. "Will not this gold be employed to provide ammunition for you against the day when you and bands like yours will sweep across Cuba fighting the Spaniards until we are free?"

Zuñega dropped the branches he held. He threw out both hands with the palms downward. His voice was full of shame.

"No, señorita; no!" he said gravely. "We are brigands— nothing more!"

Raquel gave an exclamation of keenest disappointment. She stepped backward, scorn in her face.

"You, a man, dare confess yourself not a patriot when Cuba is languishing for the strength of arms like yours!" she cried, the fire of righteous contempt making her eyes blaze. "Here in this mighty forest has no lesson been taught you but rapine? The unmistakable speech that surrounds you here is the proclamation of the tireless green life which continually asserts the sure victory of 'that which is to be' over 'that which was.' It is the prophecy Nature gives us that the old rule of Spain must give way to the young blood of freedom-loving Cuban hearts."

She pointed up to where bunches of string-like growth hung, sending down green parasitic offshoots that swayed with sinuous, snake-like movement.

Zuñega followed the direction of her glance with his own. He knew well that soon those greedy, caressing tendrils would attach themselves to the tree nearest; that they would wind themselves about its trunk, sending down to the ground long, treacherous fibres to root again and send out still more fibres which would throw themselves about their patron; that these inoffensive-appearing air-roots would drink the life and feed on the substance of their victim until finally the green growth of the matapalos would hide the skeleton of the object on which it had feasted.

"That is what Spain is doing to Cuba," Raquel told him impressively. "That parasitic plant is Spain. She quarters her soldiers on us to keep us in tame subjection while she draws all vitality from us. And this very army which feeds on us, fights us, defeats us, we are forced to pay! Where is your spirit that these things do not move you? Were I you, I would be one of Cuba's heroes, bold and noble, instead of a mountain bandit whom our countrymen fear when they so gladly would revere if they could."

The youth's mobile features changed in expression beneath her words. Into his eyes crept a light of awakening. His muscles hardened as if mentally he were measuring himself. With his uplifted head and magnificent physique, he was a fit model for a sylvan god. He had the appearance of having heard a clarion call over the heaven-piercing tops of the forest trees. The melancholy of his sombre eyes had been chased away by an odd brilliancy that burned its way into Raquel's memory as he brought his gaze back from the interlaced vines above them.

"*No es posible!*" he murmured with an accent of hopelessness. "What can I? I am Zuñega only!"

"You are a man, with courage and strength,' she returned, carried away by the enthusiasm of the moment and the fact that she had stirred perceptibly this forest denizen to the need of his land. "What more is needed but the will?"

Zuñega stood looking at her aghast. He could not grasp the possibilities stretching before his vision. This life of mixed freedom and exciting danger was the only one that he had known. The startling suggestion of this eager-eyed, white-robed creature came upon him with the tremendous force of a Niagara. It swept him from his moorings. He had an inexplicable feeling that he had been taken possession of in some mysterious way. For the first time in his life he was conscious of a sense of fear. Something cautioned him that Annizae must not return to find her prisoner standing thus before him. He motioned significantly toward the palm hut.

"Annizae!" he warned.

Raquel moved back to her position at the entrance.

Zuñega went on dreamily with his task, scarce noting that he did so. Unfledged thoughts crowded through his disturbed mind. He essayed to regain his former content. It was not possible. Everything seemed to have been torn away from him with the suddenness of a whirlwind.

No more words were uttered between them. Raquel observed his movements with a keen interest that she had not felt before. Zuñega was no longer to her mind one of the men among whom he had been reared. He was a soul capable of being moved to great achievements. She decided that as she sat there, giving feminine admiration to the symmetry of his firm, bronze, muscular development; admiration which no artistic eye could withhold. Fresh plans were taking form in her mind. She wondered if she could persuade this youth to assist her to flee from Alarcon, providing that the ransom should be delayed. She had moved him once; might she not hope to do so again?

Silent, they remained. A face that had been watching them curiously through the foliage slipped away on the approach of Annizae. It was the face of Faquita. It wore a peculiar smile.

Before night, Raquel found that the freshly built hut was designed for her occupancy. After darkness had shut the camp in as with a veil, Annizae signified that Raquel was to accompany her to the space where the members of the camp were congregated around the fire, over which simmered a garlicky soup in which all appeared to have an interest.

There was something savoring of witchcraft in the scene to Raquel. In fantastic, tropical garb, devil-may-care faces flitted back and forth through the lurid light. Each helped himself from the soup and seated himself with his portion on the spongy carpet of the woods.

Urged by hunger, Raquel was forced to accept some of the concoction; and she sat there with chills pervading her as she met the glances and sly comments cast toward her occasionally from swarthy visages. To these Zuñega responded with warning words when the offence was flagrant. Stationed on the ground flat at her feet he seemed to divine her fear, for he murmured reassuringly:

"*No tenga miedo.* Have no fear, señorita. We men of the mountains have few pleasures. You one will see."

Suddenly from out the enveloping night stole a mournful, long-drawn cry. Raquel would have leaped up in alarm had not Zuñega placed his fingers upon hers encouragingly. He withdrew his hand quickly with an exclamation.

"What is it?" Raquel questioned of him troubledly.

"*Yo no sé!*" was his mystified reply, looking from his fingers up into her face. "Your touch is fire, señorita!"

"The cry—" she repeated anxiously, not heeding his note of query that accompanied the explanation which he supposed she sought.

"Oh, Faquita?—she will dance," he said. "*Mira!* She comes. In Havana she danced. It is not always that she will. This night she wished for you to see her."

Raquel peered into the blackness out from which crept again that chilling wail. This time it dropped into a slow, mysterious chant, and Faquita flashed out of the darkness of the trees.

About her waist a dazzling girdle of iridescent light quivered, emitted by a double row of cocullos, Cuba's wonderful fire-flies, fastened to her belt by the little natural hooks at the heads of the insects.

Encircled by this brilliant zone, with wild hair and wilder eyes, she began to move slowly, rhythmically to and fro, round and round, in strange gyrations, unique, graceful, exercising on the spectators an influence which was half hypnotic.

The chant quickened into a rapid melody, high, sweet, and penetrating. The dancer seemed to become fascinated with her own music. Her motions grew wilder, more impassioned.

Those to whom this barbaric dance was not new watched curiously to see how long the performer's endurance would hold out.

The moments appeared interminable.

Raquel scarcely breathed. With every nerve tense she watched until, finally, the convolutions became less, the steps uncertain.

At last, the figure wavered, reeled, and would have fallen had not Zuñega sprung and caught it in his arms. Exhausted though she was, Faquita contrived to drop down in close proximity to Raquel.

With the tenderness of womanly interest, Raquel leaned over the prostrate form of the dancer. In spite of the perils of her position, she was attracted by this gypsyish piece of femininity. Moreover, she had hopes of exciting her pity; but, before she could frame her desire into speech even had she so dared, the soft voice of Faquita whispered cautiously:

"Steal from the hut while he sleeps, señorita. I will watch. I will take you to your father."

CHAPTER VII.

IGNORANT of the identity of this man whose salutation was so friendly; unaware that a price in excess of the ransom he demanded for the stolen señorita had been placed on his head by a nervous government, Lithgow returned the greeting of Alarcon in the sala of La Sacra Sonrisa with as much grace as his American training would permit.

M. Theuriet and Gilbert Palgrave viewed the recognition with pardonable amazement.

Lithgow explained his previous encounter with the gentleman. Alarcon remained quiet with the same smile touching his features.

M. Theuriet contemplated the athletic figure of the bandit through his pince-nez; then he turned questioningly toward the sugar planter, motioning his now removed spectacles toward the chief.

"Ees zis ze man who demands ze ransom?"

Palgrave gave an affirmative inclination of the head.

M. Theuriet inspected Alarcon again very critically, beginning at the spurred boots and mounting slowly upward to the unreadable eyes that looked out of the swarthy visage.

"You demand what sum, señor?" he inquired at length.

"Ten thousand pesos," answered Alarcon promptly.

The Frenchman gave a little shriek of expostulation.

"*Mon Dieu! C'est impossible!* I can secure cet not!"

"Ten thousand, or the señorita remains with us," replied Alarcon, with an insolence of power that stirred the hot blood in all three of his hearers.

The face of M. Theuriet purpled with rage. He advanced threateningly toward the guerrilla, looking like a bantam rooster challenging a game bird.

"*Cuidado, señor!*" warned Alarcon, with his hands on the weapons at his belt. "I have come here among you with no protection save that which belongs to one who has the friendliest intentions. I desire to aid the father of the girl to secure her. I come to warn him that no time is to be lost. Unless the ransom is produced quickly, it will be useless. The seño-

rita will have been made the wife of the chief of the band, Gonzalo Alarcon."

If the interest of the American had needed awakening, those
words would have done it.   Gonzalo Alarcon!   He remembered
that that was the name of the daring brigand of whom the captain had spoken.   He had been endlessly cautioned in the cities against this individual, in whose latest victim he now was
destined to take the keenest concern.   He was electrified by
the discovery that this man before him was the emissary of
the dreaded bandit.   For the first time he understood the real
seriousness of the girl's position.   As he looked at the firm,
hard-featured countenance and piercing, masterful eyes of
the supposed messenger of Alarcon, he felt that here was a
later-day edition of the fearless buccaneers who had plied
their illegal trade through the Caribbean waters, flying the
black flag of piracy.

M. Theuriet had stepped backward, his pince-nez dropping
from his nerveless fingers and dangling agitatedly by the chain.
He turned from the determined eyes of Alarcon to the care-
marked visage of the sugar planter.

"Can eet be—*vrai?*" he asked anxiously.

"I am afraid that it is only too true," Palgrave answered
despairingly.   "It is wisest to lose no time.   I sent for you,
monsieur, to ask you to leave no stone unturned to secure the
gold he demands."

"Eet will not be posseebl' to obtain eet for some days."
He shook his head discouragingly.

"It must be soon, señor," reminded Alarcon significantly.

"Eet can not be before four days," the Frenchman declared.
"Moreover, I can get not more zan fiv' zousand."

"It must be ten thousand!" the brigand said slowly, with a
threat in his voice.   "Not one centavo less."

"What eef I cannot?"

Alarcon shrugged his shoulders with the irresponsibility of
one who has not matters under his charge.

"You will see the fair señorita no more, señors, *Dios
sabe!*"

The father shivered with the words.   He spoke to M.
Theuriet in a strained tone:

"You swore to advance any sum, monsieur, if I accepted
your conditions.   I agree to them; I rather had see her your

wife than the mate of a renegade, a convict, if tales about him are true! God help her and me!"

The eyes of the brigand took on a sinister expression with the speech of the sugar planter. For an instant they burned with anger. He glanced comprehendingly from the Frenchman to the father. He understood with a flash the conditions which M. Theuriet had exacted in exchange for his loan. His rage at the aspersion which Gilbert Palgrave had cast at him found pleasure in the quick reflection that he had it in his power not only to thwart the designs of the avaricious old Frenchman, but also to retaliate cruelly on the planter. It was the first time in Cuba that Alarcon had heard himself called by the opprobrious term of "convict," and, though he well knew that it belonged to him by the rights of justice, the malice which it awoke in him was none the less keen.

With the arrogance of man, he compared mentally his well-knit figure and superior physical attractions with those of the middle-aged coffee-planter, and he decided that, obliged to choose, Raquel would take him, his love, and the forest life in preference to years spent in the wearisome society of old age.

To Lithgow the entire scene was more like a portion from some opera than from real life. The novel surroundings, tropical and sensuous in suggestion, the not yet familiar faces of the two planters, the half-bizarre appearance of this son of forest-clad mountains, all tended to make him doubt the actuality of the occurrence. It seemed odd to sit thus quietly while the fate of a girl not yet seen was decided by these methods. He had a wild inclination to take some part in it himself, but he was not appealed to. The issue of the entire matter appeared to rest with his host. He studied the form and countenance of the Frenchman with a wondering curiosity as to what would be the girl's feelings when she learned on what terms her freedom had been purchased. He felt an unmistakable pity for her. He could not believe that any young girl would welcome such a union. He thought of Beatrice. How she would rave over the physique of this emissary of Gonzalo Alarcon! When she should receive his letter containing a graphic account of these adventures, she would be sorry enough that she had not reconsidered her decision, he told himself with considerable satisfaction.

"Would eet not be propair to hav' an agreement drawn

up?" ventured M. Theuriet, looking at his neighbor. "Een eet I would release you, *mon ami*, from ze burden ov all previous indebtedness. I would agree to asseest you to meet othair encumbrances. Eet might be well:—ze señorita would comprehend bettair."

Gilbert Palgrave drew himself up with the sorrowful pride of a man who will accept no benefits.

"Is not my word sufficient, Theuriet?" he demanded. "If an agreement is drawn up, there must be inserted in it the clause that she is free to choose. She shall not be forced into defraying such a debt. I will work on the Havana docks as a laborer first. If she is willing to accept your offer of marriage, that is another thing. But—I prefer to remain your debtor, monsieur. Gladly I will assume this additional debt rather than permit her to be influenced against the dictates of her heart. You know the value of my word. You shall have interest on your loans, compound interest. Every centavo shall be repaid."

A wave of feeling swept from the Frenchman's face the business expression. The words of Palgrave seemed to have hurt him.

"I hav' watched her grow into ze most beautiful womanhood," he said in a pathetic tone. "I hav' desired her for my wife, abov' all othairs. She will be a parfait queen. Een Havana she will be admired. I hav' years more zan she. She will not look upon my suit wiz plaisir, but I will be so kind to her zat she will learn to lov'. Every wish shall be gratified."

His voice was freighted with anxiety. He bent his thin, small frame toward her father with the air of a supplicant.

The American glanced from the two toward the straight figure of Alarcon with scathing eyes. He would not have thought that any type of manhood could witness this conversation unmoved. He sought to fathom the thoughts of this man who watched the speakers through narrowed lids. As if conscious of Lithgow's gaze, the chief flashed a look toward him, then gave his attention to M. Theuriet again.

Though Lithgow could not read it in his face, Alarcon had decided that the ransom to be won in this manner could be secured in another way, the contemplation of which gave a little amused twitch to his mustache which he stroked reflec-

tively. What was to prevent the capture of M. Theuriet himself one of these days? The gold would be forthcoming then
speedily. And, in the interval of imprisonment, the Frenchman could have the doubtful pleasure of witnessing the señorita's happiness as Gonzalo Alarcon's wife.

"Pardon, señors," he spoke finally. "There is one difficulty; the chief will not relinquish the señorita to the arms
of a rival like M. Theuriet. *Adios!*"

He bowed with a low sweep of his sombrero and moved
with easy dignity out through the bloom of the court to the
great entrance, his spurs clattering with metallic ring as he
crossed the tiled floor.

Theuriet stood aghast. Such a possibility as this had not
presented itself to his mind. Gilbert Palgrave had sprung up
with alarm as he saw this one chance of securing Raquel torn
away from him.

"Stop him! Stop the devil!" he cried.

But it was too late. Without a backward look, Alarcon
was gone.

Making his way swiftly to the spot where he had tethered
his horse the night previous, he sprung into the saddle with
a laugh half of triumph, and soon was pushing his path through
the forest again, his thoughts on the girl he meant to make his
own despite Faquita or the murmurs of those in the camp who
would grumble at his failure to obtain the gold.

In the mean time, in the soft gloom of the taper-lighted
palm hut, Raquel's active mind turned over Faquita's words
with nervous anxiety. She peered out fearfully into the
awful blackness of the night-shrouded trees.

Had Faquita been in earnest? Should she venture? How
was she to cross successfully the prostrate form of Zuñega
stretched in front of the entrance? She knew that he did not
sleep, for occasionally he lifted his head in an alert way that
betokened ill to any hope of escape. In the opposite hut, she
knew that Annizac was stationed. Were *her* eyes wide with
watchfulness also?

She held her breath, listening, listening, desirous of attempting to slip away, yet fearful of recapture and close
guarding.

The moments seemed so hideously long that she could not
tell whether hours or seconds crept past.

Finally she dared to lift herself into a sitting posture on the side of her bed. Zuñega moved not. Slowly, on limbs that trembled, she raised herself to an upright posture. She stood thus motionless for some time, listening again. She took a step; paused; listened. Another step, holding her robe above her ankles. As she neared the entrance she could hear the regular breathing of her guard; it was not the breath of deep sleep however; she was not certain that he slept at all. She waited and waited, her heart beating so fiercely that she thought the sound of it would reach his ears.

Little by little, she edged nearer him. She lifted still higher the draperies with which she had been gowned at the time of capture, but, unknown to her, one corner dropped from her grasp and trailed behind her. Palpitating with fear, she contrived to step lightly over him and, like a bird, darted toward the dense undergrowth in a blind way. As she ran, a hand caught hers and urged her on; the hand of Faquita, who had lain in hiding for hours, watching the entrance, fearful that her bidding would not be obeyed. On they sped, ignorant of the fact that the trailing wisp of Raquel's drapery had touched Zuñega's face and brought him to his feet in time to see a faint suspicion of white disappear. He rushed after her, knowing what it would mean to her to be lost in that forest. Alone, unpiloted, she might wander for weeks only to sink to death in exhaustion at last.

As he made his way through the darkness, a revelation was borne in upon him. Without putting it into speech, Zuñega knew that with the advent of the señorita of La Sacra Sonrisa into the camp something had come to him for which he knew no name save that reverence with which he had paused before the little wayside shrines that held the tiny, weatherbeaten image of the *Madre de Dios*, Mother of Jesu. With a great light, the realization flashed over him that without her presence the camp never could be the same to him again. A glorious sense of power was with him as he dashed into the underbrush. He meant to find her if it meant endless seeking. The fever of pursuit was in his veins. Like Apollo after Daphne, he rushed headlong.

Suddenly he stopped short, with a queer, sick feeling of disappointment pervading him. There was no sign of her white garments—nothing whatever to guide him. He threw up his head and listened. His nostrils dilated with excitement. Not a sound reached him but the familiar murmur of the forest.

"She has fallen!" he whispered to himself. "She has wounded herself. She has not gone afar; not a movement can escape me."

Even as he spoke, he stumbled and fell, himself. He caught a little muffled cry of alarm. Overjoyed, he laid his hands on the object beneath his feet.

To his surprise he felt himself seized by a tenacious grasp and a hand went over his mouth, while Faquita's voice whispered:

"Hush! Not a word! Thou shalt help us to get away, Zuñega."

"*Thou?* Faquita?" he cried in amazement.

"Hush!" she repeated warningly. "What is there strange in that I am here?"

"But the señorita! Where is the señorita?" he demanded.

Faquita moved from where she crouched and revealed that her own garments had concealed the white ones of Raquel.

"I take her again to her home," she said determinedly. "Gonzalo Alarcon shall not make of her life what he has made of mine. Thou shalt help us, Zuñega!"

"*Nunca!*" refused Zuñega. "What thinkest I am? Is she not under my care? Am I not to be held responsible?"

"Thou needst fear nothing," returned Faquita. "All that thou dost need do is to secure one of the caballos and take it to the paso. We will meet thee there. Alarcon will never know that thou hadst any part in it."

"That is like thy reasoning," scorned Zuñega. "How can I account for her slipping past me? Can I say that I slept?"

"*Sí*, for thou didst," laughed Faquita cautiously. "Have it as thou wilt, but I tell thee that never shall Alarcon place her over me. If this fails, another will not! For the sake of the señorita it is well that she goes now; thou knowest that as well as I. All the camp knows it. She will die here; she fears Alarcon: *I* love him; there is the difference."

At the mere suggestion of the señorita succeeding Faquita in the affections of the chief, the blood surged away from his heart, then rushed again through it with a mighty leap that left him strangely weak.

"Gonzalo will kill thee if this is done," he told her slowly.

"What matter?" queried Faquita lightly. "It is easier to die by knife than by jealousy. But, we waste time! If thou art too cowardly to aid us, at least thou must not awaken the camp. Promise that?"

Into Zuñega's strong fingers crept those of Raquel pleadingly. He knew that they were not those of Faquita, for their touch stung his blood into riotous action as they had once before.

He heard her whisper with anxious entreaty:

"For the sake of—my honor! For the sake of my father, oh, do not refuse!"

Zuñega felt himself waver before the inexplicable power of her voice as the cane-tips bend beneath the force of the winds of the savannahs. The temptation of his life faced him there in the tropical midnight, fragrant with a thousand subtle perfumes. To help her meant to shut himself out forever from this camp which was home. He knew Alarcon; and was aware that such a violation of the trust reposed in him would be met with sure retribution even if Alarcon's hand was years in accomplishing it. But opposed to this picture was the prospect awaiting the girl; a prospect which his fiercely beating blood told him in unmistakable language was one which he never could permit to meet fulfillment.

As he stood thus, her hand pressing his hopefully in the sweet darkness, all this passed swiftly before his mental vision; the señorita the mate of the chief, or himself a wanderer, fleeing ever from Alarcon's determined revenge. With passionate disregard for danger, his heart chose the latter exultantly. At that moment it seemed an ecstatic happiness to be able to give up all for her. Then, following, swept over him suggestions of other lives than this nomad one. He knew that there were others, though their apparent tameness never had tempted him to relinquish the exhilarating experiences of an outlaw existence. There returned to him her words of the afternoon. Though the wild freedom of this brigand life might be closed to him, it was true that Cuba remained to be fought for—Cuba and the commendation of this girl who had crossed his path and strangely turned its direction, almost without his volition.

" *Vayamos!* " urged Faquita impatiently. "Let us go! Annizae will waken next."

He loosened the fingers that she held so tightly. He thought that he heard a quick sob of disappointment.

"Comest thou with us?" whispered Faquita, persuasively, once more.

His throat contracted. It seemed to him that an iron hand choked him as he made his renunciation silently.

"Go to the paso!" he answered at last. "I will be there with the caballo."

CHAPTER VIII.

STRONG with excitement, Raquel followed Faquita's lead with feet that rebelled against the slowness with which they were compelled to move through a darkness beside which night itself would be luminous. Faquita held back thick ropes of lianes to afford her a pathway, and assisted her over mouldering tree-trunks that sometimes seemed to crumble at their approach.

The suspense and exhilaration of fear that accompanied that flight by night through the mysterious Cuban forest, where there were vines the icy touch of which was as deadly as the snake-bite of the dread *fer-de-lance* of the Windward Islands!

Raquel's breath began to come in little, eager, tired gasps that revealed how near to exhaustion she was with this unaccustomed exertion of battling with the impregnable walls of Nature. She had a strange, bewildered feeling that she had lived through this identical experience before. Her head whirled with her effort to keep pace with Faquita's movements, but her mind was alert with queer thoughts that the night-hush of the forest seemed to breed. Here, one could believe in a limitless past through which one might have lived out lives without number, casting each behind him as a snake casts its skin, the butterfly its chrysalis.

They found Zuñega waiting for them in the gloom of the paso, a rift in the mountains that permitted the light of the stars to penetrate to the secrets of the softly growing forest things.

" *Dos caballos*," exclaimed Faquita, with surprise when she discerned that he held two horses. " *Porqué?* "

For reply, he silently placed her on one of the animals and Raquel on the other, vaulting lightly up behind the latter.

Tactfully, Faquita refrained from questioning. In fact, it might be said that her amazement kept her quiet. Guiding the horse himself, he took the lead, and Faquita followed, seeking in her mind some solution of this change in him. She finally reached the conclusion that, when he felt that he had piloted them beyond danger of pursuers, he would return with greater speed to the camp by means of the second horse, leaving them to find their way on to the plantation highways. But, just as she had decided this, Zuñega turned his head over his shoulder and said:

" Thou canst return to the camp if thou wilt, Faquita. Alarcon need not know of thy part in this matter. I will take the señorita to the plantation of La Sacra Sonrisa."

" Art thou mad?" exclaimed Faquita in amazement. " Alarcon will riddle thee with bullets. Return quickly, Zuñega! He will not dare give to me the hatred he will give thee. I can win him as thou canst not."

" I return no more," answered Zuñega briefly, pushing on through the thicket with an increase of speed. He felt the form of the girl that he half held in his arms give a start of surprise.

" What meanest thou?" demanded Faquita sharply, endeavoring vainly to urge her horse abreast of his. " Wilt thou desert the camp? Thy life will not be worth a medio, Zuñega."

" Not if Alarcon finds me," he admitted, " but he shall not find me !"

Faquita almost groaned.

" Thou knowest him," she reminded. " Think well, Zuñega. It is foolish to risk all for the little señorita. *I* have a reason for venturing so much. I mean to teach him that Faquita is first—and last !"

" How knowest thou but that I have a reason also?" queried the youth.

" It is because I have urged thee,'' Faquita regretted.

" Who knows ?" smiled he in the darkness. " Thou shouldst not thus grieve; I make it easy for thee to go back. Thou canst escape his anger."

"No; Faquita, no! Leave me not!" cried Raquel fearfully, suspicious that, if she were deserted by the other, Zuñega might circle around to the camp and replace her in her former imprisonment out of his sense of obedience to some bandit code of honor. . His announcement that he did not intend returning to his companions she believed was only made to increase her confidence in him.

Faquita hesitated. She reasoned that if Zuñega really was determined to risk himself thus, there was no need of both of them incurring the chief's displeasure; but Raquel's plea decided her to go on at least a little farther. Perhaps she was actuated somewhat by her indisputable curiosity to learn more if possible as to Zuñega's real intentions. Not for a moment did she attribute his strange decision to the fiery words she had heard Raquel deliver to him during the previous afternoon. She supposed of course that the declaration of her own jealousy and disinclination to be supplanted had been the spur for his chivalrous action, his effort to move from her path the rival that she feared.

"*Muy bien, señorita mia*, I will not leave thee until thou art within thy father's walls," she agreed finally. "Thou needst not fear."

Zuñega said nothing further.

With the instinct of the race from which had come his strange beauty, his waving blue-black hair, his marvellous coloring,—the Caribs—he fought undeviatingly through the forest for the straightest route to safety, battling successfully with the oppositions which Nature interposed at every step.

They went on silently for fully two hours. The stupendous radiance of another day had swept up the east, but through the dense foliage that closed about them it penetrated but little, only making their outlines appear ghostly as they stole on. Their horses' feet sank with muffled tread in the dust of the centuries that lay beneath the mighty arches of this cathedral which ever-springing green life had built with mystic touch.

Suddenly Raquel pitched forward. Zuñega's hand, holding the bridle, alone saved her from what would have been a disastrous fall had her head hit any of the thickly up-cropping tree-trunks. With an exclamation of alarm he pulled her back forcibly into his arms, and found that she had fainted from

6

sheer exhaustion.   They could not know that she resolutely
had ridden mile after mile with her teeth cutting through her
nether lip in the futile endeavor to overcome the horrible sense
of sickness that drew her the more irresistibly into its grasp
with every step that the horses took.

"*Dios mio!*" he cried in consternation.   "What is to be done?
If we dismount here, nothing will be gained.   A little further
will bring us to the *Cárcel de Diablo*.   A subterranean stream
flows through it.   We may be safe there.   Will it do to wait?"

"*Yo no sé,*" answered Faquita troubledly.   "If we had
aguardiente!   If thou wilt dismount I will rub her hands.
She may recover."

Zuñega studied Raquel's pale face anxiously.   In the wan,
greenish twilight of the trees, she wore an unearthly appearance.

"It may be as well to dismount here," he admitted reluctantly.   "I will slip her down into thine arms.   If only we
could get her to the bottom of the canyon!   There will be
water to revive her."

Faquita received Raquel's inanimate form gently and
placed her in a recumbent position.   Both of them worked
assiduously over her for some minutes, until finally, discouraged, Zuñega picked the prostrate girl up lightly and
strode on.

"Lead the caballos!" he called to Faquita.   "It is dangerous.   Every step must be taken with caution.   We had gone
farther than I thought."

After a short descent he paused and deposited Raquel on
the earth again, while he took the horses from Faquita's hold
and tied them securely until such time as he could return for
them.   Then, re-assuming his burden, he picked his way carefully down the precipitous wall of the cleft mountain to the
torrent below rushing madly over a rocky bed, foaming, seeth-
ing, whirling in its haste to reach the sea.   The green draperies of the mountain-side overhung its brink; venturesome palms
had thrust themselves out at right angles from the common
foliage; lianes had crept out over these and drooped in fes-
toons above the leaping waters, so that from mountain to
mountain, which this aqueous ribbon separated, had been
flung an arch of emerald tint that excluded the sunlight and
made the depths of the river as black as Acheron itself.

On the stones at the side of the stream Raquel was lain, while Faquita dexterously resuscitated her. Zuñega, with strange thoughts in his brain, watched her being brought back to consciousness. That perilous descent with her in his arms had given birth to ideas which never, before her coming, had been known to his philosophy. He stared at her unresponsive features with questioning eyes. What was there about her fragile, unconscious form to move him so? In that moment he touched the mystery of human life; and the forest about him might have whispered that the day never would come when he could fathom the secret of the power that shook him, any more than he comprehended it now when its blinding light fell upon him for the first time. For the one real passion that comes to the soul of the human defies description, analysis, comprehension. It only can be accepted gratefully and permitted to fulfill its destined mission of ennobling, purifying, uplifting.

When she had been brought to a knowledge of their surroundings, he went back for the horses and succeeded in leading them down the cliffs after a vast amount of persuasion. In the mean time, Faquita, urged by her own hunger, had gone in search of the forest fruits which were certain to be found near. Left alone, Raquel had remained recumbent, hoping to gain strength for the journey that lay before them. While elation was in her heart, her body refused to respond to the urgings of her mind, and she lay weak and tired close to the tumbling waters that dashed their spray on her face as they swept wildly over the rocks.

Her thoughts were with her father. Did his anxious heart have a premonition that she was coming toward him? In memory she went slowly over the entire ingenio, accosted each black and was welcomed vociferously. The mental picture won a smile to her lips. She lived her return in imagination. She touched with delight the dear old books. She felt that hereafter she should love the monotony which she had thought so irksome. But even the hunger for home could not render her oblivious to the wonders of the bloom that hung above her, a veritable Solomon's hanging garden with all the brilliant lianes, orchids of delicate hues, and strange sister parasites dangling from every limb, swaying slightly like pendulums.

"I wonder are they Nature's time-keepers," she murmured musingly. "This is the spot of which Tennyson must have been thinking when he wrote the 'Lotos-Eaters!' Here, in the heart of prolific tropical vegetation, time almost seems to swoon and pause awhile in its mad race!"

Half in dreams, Zuñega found her when he returned.

He sat down near and watched her, his great eyes veiled with the soft mist of melancholy. He was wondering what he should do when she was once again within her father's protection. He could make his way to the cities. He could secure work until the time came to enter into Cuba's struggle, but,— could he live away from the forest? He had not known that he loved it until now, when he contemplated leaving its safe shelter and nourishing resources. He reached and plucked some dark, shiny leaves tenderly. There was that in his face which riveted Raquel's attention. She remembered his declaration that he would not return to the camp. Observing him, she realized that it was the inestimable service which he was rendering her that was shutting him out from the career he had known. His manner now convinced her beyond any manner of doubt that he had had no ulterior motive in thus taking the escape into his own hands, and she was seized with a sudden desire to know what were his plans. She had not vanity sufficient to believe that her words were wholly responsible for this relinquishment of all that had made his life.

"If you go no more back to Alarcon's band, what shall you do?" she asked him as she propped herself against a giant trunk that shot upward toward the sky from this deep gorge.

"*Dios sabe, señorita,*" he replied gently. "God knows, not I. When the day comes, I will fight for Cuba as you told me; but until then,—who knows?"

Raquel was silent. This simple avowal that he had been swayed by her scorn brought to her an odd embarrassment which she did not analyze. She glanced at him from under her lids with unconquerable curiosity. He was not looking at her. His gaze was fixed on the waters that swirled by them. Finally, pointing to where sharp rocks rose out of the middle of the river, he said slowly:

"After the last insurrection, señorita, it is said that Louis Honorvath threw himself on these rocks from above. Imprisonment was to be his—or death. The home of him and his men was here in these mountains, in the caves that the rush of the underground rivers have hollowed out."

"And those same caves will be the homes of other men with the same mission," Raquel found herself saying to him. "Here and there arise the natures that are destined for such works as lie before the Cuban. They rise above their fellow-men with the same irresistible impulse of growth that sends the palm upward, far above its associates. Where is the man who will lead Cuba's next rebellion?"

"I will follow him," Zuñega replied in a low voice. "You have spoken words that will not be forgotten."

He turned his marvellous eyes toward hers. There was that in the meeting that was like a flash of recognition that neither of them fully understood. Moved by an unfamiliar emotion, Raquel dragged her gaze from his peculiar one by force of will. . That moment long remained in her memory.

Faquita came toward them, bearing the result of her search. The three ate the luscious fruit together, and Zuñega and Faquita were relieved to see that Raquel brightened visibly when thus refreshed.

"We must creep along the side of the river as far as possible," Zuñega told them. "We shall be in no danger of encountering Alarcon here as we might over the mountain. When the stream seeks an underground passage again, we can skirt the shoulder of the mountain. It will take more hours but means safety."

"How shall I ever repay both of you?" cried Raquel, with a burst of gratitude. "You, Faquita, you ought to remain and be my sister. I have had none. You would be happy so,—no?"

Faquita shook her head.

"Once I knew a home, a father, sisters," she said slowly. "They have forgotten me long ago. My only home now is the forest. I shall be happy in that I have outwitted Gonzalo Alarcon. That is all the recompense I crave, señorita."

Raquel did not glance at Zuñega as she inquired:

"Know you what I can do for you—señor? I fear there is little I can offer, save the thankfulness of the house of Palgrave."

Zuñega bowed low before her with all the courtly grace of a kingly race. His sombrero swept the moss on the stones.

"Has the señorita not given me the chance to serve her?" he asked softly. "It is sufficient."

Faquita's astute knowledge enabled her to read further than even Zuñega could into his own heart. His words and his manner revealed to her the secret of his assistance. She shot a swift look at Raquel. She perceived that the girl was as yet ignorant of the passion she had awakened in the heart of the man before her.

"*Vayamos!*" she cried abruptly. "Surely it is time to move. The señorita is better—no?"

"Ah, let us go!" echoed Raquel impatiently. "Every moment of delay means that much more suffering for my father. I am strong again. I can endure anything. Let us go!"

"Can you ride alone?" inquired Zuñega. "It is necessary that I go ahead and cut a passage."

"There is nothing I cannot do,—if I must," answered the girl firmly, unconsciously sounding the key-note of her character.

It was rough, tedious riding that followed. Many a time Faquita was tempted to go back and leave Zuñega alone to restore Raquel to her home, but each time feminine curiosity got the better of her fatigue and she pushed on faithfully, revolving in her mind what she would say to Alarcon on her return to camp.

Sometimes they were on one side of the stream and now on the other, as it admitted of being forded. Under overhanging masses of foliage, through aggravating thickets that crowded close to the verge of the water they crept, miles deep in day's death. At one point, Zuñega asked them to dismount. He tethered the animals while Faquita besieged him with questions. To these he vouchsafed no reply save a non-committal smile. Finally, he plunged boldly into the jungle-like vegetation that threatens to engulf the island. He called to them to follow. Reluctantly they obeyed, finding traces that this dense growth had been penetrated before. Moving a great boulder with a forceful push of his shoulder, Zuñega revealed to their eyes a cave of immense dimensions.

"This is one of the caves of the mountains that has proved a place of safety for many of those whom Spain believes dead," he informed them. "Brave hearts have hid here. Some of them have died here, hearts that would have won Cuba her freedom if they could, señorita!"

Raquel peered into the damp gloom of the retreat, so unknown to Spain, with eyes in which shone the worship that belongs to heroes. No premonition whispered to her that she was destined to know this historic spot inch by inch in the days to come. No voice foretold the part this Cave of Lost Spirits was to play in her future. But, as she laid her fingers on the cool, mossy rocks, she shivered.

"It is strange that liberty should be bought at the price of life," she murmured musingly, "liberty that is the right of man! And all the patriotic blood that has been shed for Cuba seems to have profited her nothing. But the memory of brave deeds burns in the heart of the Cuban people like an unquenchable fire, a fire that yet will burst forth with such fury that Spain herself will be consumed."

"Ah, perhaps," shrugged Faquita. "Long after we are dead, let us hope. I remember a little of the ten-year war. It was sad for Cuba."

"Care you nothing that Cuba lies helpless in Spain's fingers?" cried Raquel, with surprise.

"Why should I?" queried Faquita, laughing. "I cannot free her."

"But you might nerve others to," flashed Raquel.

Faquita laughed again. The subject was too stupendous for contemplation in this stifling, moist heat that the tangled mass of green seemed to hold.

Zuñega led them back to the clearer air of the gorge.

"Soon we shall strike over the spur of the mountain and descend to the savannahs," he said to Raquel. "You are not far distant from the plantation."

Raquel gave a little choked cry of joy.

From that time on she counted the steps the horses took. Each brought her nearer her father. Fresh energy came to her with the thought.

They left the river and crept upward again. Zuñega still trudged ahead, apparently tireless. Once he stopped and severed the great rope-like liantasse that tosses itself like a ship's cable among the trees; this section of the hollow tube he held to Raquel's thirsty lips, urging her to drain it of the pint or two of pure, cold water which, absorbed by the roots, was ascending to be converted into leaf and fruit.

"How well you know the secrets of the forest!" she exclaimed gratefully.

Zuñega gave no answer. The silence of the woods through which they passed was in his soul. When again would his feet fall thus softly into the ashes of the dead years? The question was in his mind continually. It grew louder and louder in its voicing as they neared the edge of the forest. It was with a pang of regret that he first caught the sight of the purpling hills to the east, rising in gentle billows up from the stretches of ochre-hued cane fields. He was sorry to have this journey done, this unpremeditated journey which was launching him on a chartless sea of endeavor to merit the praise of the girl whose horse he guided.

He had tried to formulate plans as he had cut the path through with his machete. If there were an uprising, the solution would be easy; he would join and fight with the valiant blood that was in his veins; but, for a wonder, there was not even the breath of insurrection in the air. Nothing remained but to hide his identity from Alarcon as well as he could by becoming a laborer in a distant part of the island. That decision was what made the knot in his throat when they passed at last from the shadow of the mantled mountain and came out upon the valley lands. They had yet a considerable distance to go; he had chosen a circuitous route since leaving the gorge, to prevent the slightest possibility of encountering the chief. He glanced back at the forest. The melancholy in his beautiful eyes deepened.

"*Adios! Adios!*" he whispered.

Was it only his fancy, he wondered, which made it seem that the spirits of the woods reached out after him; that all through the vast vaulted arches, hung with the delicate fretwork of laced foliage, crept a murmur of regret? Were his ears keen with that soul-sense which enables one to hear the utterances of the sphinx-like progeny of Nature?

He felt that invisible hands grasped him. He thought that he heard whispers which, with the subtleness of fragrance, cried:

"Goest thou out to avenge the wrongs of men? Thy heart will ache with bitterness; thy eyes grow weary. Many have gone before thee. Many will come after. Who shall say they pass in vain?

"Thou art built of the sinew of the flesh; through thy veins runs the red fire built by the fingers of that mysterious Life whom none hath seen. Thou of the red fire go out across the earth, seeking ever the reason of thy creation. We of the green fire stand immovable.

"Silently, we watch them of the red fire rear their structures. We perceive their blindness of vision. We learn that they hear no voices but their own. We listen to their arrogance of speech, their jest of life, their fear of death. And we push our roots deeper; we reach out with the hush of sovereignty; we spread our green mantle over the works of man. Our green fire burns through the centuries, and he of the red fire is consumed by us; his body becomes tissue of our tissue. Into the crucible of the years drop his ashes.

"It is written! He of the red fire is migratory. He flits from land to land, from sea to sea. Like the butterfly, he knows his hours are few. He craves immortality; and he builds and builds. He wars for supremacy; and builds again. He knows not the calm of the rocks and the forests. The fear of Death is with him from the hour of birth. It dogs his steps. He knows not the visage of Death nor the Light it wears! He gropes blindly and dreams not that Death and Life are one.

"Thou of the red fire, *Adios!* There are battles for thee to fight. There is work to be done for thy short-lived race. We would stay thee, but we may not. *Adios!*"

CHAPTER IX.

AFTER the abrupt departure of Gonzalo Alarcon, the three astonished men in the sala of La Sacra Sonrisa discussed the matter excitedly, striving vainly to decide what course should be pursued. Beyond petitioning the government for the services of the *guardia civile*, there really was nothing to do; and they knew only too well what the dilatory reply of the government would be. Even if the *guardia civile* did come, the soldiers were no match for a forest-ambushed foe. Both Gilbert Palgrave and M. Theuriet knew that Raquel's fate was sealed so far as their efforts to extricate her from her position were concerned.

The father had aged seemingly ten years, twenty years. All of the buoyancy of manner which the Cuban climate gives to its dwellers had been swallowed up in this terrible fear which had fallen like a blight upon him. The atmosphere of the entire plantation was depressed. The fires still remained gray in the furnaces. The blacks talked in hushed tones.

This strange stillness was not so apparent to Lithgow, who did not know the ingenio in its tumultuous activity. He and M. Theuriet sat in the sleep-inducing chairs of the estrada; the master of the house walked the floor with the wild impatience of powerlessness. M. Theuriet was very quiet. He realized that it had been the announcement of his intention to claim Raquel which had wrenched from them their opportunity of securing her. He was filled with unavailing regret. He wondered that Palgrave did not hurl anathemas at him. They were in the father's eyes, but they were not spoken.

On Lithgow's arrival with M. Theuriet, the sugar planter had offered to the Northerner the house, the plantation, and all of his worldly goods after the courteous fashion of Cuba. Encouraged by such hospitality, Lithgow now ventured to look about him. He had some curiosity as to what had been the surroundings of this lost señorita. Everywhere were evidences of refinement. The high cool-looking walls were graced here and there with reproductions of English cathedrals, and there also was a picture of "The Madonna of the Chair." He moved over to the bookshelves. They held a varied and rich collection for a Cuban household.

"Bless my soul!" he exclaimed to himself, as he glanced over the titles. "Carlyle; a Latin Lexicon; Shakespeare; 'The Iliad;' Voltaire; Hugo; Schopenhauer's 'Wisdom of Life;' Pascal's 'Thoughts'!"

He took down each volume he had enumerated and several others, whirling over the leaves interestedly. Everywhere he observed marks that indicated that the books had received much usage.

"Probably he is an Oxford man," he told himself explanatorily, as he inspected the bethumbed "Thoughts." Here and there he paused to read underlined passages, and this one: "Our whole dignity consists in thought. Our elevation must be derived from this, not from space and duration which we cannot fill," arrested his notice peremptorily; for at its margin was traced in a feminine hand the admonition:

"Take this for thy correction, Raquel, when thy soul burns —in vain—to achieve great deeds."

Gilbert Palgrave, perceiving his interest came and stood beside him, saying sadly:

"These were the poor child's treasures. They are the only society she has had except mine. Only the day that she was seized she was rebelling against the dullness of her life here. She has great longings to accomplish something; I suppose that it is the longing of youth. Perhaps her English blood is accountable for some of her restlessness."

"Does she take a dose of Pascal to quiet her riotous spirit?" queried the American, exhibiting what he had been reading. Palgrave viewed the sentence with moist eyes.

"Perhaps so. That is her writing," he admitted. "I presume that I have done ill to permit her to grow to womanhood here with only myself for a companion. It is natural that she should long for society; and I hoped to furnish it to her in a year or two. But now—my God!—the thought will drive me insane!"

Later, Lithgow wandered out into the court. It was suggestive of Moorish life. The slender, graceful columns upheld a wide upper gallery which jutted out over the colonnade that enclosed the patio with its fountain and riot of bloom. He espied the listless folds of the hammock and divined who had been its usual occupant. Through the shade of flowering shrubs he peered upward, past the bright strips of gay awning, to the brilliant whiteness of the zenith. It was past the hour of noon. The air quivered with heat. It seemed to him that all the world had swooned beneath the narcotic atmosphere that filled this little spot with such a hush. He stood still, mesmerized by the beauty of the place.

"It is ideal!" he said, with a deep breath. "One could live and die here and never drink nor dream of the poison that the world knows and with which it intoxicates itself."

He never knew how long he had stood there, but suddenly he was startled by an unearthly commotion from without. Shrieks and deep cries from the black population of the plantation arose in a chorus that brought Gilbert Palgrave and M. Theuriet from the sala to the entrance of the court in a rush of dismay.

"*Mon Dieu!* What ees ze mattair?" cried the Frenchman in alarm.

"Perhaps the plantation has been set on fire!" said Palgrave, with white lips.

What he saw, drove the blood from his heart up into his face, with a sweep of red that ebbed and left him of deathly pallor.   He caught hold of Lithgow's shoulder.

"Am I mad?" he asked in a hoarse whisper, pointing with a trembling finger to a figure in white that seemed to be carried above the heads of the excited, gesticulating blacks. "Isn't that Raquel?   O God!"

Lithgow's eyes already were fastened on that white object. So intent was his questioning gaze that he never noticed that the man by his side reeled, overcome by this sudden joy after the hours of torture and despair.

With a sob, Gilbert Palgrave fell forward on his face unconscious.

Incredulous that the comer possibly could be the señorita, M. Theuriet had stood petrified with astonishment.   Now, he bent over the prostrate form of his neighbor with fear and trouble in his face.

High above the glad exclamations of the blacks rose a shrill cry of terror.   In another instant Raquel had thrown herself down by her father, beseeching him to speak to her, to look at her.

"Ah, if he is dead!" she wailed, laying her face beside his in the frenzy of fear.

"He is not dead," volunteered Lithgow, seeing that no one else offered the consolation.   "He has lost consciousness for a moment, that is all.   The sight of you—"

"Ah, ze sight ov you was too mooch, *señorita mia*," broke in Theuriet, his excitement getting the better of his politeness.   "He was almost censane wiz ze loss of you."

Raquel gave not a glance to either of them.   She had her father's face in her hands and was caressing it hungrily.   Suddenly, she looked up with remembrance and called:

"Faquita!   Faquita!"

From out the encircling group of awed and frightened blacks, the gypsy-like countenance of Faquita peered forth.

"*Qué, señorita mia?*" she asked doubtfully.

"Help me!" pleaded Raquel.   "Tell me what to do."

For answer, Faquita dropped down on her knees, took his head from Raquel's hands, and laid it back on the tiles.

"Water!" she ordered briefly.

A dozen of the women rushed to obey, but Lithgow had been ahead of them; from the fountain he brought his handkerchief dripping with moisture. This Faquita passed gently over the features of the planter and was rewarded by seeing signs of returning life. Then she stood up and ordered the throng of gaping servants away with peremptory gesture. As though they had been accustomed to obey her all their lives, they scurried out of sight, leaving their master to perceive only the sweet visage of Raquel when he opened his eyes again.

That that was sufficient to revive him was proven in a short time. With the haziness of returning memory, he gazed on her tenderly; then, with sudden recollection, lifted himself and caught her in his eager embrace.

There were no words at first. None were needed.

If Zuñega had wished any other reward than that which he already held to be his, he would have found it in that scene which he observed from under his lowered lids. His heart was beating strongly with the sweetness of this home-coming. He knew that, no matter where he went or what fate became his, the memory of this hour would ever nestle in his mind. He turned and looked at Faquita. Was she too moved? He read in her dark, passionate face the sign of keen emotion, but he could not peer deep enough to see that her thoughts were back in the home that mourned her as one dead, dead to the pure and quiet life which had been hers as a child.

Lithgow watched the entire group: Raquel's warm coloring, Faquita's half-Spanish apparel, Zuñega's unrivalled muscular development. All of a sudden he saw that which made him take a quick step forward. He took the hand of Zuñega in his own with undisguised excitement.

"*Perdone me, señor,*" he begged eagerly, "but this ring!— Where did you get it?"

Zuñega drew his hand away slowly, with all the haughtiness of a prince in his sombre eyes.

"*Porqué, señor?*" he demanded.

For reply, Lithgow thrust out his own hand and displayed on it the exact counterpart of the ornament that the Cuban wore.

"*Caramba!*" murmured Zuñega wonderingly. "You, señor, where got you yours? This was my father's."

It had all come so quickly, with such simpleness, that Lith-

gow only stared at Zuñega for reply.   He could not believe
that thus had dropped into his hands the very individual for
whom English and American lawyers had sought so fruitlessly
for years.   Finally he questioned cautiously:

"Your father was a Cuban?"

"*No, señor, inglés.*"

Lithgow had an exuberant inclination to indulge in some
extravagant demonstration of satisfaction, but he restrained
himself sufficiently to say significantly:

"Then I have some strange news for you, if you can bring
me proof of your assertion.   Can you?"

The attention of all was riveted on them now.   Faquita
came nearer.

"*Yo no sé,*" answered Zuñega, a line of perplexity showing
between his black brows.   "I have but this ring and the words
of Annizae."

Lithgow almost gave a leap in the air at the sound of the
name that he had heard in Bertram's office in New York.

"Annizae!" he shouted.   "Where is she?"

M. Theuriet and Gilbert Palgrave regarded him as if they
thought he had lost his senses.   Raquel, her attention held by
him for the first time, turned a questioning gaze upon her
father.

"He is Monsieur's American guest," he explained to her,
and both gave their eyes to the participants in the strange
drama before them.   If Lithgow was new to Raquel, Zuñega
and Faquita were not less new to the two planters, who, in
their absorbed contemplation of the returned girl, had given
as yet no thought to the method of her coming.

"Why, señor?" queried Zuñega again, puzzled at the vehemence of this Spanish-speaking foreigner.

"What is this woman called 'Annizae' to you?" asked Lithgow, answering with another question.

"My mother," replied Zuñega.

"Are you certain?"

Zuñega turned toward Faquita with a gesture.   "Ask this
señora, señor," he advised.

Faquita, all curiosity, was nothing loath to be questioned.   Raquel urged her father and M. Theuriet nearer,
explaining the part that the two had played in her escape
from the camp of Alarcon.

Gilbert Palgrave, not to be deterred by the strange queries of the American, went at once with not yet steady step to Zúñega, He held out his hand with the grateful grasp of an Englishman.

"My daughter tells me that it is to you and your companion that I owe this joy which has come to me," he said simply. "What I have is yours."

Zuñega bowed so low that his long, wavy hair almost seemed to touch the tiles.

"I am repaid, señor," he replied softly, lifting his eye for a moment to those of Raquel. "There is nothing I would take of yours but the pleasure it has given me to give *you* joy."

It was no more than the common, courteous Spanish way of disclaiming gratitude, but his eyes gave the words a weight they would not otherwise have had. Palgrave extended his hand also to Faquita. As she placed hers within it, he bent his lips to her fingers.

"What is there I can do to repay you, señora?" he questioned anxiously, supposing her to be the wife of Zuñega.

Faquita's oriental-like face altered. She glanced at Raquel with half-amused glance, as if questioning if she should tell that she already had her reward also. Finally she said:

"You may answer a question, señor."

"With pleasure," bowed the sugar planter wonderingly.

"Has Gonzalo Alarcon been here to demand ransom for the señorita?"

Gilbert Palgrave looked around at M. Theuriet with compressed lips, then turned back to his interrogator.

"Was that Alarcon who came here?" he demanded unbelievingly.

"None other," returned Faquita.

The soul of the planter stirred with the bitterness of viewing a lost opportunity. To know that the most feared brigand of Cuba has slipped through your unretaining fingers is enough to arouse rage in any heart.

"If I only could have known!" he groaned. "He went from here only a few hours ago."

"Went he back for the señorita?" asked Faquita anxiously. "Was he to secure ransom?"

"He refused ransom," returned Palgrave, not deeming it necessary to explain why.

Faquita brought her hands together with triumphant gesture.

"Ah, what did I tell you, señorita?" she cried. "It is well that the miles of forest stretch between you and Gonzalo Alarcon now."

Faint with the realization of what she had escaped, Raquel leaned hard on the arm of her father.

"I owe it all to you," she said gratefully, "to you and Zuñega. He can return no more to the forest. He must become one of us, and you, Faquita, if you only will."

Faquita shook her head smilingly. Her fancy was picturing the rage of Alarcon. She would not miss her triumph over him for a dozen plantations like this quiet one of La Sacra Sonrisa.

"The señorita is kind," said Zuñega with a glad light in his face. "But the revenge of Alarcon will be far-reaching. I must go where my face is not known; perhaps among the tobacco fields in the most distant part of the island. Perhaps, some day, I can win my way over to the free country north. Who knows?"

Lithgow, whose queries as to Zuñega's past were trembling unuttered on his lips, now sought to make himself heard.

"I think that there is another country that waits for you, señor," he said distinctly, "the land of your father."

Each countenance was turned toward the speaker. His tone commanded attention with which even the expressions of gratitude could no longer interfere. He directed his questions first to Faquita.

"Will you tell me who you are, señora?" he begged.

"The wife of Gonzalo Alarcon," was her answer, as she glanced amusedly toward the surprised planters, exchanging mystified looks.

"And this Annizae, who is she?"

"Who knows?" shrugged Faquita. "She speaks no word ever save that which is required."

"She calls herself the mother of this man beside you?"

"It is true, señor."

"But why does he not call her by the term of mother then?"

Faquita shrugged her shoulders again and glanced at Zuñega.

"Tell him, Zuñega," she urged. "Thou shouldst know more than I."

"I know nothing," replied Zuñega reluctantly. "Always have I called her 'Annizac.' I never have thought about it. Every one calls her so, señor."

Lithgow was growing more and more certain that he had found his man.

"How came you with the ring?" he questioned. "Do not fear to answer. Great good will come to you if you are the man I think you are. If you prove not to be, you may go your way."

Zuñega looked him in the eyes for fully a minute. He appeared satisfied with what his searching glance had revealed, for he responded at length:

"I secured it from her when I had grown to manhood. She said it had belonged to my father."

"Has she told you nothing of him?"

"Nothing, señor."

"Then I will tell you," announced Lithgow. "Unless I mistake, this woman is not your mother. She exchanged her own child for you when your father and mother sailed for England years ago. All traces of her and the child she had stolen were lost. Tireless has been the search. As far as I can see, the possession of this ring proves conclusively that you are the personage for whom others beside myself are seeking. But first I must see this woman. You and she must accompany me to the States, possibly to England. Your father and mother are dead. All that they died possessed of becomes yours by right, if you can prove to the satisfaction of all concerned that you are the child who was stolen. I am willing to help you to do this. We must secure the confession of the woman. How shall it be done?"

Aghast, scarcely able to grasp the rapid words which meant so much to him, Zuñega was silent.

He was not the only one silent through astonishment.

Raquel was the first to recover.

"*Gracias á Dios!*" she exclaimed. "There are invisible fingers that guide! You, Zuñega, gave up your all in order to restore me to this safety that I craved. You asked no

7

recompense, but—has not one come? See what it promises: neither labor in tobacco fields nor danger from the vengeance of the chief! Life in a free land! Ah, it is a grand fortune!"

Zuñega did not take his eyes from her while she spoke. There was a peculiar sinking of his heart with the words: " Life in a free land!" That meant a country far away from Cuba; and Zuñega knew then, with an overwhelming sweep of realization, that he would count nothing good which took him from the skies that looked down on this maiden who had so unexpectedly crossed his path and changed its direction.

" It is not true what the señor thinks," he said slowly. " I am the son of Annizae. All believe it."

" Who knows?" queried Lithgow, employing the national question. " We must ascertain if what *you* think is true. It means more to you than you can imagine. It means that, if Annizae is *not* your mother, you can live where you will. You will be possessed of fortune, honor, place in the world of prominent men. Annizae has kept you out of your rights for years, if I mistake not. Are you willing to be defrauded longer? You will be not an unknown forest dweller, subsisting on the spoils of a doubtful occupation; you will be owner of wide lands, master of great houses. This woman Annizae must make restitution to you. She is the only one who can place you in the position that was your father's. Will she do this without being compelled to do it?"

Faquita smiled broadly.

" Compel Annizae?" she murmured. " The señor knows her not."

Zuñega's brows were drawn. He was confused. He was beginning to understand dimly what this might mean. Through the chaos of bewildered thoughts which thronged his mind, one suggestion shot, leaving behind it a track of light that dazzled him. " Fortune, honor." Those magic words. Would they not place him on a par with this girl before him whose eyes rested upon him with such unfathomable potency in their depths? With the fortune might he not be able to accomplish something that would win her praise, perhaps her love? With a fortune to back him, might he not accomplish for Cuba that which was so near the heart of the señorita? Knowing the secrets of the island so well, could he not plan and lead men against the Spanish rule in a well-sus-

tained revolt that would wear the soldiers out? There was
nothing definite in the whirl of thoughts that made his head
fairly spin as his great midnight eyes travelled from face to
face of the group before him.

"I cannot believe, señor!" he said finally to Lithgow. "You
are kind! I am indebted to you, but I cannot believe. Why
should I be what you say? I am only Zuñega. Gonzalo Alarcon has taught me what I know."

"Will you believe if this woman Annizae confesses the
wrong she has done you?" asked the American. "Will you
go to England with me in that case?'

Zuñega bowed low. His sombrero with its decorations
swept the tiles as he moved his hand gracefully.

"*Ciertamente, señor*," he agreed.

"How are we to get this woman?" demanded Lithgow anxiously.

Zuñega shook his head. He had no solution of the problem
to offer. He could not return to the camp. Annizae would
not come to the plantation. Was that not an end of the entire
matter?

Faquita's ingenuity was at work. Her eyes shone with excitement. The tale that the American had told had aroused
all of her interest. Annizae's secret, for it was known that
Annizae had a secret, had defied them all. Many had been the
bantering questions which had been thrust at the uncommunicative creature, and her taciturnity had won for her finally the
sobriquet, "Silent Annizae." To pierce this veil which had
so long shut the woman in would be an act that the whole camp
would relish. It would be a fair revenge for various indignities
which the elder woman had occasionally heaped upon the head
of Faquita for usurping the place which had been her own. It
was true that they had dwelt together with apparent amity,
but always there had been a smouldering hatred, and Faquita
would not be sorry to gain the upper hand over the black creature whose will still was law in the camp cuisine.

"*Perdoname, señor*," she ventured to address Lithgow,
"there is but one way. No word you could send would bring
her here. I think of one chance; it might bring her as far as
the shrine of Nuestra Madre de Dolores that stands on the
highway that runs through the edge of the woods at the base
of the mountains to the south. She knew not of Zuñega's de-

parture. To see him, to beg him to return, she might come
that far; but she must come without Alarcon's knowledge.
If he mistrusted, he would follow her. He will owe death to
Zuñega for robbing him of the señorita. Not even the length
of the island, not even the obscurity of distant tobacco fields
will shut Zuñega from the revenge of Alarcon. It is well that
the señor takes him from Cuba. Zuñega's life is worth nothing here now."

Zuñega made her an imperative gesture of silence. Faquita
saw it, but she heeded it not. She meant that these señors
should know the full value of this deed that Zuñega had done.
If great good came to him by reason of it, well and good.
Zuñega had known of no reward when he had agreed to help
her and the señorita; he had known only the fate that awaited
him somewhere in the future in the day when Alarcon's sure,
mean vengeance should overtake him.

"God in heaven!" cried Gilbert Palgrave, understanding
for the first time the rich measure of Zuñega's right to his
limitless gratitude. "You are of the metal that heroes are
made of! Practically, you have given your life to bring my
child to me, and I have nothing to offer you, nothing but the
unbounded admiration of a father and a man who is an Englishman. Aside from the service you have rendered me and
mine, I am proud to know you, sir. Consider me your debtor
and your servant."

Zuñega's face flushed. Save from the lips of the señorita
herself, never could words be uttered that would give him
such a thrill as these which came from the master of La Sacra
Sonrisa, the man whose consent must be gained before ever he
might look upon the señorita with covetous eyes of love.

"*Gracias, señor,*" he murmured faintly, bowing low again.

M. Theuriet had been standing silent. Though alert to
everything which was transpiring, he was engrossed with the
fact that he had, in the guise of her father's neighbor and
friend, taken Raquel's fingers within his own and was now
patting them tenderly and reassuringly, as if to remind her
that home walls were again around her. She had glanced at
him once wonderingly, but his expression of delight at her unexpected return induced her to permit her hand to rest in his
clasp without exhibiting any of the repugnance which she felt
without knowing why. Now, the Frenchman within him could

not but give praise to the spirit of the handsome youth to whom they were so much indebted. He even felt an inclination to bestow upon the fellow a tiny portion of what would have slipped from his grasp altogether if Alarcon had taken the ransom. By means of this young bandit—who might turn out to be quite an important personage—they had secured Raquel and it had cost them nothing. He could afford to be generous; besides, it would make him appear well in the eyes of Raquel and Gilbert Palgrave. He spoke in Spanish to Zuñega.

"I echo the words of Don Gilberto; and, in his name, I will ask you to accept two hundred pesos for a slight reminder of what we owe you."

"*No es posible, señor,*" refused Zuñega gravely. "I can accept nothing for what has been done. On the señora you may bestow it; all is due to her." He bent his head toward Faquita.

"Then she shall have it," declared Theuriet. "I will send for the amount at once."

"*Nada, nada, señor.*" Faquita shook her head with a little coquettish droop of her lids that M. Theuriet would have found fascinating had not Raquel been near.

"Pardon, I shall insist," swore he, feeling that the fingers of Raquel pressed his approvingly. "I will go for it now; you shall take it back to—your husband, if you care not for it yourself. He may wish now that he had waited for the ransom. God be praised that he got it not!"

Faquita's shoulders moved with the shrug which was habitual.

"As you will, señor," she smiled, "but, if you will listen, you will be careful how you travel without many outriders. It was you whom Alarcon intended should be taken, not the señorita. He anticipated a large ransom from you."

M. Theuriet turned toward Raquel as quick as a flash.

"Ah, *ma chère,* you hav' suffaired for me!" he cried with grief. "Eet ees I who should hav' been enduring zat which has fallen to you. Ze devotion ov a life could not recompense, yet I will attempt to repay you—eef you will pairmit."

Raquel regarded him puzzledly, but replied with a smile that she meant should be grateful.

"What has been, has been best—no?" she inquired. "You

have paid no ransom to secure your own liberty, as you would have had to do. These noble people have released me from what would have been a life of torture; in so doing, one of them has made a strange discovery. What God orders is well."

"Zink you zat He instigated your unhappy abduction, señorita?" smiled the Frenchman.

"Ah, who knows?" she replied seriously. "Is not He able to turn all things into a way that will bless us?"

Over four of the listening faces passed a wave of amused skepticism as to the probability of there having been any divine influence in this matter, but in Zuñega's richly colored countenance shone reverence and the knowledge that her misfortune had been the means of blessing him, even though no fortune became his, and only the fear of Alarcon was his portion in life. Raquel, with her words, thought of the opportunity which had become the bandit's to carry out the hope of Cuba. M. Theuriet thought of the chance which yet remained of making Raquel his own.

"Who is to induce Annizac to come to this shrine?" asked Lithgow of Faquita.

"I will try, señor," volunteered she readily.

"But no word must be spoken to give her an idea that he knows of the wrong she has done him," warned the American. "If she has kept silence this long, she means to keep it forever."

"How will you break that silence, señor?" questioned Faquita curiously.

"That remains to be decided when I see her," he answered. "Do you agree to urge her to meet this man she calls her son at the spot designated?"

"*Sí, señor.*"

"When?"

Faquita counted her fingers thoughtfully.

"Not before a week from last night, señor," she returned. "By that time Alarcon may be away for a time. It is only a chance; no one could promise for Annizae; she may come; she may not. I will do my best."

"*Bueno!*" decided Lithgow, with a breath of relief. "We will be there. At what hour?"

"Ten," she said. "There will then be time for us to reach

the camp before sleep is away from their eyelids. They sleep late when the chief is far."

"Ten," agreed Lithgow, "and, if Annizae is wise, she will bring her possessions with her. She will return no more to the camp of Gonzalo Alarcon."

"Then she will come no step, señor."

"She must not know it," returned Lithgow. "I rely on you, Señora Alarcon."

Faquita laughed at the title. Never had it been bestowed upon her before; it was pleasant to her ears. Exultation was in her heart. Her revenge for the slight which Alarcon had been ready to put upon her was becoming richer. Not only had she deprived him of the señorita, but she could also remove Annizae, who wielded a subtle but unmistakable power over the chief, a power that all recognized but of which none knew the secret.

"I will not disappoint you, señor," she promised meaningly.

"Annizae will not find me at the shrine," reminded Zuñega. "I must be far from here by this hour on the *mañana*. To remain here would be death. I must make my way to some hidden place. It must be so."

"*Es verdad*," admitted Faquita, troubledly. "What is it to be, señor?"

Lithgow thought a moment.

"How do you propose to go?" he asked.

Zuñega hesitated, then looked straight at Gilbert Palgrave.

"If I might have a horse," he ventured. "I would not rob the chief. He needs all that he has."

"All I have you may command," answered the sugar planter. "When will you wish it?"

"At once, señor."

Zuñega noticed that Raquel's face changed. She stepped forward impulsively.

"Can you not wait?" she pleaded. "You can hide here."

He shook his head. A wonderful softness was in his eyes.

"Some day, señorita, I will return," he replied in a low voice. "I will be all that you would desire."

"God walk with you," she said enthusiastically. "I shall watch for your coming."

And she did not know the full truth of her words.

" Where am I to meet you?" demanded Lithgow, seeing this much desired individual taking his fortune into his own hands. " We must have everything understood."

" Two weeks from to-day at noon I will be in the Campo Santo at Habana," replied Zuñega. " If you come there, you will see me. You are an Americano?"

" My name is Lithgow Hamilton," explained the Northerner, feeling that this was doing important business in as expeditious a manner as even an American could wish. " I will be in Havana at that time with Annizae."

Faquita lifted her brows and glanced at Zuñega amusedly.

" The señor has not yet met Annizae," she commented.

In less than an hour both Faquita and Zuñega were on their respective ways, provided with all that they could be prevailed upon to accept. Faquita led the animal which Raquel had ridden. She was in high spirits and had no visible fears as to her ability to find her way back to the camp.

" *Adios, adios!*" she cried over her shoulder to Zuñega.

He kept his sombrero on the pommel of his saddle until she was out of sight. He had an affection for Faquita that even Annizae's fault-finding had been unable to destroy. Now, he was conscious of a deep sense of respect for her. To her was due the happiness which now illumined the señorita's white face. He, left to himself, never would have done this deed that they called "noble." He felt that he had deserved none of the praise they had bestowed upon him. He was full of a sense of shame in accepting their thanks. But, as he sat there, his fine physique outlined against the bright light of the afternoon slipping westward, he made a vow that he would return in a manner worthy of the speech they had given him this day. If the words of the Americano were true, he could return soon, her equal. But, even if they were not true, he would return, though it might be years hence, and, when he came, he meant it should be as her equal.

" *Adios, señorita mia,*" he said to Raquel. Zuñega never forgets. *Adios, señores!* To outwit Alarcon, I must ride well and far. *Adios!*"

He replaced his sombrero. He rode through the orange grove and out upon the highway. He did not look back.

CHAPTER X.

THE greater portion of the week which must elapse before the hour to meet Annizac was spent by both M. Theuriet and Lithgow at the sugar plantation.

The Frenchman did not appear wholly satisfied unless he was looking at Raquel. That she was surprised by the unusual interest he manifested in her was evident, but it also was clear that she attributed it to the neighbor's natural desire to rejoice with her father and the entire mass of blacks, who had not yet ceased nightly celebrations.

Again and again, to different groups of listeners, Raquel patiently related her adventures, until finally they felt almost as familiar with them as she did herself. That these accounts were related again with blood-curdling embellishments in the safety of the negro quarters, none of them heard.

This frequent presence of the American changed the tenor of the days for Raquel. Instead of slipping back into the even melody of uneventful hours, she experienced the delight of having a companion who not only liked her books but understood them better than she did. So great was this pleasure that she did not even feel bored by the proximity of M. Theuriet and actually went to the extent of showing the Frenchman trifling attentions. Lithgow, cognizant of the plans in the mind of his host, for M. Theuriet made no effort to conceal his hopes from the guest who had become aware of them during the audience with Alarcon, wondered much as to what would be the girl's verdict could she know on what terms her freedom was to have been purchased.

Seeing her love for her father, witnessing how she caressed each vine and flower in the court, he could not doubt that she would have accepted anything that offered her the safety of home walls.

The curiosity he had felt concerning her deepened as he knew her. He discovered that she had thoughts as radical as Beatrice's, though in a different way. He called her a child, as he watched her lithe figure dancing gayly through the corridors on her way to and from the cocina, where she was welcomed with the joyousness of the exuberant southern natures. He called her a woman of years, as she swung idly in the hammock and argued with him over the volumes that her library boasted. She was not the usual quiet convent-bred maiden which he had fancied common to Cuba. She sometimes made him think of a volcano, smouldering, emitting occasional flame, suggestive of the fires within. She fascinated him with her quick changes, her little skips from one subject to another widely foreign. He often had the uncomfortable feeling that she had not been listening to what he had been saying, her mind seeming to have flown far after she had uttered her own words; but he invariably learned that she had missed nothing and only was laying up his thoughts against that day when the plantations would know him no more.

Those gold and sapphire days were magic ones. He knew it at the time. He knew it better long afterward. Insensibly, the soft, fragrant hours droned themselves away while he smoked and chatted with the two planters or exchanged ideas with Raquel in the cool court amid the subtle witchery of tropical bloom.

The estate was a bustling scene of activity again. With the American fondness for acquiring information, he studied the process of sugar-making, rising at three o'clock in the morning and going over the estate with Gilbert Palgrave while yet it was the violet hue of waning night through which the phosphorescent cocullo darted about, its firefly lantern not yet extinguished.

During the madrugada, those hushed hours between midnight and dawn, these little cocullos made the perfumed West Indian darkness seem as if peopled with falling stars, thousands of lost Pleiads, more brilliant than those which gemmed the purple vault overhead.

Side by side with the sugar planter, Lithgow made the tour of the plantation, up and down the wide paths that intersected the fields and formed roads through which the carts could travel to gather the cane. Returning for the light breakfast, they afterward made their way to the vast, low buildings from the high chimney of which poured the black smoke that made such a blot on the fair landscape now wakening to life.

The red-tiled roof of the mill was full to the top of the cut and bundled cane, and the sugar master nearly beside himself with the fear that the mayoral had given him more juice than he could work up in the time allotted to him. Wild appearing, half-naked negroes tramped up and down the platform of the mill, thrusting armfuls of the canes between the ponderous rollers of the crushing-machine, from which streamed continually a flow of milky cane-juice that took its way swiftly through canals of split palm trees to the vats of the purging-house. There was the scene resembling Hades. Huge furnaces glowed with the fiercely burning fuel called *bagazzo*, the dried cane-stalks. From boiler to boiler the juice passed, changing ever: simmering; foaming; sluggishly inactive; a brown mass; a tossing sea of liquid gold. Long paddles of aloes wood beat it into a creamier tint and ladled it into a trench of immense depth, where it was stirred and flung aloft in marvellously tinted showers that crystallized slowly in the falling.

Lithgow did not marvel at the Englishman's financial condition when he learned that the previous year the running expenses of the estate had been one hundred thousand dollars, while there had been realized from the output of sugar less than seventy-five thousand dollars; and that the year before matters had been even worse.

"You will be glad if Cuba ever breaks away from Spain, won't you?" he remarked while the mayoral stood near.

Gilbert Palgrave laid his hand warningly on the American's arm.

"No such words are uttered here," he replied, and the accompanying glance silenced the exclamation that was on Lithgow's lips. As soon as they were alone, however, Palgrave brought up the subject again. "When you have lived long in any land under Spanish rule, you will make sure to whose ears you are speaking before you speak," he said. "I am not certain of that fellow. He may be wholly Spanish in sympathies. He came from Havana. It is well to be cautious. Spain is not above employing spies to ascertain if she is securing her share of the output from the plantations."

"Good Lord!" ejaculated the American. "What a land!"

"What a government, you mean," corrected Palgrave, with a smile.

Lithgow accepted the amendment.

"How can you stand such an order of things?" he questioned.

"I'm afraid I can't much longer," sighed the sugar planter,

"but what is a man to do? My all is invested here. I see it shrinking daily. Each year I am deeper in debt, but we keep hoping for better things."

"Do you see any prospect of a betterment until Cuba is free?"

The Englishman hesitated. He made sure that none was near, then he answered briefly:

"No."

"What would you do if there should be a revolution?" queried Lithgow.

"Sometimes, in my hours of despair, I think I would rush in with all my men at my heels, but I dare not whisper such a thing to Raquel. The seeds of revolt seem to be in her blood. If she were a man, I really believe that she would be rash enough to throw herself into the jaws of the monster, Spain, in a vain effort to help the country. Her frail body shelters a giant soul. It's a pity that some strong man could not have her spirit."

"She seems to feel no fear of voicing her opinions," smiled Lithgow. "I have heard her utter some bitter things against Spain. I supposed that she took her cue from you."

Palgrave shook his head.

"I don't know where she gets it," he said thoughtfully; "it always has been in her. I don't think I have allowed myself to criticise Spain very much before her, though it may have been that I have done so without noticing the effect upon her. At any rate, she is a rank revolutionist at heart. It is lucky for her that she is a woman."

"Do you care if I disagree with you?" said Lithgow. "Who knows what she might accomplish if she were a man? As it is, she must submit to the uneventful, possibly unhappy, life of femininity while she has the capacity for a wider work."

Gilbert Palgrave looked at the American with some surprise.

"Have you noticed it too?" he asked.

"Noticed what?"

"I scarcely know what term to call it," answered the father, "but sometimes she seems to possess a force that, unknown to herself, makes me feel quite small and insignificant. She longs to do such things as Napoleon did. Now, I confess that no such ambitions ever entered my youthful mind. I was content to live as boys did, play their games, and not trouble myself about impossible aspirations. When I was forced to start out for myself, I came here. Raquel's mother was a Cuban. Possibly through her crept this restless streak that torments the child, and, I may confess, me as well."

" Possibly if she could have played games with companions of her own age as you did, her spirits might have passed off in such healthful excitement," suggested Lithgow. " But she has lived within herself a great deal, has she not? She worships the heroes of history, I can see that. She craves romances, yet it seems to me that she lives in a veritable land of romance."

He looked to where the hills were putting on their noonday purple in the north; southward lay the bright yellow green of the cane-fields. An African woman of stately bearing came toward them, bearing a water-jar on her head. The gentle breeze stirred the leaves of the far-above palms but touched not the dark, shining, irregular foliage of the parasitic jaguey-macho that had a giant ceiba in its deadly grasp. Despite the rush and flurry at the mills, an air of indolence lay over everything. Black judios flew chattering over the broad fields, but all else appeared to sleep in the hot sunlight.

He had not been there long enough as yet to sense the isolation which encompassed the girl of whom they had been speaking; though he felt a shadow of the sadness which seems to be a part of tropical life, the half-divine pain which haunts the heart and may be born of the constant war which the luxuriantly flourishing material life wages against the seemingly quiescent spiritual aspirations. While he revelled in the soft balminess of the air redolent with the sweetness of thousands of blossoms that rioted unseen, he knew that he was not condemned to the narcotic influence of a southern climate for the remainder of his existence, and that comforting fact made him enjoy it the more, though he might not have been conscious that this was so.

His business with the coffee planter had been consummated with ease after the anxiety concerning Raquel had susbided, and now nothing remained to keep him save the meeting with Annizae. He congratulated himself that he had been so fortunate as to complete his negotiations with other planters before coming to La Buena Esperanza; otherwise, he would

have been at a loss to know what to do with Annizae after
securing her.　As it was, he contemplated sailing at once for
New York, taking her with him whether she wished or not.
He discussed this possibility with Raquel during the hours
which they spent in the deep rocking-chairs of the estrada.
She confessed herself doubtful as to his ability to accomplish
this.　He, as decidedly, swore that nothing should defeat him.

"Our friend, Zuñega, will not be the only one to be benefited," he announced frankly.　"It will net the lawyers a nice
sum if he turns out to be the proper heir, and I shall not be
neglected, though to me belongs little credit.　Had it not
been for your capture, the fellow might have lived and died a
bandit, 'unhonored and unsung.'　He really owes his fortune
to you, señorita."

"I am glad," she answered simply.　After a pause she
added : "He will use it well."

Lithgow lifted his brows.

"Think you so?" he questioned.　"One seldom does in a
like case.　Titles, lands, mansions, descending in such an
abrupt manner, are likely to crush out what little brain the
lucky individual may possess.　I don't believe I could survive
such a surprise."

"Titles?" she echoed.　"You never spoke of titles before.
What will he be called?"

"A lord," smiled Lithgow.　"That will be fatal!　He will
be courted, fêted, worshipped, by the scheming matrons.　Poor
Zuñega, there may be times when he will crave the stagnation
of this indolent Cuban existence.　But, in all probability, he
will forget it.　The fascinations of London and Paris will force
these days of brigandage out of his mind."

A shadow crossed Raquel's face.　She remained silent.
Lithgow dwelt on the charms of continental cities in a dreamy
fashion.　Heretofore, she had exhibited the most eager interest in all that he could tell her of the world she longed to see.
Her quietness caused him to regard her curiously.　He wondered where her thoughts had flown.　Her eyes were sombre.

"*Un centavo por sus pensamientos, señorita,*" he said gently.

"Ah, my thoughts are not worth a *centavo*," she returned.
"I was thinking that I belong to the company of which Socrates
spoke to Glaucon.　Do you not remember?　No?　I have seen
only shadows passing and repassing before me like those which

Socrates described passing before the men in the cave. I have lived and loved with the ghosts of dead men's thoughts."

"And have had better companionship than you are likely to meet when you are out in the rush of the world," he remarked.

"I never shall see the world nor its glorious stir," she sighed.

The American sighed too; but for a different reason.

"You have dreamed of it as youth always dreams," said he, with a touch of pity in his voice. "I have not forgotten that I dreamed also, lying on my back under the old apple trees. What you will find, *señorita mia*, will be disillusionment. Humanity is less lofty and noble than you deem. Your heart aches here; it might break there."

He read in her face that his words had gone deep. She had not yet learned the art of wearing a mask over her feelings. She turned her eyes upon him with a surprised question in their luminous depths.

"How do I know that your heart aches?" he echoed her silent query. "You have told me in a thousand voiceless ways."

"The señor mistakes," she declared swiftly. "My heart aches not save with joy to be near my father once more. I am not content to be idle, however; I confess that. There is no work for my sex here in Cuba. In your country it is different, It is different in the land that was my father's. Know you women who work, señor?"

"Scores," he rejoined. "Many of them would fancy that such an existence as this you lead would be heaven. Where hard fate forces them to make their own living, one's pity bleeds for them, for their lot is not enviable. Where they work from choice, it is another thing. Such women are happy. Their natures demand wide fields. I have one friend whom you would be glad to know. She is obliged to work for her livelihood, but she loves her work. She supports her mother."

Raquel clasped her hands together with an exclamation of delight.

"Ah, how I envy her!" she breathed. "What does she do?"

"She is a sculptor," explained Lithgow, nothing loth to talk about Beatrice to this Cuban maiden. "She is not much older than you."

Raquel's fingers unclasped with a little gesture of despair.

"Tell me about her," she begged. "To know that others can do these things is something to comfort one."

Lithgow recounted the history of Beatrice's varying fortunes, described her failures and her successes, and unconsciously put into the tale a warm bit of feeling.

Raquel listened attentively. Once or twice her face flushed with pleasure.

"It is grand to be able to accomplish such!" she whispered half to herself. Then she looked into the eyes of the American penetratingly. "You have love for her," she said softly.

Lithgow hesitated. He was surprised.

"Why?" he demanded.

She shook her head slowly.

"I know not," she returned with a smile; but the smile was sad. "I feel it in your voice, your eyes. I would love such a woman were I a man. There are many things that I would do were I a man."

"And the first would be——?"

"Ah, you will laugh, señor," she declared. "Papa laughs."

"I promise you," he said solemnly, "but you need not confide in me. I can guess. You would fight for Cuba. Ah, I thought so! You have betrayed that intention before. That is why I ventured to affirm that your heart aches with longing to achieve. Have you never heard that 'real action is in silent moments'? Possibly, in after years, you will look back on this period of your life with eyes that can perceive that it has been most replete with mental growth. I have a little volume of Emerson which this girl sculptor gave me when I came away. Emerson is her gospel. Will you accept it when I go? I think that she would be glad to know it has fallen into the grasp of one who hungers as she has. I will bring it over from La Buena Esperanza."

"You are kind," Raquel acknowledged; "but I do not think that those words are true. In a silent moment one may gather up force and make ready to act; but if no opportunity for action comes, would not all the energy and ambition fall into disuse? A green mould would creep over weapons which might have been powerful."

"Inaction does not await you, señorita, believe me," he argued. "That which your nature demands will come to it.

'Every sound that is spoken over the round world which thou oughtest to hear will vibrate on thine ear. Every proverb, every book, every by-word that belongs to thee for aid or comfort, shall surely come home through open or winding passages.' I am quoting from the book which I will leave with you. Consider me as one of the avenues through which a volume that every life needs has come to you. It will help you. It will strengthen you for that day on which you will be forced to act."

"What day?" she questioned.

"I don't know what day," he returned; "but it is certain to come."

"You puzzle me, señor," she frowned.

"Yes: life is a puzzle," rejoined he, pushing back his hair from his forehead. "None of us solve it. Sometimes I wonder that we try so hard. Would it not be better if you could stop beating your wings, señorita? 'Sweet is the lower air and safe the homely levels.'"

"You mean to insist that I have the ache in the heart," she commented.

"Because you betray yourself," he answered. "I understand you. I appreciate how you long for an absorbing occupation; but, knowing the world, I feel constrained to impress upon you that you have much for which you may feel grateful. Love will come to you. You will marry."

"You think that is the best thing that can come to us?" she demanded hotly.

"I do," replied Lithgow honestly.

"What does this girl sculptor think?" she questioned with eagerness.

Lithgow laughed.

"I am afraid that you and she would agree," he told her.

"She will not marry?"

"She will not marry *me*."

"Yet you will not interfere with her work?"

"Certainly not; but I would take from her shoulders the burden."

"It must be a dear burden to care for those whom one loves!" murmured Raquel, wistfully thinking of Beatrice and her mother.

"Men often find it dear," commented Lithgow, with a covert smile.

"I would rejoice to be able to help papa," she continued. "All my life I have been cared for. I have been selfish. I even have rebelled against the quiet of the surroundings with which love has provided me. Now he needs aid. If I were a son I could be of use. I might take the place of the mayoral. As it is, I idle. I even came near costing an immense ransom. I am of no use in the world!"

"Coming days will teach you the falsity of that assertion." The American stretched out his long legs more comfortably. He knew it was near the hour for the three o'clock dinner. M. Theuriet was to drive over with a goodly escort. This drowsy little *tête-à-tête* soon would be interrupted. He had taken more pleasure in observing the varying expressions of her changeful face than his devotion to Beatrice would warrant. "Already you have accomplished more than many women do in an entire life," he added.

"*Como?*" She was very serious. She had none of the little arts common to femininity, but her half-lifted lids exercised a power that she little imagined. Lithgow drew his glance away with difficulty.

"What a danger to men's hearts she will be when she understands how to employ her fascinations!" he ejaculated silently. Aloud he said:

"If I should tell you, I should be trespassing on the right of the years."

"They will unfold nothing," she replied impatiently.

He heard the cracking of the whip of M. Theuriet's postilion. He saw an expression that was not gladness cross her face.

"Daily is being unfolded before your vision a little drama," he ventured to warn her. "Your gaze is fixed on a horizon so distant that you cannot see what lies near at hand."

Startled, she sought to read his meaning in his face.

"I do not understand," she finally said, with a troubled look.

"No: you do not understand," he shook his head. "But you will."

He wondered that she did not grasp his meaning when, a second later, the Frenchman entered the sala. He perceived the wave of displeasure which shot over M. Theuriet's visage with the discovery that her father was not present and that they were enjoying the chat in the estrada. He endeavored to restore his host's good humor by offering to go in search of the sugar planter, but was held by Theuriet's query given with uplifted brows:

"Ees eet more necessaire now zan before, *mon ami!* Eef you will pairmit, I will join een ze conversation."

Raquel lifted her eyes for one swift moment to those of the American, with the realization in them that the conversation had been such that it was not easy to share with a third party.

"You can give us your opinion as to the chances of my finding the bandit woman at the spot designated," Lithgow said quickly. "The señorita is skeptical."

"Still do you discuss zat question?" demanded the Frenchman, with a show of polite surprise, glancing sharply at Raquel, in whose face he read something new.

"Why not, monsieur?" demanded Lithgow, comprehending the suspicion delicately expressed.

"*Why*, monsieur?" smiled Theuriet. "Gains one mooch by speculation? Ees eet not as well to wait wizout questioning?"

"Perhaps, monsieur," admitted Lithgow graciously. "I fear that I have been so stupid as to weary the señorita with my affairs. I trust she will pardon."

He strolled out into the court with an apology. Something was coming over him which made it difficult for him to sit and observe the eyes with which Theuriet dwelt on Raquel's beauty. It offended him. He resented it. From the court he passed out at the entrance and went among the trees surrounding the house.

"He is no fit mate for that girl!" he said disgustedly. "He can make her mistress of La Buena Esperanza, and she still can be near her father. He will afford her occasional jaunts to Havana. But this is all her life is to be! Heavens! What will she say when she learns? I was fearfully tempted to tell her, just to see the look which would come into her eyes. I fancy it would be horror."

And at that moment M. Theuriet was saying persuasively to Raquel who, though her inclination was to run away, was compelled to remain and entertain him:

"Your papa ees een vera sad plight, *ma chère mademoiselle.* We must see what eet ees posseebl' for us to do, must we not?

We are ze only ones zat can help him; ces eet not so? Ah, *vraiment!* You lov' him?"

"Better than my life, Monsieur Theuriet," she cried earnestly. "I know that he is in trouble. There is nothing I would not do to help him; but what can I do, monsieur? He tells me there is nothing."

M. Theuriet's eyes wore an unholy look.

"Listen," he whispered, drawing near to her. "I will tell you zat which I am willing to do; wiz ze aid ov you much more can be accomplished. You know zat he owes me money? *Bien!* I am willing not only to cancel zat loan but I also will pay ze debts which he has made wiz ze Catalans."

"You will, monsieur?" exclaimed Raquel, grasping both of his old hands in her soft ones. "What nobility! Who will reward you?"

It was coming swifter than Theuriet had anticipated. He had intended to lead up to it in a wonderfully clever manner.

"You, Raquel, you," he whispered, his thin lips almost bloodless.

Raquel rose to her feet. She dropped his hands. A horrible premonition of his meaning froze her heart.

"How?" she asked simply, but her voice and eyes were terrible. Theuriet almost cowed beneath them.

"As my wife."

She understood the meaning of Lithgow's words now. She marvelled that she did not shriek, that she did not faint, that she did none of those things which she would have deemed natural. As it was, she never moved. She only pressed her fingers tighter on the back of the chair as she stood there, facing this suitor. She studied his graying hair, his sharp eyes peering out at her from under his heavy brows; she contemplated his curled mustache and the curve of his nose. She knew that the sight of these awakened a repugnance within her the violence of which she had not conceived. She heard him ramble on excitedly, telling how long he had worshipped her; what he would do for her; that every luxury should be showered upon her; and, crowning temptation, she should spend the season in Havana. His words entered into her ears, but made no impression upon her brain. All that she had comprehended was that this man would lift from her father's shoulders the heavy burden of debt which yearly grew more

unbearable. In exchange, she would have to give her life—
it would be the same as her life, would it not? rebelliously demanded her heart. But had she not just declared that she
would offer up everything to help her father? Had she not
told the American that she would *rejoice* to be able to aid him?
By this sacrifice would she not be caring for him in the only
way that offered?

"Does my father know of this?" she asked at last, in a tense
voice.

"*Non, non,*" Theuriet shook his head. He knew well that
her father never dreamed of the mean advantage which his
neighbor was taking. Palgrave had supposed that the matter
had ended when the ransom was not required. "He must not
be told, not unteel your mind ees made. He deems me aged.
He would think you could not lov' me. He would fear zat
your lov' for him would mak' you say zat which your heart
had no part een."

Raquel did not smile at his presumption. She only
asked:

"Would you expect that I could love you, monsieur?"

"I would make you," declared Theuriet with a smile of
fancied power.

"It would be impossible," returned the girl. "I would hate
you."

Theuriet shrugged his shoulders with an undefinable expression on his wrinkled features.

"*Tant mieux,*" he returned, "then I would hav' ze plaisair
of winning your lov'. Even eef your lov' came not, I would
be happee to know zat you were happee."

"I, happy?" she echoed. "Do you for one moment fancy
that I could be happy as your wife, monsieur?"

"Why not?" he questioned lightly. "Hav' you not believed
zat you would stop at nothing which would help him? Would
you not be happee eef he were happee?"

"But he never could be happy if I were not!" cried Raquel.

"No," admitted the Frenchman, "but how is he to know zat
you are not happy? You are romantic. You look for ze coming of a lovair who will be young and beautiful; but such an
one will not hav' ze monnaie. Your father would be no bettair off. You do not know what lov' ees, yet. I will teach
you. Will you not so pairmit, Raquel?"

Raquel shuddered from head to foot.   She turned to leave the sala.

"Perhaps you mean to be kind, monsieur," she said in a low voice.   "I can't tell."

Theuriet stepped in front of her, caught her hand and touched his lips to it.

"Speak nozing to your papa unteel you hav' decided.   He would not let you mak' what he would fear was a sacrifice.   He rather would suffair heemselv alone; oh, *oui!*   Eet ees true zat I hav' years more zan you; but, my heart ees young.   You must zink; you will be een a position to do mooch zat you desire.   You will be riche.   You can travel.   Forget none of ze advantages, Raquel.   Zey are not to be deespised even eef lov' does not come."

He relinquished her fingers and watched her pass from the sala.   She never had appeared more beautiful.   Scarlet spots burned on each cheek.   Her eyes were like molten flame.

CHAPTER XI.

RAQUEL went out into the court and up the broad staircase to the upper corridor with a feeling that she had been transformed into stone.   Her limbs moved with difficulty.   She was forced to place her cold fingers on the balustrade in order to assist herself to ascend.   All elasticity appeared to have departed from both body and spirit.

Within her chamber, she paused and pulled the gauzy portières across the doorway.   There was no other method of shutting herself in.   She then walked to the centre of the room and looked about her with a dazed expression.   Everything remained the same.   She alone was changed.   The little white net-draped bed was the same she had occupied from childhood.   There were the worn places on the rug where she had knelt before the little crucifix on which the soft radiance of the faintly burning candle shone dimly.   On the simple dressing-table still rested her open book.   Cheerless though the tropical bedroom with its bare floor and walls would have looked to eyes accustomed to the more luxurious furnishings of the North, to Raquel it was the dearest spot she knew.

She put her hands up over her head and clasped her fingers desperately. Her burning eyes seemed to peer hopelessly down through the years. She wondered vaguely at her strange quietude. She could utter no sound. Nothing that could have been uttered would have voiced the tumult within her. She was making the discovery that, under the keenest sufferings, the human is dumb. Light woes bring ready expostulations, rebellion, tears. Crushing sorrows seal the lips.

It seemed to her that she stood there years, so much did she live in those moments.

"This is what the Americano meant," she whispered to herself. "He must have known."

She turned wistfully toward the little crucifix. The woman within her yearned to pour out this anguish somewhere.

"What good will it do me to kneel there?" she said with bitterness. "No answer has ever come! Who knows if there be an ear that listens? If there were, would not Cuba have been free years ago? Then there would be no taxes that eat the profits, no debts, no—*ah, Madre de Jesu!*—no need of this which has come for me to do!"

But, she went and crouched before the white pitiful Christ.

Gradually the fire gave way to a heart-weariness; but it had burnt deep circles under her eyes.

She rested her hands before the altar. She bent her dark head upon them.

"If my mother were living!" she moaned.

The summons for the three o'clock dinner rang out.

She arose. She knew that her absence would cause her father such wonderment that he would not rest until he learned the reason of it.

She bathed her face, and was horrified to find that her diminutive mirror gave back a countenance so altered that there was no hope that it would not be perceived. She paused irresolutely. She knew of no remedy. She must descend. She shivered at the prospect of sitting through the dinner with the old Frenchman's eyes upon her.

"*Querida mia,* we are waiting," she heard her father's voice in the court.

She gathered up all her strength of will and stepped out into the corridor. Then she prayed as she had not prayed on her knees.

"Help me! Help me, Jesu!" she cried silently as she went down the stairs.

The three men stood waiting for her in the court.

She essayed to smile as she saw her father's loving face, but her lips refused to obey the mandate of her will.

She did not look at Lithgow; but he, after one glance at her, divined what had transpired in the sala. A great wave of pity rushed through his soul. He turned upon M. Theuriet with indignation, feeling that the girl had been taken advantage of. But the coffee planter was watching Raquel with eyes that did not perceive the American's fierce glance.

"What is the matter, dearest?" questioned Palgrave anxiously. "Are you ill?"

"Not enough to be frightened about," she said, with the heroic smile that women can sometimes conjure up for the sake of those whom they love. "*J'ai mal à la tête*, as monsieur would say." She purposely half addressed the Frenchman in order to get the worse of the ordeal over at first.

"Possibly you are beginning to feel the effects of the strain you were under during those horrible hours," suggested Lithgow quickly. "It has been surprising how well you have borne up."

"Eet has, *vraiment*," agreed M. Theuriet.

At dinner, Palgrave still regarded his daughter in a manner that threatened to be distressing. Lithgow exerted himself to turn the attention from her as much as possible, and succeeded to such an extent that when she finally allowed her gaze to encounter his there was gratitude to be seen in the depths of her grave eyes.

Never before in his life had Lithgow striven harder to make himself entertaining. His companionship was a boon to these two men so far removed from the bustle of northern life. They enjoyed his tales and laughed over his stories, lamenting that his stay was so soon to be brought to an end. Occasionally, M. Theuriet threw Raquel a searching look, but he failed to meet her eyes. He knew, however, that they no longer wore the expression which had been theirs when she left the sala. That was some comfort. He knew also that she had not told her father. He did not believe that she would. He felt certain that he had handled her with consummate skill.

Once she spoke.

"Do you know what the liantasse is, señor?" she asked Lithgow, without lifting her lids.

"I must confess my ignorance," he returned, aware that she was trying to supplement his efforts. "What a brave heart she has!" he told himself admiringly. "No one dreams what she is suffering, not even he who is the cause of it." He was conscious of a growing aversion for M. Theuriet. What business had a man of his years to crave a child for a wife! He was asking this question in his mind over and over during that dinner. His sympathies were awake.

"What *is* the liantasse, *querida mia?*" queried her father curiously.

"One of the forest's treasures," she exclaimed. "It is to the foresters what the cups of the wild pines are to the bird tribe. It contains that which quenches thirst. Mr. Hamilton is a liantasse to us. We have taken a little section out of his life and have replenished our own minds from his store. When he goes, we shall thirst again."

Lithgow's ready tongue failed him. He was silent.

The two planters applauded Raquel's metaphor.

Lithgow compelled Raquel's straight gaze to meet his. He sent down into the depths of her consciousness a look that stirred her vaguely. He had hoped to convey to her that he understood and desired to·be of service to her. She did not know what she read, but she was aware of a subtle sense of comfort which had been absent before.

In the evening, there was to be the final celebration among the blacks. Raquel's return had afforded them a legitimate cause for rejoicing which they had not been slow to improve.

Already a score of little black imps of the negro quarters were armed with nets attached to poles by means of which they contemplated snaring the fireflies for decorative purposes.

The afternoon had melted away imperceptibly to all save Raquel. To her the long, luxuriously served dinner had seemed interminable. It was with a sigh of relief that she passed into the court again while Lithgow held back the curtain for her. He ventured to follow her.

"Do you know," he began, thinking it best to make conversation, "people believe what is not true about southern countries. Really, tropical lands are the most temperate in all things." Seldom are committed any of the excesses with which the frozen blood of the North warms itself. The southern nature is volatile, not brutish; graceful and happy; never clumsy and morose. I have heard it declared that this climate was conducive to physical perfection, but fatal to the spiritual. Compare the tropical man, however, with—say, the Esquimau. Northern latitudes fail to produce the spiritual yearning that this marvellous clime awakens. There is something in this air that seems a perpetual promise or warning, I have not been able to decide which. These are the words which have sung themselves in my ears ever since I came:

> "'O world! so few the years we live,
>   Would that the life which thou dost give
>   Were life indeed.'"

"Don't you think we should be glad that it is not?" said Raquel quickly.

"But we don't know what the other life may be," he smiled.

"At any rate, it could not be worse than this threatens to be," she flashed, before she was aware how much her words betrayed.

"Is it as bad as that?" he asked gently, stopping and leaning against one of the pillars of the corridor. "Won't you tell me what has brought that look of dread into your eyes? Perhaps I can help you."

She shook her head. There was that in his voice which was almost as tender as she fancied a mother's tone would be. She felt tears creep under her lids.

"I am a stranger; you never will see me again, what difference will it make if you unburden your heart to me?" he questioned, throwing all possible entreaty into his words. "You must tell some one. You will not confide in your father."

She looked at him half defiantly.

"How do you know that I will not?"

"Because you concealed as much as you could at the dinner-table."

"You tried to help me, señor," she returned gratefully, plucking and pulling into fragments a gorgeous purple blossom.

"I saw that you suffered," he replied. "Mere headache does not bring to one's eyes the expression that you so nobly endeavored to banish with a forced smile. This look was not in your face when we were chatting in the sala. Did anything that I said bring it?"

"No, señor," answered she truthfully.

He waited an instant. Then he asked in a still lower tone:

"What did M. Theuriet agree to do if—you would marry him?"

She drew herself up proudly. Her eyes blazed as they had in the sala at the Frenchman.

"He has told you!" she cried in a whisper replete with scorn. She would have been past him and up the staircase if he had not dared to restrain her.

"Let me speak of this to you," he begged. "How can you, a mere girl, judge what is best to do? I fancy that already I see in your face the determination to submit. Your father will not permit it if he reads in your countenance what I do."

"He shall read nothing but what I mean that he shall," she averred.

"But a broken life has a language of its own," he told her. "It can be read like an open book. You will fail to disguise it."

"I can try," was her answer.

Gilbert Palgrave and M. Theuriet came out into the court at that moment, each smoking a cigar. Theuriet glanced at the nearness of his guest and Raquel. His already lined brow took on another line.

"We may as well sit here until the contradanza is given," suggested the sugar planter, selecting a seat near Raquel's hammock. "Come here, *mi cara mia;* take your hammock as usual. It will rest your head. Is it better? Yes? The gentlemen will pardon your freedom. I will sit beside you. I almost am afraid to let you out of my sight."

Raquel complied, glad to shield her face from too direct gaze. She thrust her fingers within those of her father. Through the strips of bright-colored awning she caught glimpses of the darkening heavens.

"Your Cuban skies are a combination of our brilliant ones and the luminous ones of Europe," observed Lithgow, settling himself comfortably in a manner that obscured M. Theuriet's view of Raquel. "The way in which you sweep from sunlight into starlight reminds me of that wonderful moment when one shoots from the glow of the Bay of Naples into the cool, blue restfulness of the cave of Capri."

"How much you have seen, señor," sighed Raquel, all her old longing for a glimpse beyond Cuba rushing over her.

"You hav' ze years een which to see zem also, señorita," reminded M. Theuriet with a meaning which only Gilbert Palgrave missed.

Lithgow lighted a cigar and smoked a few moments before he remarked:

"In the little book of which I spoke, señorita, you will find something like this: 'Not in Nature, but in man is all the worth and beauty he sees. The world is very empty and is indebted to this gilding, exalting soul for all its pride.' Go where you will, if the soul is sick within, there is little beauty even through it throbs around you."

"You believ' een ancient philosophie, *mon ami*," observed M. Theuriet.

"I am inclined to believe anything that my own experience proves true," replied Lithgow. "Has not some one said, 'the universe is represented in an atom, in a moment of time' ?"

"Mr. Hamilton has discovered my fondness for books," Raquel said to her father. "He promises to leave me the one he spoke of."

"I dislike to be reminded that he is going to depart," Palgrave confessed. "We shall miss our *liantasse*, shall we not?"

"I little dreamed that I should be welcomed so hospitably into your home," returned Lithgow gratefully. "You will not be half so sorry as I when the hour comes for me to make my farewells; and I suppose that that time will be soon. Is it not to-morrow that I am to meet my forest lady?"

"She is more likely to be an African Amazon," laughed the sugar planter. "You will go well armed, of course; and I shall do myself the pleasure of supplying you with a mounted force of my men."

"You are too kind," expostulated Lithgow. "I could not think of permitting such a thing. You need the services of every man Jack of them now in order to make up for lost time. I shall get on famously, believe me."

"Eet will be possebl' for *me* to send men wiz you wizout inconveniencing myselv one parteccl'," announced M. Theuriet. "I even am desirous ov accompanying you to see how ze madame accepts your words."

"I shall feel relieved to be thus guarded," admitted Lithgow, "and I trust that you will not witness my defeat. I hope to make the woman confess the deception she played, and acknowledge that Zuñega is the child for whom she heartlessly exchanged her own."

"What was her object in so doing, do you imagine?" inquired the owner of La Sacra Sonrisa.

"She might have thought her action would place her own child where she evidently felt that he belonged; or her maternal sentiments may have been swallowed up by her overwhelming desire to rob of joy both her master and mistress. Did any man yet ever succeed in fathoming a woman's reason?"

"*Holà!* The dances are beginning!" exclaimed Palgrave, rising to his feet. "We must go out and watch them. They will be new to you."

In the open space between the mansion of the master and the plantain grove behind which stretched the negro quarters, all of the unoccupied members of the plantation were gathered to the lugubrious music of a drum. Already a circle had been formed within which two dusky figures of superb development were moving slowly in the prelude to that rhythmic, sensuous utterance of the life that beats with tropical languidness. Lithgow had witnessed the wildness of the Tarantella danced on the white sands of Italy, but never had he beheld anything of the nature of this movement of which only Cuba knows the secret.

The scene reminded Raquel of Faquita's passionate dance in the heart of the forest, and she drew closer to her father. Her soul had been filled with apprehension then; now, it beat with the sluggishness of despair, a despair which he must never discern. He folded his arm around her tenderly.

"Their rejoicing takes an audible form," he whispered softly, "but it is as a wisp of vapor compared to mine, which is silent because of its magnitude."

There was no visible instrument from which the plaintive cadences of the music for the contradanza could come, yet there crept up through the purple night air, heavy with sweetness, the most thrilling melody the American ever had heard.

It chilled him even while its passion was stealing like a seduc-tive poison through every nerve. Fascinatedly, he watched the two shadowy forms, one of which was sparkling with the phosphorescent flash of the insect jewels that, still alive and unharmed, hung by natural hooks in her drapery and hair.

There was something entrancing in the grace and precision of the step of the bronze fauns thus disporting in the marvel-lous moonlight known to the Caribbean and its islands. There was that in the weird music which enthralled. The soft night winds seemed filled with a mystery which the music strangely voiced. It wailed, it swelled into voluptuous tones, it rioted in passionate tumult, it sank to tenderest whispers; and all the time the dancing forms silently wove their spell about their watchers, mesmerizing them into experiencing all of the emotions with which the music throbbed.

Afterward, Lithgow never could explain satisfactorily to himself how it happened. He only remembered that, moved by that mysterious, luxurious melody, he had in some way caught hold of Raquel's fingers; that they quivered within his retaining clasp but were not immediately withdrawn.

No thought of Beatrice's calm face crossed his memory. He was conscious of nothing but the girlish figure beside him whose draperies touched him, whose hand palpitated within his like a frightened bird. All past, all future, vanished in those moments while the music bent them with its magic and swayed them from their moorings with its subtle witchery. And she, did she know the force of this unfamiliar tide that rocked them with its surging? He sought to read her face, but it was turned from him.

The movements of the dancers had become wilder; the melody crept upward with a cry of hungry longing, the sus-pense grew almost too tense.

Suddenly Raquel snatched her fingers away from him.

"Not another moment! I can't endure another moment of it!" he heard her say to her father pleadingly. "Let us return to the court."

M. Theuriet turned backward with them.

"Eet ees not necessaire for you to come," he said to the American. "Remain eef eet please you. We hav' seen eet before. To you, eet ees new."

And Lithgow remained out in the moonlight.

He no longer watched the dancers. He strolled among the orange trees. He threw himself down on the ground and stared up through the foliage at the wide, indigo heavens.

"I had no more right to touch her hand than I would have had to kiss her lips," he swore at himself savagely. "It was sacrilege. She is a child."

He lifted his hand until the bright moonlight fell full upon it. A tender look went over his face. He brought the hand to his lips. A faint fragrance seemed to cling to his fingers. He sighed. The stir of the music was still in his blood. He could hear it rising and falling in that circle beyond the trees. He knew that it was responsible for his lapse from fealty; but the lapse had been so full of sweetness! An unreasonable exultant joy possessed him. He endeavored to crush it out of recognition.

"She is the personification of the mystical being who figured in my dreams under the old apple trees," he told himself with a smile that was sad. "She will be one of those women who move men unwittingly. She may go through life ignorant of her fatal power. I don't know but that I hope she will. Yet, —the thought of her as the wife of Theuriet is——" He sprang to his feet. He turned toward the white walls of the house that held her. "——I must not let it be anything to *me!*" he said resolutely.

He found the two planters lounging in the deep easy-chairs in the court.

"Ah, wearied at last, eh!" saluted Palgrave. "Raquel has begged to be excused. I believe that she has retired. Her head was aching. She requested me to give you her *buenas noches.*"

"It will be some time before your escort can tear itself away from the fascinations of the celebration, M. Theuriet," the planter continued. "There have been extensive preparations going on all day. No doubt a feast is in store. Would it not be better for you to remain the night."

The Frenchman would not be persuaded.

"You forget that Mr. Hamilton starts for ze forest een ze early hours," he reminded. "I will wait unteel midnight has come. Ze men must be ready to accompany us to La Buena Esperanza by zat time. Ze numbair ov zem will remov' all danger ov a posseebl' attack from ze dread Alarcon. I am verra cautious since ze warning ov ze *bizarre* creature called 'Faquita.'"

" If only we had suspected the identity of that daring fellow, we should have done the Spanish government a good service and enriched our coffers," sighed the sugar planter.

" Ah, wiz him een ze safetee of ze Moro walls I certainlee should feel more comforta-a-bl'," agreed M. Theuriet.

Listening to their conversation but taking small part in it, Lithgow sat till midnight in the odorous hush of the quadrangle. The moonlight illumined the square and dimmed the brightness of the ends of their cigars. The waters splashed lazily in the fountain; the thin curtains in the upper doorways fluttered with the cool, night winds; the palm shook its crest with a shuddering breath as if it scented danger in the air.

Without, the plaintive melody gradually died away. The dancers had been succeeded by other dancers who also had given way in their turn, until, finally, the entire circle had taken part in the entertainment and were ready to seek spots of repose.

M. Theuriet's blacks presented themselves for service, rather worn but still jubilant.

The drive to La Buena Esperanza was unusually silent.

M. Theuriet dozed a portion of the distance despite the noise made by his accompanying guard galloping alongside. Occasionally he aroused himself sufficiently to address his companion in a polite attempt to disprove any possible accusation of somnolency.

Lithgow lent himself to the sinuous motion of the volante, but no sleep came. He was more keenly awake than he ever had been in his life.

' This moonlight would have driven Shelley mad!" he commented reflectively. " Perhaps there is some excuse for me!"

CHAPTER XII.

The cavalcade which was to show the American the route to the shrine chosen by Faquita started from the coffee plantation before the fragrance-steeped darkness had been lifted from the crowns of the hills. The melligenous dew dropped

noiselessly from the leaves to the earth.   Here and there a be-
lated cocullo flashed with the indecision of firefly nature.

Though Faquita had said that the meeting would be at
night, Lithgow was anxious to reach the rendezvous early
enough in the afternoon to be certain of his plans.

The dissipation of the evening previous had left the blacks
very quite.   So silent was the company that the hook-billed
judios scarcely were disturbed by this matutinal procession,
and only fluttered occasionally to a lower bough.

The foliage by the highway assumed fastastic and sometimes threatening shapes, but nothing stole out upon them
save the narcotic perfumes of a southern night.

" How the artistic soul of Beatrice would revel in the novelty
of these scenes, as widely dissimilar from prosaic New York
as would be the life of far-away India!" he exclaimed to himself as he observed the muscular forms of the blacks becoming
gradually more distinct with the approach of day. There was
not the long, lingering grayness of the north ere the first, faint
tinge of color appeared. With a suddenness that was bewilder-
ing, they found themselves in the midst of a marvelous glory
which seemed to have been created solely for them. The
mists still hung about them, reluctant to lift their white wings
and leave the vegetation to be again scorched by the heat of
the sun-god's passion. Every leaf dripped and crystal beads
clung to the manes of the horses. The hills were transfigured.

Lithgow had witnessed sunrise from the Mongibello of the
Sicilians. He had stood awed while the huge monolith cast
its purpling shadow far across the world; but he had not experienced the emotions which swayed him now in a valley
shut in by mountains of Cuba.

" It is a dream!" he said softly. " If I could choose the hour
of my death, I would wish it might be when the sun rises over
Cuba!"

" Ah, you are beginning to feel ze lov' zat all ov Cuba's inhabitants grow to experience for ze beautiful island," remarked M. Theuriet, suppressing a yawn. " Despite ze extor-
tions ov ze Spanish and ze drawbacks ov a life here, zose who
once know Cuba hav' for eet ze most maddening devotion."

They talked on desultorily while their horses steadily pursued the easy gait known as the Cuban " march." Lithgow

thought that possibly the Frenchman would mention the result of the conversation he had had with Raquel in the sala,
but M. Theuriet now was silent on that subject, though pre-
viously he had shown no hesitancy in discussing his hopes
with his whilom guest.

" It is none of my business," the American told himself with
prudent recollection.   " If I had not chanced this way the
thing would have happened, and I been none the wiser or
sadder.   Certainly I am not called upon to interfere.   It is
past the days of knight errantry.   What possible good would
it do if I should venture to overstep the bounds of etiquette
and expostulate with the old rascal?   Already I have shown
him quite pointedly that his views are not in conformance
with mine.   He means to secure—Raquel—" he hesitated
over the name.   The fever of the music and the moonlight
was still in his veins.   " Perhaps the union will be no worse
than those which are consummated yearly between impecu-
nious noblemen and wealthy American beauties, yet the heir-
esses are willing to assume the marriage bond, while she—the
child shrinks from it.   She will sacrifice herself wantonly for
the sake of her father!   Dare I warn him?   What is permissible in such a case?   I am a stranger, but would he not condone
my interference?"

These thoughts came and went through his mind repeatedly
in various disguises while he conversed with his host and the
morning hours crept by.   The penetrating sunlight revealed
flashes of brilliant red and green plumage among the branches
that spread above their path.   Discordant shrieks of fright
and displeasure convinced them that the feathered tribe resented this invasion of their realm.

They passed one dilapidated shrine where the entire group
of horsemen made obeisance to the grotesque little image
meant to represent the beautiful Mother of the Immaculate.
Lithgow removed his sombrero as the others did, but he
looked instead up at the towering mass of vegetation toward
which they were wending their way.

" Obediently they worship the symbol," he murmured, " but
can they entertain no conception of the magnificent Force
which builds and builds tirelessly while the Ages creep away?
This glorious burst of ever-renewing green life voices a ser-
mon that tongue of man never uttered and never can!"

"Zees ees not ze shrine, but we might eat our *almuerzo* here by eets side," suggested M. Theuriet, ordering his men to dismount and spread out the slight breakfast which had been brought by them.

The hunger of the American made him appreciative of his host's thoughtfulness. He threw himself down by the shrine and sought to make himself more companionable than he had been. For the hospitality which the coffee planter had accorded him, he knew that he had been contemplating making a poor return by attempting to thwart the plans that M. Theuriet had entertained for so long. He felt guilty one moment and justified the next.

"The sooner that I secure the woman Annizae and leave the island, the better it will be for all concerned," he decided as he drank a bottle of Catalonian wine with the Frenchman, who, ignorant of the designs which he could not avoid nursing, wished him all possible success. "If Beatrice possessed the power of projecting her astral self through space and could read my present dilemma, she would declare that she had won her wager. But that I have wavered for one instant in my allegiance to her she never shall know. She could never understand the power of Cuban moonlight, the contradanza music—and Raquel! The child does not understand her own power, that is what makes it so irresistible. Heighho! This is a queer world!" With which reflection he endeavored to banish from his consciousness the realization that this girl of an isolated sugar plantation had moved him as never woman had done before. But when they were again mounted and skirting the edge of the forest, he learned the troubling truth that the memory of those fatal moments would not be consigned to oblivion. Back into his thoughts it crept with insidious sweetness, and he dwelt upon it with that weakness which cries:

"It is only for this moment, this one moment out of life. I will feed upon it while it lasts. None shall know of the poison which it leaves in my blood. None shall dream of the barrenness it seems to cast over all the years in which it must be forgotten."

He remembered those lines of Jean Jaques Weiss: "The human mind is twice limited. It may love several times and it may fully enjoy love but once."

"I will enjoy it while I may," he resolved, "but Raquel shall be none the wiser. Beatrice will be conscious of no loss. I alone will be the one to suffer."

Wild pigeons flew among the foliage. M. Theuriet called his attention to their lovely tinged necks and breasts. The red throat of the bright green pedorreva attracted notice to its fly-catching abilities by its sharp click. To the south rose the mountain which Faquita had designated. Veiled in the softest of greens, one never would have imagined how precipitous the range was to which it belonged. By the side of the highway foamed an angry little stream that finally would spread into a river and gnaw its way through the hills to the sea.

The sun had grown hot. The road was dusty.

"We shall hav' long to wait, but ze rest will be refreshing," said M. Theuriet. "Eet will not tak' us more zan two hours to reach ze spot now."

"I am consumed with regret that I permitted you to undertake this tedious trip, Monsieur Theuriet," declared Lithgow. "Nothing but your unexcelled courtesy is responsible for this self-abnegation, I am sure."

"Ah, pardon, you mistak'," protested M. Theuriet. "I am anxious to perceiv' how you conquer ze madame. I am interested in ze fortunes ov ze magnifique caballero who so proudly refused to be rewarded. His story, eef eet be true, ees most wonderful. I should be stupced indeed did I not mak' your efforts as easy as posseebl'."

The afternoon whiled itself away with languorous content. With their horses concealed from view, the men arranged themselves comfortably in the ambush that the underbrush and vines afforded. Here they were comparatively safe from attack in that they would have the advantage in case that Faquita played them false by allowing Alarcon to learn of the rendezvous.

It was the first time that the American had stepped within the brooding gloom of a Cuban forest. Though just on the edge of its mysteries, he was held speechless by what he beheld.

He waved his hand upward to where he caught glimpses of brilliant florescence high amid the canopy of emerald, through which fell dim rays of sunlight that possessed the shadowy refulgence known to groined cathedrals.

"Perhaps it cost that boy nothing to go out from the slumberous beauty of this strange world, peopled with stalwart sentinels of the years," he commented to M. Theuriet, "but I count it an act of heroism. He did not know that he, was walking into a fortune. He supposed that all that remained for him was voluntary exile."

In the mean time Faquita and Annizae were threading the labyrinthine forest paths with the speed which familiarity gave. Alarcon and his men were absent from the camp. They had been gone for three days. And those days had been full of trouble to the woman who followed the steps of Faquita. Her taciturn visage was heavy with anxiety, which she endeavored to conceal beneath an affectation of her usual indifference.

Faquita moved with light tread. Most of the time her face wore a smile that was excessively irritating to the older woman, who shot angry glances at her as an occasional snatch of song burst from her lips.

"*Cuidado!*" she warned once. "How knowest thou that Alarcon will not hear and follow? Thou art aware that he is a chameleon; can he not even change himself into a tree?"

Faquita shrugged her shoulders.

"Gonzalo is far from here," she declared.

"*Quien sabe?*" retorted Annizae. "Thou wouldst like nothing better than that he should discover that I go in search of Zuñega."

"Ungrateful! Why then should I accompany you?" demanded Faquita. "Gonzalo is on the wrong track. Did I not tell him that Zuñega had gone south?"

"Ah, but he had not, you say. Who knows? Alarcon may have found him here in these caves. What may not happen in three days? Even now Zuñega may be hanging between two trees. When Gonzalo Alarcon's face wears the look it does, it speaks of ill to him he hates."

Faquita said nothing. She had been too late to witness Alarcon's anger when he discovered Zuñega's treachery. She had ridden into camp with the two horses when the wildness of his rage was past; but there had been that in his eyes which warned her it were not wise to vaunt her triumph. On the spur of the moment she had resorted to an expedient which seemed preferable to sudden death. She had pretended that, discovering the absence of Zuñega and his charge, she had taken a second horse and had followed them in the hope of persuading Zuñega to return. This he had refused to do; and she had gone on and on with the expectation of discovering his plans. He had outwitted her, however. He had proceeded south over the mountains. Alarcon could go himself and see if he could do better than she had. All this she said with the appearance of truth in her face; and Alarcon, relinquishing the madness which had made him swear to shoot her through the heart when he succeeded in tracking her and her companions, credited her words and started over the range in pursuit. He knew every hiding-place in the range. Zuñega could not escape. The dog should meet the death of a traitor, and the señorita should be his again. So he swore as he rode. And Annizae, knowing what the anger of Gonzalo Alarcon meant, trembled for the safety of Zuñega.

The falsehood had not lain heavily on Faquita's conscience. She knew that Zuñega was far toward safety before Alarcon started in the opposite direction; but she dared not tell Annizae. While she regretted the loss of her triumph she reasoned that it was better to be alive and able to win future conquest than it would be to be dead and powerless to enjoy the victory she had.

Her apparent heartlessness made Annizae raging. Nothing but Annizae's fear for Zuñega, and her desire to see him and urge him to fly far from the mountains, allowed her to endure the presence of the girl. For some reason which she could not explain to herself, she doubted the tale which Faquita had related. It looked honest enough; Zuñega was gone; Faquita had returned. In spite of effort she failed to fathom the reason of Zuñega's action. She was wrathful at him even while her mind was filled with fear for his safety. What had there been about that little muchacha to make him faithless to his chief? She had bitter words ready for him when Faquita should at last lead her to the spot where he was in hiding. It was a long journey; long even for her who was accustomed to the wearisome struggles with forest tangles.

It was past ten when they emerged from the blackness of the trees and approached the shrine. Faquita's heart sank within her. There was not a sign of life. She bent before the Virgin and said a prayer. But Annizae stood upright, looking into the night with piercing vision. The glorious moonlight flooded the scene. Suddenly she caught Faquita's arm and half dragged her to her feet.

"One comes," she whispered. "Hast thou no signal?"

"No," answered Faquita. "I will go and see if it be Zuñega."

Annizae remained motionless. Her lips were tightly pressed. She heard the crackling of bushes. She could not yet distinguish the cause. Then Faquita's voice said cautiously:

"Advance, señor! It is Annizae."

Annizae shrunk back against the shrine. She gave a low cry of anger.

"Faquita betrays me! It is not Zuñega!" she cried fiercely.

She could have darted into the shadow of the woods and escaped, but her desire to be certain held her. Lithgow approached. She trembled, though she knew by his costume that he was not one of the *guardia civile;* consequently what should there be to fear?

"It is one who brings news of Zuñega," Faquita told her breathlessly. "He is safe."

Annizae was full of suspicion.

"*Dónde?*" she interrogated cautiously.

"In Havana," replied Lithgow. "He is going to the United States."

She was silent through astonishment for a moment, then she demanded:

"How know you, señor?"

He flashed into the moonlight the ring which he wore. Wondering what would be the result, he answered:

"This ring tells me, *Brown Annizae.* Shall I mention what else it reveals?"

Her eyes travelled from his face to the ring and back again. Her limbs seemed to give way beneath her. Her voice was hoarse when she accused:

"He has been killed! These are lies that you speak!"

"Listen, *Brown Annizae,*" advised Lithgow impressively. "You shall hear what this ring makes known." He was positive that she crouched backward with the repetition of her name as it had been spoken in the years past. He wished that it were daylight that he might better study her face. He changed his position so that the moonlight fell full upon her. "Zuñega goes to the States and he goes to England. He crosses the deep waters that his father did. He must claim the fortune which his father went to claim at the time when you stole Zuñega from the ship and put your own child in his place."

He did not have to watch closely the effect of his announcement. Annizae was huddled together, her face in her hands. To her superstitious mind this man was possessed of the Evil One or was that personage himself. How could he know so much if he were not? No one but herself knew this which he was uttering. No priest had won it from her breast. She had whispered it before no cross. She shook with a fright in which was mingled her old-time hatred. If he knew so much he must know more, she argued to herself vaguely. She lifted her great eyes with a question burning in them.

"*She?* Where is she? Does the ring tell that too, señor?" she demanded, never for a moment dreaming of denying it all. What was the use of declaring it false when he knew? He possessed the "evil eye," or he could not look that far back in the years. No doubt his glance would poison her; she would die as the victim of the *fer-de-lance* dies, the rotten flesh dropping from her bones! But—she would ask one question. Out of the silence of the years which had elapsed she would wring one satisfaction. She would know the fruits of her revenge.

"She is dead!" answered Lithgow solemnly.

"*Gracias á Dios!*" she shrieked ecstatically. "*La Madre de Jesu* has heard my prayers. I have burned candles on every shrine, praying that death would take her from him. But it has been so long—I grew tired; sometimes I almost forgot. Now, I remember again! Where is *he?* Are you of his blood?" She leaned nearer him. The sudden savagery in her face made the American experience a chill in spite of himself. "Is that how you can tell things which even the priests themselves cannot bring to light, or, are you *el diablo?*"

"I am neither," returned Lithgow. "I have come to tell Zuñega that you are not his mother; that you have robbed him of all his rights. I have come to take both of you to England, where you are to make reparation for the wrong you have done him."

"I go never, señor," she said defiantly.

"Those whose hearts you broke are dead," Lithgow told her solemnly. "You need have no fear. No punishment awaits you."

"Is *he* dead?" she repeated. She leaned heavily against the shrine.

"He is dead. Zuñega goes to take his place as Lord Harberton."

She remained silent.

Faquita had stood spellbound. She had expected anything but this strange, submissive manner, so unlike Annizae.

"There was another child," reminded Lithgow. "Have you forgotten?"

An unexpected fury flamed into life. Her entire manner altered. There in the moonlight, in her unkempt attire, with her hair loose and wild, she looked like a Medusa.

"What did she do with him?" she cried wildly. "She took my place; it was right that my child should take the position of hers. Was it not all that I could do? Sorry? *Nunca! Nunca!* I know that it cost her tears; I meant that it should. It was her time to weep, as I had done. Did she kill him? That would not give her back her own. No! I thought of all that. I put her own beyond her reach. She can never have him. She is dead? It is just!"

"She educated him," replied Lithgow, excited with this certain proof of Zuñega's identity. "You made a bandit out of her child. She tried to make a gentleman out of yours."

He watched every change of her dark features. He read that to win her to accompany him, he must play upon the delights of the triumph which the years had brought her.

"No power now can keep you from walking through the rooms where she was known as mistress," he suggested. "The time was when *he* would not permit you to be taken to his country; now, there is nothing to prevent your going as she went. Once in England you can learn for yourself if my words be true. You will taste the sweetness of the vengeance you wrought. You no longer will be one who hides from pursuit. You believe that Heaven has placed your triumph in your hands—no? Will you let it slip through your fingers? Will you not see for yourself what was done with the son you relinquished? I have come far to tell you this.

but had it not been for Zuñega's nobleness in restoring the señorita it would have remained untold. You never would have known the satisfaction which now shines in your eyes. You would have lived and died an outlaw. As it is, the ease and luxury which were hers will be yours."

She shook her head. But the long-smothered instincts of femininity had received an electric touch. They sprung into energetic life with a suddenness that surprised her. "The things that were hers will be yours." That was a temptation which stirred her to her very depths. All the wild hunger and ambition that had been her misery in the days gone by now swept over her resistlessly with the strength of pent-up force. The poison of the malice which had burned in her blood ate into her heart once more. Memory was alive again. The narcotic influence of the forest had lulled it into a repose which had been deceptive. The fury of the passion which had caused her to forfeit her own flesh and blood in order to rob her rival of happiness stormed within her in all its old mastery after this long stretch of years. Go? Was there a spot on earth to which she would not go if she might drain this triumph of all its joy?

She did not know what time sped by while she relived the past and dared to peer with victorious gaze on into the wonderful future which her uneducated fancy opened before her. With drawn brows, a cruel smile, and demoniacal-looking hair, she half knelt in front of the shrine, but there was no supplication in her breast that the unholy pleasure which was affording her unbounded satisfaction might be removed from her for the good of her soul. Neither was there thought of possible good to Zuñega in her mind. Everything was consumed in the selfish fire of jealousy and hatred, on which fresh faggots had been piled.

M. Theurict had crept carefully from his place of concealment and stood behind her.

She appeared oblivious to them all.

Lithgow observed her anxiously. He realized that she was undergoing a struggle, but of its fierceness he had no conception. He had resolved that if she refused to go peaceably he would have her taken by force. He knew that the men were in readiness. He glanced up at the heavens. The cross was not visible, but he felt the hour was late.

"Midnight is near. We must be gone. Go you with us, Annizac?"

She lifted herself as from a dream. She arose to her full height. There was something magnificent about the creature. Her life in the midst of cultured people had given her a grace of bearing and a refinement which had not been wholly lost in the nomadic existence she since had led. The American was conscious of a wave of surprised admiration. That she had possessed in her youth the matchless beauty which a mixture of blood sometimes bestows was not to be doubted.

"If your words be true, señor," she said with a decisive tone he had not expected.

"How can I prove their truth save by this ring?" he questioned, going close to her and holding his hand so that she might inspect the ornament as well as was possible by moonlight. "You recognize it?"

"It is Zuñega's, señor," she declared.

"No; Zuñega wears his still. This is what was sent to convince you of what I have said. When we reach Havana you will see that Zuñega's is where he placed it when you gave it to him."

"How know I that I will not be imprisoned, señor?" She looked out at him sharply.

"You do not know unless you can believe my word," he admitted. "I promise you that no harm shall be yours. When Zuñega is proven to be the rightful heir to Harberton Towers, you may return to these forests if you will. You will have gold of your own. You may do what you please."

Though no idea had been suggested by the lawyer as to what disposition would be made of Annizac, he thought he was safe in making the assertion. Those last words of his were happy ones. They appeared to decide her. She threw out her hands and permitted them to drop at her sides with an air of capitulation.

"I go, señor," she agreed.

Lithgow gave a quick signal, and immediately they were surrounded by M. Theuriet's men.

Annizac did not suppress a start of surprise at their appearance. She understood now that had she not gone willingly, she would have been taken. Fear seized her, but she reflected that if she did not see the ring on Zuñega's finger in Havana she would know that deceit was in the stranger's mouth and she then could effect her escape. She comforted herself with the thought that her wits were liable to be as sharp as those of an *inglés*, and she resolved to trust to luck.

The horses were brought forth and Annizae mounted with the ease of accustomedness.

Faquita leaned against the shrine. A depression was creeping over her. She meant to retrace her steps through the forest with haste. It would not do for her to be absent from the camp if Alarcon should return. She wished to seem to have had no part in this disappearance of Annizae.

Lithgow held out his hand to her in farewell.

"Why not go with us?" he said gently. "This forest life is not for such as you. You have known other things."

"And if I have, what then, señor?" she queried in the same tone.

"Does your heart never turn back toward them?"

"My heart is here, señor," she said with a sort of sad joy. "I have followed it, that is all."

He looked up to where Annizae sat motionless, waiting.

"It is to Faquita that you owe your triumph, *Brown Annizae*," he said. "But for her Zuñega never would have brought the señorita to the walls of La Sacra Sonrisa."

Annizae expressed no gratitude. She only looked down at Faquita with a knowing smile and said:

"That was better than the manchineel apple, Faquita—no?"

Faquita's eyes flashed. She dimly understood Annizae's accusation, though it was unfounded.

"The manchineel apple would have been preferable to the fate that thou wert willing the señorita should have," she cried bitterly.

Annizae's broad shoulders shrugged with irresponsibility.

"Thou wast thinking of thyself as ever, Faquita," she returned. "I know well that thou wouldst have brought no good to me if thou hadst known what thou wert doing."

"Who knows that it is good that will come?" queried Faquita.

"Hush!" begged Lithgow. "The service you have done has been too great to spoil in this manner. If Annizae has no thankfulness, I have. But for you my success in restoring Zuñega to his rights would be out of the question. There are other ways than words by which to show appreciation. Is there no manner in which I can communicate with you to tell you if Zuñega comes into his own?"

Faquita hesitated.

"You have kindness, señor," she said finally. "Perhaps a word to Benito Sanchez at San Juan might reach me."

"The word shall be there," he promised. "*Adios!*"

"*Vaya V. con Dios, señor,*" she said as he took his seat in the saddle.

The line of horsemen filed away.

Annizae glanced back over her shoulder. Faquita still leaned against the shrine. Annizae pulled up her horse. She scarcely could believe that this woman riding away with strangers was herself. She felt an almost irresistible inclination to wheel, ride back for Faquita, and then fly into the retreats of the forest away from this temptation. But the hand of the American was on her horse's bridle. On his features was a smile of comprehension.

"The forest may know you again, Annizae," he said, "but not now."

CHAPTER XIII.

Annizae was established at the coffee plantation and, though she was ignorant of the fact, was well guarded. This *entrée* once again into a home was not without its charm to the woman, though she was reminded of earlier days in a manner that was distressing. She was moody and ill content, and Lithgow perceived that he must lose no time in getting to Havana.

But the elation which he would have expected to experience in connection with his success was wholly lacking. He was conscious of an absolute pain with the thought that he could count the hours that remained for him of this *dolce-far-niente* life.

He had one more day only. He shook his head at his own reflection that morning as he shaved himself.

"I suspect that it is a lucky thing that you've got to go, my boy," he remarked. "It would be scarcely permissible to snatch the girl from her elderly suitor and take her to America to present to Beatrice; yet I believe that is the suggestion which has come to you in the disguise of a noble action."

He rode over to La Sacra Sonrisa with M. Theuriet in the afternoon. They were to dine with the sugar planter and return home early, as the start was to be made before day-break.

That subtle sadness of the south was in the air. It weighed upon his heart. With a pang of genuine reproach Lithgow realized that in leaving Beatrice behind him unwed, he had not suffered the heaviness of soul which encompassed him now.

"It is because I know what lies in store for Raquel," he told himself excusingly. "None could fail to be moved by the contemplation of such a sacrifice."

He was hoping for an opportunity to have a word alone with her, but there appeared to be little prospect. He had not seen her since the night of the contradanza. Covertly he watched to see if any remembrance of it lay in her manner. When he failed to detect any he caught himself wondering if he had dreamed that thrilling clasp of the hand.

"She is not the child that I thought," he commented silently. "She has the power of concealment." And, manlike, he became more anxious to peer beneath the surface which Raquel had succeeded in making appear so unruffled.

Both she and her father were exceedingly interested in hearing the full account of the meeting with Annizae. When Lithgow declared that in his own mind he was convinced that Zuñega was the long-sought heir to Harberton Towers, Raquel voiced the most exuberant gladness and inspired the others with her enthusiasm.

"Will he have much money, señor?" she queried.

"Money to burn, I fancy," he replied, "though I am not certain as to the extent of the estate."

"Why, Raquel?" asked her father. "What is it to you?"

"Nothing, of course," she returned. "I simply felt some wonderment as to what use he would make of it. He never has had money; it will seem strange to him."

Her father laughed.

"You speak as with the familiarity of long acquaintance," he told her teasingly.

"Sometimes with the acquaintance of a day friendships are

formed more strong and enduring than those which have been years in growth," Lithgow observed, speaking to Palgrave but looking at Raquel.

He was rewarded by a glance from her, one that led him to add:

"I hope ours will prove such."

"Thank you," smiled the Englishman. "Why should it not? You are our liantasse, remember! I trust that you will come down to see our friend Theuriet here every season."

"I am afraid that luck like this will not fall my way again," Lithgow replied regretfully. "In all probability I shall not see Cuba's shores for many years." He was watching Raquel's face.. He saw it change. A warm glow crept through his heart. Faithful or unfaithful, the man does not live who does not feel gratified to learn that his comings or goings are no longer a matter of utter indifference to a beautiful woman.

"Who knows what may have befallen us before then?" mused the sugar planter. "These walls may encircle other faces than ours by that time, Raquel! La Sacra Sonrisa may have another master."

"It never shall have other master than you, *papa mio*," Raquel said, with a significance that he did not perceive.

"That is woman's hopefulness," smiled her father, reaching out his hand to touch her dark, insubordinate hair with tender fingers. "After all, I shall care little what fortune comes so long as I have you. My late hours of torture have taught me that, *querida mia*."

"And they taught me the identical lesson," she replied, turning her face upward with a resolve written upon it that it turned Lithgow's heart cold to see. "Nothing is of any value to me except you and your happiness."

"Ah, saw you ever such devotion?" cried the man to his friends. And they observed that tears were in his eyes. "We owe that scoundrel, Alarcon, something after all. He revealed to each the worth of the other, eh? I will be worthy of your affection, sweetheart; the plantation shall be held if wits and energy can do it. If not, we will shoulder our traps and move on. 'While there is life, there is hope'!"

"But it would kill you to relinquish this place," sighed Raquel, with her eyes on his face.

"Almost, not quite," he admitted. "I love it for many reasons. It was here that I brought your mother. The few years that were ours together were spent here, and they were the happiest of my life. I pray that as happy ones will come to you."

Raquel's eyelids quivered and fell. A great wave of blood swept up over her face, then ebbed, leaving her a deathly white. She leaned back in the deep rocking-chair. Only Lithgow noticed that her fingers were clasped convulsively in her lap.

"I shall be happy," she said slowly and distinctly, but the voice did not sound like her own. All of the caressing music and soft cadences seemed to have died out of its tones. "I am going to marry monsieur, *papa mio*. You and I never will be separated."

Lithgow could not have moved if his life had depended upon it. He felt as if every portion of his physical mechanism gave way with a sickening sensation that made his eyes blur and his brain reel. He saw the master of La Sacra Sonrisa lean toward his daughter with unmitigated astonishment on his features.

"Marry—M. Theuriet?" he repeated dazedly. "Has he dared to—to ask—you?" He now was on his feet and advancing threateningly toward his neighbor of years. Rage, wounded honor, all the passion of a father's love was in his manner. M. Theuriet shrank perceptibly before him, though he had risen also and stood with his arms folded.

"You have betrayed the fact of that despicable contract," accused Gilbert Palgrave in the voice that only an aroused Englishman can assume. "I relied on your honor as a man never to reveal it. Nothing but the horrible circumstances forced me into it, and you know it."

"Pardon, *mon ami*, ze contract has not been mentioned," declared the Frenchman. "I believ' zat ze señorita knows not of eets excestence. I hav' asked her to be my wife. What more or what less can a man do when he loves a woman? Eef she consents not, eet ees my loss. Eef you pairmit her to accept me, my love, and my fortune, neither you nor she ever shall regret eet, as *le bon Dieu* loves us all!"

Gilbert Palgrave paused irresolutely. He looked from M. Theuriet back at Raquel. He could not doubt the Frenchman's words, yet he felt that he also must hear from Raquel's lips that no mention of the unfortunate contract had been made to urge her into this inexplicable acceptance of the aged neighbor's suit.

"What has led you to make this decision, Raquel?" he demanded.

There was a little fright in her eyes as she looked up for the first time. She glanced appealingly at M. Theuriet. Would he not help her to keep from divulging the real reason?

She knew that to reveal it would be to forfeit this opportunity of placing her father on his feet financially; for if he divined that she was making a sacrifice he would lose both estate and life before he would allow it.

"I hav' offaired her ze delights ov Havanese society, ze fascinations ov travel, ze gratification ov all her desires," interposed the Frenchman quietly. "Pairhaps zose hav' influenced her. She loves me not now, I am aware ov zat. But I hop' to mak' her feel affection for me, *mon ami*, wiz your pairmission."

"Is it true, Raquel?" questioned Palgrave anxiously. "Do these promised things make you content to marry this man who is old enough to be your father?"

Raquel dared not lift her lids. She was afraid that he would read the truth. She went toward him swiftly and hid her face against his breast.

"I wish to marry monsieur," she said faintly, "if you have no objections."

Palgrave lifted her face and looked into it searchingly, but the horror which the closed lids shielded did not reach his troubled heart.

"I should have mountainous objections if I thought that my fears were true," he answered, "but if you really desire to become the wife of our life-time friend, it is not for me to interfere. I don't know as a better man could be found anywhere, or one who would make a kinder husband. He cannot take it amiss if I confess that I had desired a younger mate for you, one more in keeping with your own youthfulness. You have seen nothing of the world yet, *cara mia*; it might be better to wait."

"You speak of a contract," she reminded. "What was it?"

Gilbert Palgrave hesitated. He was much averse to telling

10

her its conditions, but he reasoned quickly that it might be wiser for him to explain the matter himself than to permit M. Theuriet some time to do so.

"Simply this, dearest," he began with a long breath, "in my trouble, M. Theuriet suggested a way out of the dilemma. He offered to furnish the amount of the ransom—you understand that I was utterly unable to furnish even a centavo myself—on the condition that I gave my consent that you should become his wife. This I would not do; but finally I was forced, when Alarcon came demanding the gold, to send for our friend and tell him that I agreed on the condition that you should be allowed to choose. I felt certain that you would refuse to comply with his request, and, in that case I would be only glad to forfeit everything and start out fresh in life on some other basis than that of sugar production. We could go away somewhere and live in a meagre way. All I was anxious about was you; you are so—so dissatisfied, I feared you might weary of poverty." He felt his daughter cling tighter to him and he went on: "Then the opportunity to secure you by even that means failed. We were frantic. Possibly you have not been told, but Gonzalo Alarcon refused the ransom because he said that he would not relinquish you to the arms of a rival like M. Theuriet. I hope you comprehend, Raquel, that it was only the terrible position in which I was placed that made me contemplate such a contract with quietude. As it was, I sought to make it one that would be binding only to me; you were to be free to follow the dictates of your heart. Finally, through the brave action of that one whom you call Zuñega, you were returned without any ransom, so that relieves both of us from its terms. Were you unaware of all this?"

"Yes, papa," she nodded, her resolution only the more firmly fixed in her mind. Ignorant of life save as she knew it from books, she really had small comprehension of all that this decision actually meant to her future. Moved by a noble spirit of filial love, she imagined that the strong uplifting that she experienced at this moment of self-renunciation would enable her to bear herself through all the suceeding days.

"Then nothing influenced you in this decision which you have given M. Theuriet?" he questioned.

Raquel not once had permitted her glance to wander in the

·American's direction. Now, however, it was almost as if his powerful, keen gaze had compelled hers. Beneath her languorous lids her eyes wavered. She read in his that he had not forgotten the night when their hands had met as their eyes met now. And she knew that he now discovered that she also remembered. Nothing had influenced her? She was ashamed to feel how the careless words of this northerner uttered a few moments previous had made her present decision possible and in her mind half necessary. He was going away. Neither she nor Cuba might see him again. What more was left to life save this sacrifice, which would benefit her father more than any other thing on earth—except Cuba's freedom—could? And the American should know that he was nothing to her. This declaration of her acceptance of M. Theuriet would prove to him that the startling revelation which had borne itself in upon her with such force, that rare moment in the moonlight when the subtle frenzy of the music pulsed through her veins, had been unwelcome.

She managed to tear her eyes away from the magnetic ones of Lithgow before she answered her father gently, in a way with which he was forced to feign content:

"Nothing has influenced me—except love—for you," and the fact that the last two words were inaudible to any but her own soul made her reply something surprising to M. Theuriet as well as to the father.

The accepted suitor moved toward her in a reverential manner that did him credit. He bowed his gray head over Raquel's cold fingers with a murmur of joy to which she gave no heed. She was aware only of the American's set mouth and stern eyes, and she was woman enough to take a certain pride in her sad triumph.

"Señor, you do not congratulate me," observed M. Theuriet, smiling, rejoicing because of the unexpected tact with which Raquel had engineered the announcement. Despite his anxiety to secure Raquel, he had experienced some trepidation concerning the manner with which Gilbert Palgrave would receive the news. The girl's care to keep the true reason for her decision from her father did not offend the Frenchman. It simply made him commend himself for his astuteness in reading her character aright.

Lithgow arose to his feet and bowed gravely. Fiercely he

was condemning the conventionalities of life. In the knightly days it would have been quite permissible to seize this maiden and ride away with her to safety and to love; but in this end of the century nothing remained but to shake her aged lover by the hand and wish him the good that the gods provide.

"I have the warmest desires for the happiness of both of you," he contrived to say; "the celebration of your betrothal brings my visit to a more joyful close than I had anticipated. Señorita Raquel honors me by announcing it in my presence."

He made his exit into the court gracefully, as if he deemed it the most natural thing that they should be left alone. There he stood very still. He inwardly felt like uprooting every growing thing in the place, but he remained as calm as one must in this age of self-repression. Gilbert Palgrave came out to him there, after having taken Raquel in his arms to wish her all of the joy that possibly can come to mortal. The sugar planter offered him a cigar and lighted himself one. Lithgow debated within himself whether silence was the honorable course to pursue.

"I wonder if a man ever learns to understand women," Palgrave said half to himself. "How that child can marry Theuriet, though I must confess that I like him well enough myself, is beyond my comprehension!"

Before Lithgow could answer, Raquel's voice was at his elbow. She seemed to be afraid that he might betray her. He understood her when she said:

"Your hours with us are to be so few that I do not mean to be deprived of any of them, señor."

"That is right," cried her father. "We have dubious days in store, but let us banish them while we may."

Lithgow felt that he never should forget the awkwardness of that otherwise delightful dinner which consumed the remainder of the afternoon. He was conscious that his own manner had taken on an air of restraint, and he could see that Raquel's had also. They talked at each other as if miles intervened; and all the while each counted the minutes which were drifting dreamily away. Under the spur of his happiness Theuriet became very talkative, and even went so far as to plan the little journeys into the outer world with which he hoped to buy Raquel's love. Lithgow was very quiet. Once he said:

"And you will come as far north as New York, of course."

"*Ciertamente*," agreed the Frenchman, feeling that nothing was too much to promise on this occasion. "In zat way we may hav' ze plaisir ov seeing you again, eef you come not more to Cuba."

To Lithgow there was something gruesome in this familiar manner in which the prospective bridegroom spoke of himself and Raquel as "we." He found himself objecting to it silently again and again during the course of the afternoon. And he smiled at himself with mingled amusement and reproach as he realized how completely he was making this girl's troubles and sorrows his own. He fashioned to himself the comments which Beatrice would give, providing that he ever made her his father confessor in this affair as he had in others. But in his heart he knew that the thoughts which he entertained toward this unsophisticated maiden of a sugar plantation were such as would be locked up securely forever.

When, just a short time before the hour for departure, he suddenly discovered that both of the planters had withdrawn for a moment and he was alone with her, he became afraid of himself.

"Be careful, my boy," he cautioned. "It is better to say nothing than to say that which were better unsaid."

The silence between them grew full of meaning. To break it he ventured finally:

"You soon will become of the larger life of the world, señorita. Your dreaming will be past. It will be as if you had drifted from some shady, quiet river-cove out into the tempestuous waters of the sea. Your course will be crossed by crafts from other ports. You will speak them and go on your way wiser, possibly happier."

Raquel sat dipping her finger-tips thoughtfully into the water of the old fountain. She was thinking what the days would be like, when this man with his companionable ways was gone. She had had a foretaste of them during the short time he had been away in his search for Annizac. And the American was telling himself that the curves of the girl's lovely lips had grown firmer, the eyelids heavier, the oval face paler.

"You are a craft from another port," she remarked in a low tone.

"Yes, the first, but not the last," he assented, loosening the curb a little. "There will be many. I only pray that one will not come whose course you will wish to make your own—but cannot because of the one you have chosen to-day."

"You are unkind, señor," she said coldly.

"I do not mean to be," he returned gently. "I think you are unkind to yourself. I am torn by conflicting desires; to tell your father of the mistake you are making; to do as you appear to wish me to do—keep silent."

"It would be cruel to both of us to tell him," she declared. "Here is my opportunity to make my life worth something."

"I fail to see it in that way." Lithgow shook his head. "You are throwing it away, from my point of view."

"If throwing it away benefits another, will that not be well?" she asked. "Lives are wasted yearly in famine, pestilence, war. I should count myself happy if I might lose life in fighting for Cuba. Is it less noble to—die daily through long years?"

"But, child, it is unnecessary," he cried despairingly. "You feel capable of it now, but you don't begin to know what you are talking about. And the years are so long when one lives them."

"What is life, after all?" she murmured wearily.

"Something that most of us willingly would relinquish if we knew just what lay beyond," he answered. "When all is said, it is true that there does not seem to be much use in living. The individual appears to count for little save in isolated cases, where a rare soul makes itself felt in work for its race. My life, for instance, has never been worth anything, even to myself. I struggle, achieve a trifle, suffer, enjoy—and for what? I benefit no one in particular. My only battlefield is myself, and even on that arena I fear that I do not fight very valiantly."

"You have benefited *me*, señor," she affirmed quietly, "this moment."

"How?" he queried with surprise.

"You say that even you, a man with a man's splendid chances—benefit no one, that all your efforts are for naught. Should I not then more joyfully embrace this which will make *my* battling not wholly worthless and without fruit? No doubt I always will war, if not for Cuba, then against existing conditions; it seems to be my nature. As it now is, the battle simply will be the silent one between my two selves: the new, subdued one, burdened with the sense of debt and duty, which has betrothed itself; and the old one, restless, ambitious, determined to do, not simply to be."

"Which self do you fancy will win?" Lithgow was very earnest.

"Ah, who knows?" she breathed. "Might not the contending forces wear the battlefield out?—make a wreck of it?"

"They would be likely to leave irremediable evidences of the merciless ravages of war," warned he. "Many faces bear witness to such concealed struggles. It grieves me that yours is to be of the number."

He arose and began moving about the court restlessly, hands behind him. Words rushed to his tongue. He shut them back resolutely. Something—some other calmer self— seemed to be comparing this moment with that one in Beatrice's studio, when he had asked her to be his wife. He had felt timid then, a little doubtful, but no such wild emotions had warred within him as these, which threatened to leap up volcano-like and rush with dangerous force outward in a glow of burning speech. At last he brought himself to a pause in front of Raquel.

"Shall you care to hear if Zuñega gets his rights?" he asked.

Eagerness once more shot up into her face.

"If I may," she answered. "None could be more interested than I. Will you tell him so?"

"With pleasure," he replied. "May I write you—through your father?"

"A letter from the outside world! You cannot dream what that would be to me," was her answer, given without looking at him.

Lithgow knew that the volcanic fire was breaking its bounds. It burned in his eyes, on his lips. He bent his head nearer hers. Only the palm would have heard the next words, but——

"Ze caballos are at ze entrance, Monsieur Hamilton."

The voice of M. Theuriet came between them with the force of a dynamite bomb, that seemed to hurl them leagues apart.

"Eet ees ze saddest part ov life zat adieus must be spoken," the voice went on, "but you will veseet Cuba again, let us hop'. And you will find ze señorita a happy wife, eef lov' and devotion can make her so, while ze happiest man in ze island will be *su seguro servidor*, as ze Spaniards say."

"You have not neglected to bring me the book you promised, I hope, señor," Raquel said quietly, ignoring the speech of the coffee planter. In the knowledge that Lithgow was going to leave something which had been his, there was a consolation that nerved her to witness his departure with a face on which was mirrored none of the dread that her soul felt. He was only too well aware that she did not love the Frenchman, but she was determined that he should not read to what depths he had stirred her nature in these brief days during which their lives had touched.

"I had not forgotten." Lithgow took it from his pocket and placed it in her hand. "I prefer not to say 'good-by.' Life is long and the world is small. We may meet again; until then, permit me to speak as you Cubans do: God walk with you!"

He shook hands with Gilbert Palgrave, then mounted, and by the side of M. Theuriet rode in the direction of La Buena Esperanza. Before out of sight of the white walls he halted, turned, and lifted his hat.

Raquel still stood in the entrance.

The purpling shadows crept stealthily up over the mountains, weaving with mystic touch the web of darkness. The sword-thrusts of the morrow's sun would make a nothing of this heavy veil of night, but she knew that no morrow would lift the shadow which now lay upon all her days to come.

The great golden moon rose grandly over the forest.

She went slowly back into the empty court. She held the book tightly against her. She put one arm around the staunch old palm tree and laid her face against it, as she had done on one other occasion. Then her heart had been rebelliously eager to live; now it shuddered at the thought of what life held. Then queries had been on her lips; now there was only the silence of the anguish which knows that it will continue to live and wonders how it can.

Tears were on her cheeks. They fell on the gray coat of

the palm. Far above the green plumes quivered, and the night winds heard them murmur:

" We of the green fire have storms that bend our heads and drive our roots deeper for nourishment and larger growth, you of the red fire have sorrows. Only thus attain you the full stature of that soul called Man."

CHAPTER XIV.

When day broke over Cuba, Lithgow and Annizae, in the depths of M. Theuriet's volante, were well on their way to Taguayabon, from which point the coffee planter's conveyance was to be returned to La Buena Esperanza.

Lithgow contemplated taking from Taguayabon a train to S. Juan de los Remedios and from there to the port of Caibarien, providing that he was so fortunate as to find that the railroad officials had the intention of running a train that day or the next. He had no doubt that he could secure transportation through the interior, but he was not certain enough of Annizae to feel that it was wise to adopt such a method. On the railroad and on the steamer to Havana she would be in his hands; she would have no opportunity of escape should she alter her mind. In the interior, who knew what might befall? It was well to be out of the reach of Gonzalo Alarcon as quickly as possible.

Annizae asked no questions, though her mind was filled to overflowing with queries concerning the future. She appeared to be not wholly without suspicion, for she was very much alert and watched studiously the country through which they passed. She was not without appreciation of the indubitable comforts of this ride in the volante, however; perhaps it seemed to her a sort of surety of the greater luxuries which awaited her in the land where her rival had died.

Little by little the mountainous district slipped back of them. They advanced into a section given up entirely to the cultivation of cane. Acres upon acres of gleaming yellow stretched along their route.

The postilion allowed the horses to assume a walk. At the side of the animal harnessed to the vehicle paced the free horse, who evidently enjoyed his supervision of his mate and keenly appreciated the honor of bearing on his back the gayly attired individual whose duty it was to guide him.

Lithgow endeavored to engage Annizae in conversation, but she was extremely wary. Her accustomed reticence had settled back upon her. Not until she saw Zuñega with her own eyes in Havana did she mean to believe implicitly in the promises held out by this stranger.

She derived considerable amusement from picturing to herself Alarcon's unbounded amazement when he should discover that she returned no more to the camp of which she had been a member these many years. He would think that she had followed Zuñega. Some day he should know why. He would be more astonished then; for she would return to Cuba with evidences of her rightful position. She would wear the gowns, the jewels, and she would spend the gold which had belonged to the woman who had taken her place. Those who had deemed her a half-menial should learn what a secret it was which she had kept with unsmiling lips. A laugh was in her heart; it almost crept into utterance. Surely, she could laugh again when she had achieved her full triumph! Even in her wildest moments of hatred she never had dared to think of such a victory as this. It seemed to grow in immensity as she viewed it. To have had it snatched from her now would have been the most bitter of all punishments. Now and then she stole a glance at Lithgow out of the corners of her black eyes. She had no thought of escaping unless she should see signs of deception on his part. She realized what a risk she was running. She might be going to life-long imprisonment. But the glamour of this late triumph was before her mental vision, and she was willing to venture much in the hope of obtaining it.

Lithgow interrogated the postilion on various subjects and had quick replies flashed back at him over Diego's embroidered shoulder. But for the most part of the journey he occupied himself with thoughts of the white figure which he had left standing alone in the entrance. He had noticed that her father had turned off toward the plantain grove after their departure, and he knew that Raquel had gone back to the court alone. He wondered what her thoughts had been. He scarcely dared face his.

Dreamily he fancied Raquel in Annizae's place. Instinctively he knew how this entire scene of golden monotony · would have been changed to a fairyland, through which he would have moved in a delirium of joy.

"She liked me," he said reflectively. "I was new, a breath from the great palpitating world-life which she longs to know; but—was she conscious of keener feeling? God forgive me if I awakened a suspicion of that intense passion of which a nature like hers is capable!"

The day deepened into noon and mellowed again into those entrancing hues which are so speedily blent into the star-gemmed robe of night. It was dark when Diego drew up the horses before a tienda and prepared to give the animals food and shelter.

Lithgow assisted Annizae to alight and went to make provisions for their own comfort. As he had expected, there was no likelihood of being able to proceed to the coast under one or two days.

On the following morning, Diego and the volante wended their course back to the coffee plantation, bearing with them a letter to M. Theuriet, in which the American had sought to render appreciation of the Frenchman's hospitality. At the close of the communication he had dared—after considerable deliberation—to add, as if urged by sudden recollection:

"I neglected to call the attention of the Señorita Raquel to some favorite passages which she will find marked in the 'Over-Soul.' Will you have the great kindness to ask her to glance at them? Possibly you may enjoy reading them yourself, Monsieur Theuriet."

That last suggestion, he anticipated, would be successful in allaying any fears which his late host might entertain in regard to the mentioned volume.

Two mornings later, the boat on which he and Annizae had embarked began winding its way through the cayos (shoal-rocks) which dotted the waters in every direction. Emeralds sewn into the intricate embroidery of earth's robe of beauty they seemed, strewn with a lavish hand.

Cranes and curlews could be detected on the large islands wading about among the mangrove roots. A long pink line swept across the sea at a distance. It was a flock of flamingoes, in search of a tempting reef on which they could station

themselves to interfere with the government's fishing inter
. ests, as is their wont.

It was easy to see why smugglers and pirates reigned for
so long in these regions.

Annizae hung over the rail in a maze. The marvellous
marine vegetation was new to her. Never had she been out
on the water, save on the memorable occasion when she had
taken the first move toward the vengeance which had brought
her the satisfaction she now was hugging joyously. From
under the hull of the vessel finny creatures of astonishing
colors shot and darted about in alarm, diving down to the
coral sand as though to startle the conchs and star-fish lying
motionless and untroubled by what was passing on the surface. She peered down through the clear, green waters with
a childish curiosity. Never once did her interest appear to
abate until they reached Matanzas and were *en route* for
Havana. Then she lapsed once again into the morose woman that her confederates had known.

Secretly she was exceedingly anxious.

If this señor failed to produce Zuñega, what was best to do?
She contemplated several methods of escape. She did not
intend to be caught napping.

Lithgow's entrance into the Hotel Inglaterra accompanied
by Annizae excited a ripple of comment. Her bizarre attire,
her defiant dark face, her Juno-like proportions, would have
attracted notice anywhere, even on the streets of cosmopoli-
tan Havana. The American saw that she was established as
luxuriously as was possible before he gave a thought to other
matters. He was relying in no small measure on the long
smothered feminine inclinations of her heart, and he catered
to these as best he knew how, in the hope of having them add
their silent importunities to his when the moment came for
departure from Cuba. He took the precaution to place her
under surveillance; but of this fact Annizae was not aware.
There yet remained three days before he was to meet Zuñega
in the Campo Santo. He anticipated that it would take all
of that time for him to make the arrangements for sailing.
He went to confer with the consuls, meaning to lose no moment after securing Zuñega, for a ship would leave the harbor
the day following.

Now that he was back amid the whirl of Havanese life,

which he had left only a month previous, his strange discovery of the heir for whom Mr. Bertram was so anxious seemed even more wonderful than it had on the plantation. He found himself surprised at his own success. The elation which had been absent before now began to make itself apparent. He concluded not to telegraph the information, but to wait and take the lawyer by surprise. In that way he would miss none of the excitement which would pervade Bertram's office when the announcement was received, an excitement which he felt that he deserved to witness.

At the hotel he found an immense amount of correspondence awaiting him. He had not fully realized how far away from Beatrice his thoughts had drifted until he saw, with something of a start, her chirography boldly traced across two envelopes. He reserved them until the last. They were her usual bright, chatty letters, relating all that was being done and said in their world. He perused them with a feeling as if he had been long separated from this life of which she spoke. He was conscious of a wave of regret that he must return to it. That soft, narcotic perfume of the south seemed to have crept into his veins, quieting the wearisome energy with which his blood had pounded resistlessly through year after year of business life. At the close of the second letter he saw written:

"You once said, Lithgow, 'It is well to have a master, but it is far better to have slaves.' To that I append this recent discovery—it is better to have *a friend.* Your prophecy has proven true—I do miss you."

Lithgow looked down at the cool tiles of the office floor many minutes after reading that.

"When Bee says a thing like that it means much," he told himself slowly. "It means everything almost—after those words in the studio."

He straightened the paper out and read the lines again. He marvelled vaguely as to the unstableness of the human mind. He recollected that the mere anticipation of such an intimation from Beatrice would have moved him to gladness a short time previous. Now he accepted it in a dull, leaden way that angered him, though, to have saved his life, he could feel no other emotion.

"What am I?" he demanded fiercely. "Am I no better than

the great mass of men—carried away by a pair of wonderful eyes? Have I no strength of character? My love for Beatrice was the growth of years. It was the outcome of a study of her nobility, her fitness to make a man noble himself. Surely it can't have been swept away by—by—this which—by the sight of Raquel's trouble! I have allowed my sympathies to run away with me!" But those reflections did not bring back his old joy in Beatrice nor banish the constant thought of the girl at La Sacra Sonrisa. He arose with the most bitter disgust for himself. He went out into the streets to escape from the accusations of his mind. He joined the procession of feet that made a continual whispering in the streets. But his thoughts went with him. They said:

"What if you had given utterance to that which was in your heart and on your very lips that last night in the court?"

"I am a scoundrel!" he declared with conviction, "and nothing but M. Theuriet's entrance at that moment kept me from making it public! In another instant I would have told Raquel that I loved her. I would have begged her to fly with me. I would have forgotten Annizae, Zuñega, everything but that which burned in my veins—and burns there yet!—a fire which has two powers: to burn away the old and leave the world like new, untried, full of delightful promise; or, never satisfied, unquenchable, to eat into the heart while the years pass by and death delays!"

A mounted montero, galloping past with a jingle of coins on his broad sombrero, would have swept him down had not a muscular arm pulled him out of the way, while a voice oddly familiar in its caressing cadences said amusedly:

"El Americano thinks much, but sees little."

Lithgow caught his rescuer with a grasp that was more retentive than was necessary.

"Zuñega!" he exclaimed.

"*Bien,* am I he whom you call 'Zuñega'?" demanded the rescuer, smiling.

Lithgow hesitated. He could have sworn that the voice was that of the forest lad, but as he studied the face of the man before him he was obliged to admit that he might be mistaken.

"*Por supuesto,*" nodded the rescuer. "I am called Manuel. Want you one named 'Zuñega,' señor?"

"*Sí, sí,* know you such an one?" questioned Lithgow.

" *Es posible,*" admitted the man. " What then, señor?"

" Tell him that the Americano is here in Havana."

" Alone, señor?"

Lithgow regarded the interrogator keenly, but the meagre garb of a dock laborer and the heavy beard which he wore convinced the American that his suspicions were inaccurate.

" Not alone," he replied. " Tell him I bring the one I said I would bring."

" *Muy bien,*" bowed the fellow, with that indubitable grace characterizing all Cubans. " If I know such, I will tell him."

Lithgow went on his way. The Cuban watched him with a peculiar smile, then took his own path with a shrug of the shoulders, but it was a satisfied shrug.

Havana is not the best spot in the world in which to seek a season of introspection, but Lithgow succeeded fairly well in his endeavor to understand some of the secret working of the masculine nature as revealed in his own experience. It was an edifying task, but not a particularly enjoyable one. Right in the middle of a most complete summing up of the whole matter he would discover that his mind had wandered truantly to the fragrant court. He relived the few days in which he had known Raquel and then relived them again, until, finally, in sheer desperation, he said as he had said once before: "It is only for this moment, this one moment out of life. I will feed upon it while it lasts. None shall know of the poison which it leaves in my blood."

Annizae was not left wholly to her own reflections during those days. She was given a taste of gay life which had never been hers before, and she evidenced plainly that it was not disagreeable. The festivities at night were what delighted her most, though her immobile countenance never revealed the fact to Lithgow. In her own mind she determined to return to Havana as soon as the possessions of her rival became hers. Here, with such finery, she felt that she could enjoy herself as she had dreamed of doing before the hope of revenge and the subsequent forest existence were hers.

On the day that he was to meet Zuñega, Lithgow took Annizae with him to the Campo Santo.

Zuñega was not at the rendezvous, and the American walked about among the graves with a sort of morbid restlessness. The little stones with the cross at the head looked sphinx-like. What mysteries might they not have absorbed from the forms that they covered? They appeared more fitting for the dead than the more impressive tombs and monuments. What more emblematic shaft was needed than the palm, type of the immortality of the soul which, for a brief time, had vitalized the crumbling material once more returning to nature!

Lithgow watched the lizards sleeping in the sun. They reminded him of the lizards that hid in the fountain in the court. Everything seemed to carry his memory back there as if by magic.

Here and there the creeping, thread-like tendrils of the roots had thrust themselves upward and had pushed aside even the stones, or—had some ghostly fingers tried to raise them?

The mystery of existence, the reason for being, the ultimate ending, rose in one mighty question before him there, where nature absorbed the tissues which once had drawn their sustenance from her voluptuous breast but now returned to be re-created into other forms of life.

"Does one great Mind absorb all individualities into its perfect Self, as nature absorbs all personalities?" he wondered. "Or, is there an unfailing love which provides other lives in which can be worked out the problems over which we labor and falter in this?

"Some day, though far apart, both Raquel and I will lie in this same way, hushed, buried, forgotten; and all of the present occupants of the world will be sharing the same fate! How simple it all seems! I suppose that we will look back on this stage of our upward journey and see how trivial are the sorrows, how ephemeral the delights, of these senses, which in an incredibly short time sink to their native nothingness. What was I in previous lives—if such there be? Did I possess Raquel? Like Yasodhara and Gautama, we might have been tigers in some unremembered cycle. Now,

> "'Our past is clean forgot,
> Our present is and is not,
> Our future's a sealed seed-plot,
> And what betwixt them are we?
> We who say as we go—
> "Strange to think by the way,
> Whatever there is to know
> That shall we know some day."'"

"*Buenos dias, señor.*"

The salutation caused him to turn quickly. He found that he was face to face with the individual who had called himself "Manuel."

"Ah, then I was not mistaken!" exclaimed Lithgow with a self-congratulatory tone. "You and Zuñega are one."

"How knew you me so quickly, señor?" queried Zuñega, glancing cautiously about them and espying Annizac in the shade of a tomb.

"By your voice," replied Lithgow. "Why did you not then acknowledge that I was right?"

"I had a wish, señor, to learn if my disguise was sufficient. If you, a stranger, knew me and could not be persuaded otherwise, I feared that those of Alarcon's friends who might have been notified of my disappearance would recognize me also."

"Alarcon? Has he friends in this city?" questioned the American.

"Ah, señor, has he not?" smiled Zuñega. "There are times when he spends weeks right here in Havana; but the guardia civile know him not as the bandit. To them he is Señor Figueras. One word from Señor Figueras to them would put them on the lookout for me. One word from Gonzalo Alarcon to his friends would also place pursuers on my track. I have had two dangers to fear."

"You are well disguised," complimented Lithgow. "Had it not been for your speech I never should have thought of recognizing you as you are. Possibly I have a good memory for the peculiarities of a voice. Every voice here is so musical that each leaves a strong mental impression. You perceive that I have succeeded in bringing Annizac."

"You must be a magician, señor," acknowledged Zuñega. "Not yet has she seen me. Wait, señor; let me discover if her eyes are wise."

He approached her stealthily, appearing suddenly before her. She gave a start of surprise but remained silent, evidently seeing in him only a stranger, from whose presence she shrank without wishing it to appear that she did so. When he was well convinced that even her visual sense was deceived, he said softly:

"Annizac?"

With a cry of delight that astonished both men she slipped down at his feet and clasped her arms around his body.

"*Gracias á Dios! Gracias á Dios!*" she murmured, with her dark face upturned to study his features better. "It is thou—no?"

It was the first time in his life that Zuñega recalled the faintest show of affection on her part, and he was amazed and touched by it. He had known her only as a seemingly callous woman. Motherly tenderness he had not missed, because he never had been acquainted with it, so far as he remembered. That Annizae had been derelict in maternal emotions and cares never had been brought to his notice. Resentment had arisen in his heart against her since he had learned of the injury she had done him, but it melted beneath this unexpected exhibition of remorse on her part. It was not remorse, however. It was gladness to find that he was safe and that the words of the American thus far, at least, had proven true. The possibility of Zuñega's wrath had not yet occurred to her. It was not for his sake that she was willing to undertake this journey across the waters; it was for the joy of her final victory.

Zuñega drew himself away from her grasp.

Lithgow approached.

"Annizae acknowledges taking you from the ship," he said meaningly. "She is ready to go to England to restore you to your rights."

Annizae lifted herself to her feet. She cast a suspicious look at Lithgow.

"Wait, señor," she said with a cunning smile. "Told you not that there were two rings? Zuñega's is gone!"

Lithgow took a step forward. His heart sank. That ring was the most important evidence. The only incontrovertible one.

"You have not lost it, Zuñega!" he exclaimed, dismayed.

For reply Zuñega drew forth the little reliquary which hung at his neck. By whom it had been placed there he knew not. The possession of it had been one of his earliest remembrances. From its secret contents, blessed by some padre at his birth, no doubt, he extracted the ring unsmilingly. He held it up before Annizae's eyes.

"Dost thou remember the day when thou didst reveal that my father was *inglés?*"

Annizae bowed her head. There was that in the eyes of Zuñega which she never had faced before. That his condemnation could have power to shake her was a revelation to herself.

"On that day did I not swear to avenge thee?" he demanded. "Did I not swear it over this ring which thou hadst said was his own? Were not my words these: 'I will have no mercy for an *inglés* since thou, my mother, hast suffered because of one?'"

Annizae could not meet his eyes. She endeavored to, but her own fell. They were no longer fearless.

"Why didst thou not speak the truth, then," he questioned sternly. "Thou wert willing that I should vent fury on those of my father's nation, when thou alone wert the one on whom revenge should fall."

With his magnificent figure drawn up to its fullest height, his long black orbs blazing with righteous indignation, his blue-black hair quivering with the motion of his perfectly poised head, Zuñega looked a prince of blood royal.

Lithgow stared at him fascinated. Beauty in a man he never had admired, but this creature before him was more than beautiful; he was grand, impressive, a young god. Every muscle stood out saliently. He appeared like a living piece of golden bronze.

Annizae threw out her hands with the palms upward.

"Suffered I nothing? Did not thy mother win that which was mine? Had I no wrongs?"

Zuñega threw his head backward and looked up into the blue-white of the zenith. He did not answer at once. When he did his voice had changed. It again held its caressing cadences.

"It is possible," admitted he softly. "I knew not my father. If he wronged thee, I, his son, will make amends. Why should I bear thee malice? Hast thou not made me a Cuban? I have much for which to be grateful. Cuba shall have reason to rejoice that I have been reared a son of the forests."

His thoughts had flown back to that day when he had built the palm hut. Raquel's ringing words were yet in his mind.

Lithgow's admiration for Zuñega's physical perfection

passed into a like feeling for the mental development which had made such a reply possible.

"Neither English nor Cuban blood are wholly responsible for such fine nobility," he told himself. "He has sapped it from the vaulted arches and silent naves of a cathedral grander than brain or fingers of man can build." Aloud he said:

"Both of you shall have your wrongs righted. I have made every preparation for sailing on the morrow. You, Zuñega, have nothing to fear more from Gonzalo Alarcon. You leave Cuba now, as you came near leaving it in your babyhood, under your rightful name, Robert Deene Percival, heir to Harberton Towers and the title its owner bears."

"*Gracias, señor*," smiled Zuñega. "I am obedient to you, but always remain I a Cuban. He who once is Cuban is Cuban ever."

CHAPTER XV.

When their ship cut through the sapphire waters of the harbor on its way to the open sea, Zuñega stood on deck shading his eyes with his hand. The sunshine on the quivering expanse of liquid sky through which they swept, the glare of the brilliant façades of the dwellings in the city, was more than human vision could endure without blinking. He was very grave. His gaze was riveted on the mountains, which from the distance looked softly undulating, bathed in an emerald refulgence that slowly faded to blue before the most perfect jewel of the Caribbean slipped below the horizon.

No word of farewell was on his lip, but his heart seemed to him to be pent up in so small a compass that the blood stood still in his veins, being unable to force itself through.

"When my eyes behold thee again, it will be when I come to fight for thee," he said, ignorant that he spoke aloud.

Lithgow, standing by his side, also watching the disappearance of the island with yearning look, gave him a glance of inquiry.

"You never will return to Cuba," he prophesied, knowing some of the temptations which would be likely to keep

Zuñega on English soil and drive all thought of this spot from his mind.

"When the hour to struggle for the island's freedom comes, I will be here, señor," Zuñega declared firmly. "I so have vowed to the señorita."

"Do you mean the Señorita Raquel?" questioned Lithgow with some astonishment.

"*Si, señor mio*, the Señorita Raquel," nodded Zuñega.

"What difference does it make to her if you come to fight for Cuba?" Lithgow's voice had a tone in it that attracted the Cuban youth's attention. He turned his eyes upon Lithgow.

"She longs to do what a man might for Cuba," he explained naïvely. "She is a woman; she can do nothing—only with her fiery words breathe that into the heart of man which was not there before. I will fight for her. I will fight for myself. If what you speak is true, if gold is mine, I can do more than fight. I can provide other men with arms and ammunition. All Cuba would fight if it had weapons. Unarmed, it can do nothing but submit."

As by a flash Lithgow understood several questions which Raquel had asked concerning Zuñega's fortune and what use he would be likely to put it to. His explanation that the property was entailed had appeared to depress her. He had wondered at the fact at the time.

"Her sojourn in the forest was not an idle one, then," he commented, aware of a foolish feeling of pique as he regarded the fine stalwart figure before him. "She inspired you with patriotic motives—when? On the journey toward the plantation?"

"Before I knew that she intended to escape, señor. She had bitter words for him who lived without thought of Cuba's future. They were words that stung. I shall not forget them. I shall not forget *her*."

Lithgow leaned hard back against the taffrail.

"Why not?" he demanded sharply.

Zuñega shook his head.

"I can tell you not why, señor," he replied, looking far out across the sea. "But I think of her always, always, asleep or awake. I see only her eyes, even now while I seem to watch the sea."

Lithgow waited a long moment. There was a glow on the

beautiful southern face that a man may see once in a life-
time. He knew what had come to the lad if the lad himself did not. His voice was tender when he finally said
slowly:

"You do not know that she is to marry—the old M.
Theuriet?"

Zuñega stepped backward. His fingers, which had been
lying lightly on the taffrail, tightened spasmodically. His
lips lost their crimson. The sweet melancholy of his eyes
deepened into surprise, a growing realization of what it
meant to his hopes, then—dismay. He caught the American
by the arm.

"It is not true?" he pleaded.

"It is true," Lithgow returned sadly, going on to explain
the conditions which had urged her into the agreement.

Zuñega turned once half around and looked at Annizae as
she reclined contentedly in a sea-chair. His brows were
drawn together.

"But for her," he said under his breath, "I should have that
which would make me the equal of the señorita! I could free
her father from debt. I could do all that M. Theuriet will
do! Annizae shall suffer."

"But for Annizae you never would have known the Señorita Raquel," reminded Lithgow. "Instead, you might have
been married to some English maiden whose mamma had an
eye on your title."

"*Es verdad*," admitted Zuñega reluctantly.

"You owe Annizae more than she has deprived you of,"
Lithgow said quietly. "Ignorantly, she has benefited you.
Though a bandit, you have breathed an atmosphere clearer,
cleaner, than that of most cities. The moral poison of Paris
never has entered your brain. And you have seen a white
soul. White souls are so scarce in life. Be guided by its enthusiasm. Go back and fight for Cuba if you will. You will
win Raquel's gratitude, her praise. The fact that you must
fight for two will make you wise and strong. Live to carry
out your promise to her, Zuñega. You are going to be placed
where you will be besieged by temptations, the subtle power
of which you cannot even imagine. Keep her face before
you. The thought of it will save you from much the mere
memory of which would cause you to hate yourself."

Zuñega held out his hand.   He grasped Lithgow's fingers almost fiercely.

"Heard you not my words to her when I turned my face away from the sugar plantation?" he asked.   "'Zuñega never forgets.'   I repeat them to you, señor.   Some day you shall learn how true they are."

Through the days which followed, they spoke often on the same subject.   Lithgow was not averse to discussing her with this clean-hearted boy, and he sought to impress upon Zuñega the full worth of her rich nature, as he divined it.   Once Zuñega murmured astutely, as he glanced up with his soft, powerful eyes:

"The señor, he will not forget her either!"

Lithgow was conscious that the color swept over his mature features as it had been wont to do in his boyhood days.   Zuñega's observation had surprised him.

"I must forget her," he replied meaningly.   "There is another."

"A wife?" queried Zuñega with a touch of indignation.

"One I have asked to be."

"Oh!" Zuñega's tone was apologetic.

"You will see her," promised Lithgow.

"Is she as beautiful as the señorita?"

"Wait.   You shall answer that question to me after you have seen her."

The days of inaction on shipboard seemed well-nigh interminable to both Annizae and Zuñega.   The muscles of the latter appeared to be striving to break through the skin in their imperative desire for exercise.   Lithgow exerted himself to provide entertainment for both of them.   And as the ship advanced into the colder atmosphere of the north, the lassitude gradually dropped away from him.   He found himself sniffing the sharp, invigorating air with the same pleasure with which he had swooned beneath the balminess of the south on his downward trip.

They passed the heights of Neversink as the night closed in, cold, snowy, dreary.   They would be riding at anchor in the morning.   Annizae was in a state of perpetual chill.   Her face was gloomy.   Her triumph appeared afar off.   Zuñega was full of alertness.   He had made friends for himself everywhere.   The fascinations of his venture out into the world were taking hold of him. Lithgow watched him and smiled.

"Zuñega will forget," he said, "when he is master of Harberton Towers."

Not until they had driven from the docks to a quiet hotel and Annizae had made the discovery that, though the breath of winter may be in the land, the Americans know how to have the warmth of summer in their houses, did her moroseness abate. She then looked out on the marvellous sight of a white shrouded city with some show of interest. She was thinking of what an awful punishment it would be if she should be held a prisoner in this frozen land. The dazzling snow was not beautiful in her eyes. She hungered for the greenness of Cuba.

Zuñega was enthusiastic. From the windows of the carriage he had peered out at the rushing, busy world into which his fortune was leading him. It bewildered him. The throbbing of its mighty heart beat in upon his ears distressingly, but his muscles twitched and his nerves tingled with a desire to join the mad throng.

Lithgow had breakfast served in the little parlor adjoining Annizae's room. Her strange attire would have made her an object of curiosity to the hotel guests, and he was desirous of not calling her attention to the fact that she appeared any different from others of her own sex. Her unshod feet, her short dress characteristic of her class, her head wound with a turban that had one end brought up artistically through the top in the form of a "castle," combined to give her an unusual style that Lithgow did not wish should be interfered with until Mr. Bertram had had the pleasure of viewing her. Zuñega was not as conspicuous in the way of garb, but his eyes, wonderful tinting, and superb physique caused glances to be turned toward him admiringly, wonderingly.

When they were thoroughly refreshed, Lithgow summoned a carriage and, accompanied by them, was driven at once to Mr. Bertram's office. Their entrance into the ante-room caused the office boy and the typewriter girl to exhibit undisguised signs of curiosity.

Lithgow prevented the announcement being made of his arrival, and gratified himself by walking in upon the lawyer, after ascertaining that he was unoccupied.

"Good-morning, Bertram," he remarked coolly, seating himself. "It is rather cold up here."

Bertram removed his eyeglasses in astonishment.

"Lithgow Hamilton! Why, it can't be you!" he exclaimed, springing up with his glasses in his left hand. "Why in the world didn't you write? Haven't heard a word from you. You might have wired that you were on the way home! It would have saved me considerable speculation, I can assure you."

"Well, I've been busy, too busy to write," answered Lithgow, with an assumed air of having little to say. "And, I didn't think there was much use in wiring you."

A look of disappointment passed over the lawyer's face. It was plain that he had hoped. He settled himself comfortably in his chair again, got out some cigars, offered Lithgow one and helped himself.

"We've been afraid that our business had gotten you into some trouble," he said, lighting his. "We sent over to your firm, and even they said that they had not heard from you."

"I was down in the interior," explained Lithgow. "I wired them on reaching Havana."

"Well, what luck did you have?" Bertram ventured to ask finally. "I mean in regard to your own business; I know by your face that you were not successful in regard to the other."

Lithgow laughed.

"Do I wear my heart in my face?" he asked.

"No, of course not, but if you had learned anything important you would rush to tell me."

"I am sorry to show you what a miserable mind reader you are," Lithgow returned. "I am congratulating myself that I have not been an utter failure. I will exhibit what I have in the way of a clew."

He arose, opened the door, and motioned for Annizac and Zuñega to enter.

Bertram stood erect, with an eager expectancy that he concealed beneath a dignified and half-skeptical exterior.

As the two entered, he fell back a step involuntarily.

"Permit me to present to you *Brown Annizac* and the child that she exchanged for her own," said Lithgow, wholly satisfied with the effect produced on the lawyer.

Annizae herself was trembling in every limb, ignorant of what awaited her; the judicial bearing and keen blue eyes of the lawyer were not calculated to inspire other than a certain feeling of fear and awe, but the expression of mingled incredulity and delight which overshot his visage visibly lessened Annizae's affright. He appeared rooted to the floor for a moment, then he advanced toward them with a summoning back of his usual non-betraying manner.

"I hope this is no joke that you are playing on me, Hamilton," he remarked, as he welcomed the new-comers and placed chairs for them.

"It is no joke unless I am very much mistaken," replied Lithgow. "Zuñega, hold out your hand."

Zuñega complied. Lithgow extended his own at the same time. The two rings stared the lawyer in the face. Bertram leaned forward excitedly and inspected Zuñega's through his glasses.

"Zuñega was in possession of this ornament when I first saw him," Lithgow stated. "I then learned on reputable authority that his father was an Englishman, whom the lad never had seen, and that his supposed mother went by the name of Annizae and was a member of a mountain band of bandits, in whose society she had reared him. That and the possession of the ring seemed conclusive proof that they were the individuals you desire."

Bertram seemed half incapable of crediting such good fortune.

"If I did not know you thoroughly, Hamilton, I should be inclined to believe this thing a 'fake;' it is too good to be true," he exclaimed. "But your word and—this other ring are sufficient to convince me that you have made a brilliant success of what others have failed on year after year. All that we get out of it we will share with you, but even that will not repay you in proportion to the value of the discovery. Let me hear how you managed it?"

"It really seemed to manage itself," said Lithgow. "I am less wonderful than you think. Nothing but a chain of circumstances, seemingly disastrous but really fortuitous, so far as Zuñega was concerned, brought him into my presence. The ring attracted my eyes. The remainder of the discovery followed as a matter of course, with the result that both of

them are here in your office. To give you all the details I
shall be obliged to relate all that occurred before and after I
reached the estate of La Buena Esperanza, the last one on my
list, and one with which the firm had expressed a particular
desire to open trade."

"Go on," requested the lawyer. "Leave out nothing."

Lithgow recounted the abduction of Raquel and the events
which strangely had sprung from it.

"It sounds like a fairy story," commented Bertram when all
had been told. "But the ring—I fancy that the London solicitors will deem that pretty conclusive. I shall wire them at
once. Greene, my partner, is out of town. I cannot leave
until he returns, but we can make preparations for going on
to England. I shall want you to accompany me, Hamilton."

"I'm willing enough," responded Lithgow with a laugh,
"but the firm may not be. I have not been around to the
office yet; telephoned them of my arrival and thought that I
would apprise you of this affair's progress first. I shall have
to leave our friends here in your care while I attend to my
own business."

"How am I to get on without an interpreter?" queried the
lawyer. "I know only two words of Spanish?"

"I think there is a little cigarmaker in the basement around
the corner," suggested Lithgow. "He might be willing to
serve—for a consideration. I couldn't possibly remain with
them all the time between this and the hour of sailing, if I am
so fortunate as to be permitted absence and an ocean voyage."

"No, of course not," returned Bertram. "You certainly
have done your part. I'll manage all right if they are willing
to place themselves under my care."

"I'll remain at the hotel with them and be with them as
much as my duties and social obligations will allow," volunteered Lithgow. "I'm really very fond of Zuñega."

Bertram glanced at the physique of the former bandit.

"I don't think that I ever should employ the term 'fond,'"
he remarked; "the word 'afraid' strikes me as being more ap-
plicable."

Lithgow laughed and repeated the speech to Zuñega, who
looked somewhat bewildered. It was evident that he did not
realize his own attractions.

"He is magnificent, isn't he?" said Lithgow proudly, as if

in some indefinite way on him the credit reflected for the youth's perfect build. "I am sure that the Harberton title never had a more lordly bearer."

"Should we not begin to call him by his proper name?" asked the lawyer.

"As you please," replied Lithgow, "if he will answer to it. To me I fear he always will be 'Zuñega.' It seems to fit him in some way better than the English cognomen."

He explained to the two Cubans that he now must leave them in the hands of the lawyer and promised them the most perfect courtesy and hospitality. Annizae's features expressed the utmost consternation when she perceived that she was to remain with the stranger. Lithgow's assertions of complete freedom from punishment scarcely quieted her.

"I will send you one from your own country," he told her finally. "He may take you among those who speak your own language. Mr. Bertram will make arrangements with him regarding that."

"Caution her against speaking of this matter," suggested the lawyer. "Too much reticence cannot be preserved in affairs of this kind."

"You would deem no caution necessary if you knew her better," observed Lithgow. "Those she had lived among for years were ignorant of her story."

Bertram regarded her with a show of compelled admiration.

"I wish more of her sex possessed her faculty of silence," he commented. "Wouldn't it be advisable to buy her—some shoes or something?"

"I would make no change in her appearance until you had seen her," said Lithgow. "She is your charge now. I'll send Felipe up to you, and he can bring some of his female relatives. Under their tuition she may make what changes the difference in atmosphere warrants. She's fairly frozen in this ice-locked land."

"Wait; let me reimburse you for all the expense to which you have been put," urged the lawyer, going to his safe.

"Another time," pleaded Lithgow. "I really should be off now. Shall I stop and see if Felipe is at his old stand? He's a nice fellow. Has provided my cigars for two years."

"I wish you would, Hamilton," Bertram said gratefully.

"With him to act as interpreter I'll search her past as thoroughly as my wits will suggest. I almost am afraid to let myself accept them as the persons for whom such fruitless searches have been made."

"I don't see how you can hesitate," Lithgow answered. "It's as clear as daylight to me."

"Do not fear, Annizae," he said reassuringly. "Remember that you have come to prove that you are not without your own wrongs. We will dine together to-night, and you will find that this lawyer is your best friend. He it is who will win for you your triumph. If you are to have all that you claim should have been yours in the first place, he is the one who will help you to secure it."

Then he took Bertram apart and explained the inducements which he had held out in order to hold the woman.

"She must meet with no punishment," he insisted. "I have promised her things that please a woman's heart and gold enough to enable her to return to Cuba and live as she will. She shall have my share of the 'profits,' if there is no other way of keeping my word good."

Bertram looked doubtful. He pursed up his lips.

"I don't know what disposition they will make of her," he said slowly. "I suppose that is not for us to say. I should think the—the heir—himself would bear her some malice. I think I should desire some punishment to be inflicted on one who had deprived me as she has him."

"I believe that Zuñega has decided that he owes her something for having made him a Cuban," returned Lithgow, smiling at Bertram's surprise. "Well! I'll see you at the hotel to-night? All right! I'm glad you are satisfied."

He took his way to the offices of his firm and was closeted therein for the greater portion of the day.

It was near four o'clock before he felt at liberty to turn his steps in the direction of Beatrice's studio. He had not written or notified her of his arrival in town.

"If the words at the close of her letter were significant, I can detect the truth when I walk in upon her unexpectedly," he said to himself, as he strode along the familiar pavements.

CHAPTER XVI.

As he went up in the elevator and stepped out at the top floor, Lithgow found it difficult to believe that he had been away from New York. It seemed only the yesterday that he had come up to Beatrice's atelier in this same way. He was conscious of a foreign timidity as he knocked gently. He knew that his heart beat a trifle faster than was its wont, but not with the tumultuous eagerness which it would have experienced two months previous. It was wonderment which was stirring him now, uncertainty as to what Beatrice might reveal in her surprise.

Beatrice opened the door.

For an instant she stood amazed by what seemed like his apparition, then she cried:

"Why, Mr. Hamilton! How you delight in astonishing people! I thought that you were in Cuba!"

She held out her hand cordially and drew him into the room, where he discovered that her little tea-kettle was steaming hospitably on a Turkish tabouret, around which were clustered a few of the artists who had studios in the building. These, with their teacups in one hand, rose to be presented to him; and he seated himself in their midst, feeling that their presence was responsible for the perfectly conventional greeting that had been accorded him.

"When did your boat get in?" questioned Beatrice. "I saw no account of arrivals in this morning's paper."

"Too late to be inserted, perhaps," he replied.

"Do you know, at first I thought that your ghost had appeared to notify me of some dreadful accident happening to you," she declared.

"You did not appear exceedingly alarmed," commented Lithgow, slightly laughing. "If the news of my discontinuation arouses no more grief than you then displayed, I fear that I am held but lightly in your esteem."

"I would perpetuate you in marble," apologized Beatrice. "What more could the vain heart of man desire?"

"I have brought you two fine subjects," Lithgow went on

to say. "You will have time for only a snap shot at them, however. They are birds of passage."

Beatrice looked at him inquiringly.

"You don't mean to say—" she began.

"Yes," he nodded, without waiting for her to complete her supposed conjecture. "I was successful in my ventures, and you may profit to the extent of having for a model one of the most superb specimens of the genus man."

"Your honored self?" queried one of the artists, making a pretense of getting out a sketching-block.

"That's quite clever, Miss Durame, but sarcastic," frowned Lithgow. "As punishment, you shall not be permitted to look upon the charms of the model mentioned. In fact, I will not let him be made cheap by water-color sketches and such. Clay and bronze for him. The woman would do excellently for you, however."

"Oh, then there is a woman in it!"

"Isn't there always?" demanded the impressionist Brandt from his corner of the old Dutch settle, which Beatrice had picked up at an auction from a neighboring studio.

"That is too stupendous a question, Brandt." Lithgow shook his head as he took a cup of tea and a biscuit from Beatrice. "I wonder at you for introducing it."

"Yes, time is too limited," agreed Brandt, looking at his watch. "How many dozen more cups of tea are you intending to drink, Miss Durame? You know that you promised to walk about with me to take a peep at that exhibition of Vonnoh's pictures. I want to convince you——"

"Oh, I know," she interrupted, putting down her cup reluctantly. Mr. Hamilton was a much more attractive personage than Mr. Brandt, and she would have preferred to stay. "You may insist on your splashes of purple and your dazzling greens, but Nature is soft and harmonious, not glaring and offensive to one's visual organs."

"You don't know how to look at Nature," the impressionist declared. "Your sight must be trained as one's ear and voice are trained in the study of music. Won't you come with us, Miss Faber and Miss Lacroit?"

Lithgow felt like shooting him a grateful glance, as the artists mentioned placed their cups on a convenient chair and proceeded to accept the invitation, arguing within themselves that, though Mr. Hamilton was nicer, it was an honor seldom conferred on them to visit a collection in company with one of the foremost artists of the city.

"They would have staid until the cock crew," breathed Lithgow when the door had closed upon them, "if it had not been for Brandt."

"Have another cup of tea," urged Beatrice, "and tell me all about everything."

"I have not drank this yet," answered Lithgow. "I don't see how women manage to talk and drink tea at the same time."

"Your English education has been neglected," Beatrice informed him. "It is quite an art to take tea and chat, I assure you. I believe that Englishmen are obliged to take a regular course of it at their colleges."

"I must come up every afternoon and practise, then," he said, "for I sail for Liverpool within a week."

"You do not mean it!" Her voice was full of genuine dismay.

"Yes," he nodded, sipping away assiduously.

"Why?"

"I am going over to help establish the claim of Robert Deene Percival to the title of Lord Harberton."

"Do you really mean that the commission that Mr. Bertram gave you was actually successful?"

"Perfectly," he declared.

"Don't be aggravating! Do tell me how you came to find the baby!" she begged.

Lithgow bit through a biscuit with decorous gravity.

'I'll bring it up to-morrow," he promised. "It's about six feet tall!"

Beatrice gave a little shriek,—then, as she realized that the child had grown with the years, burst into laughter.

"Is he the superb specimen?"

"Of course. What did you suppose?"

"Why, I did not understand you at all. I thought—you know you seldom are in earnest, Lithgow."

"I can't imagine where or how I won that reputation of being a jester," groaned he. "I always am in earnest, only people don't believe it."

"Your tone is generally bantering," Beatrice sought to explain. "I have seen people look at you questioningly, uncertain whether to laugh or be solemn; then they see the quizzical light in your eyes and they laugh, thinking they are safe."

"Then my eyes deceive them instead of my tone," corrected Lithgow.

"I am afraid that neither are to be trusted," remarked Beatrice with a sidewise glance.

"When my oldest friends turn against me, then am I forlorn indeed!" Lithgow emptied his cup dolorously and asked for more.

"Not until you retract your words," she refused. "Any one would think that I boasted seventy summers! I do not choose to be numbered among those ancient individuals called your ' oldest friends.'"

"I'll retract anything if you will tell me if you were in earnest when you wrote that you missed me."

"Of course I was in earnest," she declared calmly. "I really did not dream that you were so much a part of—New York. When you are away, the entire city might as well be gone."

"I wish you would put more feeling into your words," he complained, "they sound like papier-mache images—hollow."

It was true that her tone forbade any demonstration, though her words seemed to invite.

The tea-kettle crackled. Beatrice lifted it and shook it.

"It is empty," she said. "It is too bad that you can't have another cup. Won't you come and dine with mamma and me? I wish to hear of your adventures."

"I have not been so lucky as to have any," he said with an air of confession. "I would be glad enough to accept your invitation, but I can't to-night; I'm to meet Mr. Bertram at the hotel with—the claimant. May I come to-morrow night?"

"Yes; and bring the 'superb specimen.'"

"Shall I?" he queried. "I am afraid you will fall in love with him; or do you consider yourself proof against even—" '

"Because I don't fall in love with you, you think possibly I am proof against all masculine charms?" she demanded laughingly. "I really am very susceptible."

"When I relate what a delightful trip I've had, you will be

12

consumed with regret that you refused to accompany me," he prophesied.

"I actually did mourn that I was not there to see the girl whom the bandits stole," she admitted. "Was she a disappointment? You remember that you wrote after you had reached the coffee plantation of M. Theuriet, and you said that as soon as your host returned and you learned more of the matter you would write again. Not another line arrived. Did you write?"

"No," answered Lithgow honestly. "I expected to be here almost as soon as a letter would."

"Well, did her father find the brigands and kill them all?"

"No; he returned from the search utterly discouraged, the morning following my letter to you which the guide mailed. What did happen was romantic, almost too romantic, for this end of the century."

"Which means that you were the one to rescue her and, subsequently, you fell in love," decided Beatrice.

"You are no Yankee, Bee," he declared; "you never could win a prize at guessing! This was the way of it: the future Lord Harberton was the noble individual. He saved her from becoming the wife—the second wife—of the chief, and in so doing he discovered himself, so to speak. Not until then did I advance upon the scene, and then only to make inquiries and such trifling things, with the result that he and the woman who interfered with his fortune are here in New York *en route* to England."

"It is fairly incredible, isn't it?" exclaimed Beatrice. "And what about the abducted girl?"

"She? Oh, she is to marry a neighbor who was willing to ransom her if need be. I'll tell you the whole story some time. It is too long for hasty rehearsal. Zuñega fell in love with her, I fancy."

"Zuñega?"

"The future Lord Harberton."

"Oh! And she is going to marry another?"

"Yes; M. Theuriet, my host."

"A young man?"

"No-o-o; a man about seventy, possibly."

Beatrice rose to her feet. She began putting the tea things away.

"She couldn't love him!"

"No."

Beatrice looked at him sharply. There was a note in his voice that was suggestive of pain.

"Why does she marry him then?"

"I believe that M. Theuriet is going to pay all of her father's debts."

"And—her father permits it?"

"He does not know that is what influenced her. The debts are to be paid without his knowledge; something of that sort."

"And she loves this brigand lord! Isn't it awful what mistakes we women make, or think it is our duty to make!"

"She does not know that Zuñega loves her; at least, I imagine that she does not."

Beatrice tried an experiment.

"Why didn't you promise to pay her father's debts and take her yourself, Lithgow?" she asked.

She saw the start that he gave, but she could not be certain as to what had caused it; for he sprang to his feet and came close to her, taking her hands in his.

"I am going to marry you some day, Beatrice, am I not?" he asked.

"I thought we had settled that in the negative," she replied.

"Do you still prefer to have it so settled?" There was unmistakable anxiety in his question.

Beatrice hesitated. She knew what had come to her during the hours and weeks of his absence. She was not yet willing that he should know. She drew a halting breath that was half a confession, only Lithgow did not recognize it as such.

"While I may not be ready to marry you myself, I think I should object vigorously if I saw another about to become your wife," she told him with an attempt at lightness.

"You care enough for that?" he asked.

"Yes," she said.

Lithgow knew then that she had meant all that the little line in her letter had betrayed. He would have drawn her to him, but she released herself gently.

"It is not enough to satisfy me." She shook her blonde head. "I am determined to love fiercely, completely, absorbingly. Until then, I shall not marry."

"Do you know what it is that teaches most people that they love?" he queried smilingly.

"Absence?"

"Possibly, but that which I meant was jealousy."

"Then I must ever remain in ignorance that I love," retorted she. "I have not a spark of it in my make-up."

"I will show you that I have if you allow yourself to become enamored of Zuñega," he warned. "Shall I bring him up here to-morrow? He and Annizae are certain to be lonely and I shall be busy. I know that you will be glad to model a face like Zuñega's."

"Bring them," she urged. "Miss Durame can make a study of the one you call—Annizae? yes, Annizae. She can send it to the coming exhibit. She has not been very successful of late."

"I'll ride out on the cars with you," said Lithgow, as she made preparations for home-going. "I wish to see the mother. Then I'll come back to the hotel. Oh, yes, there is time."

He was very tender in his manner. He realized how far he had deviated from his allegiance, and sought to make amends for it in a way that would satisfy himself without exciting her suspicions. His swerving had not been of the nature that some men would call swerving, but in his heart he knew that it really had been more fatal than a palpable faithlessness. The latter he could have forgotten.

When Lithgow went up to the parlor which separated Zuñega's room from Annizae's, he found Felipe and his pretty wife ensconced there, having been invited to dine by no less a personage than the lawyer himself. Annizae had been somewhat metamorphosed by the addition of a longer skirt and a visit to a neighboring establishment for footwear. Zuñega's soft, black beard had disappeared, leaving his features remarkable for their purity of outline. Otherwise he was unchanged. Lithgow viewed him with renewed admiration.

Zuñega drew Lithgow aside.

"Felipe tells me of a band of men, señor, who are united by the hope of freeing Cuba," he whispered. "Felipe himself belongs to it. All who can prove themselves true-hearted Cubans may join. It is there that I wish to go. To-night they meet. The señor has no objections?"

"Certainly not," replied Lithgow. "But what do they do?"

"That is what I wish to learn, señor. I would be one of their number. The day may come when I could help as Felipe helps. He gives all that he can to push the work on."

"I will ask Felipe if I may go with him," decided Lithgow. "I can tell better than he, perhaps, whether it is a legitimate affair or one for the sole purpose of drawing just enthusiatic fellows as he."

So it came about that the whole party, with the exception of the lawyer, went to attend a meeting of those dauntless, heroic souls whose hearts never will rest until Cuba is free or until they have died in attempting to free her.

Fresh from the island, Lithgow understood fully the great depths of the wrong which constantly was being wrought against Cuba by the power that called itself the "mother country," but might more truthfully have termed itself the "monster country." He listened to the grave, earnest speeches that were made. He watched the strong, passionate visages lighted by the pure fire of patriotism. Exiles, whose all had been swallowed by the confiscating government; soldiers, who had fought valiantly in the ten-year war; youths, in whose veins beat the elixir of liberty—a striking assemblage, and one which was destined to write its hopes in a language that Spain could not feign to misunderstand.

Lithgow felt that he was in the solemn presence of that mighty Spirit which "was in the Beginning," and broods yearningly over every nation—deathless, starry-eyed Liberty. His pulses throbbed in sympathy with the heroic utterances that found voice about him. He was charmed by the calmness and deliberation which characterized the speeches of one lofty-browed man, to whom all appeared to look as to a leader.

"Who is he?" he inquired of an enthusiastic Cuban, who applauded vociferously.

"Marti—José Marti. Dios guard him! He and the council of direction alone stand between the government and immediate insurrection."

"You can't mean it!" exclaimed Lithgow in a low tone. "I have but just come from Havana. Everything is as quiet as a—Campo Santo. There is no suspicion of an uprising."

"And there must be no suspicion, señor," smiled the Cuban.

"When the leaders are convinced that their plans are perfect and there can be no chance of failure, the word will be given, and before Spain has time to send over fresh troops the Cubans will begin their fight for independence under the same generals who led them twenty years ago."

"These are the souls with whom Raquel, on a far-away sugar plantation, ignorantly is *en rapport*," he thought, feeling that he had in some measure discovered the reason for her wakeful patriotism, kindled by unseen fires. "The subtle power of the freedom-hungering minds convened here is flashed straight through space to whatever heart beats in unison with the movement for liberty. The mental ear of the poet, the prophet, the hero catches the bugle-call long before those in the valleys are awakened. A mind can receive only that for which it is ripe. She shall hear more specifically of these voices that proclaim that Cuba shall be free. I will show her the truth of those words which I quoted to her half idly: 'Every sound that is spoken over the round world, which thou oughtest to hear, will vibrate on thy ear.'"

He was won from his thoughts by a movement from Zuñega. He turned to see what occasioned it. He was startled almost by the expression on the youth's face. It seemed transfigured by an inspiring passion that flamed in his wonderful eyes and fairly blazed through his marvellous gold tinting.

"*Cuba libre! Cuba libre!*"

Every voice took up the musical, impassioned cry.

Zuñega's was more musical, more impassioned than any. It attracted the gaze of the leader. The eyes of the two men appeared to meet in a recognition that each felt perceptibly. José Marti spoke to the man nearest him. That man made his way in Zuñega's direction. He approached to the side of the youth.

"You are a stranger—no?" he inquired in a low tone. "Señor Marti wishes to speak with you."

When the meeting broke up and a babel of speech ensued, as each exchanged greetings with his neighbors, Lithgow followed Zuñega and his guide to where the dreamy but forceful countenance of the leader was visible.

"You are a stranger. Tell me of yourself," he said simply.

Lithgow, looking from one face to the other, was astonished

to see that the two possessed a resemblance that, while intangible, was noticeable. He could not locate it, unless it lay in the eyes, which were liquid with a melancholy that the fever of patriotism did not burn away. To this natural melancholy was added, in Marti's orbs, the sadness which had come from watching over the woes of his crushed land. His glance had a peculiar far-reaching quality, as if he peered through the mists of the future. Did he perceive the death that waited for him on a Cuban battlefield?

"To-day I set foot on free soil for the first time," Zuñega said. "When I return to Cuba, it will be to make her free also?"

Marti smiled. The smile had the virtue of a caress, so sweet was it.

"You will return?"

"When you bid, master." Zuñega bowed low.

Marti watched him with visible interest; then he turned his glance upon Lithgow inquiringly. Lithgow held out his business card with a word of explanation.

Marti extended his hand cordially.

"Then you are one I wish to see," he said. "If you have been going through Cuba on business, you have done so with observing eyes. I have some questions that you, unprejudiced, may be better able to answer than a Cuban. Will you come to see me to-morrow?"

"With unbounded pleasure," agreed Lithgow. "May I petition that this youth who has won your attention may accompany me? He has come from the island with me. I can satisfy you in regard to him; and he is of a mind to be of great service to the cause."

"He is needed," answered Marti. "He has the face of a hero. There will be work for him to do. Bring him. All Cubans are brothers."

Thus was forged the link that united Zuñega with the chain of dauntless hearts that hoped to draw around Cuba the magic circle of freedom, within which the iron heel of the tyrant could nevermore enter.

They made their way back to where they had left Annizae with Felipe and his wife. Felipe regarded Zuñega with reverential glance. His manner was full of respect. He did not understand why the one so lately from the island and so igno-

rant of this Cuban movement had been summoned to the side
of the beloved Marti; but there was no envy in his breast.
He pressed his wife's hand close to his side, and told her that
they were honored in that they had brought him here.

On the way back to the hotel, Zuñega's finely poised head
turned neither to the right nor to the left. There was an elation in his soul that had not been there when he had been told
that he was heir to an estate and title. He felt that a more
important legacy had fallen to him, that of striking blows
which should rend Cuba's gyves asunder.

CHAPTER XVII.

WITH his slippered feet stretched out in front of a cosy fire,
that night after the Cuban assembly of patriots, Lithgow sat
long. He smoked many cigars, and their delicate fragrance
made him half fancy that he was back in the sunny court with
Raquel. He was trying to convince himself that he owed it
to her and her father to write and report concerning the voyage and the lawyer's reception of Annizae and Zuñega. He
wanted to tell her about this club of liberty-loving men with
whom Zuñega was to become identified. The pleasure with
which he dwelt on the thought of writing to her showed him
clearly that he was unfaithful to Beatrice in heart. He argued
first one way and then the other, as he smoked. But all the
time he knew that he intended to write. Finally he drew
the table up to him and began.

With his swift, business hand he covered sheet after sheet,
while the fire grew low and the gas-lights dim. He wrote as
he never had written before, as he never would again. When
he had finished, he read the words over, arose, thrust back
with the toe of his slipper the graying ashes, and held the
closely penned pages over the dying coals. The blue tongues
of flame reached up feebly and touched the edges of the
sheets, blackening them. He watched while the paper curled
and the ink faded. Finally he loosened his fingers and let
the letter fall. It blazed up fiercely; but in another moment
only black shadows lay where the written passion of a life had
been.

"The story it told is better there than in her heart," he said with a sigh. "If she loved, it could but make her unhappy. If she loved not, it would be of small value to her. I did not dream that I was going to reveal that."

Resuming his seat, he wrote a description of the things which he knew both she and her father would be anxious to hear relative to his erstwhile brigand charges, and terminated with an account of the manner in which they had spent the evening. At the close, he added:

"Your revolutionary spirit will be gratified to learn that Zuñega is determined to devote his fortune to the liberation of Cuba. He has taken the first step in his career as a Cuban patriot this night. He requested me to say to you, 'Zuñega will not forget!' I know its significance. You are responsible for the noble resolution which burns within him; he has told me so. Cuba may owe a portion of her freedom to the efforts of an isolated maiden who mourns her powerlessness. Who can tell?"

According to arrangements, Lithgow took Annizae and Zuñega up to Beatrice's studio the following morning, with Felipe's little wife, Anita, to act in the capacity of interpreter.

Beatrice made no attempt to hide her delight when she beheld Zuñega.

"Superb!" she cried. "Why, he might have come down from Olympus!" And she lost no time in getting to work. Annizae and Anita watched her curiously. Zuñega feigned indifference, to hide the timidity which beset him with this open admiration bestowed upon him, as if he had been an animal at the Zoo, or an object of art. But he watched the sculptor from his lustrous eyes with a critical examination. He noted her blonde head, the straight, fearless look from the blue orbs, the supple figure. He divined that this was "the other one" of whom Lithgow had spoken; and he compared her with Raquel. It was a difficult thing to accomplish satisfactorily, because they were so dissimilar. This northern girl chilled him with her pale beauty; her business-like method bewildered him. She seemed to look at him without seeing him at all. He felt half afraid of her. Yet, when she smiled into his questioning eyes, and appeared to recollect that he was alive, and not like the plaster casts which peered down upon him from the wall, he liked her.

She occasionally plied both him and Annizae with queries concerning themselves, and he answered through the lips of Anita.

"Tell me, please, how you saved the stolen señorita from becoming the wife of the chief?" she requested at last, wishing to awaken in his face something which seemed to slumber there, defying her efforts to arouse it.

He obeyed reluctantly, fearing that it would not be courteous to refuse, but he made his part of the undertaking very small indeed.

"You are humble, as befits a knight who loves a lady," smiled Beatrice, working very rapidly to snatch the expression in his eyes. Translated by Anita, the sentence reached Zuñega differently, and he answered quickly:

"Who once has seen her, loves her; even the Americano."

Not until Beatrice lifted her head with the startled motion of a bird did he realize what he had said. He would have rectified it if he had known how, but Beatrice had gone on with her work again, and he tried to make himself believe that she had not heard it. To satisfy himself, he asked Anita to repeat to him what she had said in the way of translation.

"Tell the señorita that you did not understand it properly," he told her anxiously.

Anita looked a trifle rebellious, but complied.

Beatrice smiled at him reassuringly over her heap of clay.

"I am certain what Anita repeated was the truth, whether or not it was what you told her to speak," she said with a conviction that was disconcerting. "Had I been either of you men, I would have robbed the old Frenchman of her by running away with her myself. I can't imagine where was Lithgow's American spirit. You talk of giving freedom to your island, yet you took her from the chief only to let her become the purchase of another!"

Zuñega looked troubled. He did not understand that she spoke half lightly. Her words brought up before him the very thing which he sought most strenuously to keep from sight, the picture of Raquel as a wife—another's wife.

He got up from his chair abruptly and began moving about the room. When he saw that they all observed him, he remembered where he was and came back and sat down.

"I was wishing I was in Cuba," he explained simply. "I shall go there again, please Dios, soon!"

His face had settled again into its gentle sadness.

Beatrice worked away nervously. Her eyes were very bright and very difficult to read. She was in that mood when every touch of her fingers was decisive and told on her modelling. She knew it and made the most of it. She asked no more questions concerning Raquel. She simply bestowed a quizzical glance upon Lithgow, when he came up to see how the work was progressing.

Miss Durame had taken possession of Annizae and was enthusiastic over the effective sketch which was emanating from beneath her brush. Other artists came in to look enviously at the models, and, altogether, the studio wore an air of bustling activity.

Lithgow came again late in the day, and remained to pass his criticisms upon the productions until darkness compelled cessation of work; then he escorted Beatrice and the two models out to the delightful home where the gentle, gray-haired Mrs. Warrington presided, as dignifiedly as she had in more prosperous days over the luxurious mansion which had been hers before misfortune had overtaken the family.

Some little awkwardness was noticeable on Annizae's part, at first, but the apparently unseeing manner in which they glossed over her *gaucheries* did much to re-establish her self-esteem and prepare her for the more trying ordeals which were likely to await her on the other side of the ocean. With some trepidation, she dimly discerned a few of the difficulties which might beset her in the way of etiquette as mistress of Harberton Towers, and she covertly essayed to make her own some of the ease which distinguished her hostess. She stole stealthy glances at Mrs. Warrington's well-arranged coiffure, her beautiful white skin, her manicured nails. A medley of troublesome suggestions went rioting through her brain. She was not wholly without adaptability. Life in the family of an English gentleman had not been without its salutary effect upon her, but the free-and-easy existence which she had led since that time had not contributed to perfection of table manners.

Zuñega's opportunity for observation in Havana and on the voyage to New York had not been unimproved. His dreamy eyes made a note of everything, no matter how trivial. Lithgow even felt some alarm lest his assertion that the youth had been forest-bred would be discredited.

Mrs. Warrington gladly would have entered into conversation with Annizac, but that being a difficult matter, owing to the difference in their languages, contented herself with plying the woman with northern comforts. She was intensely interested in this little romance which had come to their knowledge through Lithgow, and she was infatuated with Zuñega's beauty. The fact that he really was motherless appealed to her wonderfully, and she allowed herself to fancy that her own dead son would have looked like this young Apollo had he lived. She was very tender in her glance and speech toward the young fellow, and he appreciated and responded to it with the open-heartedness of a boy.

Lithgow noted, smiled, and commented to himself.

"Zuñega is safe here, but when he becomes Lord Harberton he will have to be careful how he succumbs to the gentle arts of womankind. All of the British matrons will not be as innocent of intention as dear Mrs. Warrington."

This was but one of the occasions on which Zuñega and Annizae partook of the Warrington hospitality during the days that intervened before Mr. Bertram had made all arrangements for departure.

And, in all that week, Beatrice, unlike her sex, resolutely refrained from making any inquiries regarding Raquel. "He must tell me voluntarily," she decided to herself during night hours, hours which heretofore had been given over to sleep, "Certainly something has altered him. He cannot pretend it was my decision in regard to our marriage. He is preoccupied half of his time, and his eyes—they seem to have absorbed some of Zuñega's melancholy. There is but one explanation, seemingly; but why under the sun does he let her marry that old Frenchman?"

All of which seemed to point to the suspicion that Beatrice Warrington was on the eve of making a few additional discoveries in regard to herself and her emotions.

Saturday's sunrise saw the great ocean liner at its dock, waiting for the signal to depart. Its taffrail was lined with the faces of voyagers, eager and indifferent; happy and sad; hopeful and *blasé*.

The Cubans, with Lithgow and the lawyer, stood looking down at the upturned faces on the pier. To Annizae's eyes, the unfamiliar, gesticulating multitude seemed half crazed. Lithgow was watching to see if he could find the countenances of Beatrice and her mother, for Beatrice had wagered that she would be down to see them off. But the ship moved slowly out of the slip and the visages on shore began to fade. He waved his hat gayly at some of his friends who had chartered a tug, which was whistling and puffing strenuously in an effort to see the steamer safely out of the harbor.

When fairly *en route*, he busied himself in ensconcing Annizae comfortably. This wintry Atlantic voyage was likely to test her much more severely than the calm, balmy passage up from the Gulf had done, and he was anxious that she should suffer as little as was possible.

The days which followed were such as belong to the life of one of the floating hotels that cross the deeps so blithely through all seasons. Annizae never emerged from her stateroom until the morning before they reached Queenstown; consequently the men were left free to occupy themselves as they would.

Zuñega, with a spirit of inquiry of which Lithgow had not supposed him possessed, made himself thoroughly familiar with the ship and its workings, and seemed to derive information by absorption, for he asked few questions, but appeared to have found out everything that was worth knowing.

"You put me to shame, *my lord*," the American said one day facetiously.

"*Porqué, señor?*" questioned Zuñega wonderingly.

"You have learned so much in the short time which has been at your disposal. I might have been a walking dictionary if I had half of your enterprise. To shame an American in the matter of energy is quite an achievement, I assure you."

"I am but making up for lost time, señor," returned Zuñega. "What is there not for me to learn if I am to succeed my father? What must I not accumulate in the way of information if I am to be of service to Cuba? It is well to know about the workings of an immense vessel like this. Cuba may need such some day, only they will be manned for war."

"Ah!" murmured Lithgow comprehendingly. "If you will

allow me to play any part in the struggle, I believe that I will choose to follow in the steps of those famous buccaneers who made the Isle of Pines their rendezvous. You will need ammunition, all of the paraphernalia of carnage. What could be more to my taste than to carry contraband goods? You do the fighting and I can do the necessary supplying of munitions of war. Life is not exhausted yet! We will deserve the approbation of the little señorita."

Zuñega threw himself down on a coil of rope sombrely.

"She then will be the Señora Theuriet," he reminded. "She whom you call Miss Warrington said that if she had been either of us she would have taken the señorita from the Frenchman and have run away with her."

Lithgow straightened himself up from his lounging attitude.

"Oh, did she talk to you of Raquel?"

"Once only, then she said that which I have repeated."

Lithgow lapsed into ruminating silence. Zuñega, with his hands clasped back of his head, stared up into the pale blue of the sky. Already he was hungry for the deep, rich tints of his birthplace. England could never hold him, he said decisively. There was but one land in the world for him—Cuba.

Sitting abaft, night after night, chilled by the sharpness of this atmosphere, which was so different from any he had known, he had formulated plans that appeared magical, but which he dreamed that he would be able to carry into effect. From a youth he had expanded into a thinking, reasoning man, during this period which had elapsed since his passing out from the forest. It seemed to him that he had lived years upon years in the days following his decision to forsake the brigand camp. All the life previous was now like a dream. He had ripened under the stress of action as fruit ripens under the torrid heat of noonday.

Annizae, convalescent but irritable, and craving the warmth of the tropics, claimed their attention the next day. At sundown they caught sight of Fastnet, and at midnight the mails were taken off at Queenstown. The next morning they rode at anchor off Liverpool.

Even Annizae betrayed a trifle of excitement at the prospect of soon setting foot on the soil which was denied her in years

past.   Both she and Zuñega, accustomed to tropical dilatori-
ness in all matters, awaited with enviable patience the coming
of the second tender, while the two Americans were irked perceptibly.   There was the usual scurry to get through the cus-
toms and book for London by the first train.

The two Cubans exhibited intense curiosity in the garden-
like country through which the train swept, and Zuñega
looked with interest upon the various parks, turreted towers,
and magnificent façades, which Lithgow pointed out to him
in the distance as homes no finer than his own was said to be.

With American extravagance and faith in the power of appearances, Mr. Bertram insisted on registering at the Metro-
pole and established Zuñega in the finest suite procurable.
Confident that Zuñega was the long-sought heir, he meant to
spare no expense in proving the validity of the claimant's
rights, even if the solicitors should decide that the proofs were
not conclusive.   Taken before an English court, he thought
that the decree would be that the heir to the Harberton title
had really arisen; and he intended that Zuñega should attract
all of the attention which his appearance was sure to command.   Mr. Bertram was full of excitement; but he successfully concealed it beneath a most business-like exterior.   He
had notified the London lawyers that he thought he had secured the right man, but he had not apprised them that he
would sail on that steamer.   For reasons of his own, he wished
to take them by surprise.   And he did so.

After becoming established to his entire satisfaction, and
thoroughly recuperated after the voyage, he called a four-
wheeler and, with his three companions, was driven directly
to the office of Lambert and Milman, Q. C., Holborn.

Zuñega, Annizac, and Lithgow seated themselves in the
anteroom while Mr. Bertram sent in his card.   Zuñega glanced
about him curiously.   His retentive memory took in every
detail of the dingy, vault-like apartment.   Compared with
the luxurious appointments of the American office buildings,
through which he had been escorted by Lithgow, this little
room, presided over by a gloomy looking young man, appeared like a dungeon.   He could scarcely realize that he was
on the point of meeting the men who had managed his father's
business, as well as that of the previous incumbent of the title.

At a signal from the imperious "Buttons," Mr. Bertram

went forward through a heavy nail-studded door into the inner sanctum of Mr. Lambert, who, with surprise on his features, stood to receive him.

"If you had notified us of your coming, one of us would have met you at Liverpool, Mr. Bertram," said the Englishman, welcoming his American colleague warmly. "Mr. Milman has stepped out. He will return in a short time, no doubt. You have brought the claimant with you?"

"He is in the outer chamber," replied Mr. Bertram. "Shall I call him in?"

Visible curiosity shone in the solicitor's blue eyes, but he pulled his nether lip reflectively.

"Perhaps we would better wait until Mr. Milman comes in," he hesitated. "I will confess that we are anticipating more than we ought, possibly, from this discovery of yours. I should not wish to deprive him of the first—oh, here he is! Milman, this is Mr. Bertram."

The younger lawyer greeted Mr. Bertram with trenchant glance. He had come through another entrance into his own office, and had not observed the occupants of the anteroom.

"Why, you have taken us by surprise, Mr. Bertram," he exclaimed. "I hope that your success of which you wired us has not proven to be a hoax!"

"I think not," Bertram answered modestly. "I believe that I am prepared to furnish you with the lost heir to Harberton Towers."

"Will you tell us by what process you found him?" requested Mr. Lambert, settling himself comfortably in his leathern chair, and placing his hands before him in an attitude suggestive of prayer. Mr. Milman took a seat and leaned toward the American interestedly.

"Really, I did very little," confessed Bertram. "A friend of mine was going down to Cuba on business. I told him the story and asked him to keep his eyes and ears open during his journeyings through the interior of the island. The detective whom I had engaged there was discovering nothing, and I thought this chance was too good not to be employed. What the result was, I think that I would better allow my friend to relate himself. He has accompanied me over in order to do this. He is in the anteroom."

Mr. Lambert looked over his shoulder at Mr. Milman.

"The claimant is there also," he informed his partner.

Mr. Milman thrust his fingers with a degree of excitement through his rough, bristling hair.

"We appear to be getting down to business," he remarked. "Shall we have him in?"

"I think that you would understand how simply it all has come about, if you were to hear Mr. Hamilton tell of the singular circumstances which led to the accidental discovery of the heir," suggested Mr. Bertram.

"Mr. Hamilton is your friend?"

"Yes; he visited the island in the interests of his firm, a coffee company."

"Pray ask him to enter."

Lithgow obeyed the signal from Bertram, and was introduced to the judicial-appearing English solicitors. In a rapid, concise manner, he rehearsed all the events which had culminated in such an unexpected way for Zuñega. The lawyers were very passive at first, but, as the story unrolled, their interest and belief in its verity increased, until, when Lithgow finished, they were enthusiastic over what appeared to be success to all of their hopes.

"It seems incredible," commented Mr. Milman; "its very simplicity and lack of complication is all the more remarkable in that we have struggled through so many tangled-up affairs during the years in which we have prosecuted this search. There have been other claimants, you understand; they have been disposed of satisfactorily, however. If any difficulty arises now it will be because of those who believe themselves to be the next of kin, and they will resent this Cuban heir being brought forward. There is sure to be some fighting on that score, but, if we are convinced that this man is what you believe him to be, we shall be able to place him in possession of his rights. Am I not correct, Mr. Lambert?"

"You are correct," bowed the elder man. "Let us have *him* in now."

And Zuñega was summoned.

Lithgow's eyes were on him as he entered. His magnificent physique had never appeared to better advantage than it did at that moment in the doorway. His well-set head was thrown back with that alert, proud air which was a part of his forest heritage. Framed in its jet waves, his gold-tinted face,

13

with its dreamy eyes and firm, scarlet mouth, was startling in its impressiveness.

Bertram's gaze was fixed on the countenances of the Englishmen. This was the surprise which he had not meant to lose. He noted the changes which passed over their visages in quick succession. The expression which remained, in spite of their facial control, was one of astonishment with which was mingled satisfaction. The room was perfectly silent for a full minute, while the two men leaned forward eagerly, unaware that they did so. Then they turned their eyes upon each other, as if to ascertain if the effect had been the same.

Mr. Lambert was the first to recover himself sufficiently to rise and extend his fingers to Zuñega.

"We are glad to welcome you," he said, with his eyes still on the youth's face. "This is Mr. Milman. Will you be seated?"

Milman shook hands somewhat as one might with an apparition, and placed a chair for him.

Zuñega looked at Lithgow for encouragement. The manner of these men bewildered him.

"You may desire to procure an interpreter," suggested Mr. Bertram. "He has picked up a little English, but not enough to carry on a conversation of this nature, while the woman, Annizae, speaks nothing but Spanish. Of course Mr. Hamilton will act in the capacity, but you would be better satisfied to obtain one who knows nothing of the story."

"The suggestion is a good one," nodded Mr. Lambert, "but in that case we will have to postpone investigation. I confess that I am anxious to waste no time in satisfying myself as to the reality of all this. We can secure an interpreter for to-morrow; in the mean time, may I inspect the ring which this individual is said to possess?"

Lithgow repeated the request to Zuñega, who drew the ornament from his hand. Together with the one which Lithgow had been given by Bertram on his departure for Cuba, it was placed in the outstretched palm of the old lawyer. He reached over his desk for a strong magnifier, then passed to the window and stood with his back toward them. Presently he called his partner to him. They conversed in cautious tones that did not convey any information to the three other occupants of the room. Finally Mr. Lambert moved to a private safe, and, after some peering, brought forth something which they studied together, glancing now and then at Zuñega with half-closed, calculating eyes.

Under this trying ordeal, Zuñega sat imperturbably. He had no idea what they were doing. Lithgow was wondering; Mr. Bertram divined, and found his conjectures were right when, some time after, he was summoned to their side.

Mr. Lambert held a daguerreotype of a strong English face, on which a dogged self-will was emphatically written.

"This is a good likeness of the late Lord Harberton after he returned from the Indies," explained the solicitors.

Bertram looked from it to them meaningly.

"Other evidence would scarcely be necessary," he commented, "though the eyes are quite different. This daguerreotype possesses the round English eye. Zuñega has the long, sad orb that is said to belong to those of Carib extraction. I understand that his mother had a suspicion of Carib blood."

"His eyes are exactly like those of Lady Harberton," pronounced Mr. Milman with decision.

".His face has the intensity that is a characteristic of tropical natures," Bertram continued thoughtfully, "yet it retains the dominant features that this picture of Lord Harberton exhibits—chin of great determination, immense width of forehead."

"His nose is like his fa— like Lord Harberton's, also," said Mr. Lambert.

Mr. Milman laughed.

"I believe that both of us are inclined to agree with Mr. Bertram and Mr. Hamilton that the Cuban claimant's chances are phenomenally good," he remarked, no longer attempting to conceal his pleasure.

"Things as certain have been known to disappoint," warned the older lawyer, returning to his chair and passing three rings to Zuñega for inspection.

"Ask him to select his own from among them," he said to Lithgow.

Zuñega studied them well, then handed them to Lithgow with a shake of his black head.

"They are alike," he said.

Neither Lithgow nor Mr. Bertram were able to detect difference between the three.

"Yet there is a decided difference," Mr. Lambert informed them. "All of them are copies of the original ring, which never becomes the property of any one but the reigning lord. It has a strange history. No one ever thinks of wearing it as you wear this," he told Zuñega, as he returned to the youth his own ornament. "It is called a dangerous possession and is employed only as a seal. If you are proven to be the heir to the Harberton title, you will become the owner of it and its unique history. The ring which I have given back to you will belong to your second son. You see the first son always stands the chance of getting the original; it descends to him as surely as the lands. Your possession of that ring would seem to prove that your father was he whom you claim. He was a fourth son and he possessed such a ring. These others are merely perfect copies, made to assist us in our search."

"Does not the possession of the ring prove his identity conclusively?" questioned Lithgow.

Mr. Lambert shook his head.

"We must learn beyond all manner of doubt how this ring was obtained," he explained.

"That Annizae can tell," Lithgow declared.

"But I fear that we must have other susbtantiation than merely her word."

"I don't know how we are to procure it," Bertram said.

"There is her own child," reminded Lithgow. "Could not that personage be employed in such a way that she might be betrayed into some show of maternal feelings?"

"That would prove little."

"But she desires that he shall share with Zuñega in this matter of the Harberton fortune."

Mr. Lambert lifted his brows and Mr. Milman smiled inscrutably, while Lithgow went on to explain that the chief lever used in getting her to England had been the suggestion that the place waited for her which would have been hers had Lord Harberton married her instead of Zuñega's mother.

"And she wishes to see the child whom she had no scruples about abandoning in his infancy," commented Mr. Lambert.

"She does not consider that she abandoned him," corrected the American lawyer. "As I understand, she thought only, in her heat of revenge, of placing her own child in what she deemed his rightful position, and—of breaking the heart of the woman whom she felt had usurped her."

"She secured her desire so far as Lady Harberton was concerned," returned the old Englishman slowly. "The most beautiful woman that I ever saw, she cared nothing for the admiration which was lavished upon her. She never was happy in England, and mourned unceasingly for her lost child. The sight of the one which had been foisted upon her never failed to irritate. It was a source of considerable trouble between her and her husband. She would have cast the little one off, but the justness of Lord Harberton's nature would not permit him to do that. He had the lad well-reared and gave him a fine education, providing him with a fair allowance, which still continues. Certain conditions were mentioned in the will, however, which remain to be fulfilled. I am sorry to say that the young fellow does not conform to those conditions, in which event the allowance stops. It would be much better for Carlos Vaschez if he were forced to work, and work hard. He squanders everything. An inveterate gambler, the passion seems to have been in him from earliest boyhood. He knows nothing about himself. The reason for Lord Harberton's interest in him has never reached his ears; in fact, he does not know that Lord Harberton ever was interested. All was intrusted to us. He is certain of his allowance; but, at the pace he moves, he will not be certain of that long."

"Annizae is very suspicious," remarked Lithgow. "She is fearful that she is brought over here for punishment, but I have promised her that, instead of retribution, she shall meet with gain. On those grounds alone would she come."

Mr. Lambert closed his lips very tightly and worked them cogitatively.

"What do you think about it, Milman?" he questioned at last. "Would Lady Harberton rest in her tomb if we did not see meted out to the woman the punishment that she devised?"

Lithgow had been translating to Zuñega all that transpired; now Zuñega spoke rapidly and earnestly to Lithgow.

"The claimant says that he will see no harm come to Annizae," Lithgow repeated to the lawyers. "He considers that the one whom you call Carlos Vaschez is his brother, in that

they had the same father.   He is willing to share with him,
but he insists that nothing whatever shall be done to Annizae.
Rather than that he will give up all idea of claiming his
rights."

The lawyers regarded Zuñega with mingled feelings, principal among which was surprise.

"Will he tell us why he entertains such warm affection for
the person who not only deprived him of all his heritage but
broke his mother's heart?" inquired Mr. Lambert, a trifle sar-
castically.

Zuñiga turned his face gravely upon the questioner.   Lithgow gave his answer:

"She wronged me, but she made me a Cuban.   I had rather
be a Cuban than an Englishman."

Both Englishmen smiled.

"Ah, you do not know us yet," replied Mr. Milman, "and—
you have not seen Harberton Towers."

A sudden thought seemed to strike the older solicitor.

"What do you say to a trip down to the Towers to-morrow,
Milman?" he said suggestively.

"I don't understand," confessed Mr. Milman.   "Why?"

"I would like to see the effect the place would have on the
woman."

"Oh, you mean to—take these—friends down?"

"Certainly.   What could be better? There is a full length
portrait there of Lord Harberton, which I imagine this young
man will resemble even more than he does the daguerreotype;
and there are other reasons."

"It is a good idea," acquiesced Mr. Milman.   "I will wire
down to Wickham to meet the eleven-forty. Will that be right?"

"Yes.   Suppose that we take a look at this Annizae."

Mr. Bertram ushered her in.   She shook with unconquerable anxiety that was evidenced in her bearing.   Left alone
in that outer office, she had sat in a shiver of apprehension,
which rapidly was culminating in terror when Mr. Bertram's
kindly visage appeared.   What awaited her, her imagination
pictured in colors that drove the blood from her heart.
What she really encountered when she faced the five men
were simply looks of keen curiosity on the part of the two
Englishmen and glances of reassurance on the part of the
remainder.

No questions were asked her. She was allowed to maintain silence, while arrangements were made for the following day. Her spirits began to rise insensibly.

Surreptitiously she took two or three long breaths, of which her fear had deprived her during the last hour.

When Lithgow explained to her that they were to go on the morrow to the place over which Zuñega's mother had reigned as mistress, all anxiety on her features gave way to an exultation. She supposed that the entire matter had been settled, and she was grateful to the Americano for keeping his promise so well that not a query had been put to her.

"*Gracias á Dios!*" she murmured fervently. "Who would have thought that my prayers would be answered?"

CHAPTER XVIII.

THE members of Mr. Bertram's party were not the only ones who accompanied the solicitors to Harberton Towers the next morning. An imposing lawyer of title and a dapper gentleman who boasted that he could speak seven languages completed the group.

Lord Lestonbridge inquired occasionally of Mr. Bertram regarding his country much as people interrogate African explorers concerning the savages. The dapper interpreter occupied himself in conversing with Zuñega relative to his impressions of England.

Annizac was busy peering through the car windows at the rapidly passing panorama of exquisite country. Suppressed excitement was visible in her manner. Again and again she whispered to herself that over this ground had travelled the woman whom she had hated. These fair English scenes had been familiar to the eyes of Zuñega's mother. Had they become hateful to her because of her hopeless grief? Annizac was tasting the sweets of revenge.

"*Dios es bueno!*" she said joyously. Had God indeed not brought her to this enjoyment of what had been another's pain? Her belief that He had was a source of much satisfaction. On their arrival at the little station they found two conveyances in waiting. Lithgow, Mr. Milman, Zuñega, and Annizae took places in the first. As it rattled over the stones of the village street, the two from Cuba looked out curiously and encountered the questioning gaze of villagers at windows and doors.

The red-tiled roofs of the cottages gave back the brightness of the morning sun; the tiny front gardens gloried in a riot of bloom.

At the extreme end of the long street they came to the ivy-covered church, with its great tower on which yet remained the beacon that had carried intelligence to twelve counties in earlier times. Out from the mass of green gleamed the face of the clock.

Zuñega observed these things with a peculiar sensation creeping over him. How many times had the father whom he never had known looked up at this clock-face as he now was doing?

"The Harbertons have been buried here for centuries," spoke Mr. Milman. "Would you like to see the interior of the church?"

"Of course," answered Lithgow for Zuñega, "if we may."

The cool, damp air, which seems inseparable from old English edifices of worship, rushed out and chilled them as they entered. Passing through the base of the tower, they stepped into the nave. High, cushioned seats shut in the aisle which led to the reading-desk, back of which rose the organ, domed by a ceiling frescoed in semblance of starry heavens.

At the right, closed in by iron gates, were the tombs of the Harbertons:—great marble sarcophagi upon which the recumbent effigies of the dead were stretched in silent majesty.

It was the first time that Zuñega had seen such pomp and splendor for the dead. In the gloom of the old church the tombs were more impressive than those in the Campo Santo at Havana. A certain pride became his. These were his kin! Their lengthy title was his! He gazed at the white marble image of her who had been his mother, and a thrill of tenderness went through his heart. It seemed to him that she looked like Raquel. And, with that thought, a great joy filled him. Did not these things prove that he indeed was Raquel's equal? He bent and touched his lips to the white marble feet.

In the mean time, those who had been in the rear had seen

Annizae fly out of the church as if pursued by the evil one. In her mad rush she had tripped over a low gravestone, and now lay prostrate, groaning.

When once more placed in the carriage, she sat with her face buried in her hands, as if to shut out the sight of those white images, which had carried such unreasoning terror to her heart. Mr. Lambert regarded her with much interest. Zuñega was unable to elicit any information in response to his inquiries. She would not lift her eyes, and did not observe when the lodge was reached.

The old keeper, who came at the signal to swing the iron gates, stood bareheaded, staring with wide gaze at the face of Zuñega.

Mr. Lambert placed his hand on the arm of the lawyer of title.

"What do you think of that, Sir Lestonbridge?" he asked smilingly. "Even old Jepson perceives the resemblance."

"Did he know whom you intended to bring down?" inquired Sir Lestonbridge cautiously.

"No."

"Well, if this young fellow really is the heir, he will prove a valuable addition to the county. The Harbertons have always been in the House."

"He will be a very eligible *parti*," smiled the interpreter.

The carriages moved rapidly through the park.

"This is the place you have come so far to see, Annizae," said Lithgow remindfully.

Annizae lifted her face. It wore an expression he never had seen on it before. He could not decipher it.

A broadening expanse of acres, darkened occasionally by small forests of valuable trees, came into view. When the horses swung into the avenue of copper beeches, Lithgow could not repress an exclamation. An impressive gray pile of masonry had become visible. The magnificent colonnade of richly hued trees acted as a field-glass, at the far end of which arose massive Harberton Towers.

Situated on an eminence from which the ground swept away grandly to forest and river, two ivy-girdled towers jutted out from the north and south extremities of the many-windowed façade. Successive generations had added to it, and the style of architecture differed. Oriel windows peeped audaciously at mullioned windows.   Two huge wings extended toward the rose garden on the east; but these were not to be seen from the state entrance, above which rose a slender clock-tower, which bore the Harberton arms.

Annizae's eyes opened wide.   She seemed to hold her breath.   Zuñega was motionless.   Spell-bound, he watched his heritage draw near.   It was unlike what his wildest imagination had pictured.   These walls appeared to have stood there for ages.   He would enter them as his ancestors had entered them—for a brief space; then, rest in the cold quiet of the ivy-grown church.   Dimly he comprehended the responsibilities which would be his with these lands.   No more would he be free as the winds.   It almost seemed a bondage that he was coming into, a compact with the past and its actors; he was to step into their shoes, fill their places, eat on their plate.   He shot a swift glance back down the beech avenue.   For the moment he would have given all, Harberton · Towers itself, could he have found himself in Cuban forests and this a dream; but the next instant he had regained himself, with the thought that only thus could he secure that which would enable him to return to help the land for which his heart yearned.

The entrance was open.   Wickham, the butler who had served in the time of the former lord, stood ready to receive them.

Zuñega was conscious of a tremor as he stepped from the carriage, and, side by side with Mr. Milman, walked up the grassy terrace to the stone steps.   There, they paused for the others to come up abreast.   Mr. Lambert stepped ahead.

"Wickham," he said to the butler, "this is the latest claimant."

"Ay, an' 'e be the true one, sir," Wickham said with conviction, bowing low in front of Zuñega.   "My old heyes saw at a glance that 'e is the himage of the lamented Lord 'Aberton!"

Mr. Lambert glanced around triumphantly at the others. He acted as if he were trying to convince the Americans, when it was himself that he meant to convince.

"Were you here, Wickham, when the late lord returned from the West Indies?" queried Lord Lestonbridge.

"I 'ave bean in this 'ouse all my life, as I might say,

sir," replied Wickham proudly, "though I was but a lad then, sir."

" And this man looks like Lord Harberton?"

" Like both Lord and Lady 'Arberton, sir."

Mr. Bertram and Lithgow exchanged satisfied glances.

" You appear to be willing to accept him as genuine, Wickham, if no one else is," smiled Mr. Milman.

" Perhaps there be one who will see as I see, sir," Wickham said, struck with a sudden thought, as, from in front of the great hall fire-place where he had been lying, a hound raised himself dignifiedly and moved inquiringly toward them. " Beppo! Beppo, come 'ere!"

The beautiful creature advanced, contemplating the new-comers critically.

" Who be this, Beppo?" Wickham demanded, touching Zuñega deferentially on the arm to call the dog's attention to the stalwart figure.

Beppo obeyed by appearing to study with intent intelligence the face of the man thus indicated. Suddenly, unexpectedly, he raised himself and placed his paws on Zuñega's breast, bringing his own nose in close proximity to Zuñega's. The Cuban had stepped backward with surprise. The canines he had seen roaming through the streets of Cuban cities were more like the dogs of Constantinople than this wise-faced creature, who seemed to know as much or more than himself. There was something almost pathetic in the animal's examination of his features. Watching with some amazement, the group remained silent. The human expression in the dog's eyes was touching; it held anxiety, curiosity, wonderment, all that any features possibly could voice without words. As if not satisfied, he dropped to his feet, walked twice around Zuñega, then resumed his position of inquisitor, as if he were striving to recall some almost forgotten remembrance.

Zuñega suddenly realized that this dog had known his father, possibly had missed him. There was a strange comfort in the belief that the animal recognized something familiar in him, who never had set foot within these walls. Scarcely aware that he did so, he smiled into the creature's great, brown eyes. Instantly, Beppo dropped to his feet and thrust his nose into Zuñega's half-closed hand.

"See that? 'E knows!" declared Wickham decidedly. "'E never was far from the side of my master. Since my lord died, Beppo never 'as bean the same. 'E grieved like a babby for months, 'e did, sir."

Zuñega caressed Beppo tenderly. When he smiled, the dog pressed closer to him.

"'E 'as my lady's smile," Wickham commented to Mr. Lambert. "Beppo was fond of my lady."

"It is a pity that Wickham's and the dog's recognition would not be considered sufficient in law," said Mr. Milman to the others. "This was a confirmation which we had not thought of looking for. Will you permit me to take the keys, Wickham? Other people besides yourself remain to be convinced. We came down to go over the house. We wish him to see what will be his if he is what he thinks he is."

Wickham yielded up the keys reluctantly. It was one of his delights to lead a procession over the house, through room after room, up staircase after staircase of this massive structure, in the care of which he had been foremost servant for so many years. To be deprived of watching the effect produced on this one, whom he already considered the prospective master, was a hardship indeed. He stood and surveyed Zuñega as he followed after the lawyer with the dog closely pressing his side.

"If that do not tell them, what will?" he queried to himself. "Beppo hain't done that way since the master died; not even to me 'e hain't done so, me that 'e knows better than 'e knows 'isself!"

With pride that grew, Zuñega took in with comprehensive glances the details of the hall, dark with age-rich panelled oak. Trophies of the chase adorned its walls; armor gave back the flash of the sunlight; mailed knights, halberd in hand, appeared to stand guard over this vast home which awaited the coming of a master. Looking up, he could see them on the landings of the grand staircase, up which four horses could have been driven abreast. Through the opposite windows the leafless rose-garden was visible and the smooth lawn stretching to the river. To what a beautiful home had his mother been brought!

"I think that I will show you the marble hall first," said Mr. Milman, ushering the way. "More royal legs have been stretched under this board than under any other in England in times past, I will wager," he added, thumping the massive banqueting table with his knuckles. "Some of these family portraits are by Lely. Wickham has the whole thing by heart. This wonderfully carved screen at the end over the great fireplace is where the musicians have been concealed while royalty disported itself gayly."

Zuñega looked about at the tapestried walls, without realizing the historical value of what he viewed. To him it was all very magnificent. There had been nothing in his experience with which he could compare it. Annizae stepped along with a sense of her own insignificance. She was overpowered by the surrounding grandeur. She glanced at Zuñega and secretly marvelled that he appeared to be so at home in the midst of it. Lithgow and Mr. Bertram gave free vent to their unbounded admiration.

Mr. Milman unlocked a door near the fireplace. This revealed a flight of steps which conducted them into a broad, upper hall. From this they passed through the state drawing-rooms. These apartments were filled with curios from all quarters of the globe, and seemed replete with romances, in which the actors had been the personages whose painted semblances looked down upon them from the high walls.

"How delighted Mrs. Warrington would be with these 'ancestral halls'!" exclaimed Lithgow to Zuñega. "I cannot realize that they belong by right to you."

"It is a dream!" replied Zuñega softly, but his eyes shone. "What would I not give if the señorita could see! She was meant for such a place—no? When it all is mine, I would be able to pay her father's debts, is it not so? But it is too late! I only may fight for the country she loves!"

Mr. Milman was holding back a tapestry behind which the others had disappeared as if by magic. He looked smilingly at Zuñega's face, lighted with a fire that was not pride of possession, as the lawyer supposed.

"He will enjoy these things that seem to be claiming him," Mr. Milman remarked to Lithgow.

"Perhaps," admitted Lithgow, "but, unless I am mistaken, they will irk him. He is accustomed to freedom. He will have to be trained to bend his back and brain to the cares that weigh upon a master and a landlord."

" Most people would deem such cares agreeable ones," commented the Englishman.

" But they have not known what it was to be a Cuban brigand," returned Lithgow laughingly, passing behind the tapestry and through a sliding panel, which disclosed another flight of steps. " This savors of kingly escapes. I suppose these walls could tell strange tales."

"Indeed they could," Mr. Milman answered enthusiastically. " This is the secret entrance to the chapel. Many an ear has listened to prayers here while the worshippers have gone through the service little dreaming of the secret auditor. Many were the ones who were sheltered in the hidden passages of this house until the hour of political danger was past."

Mounting the steps they emerged into the gallery of the chapel. Right in the centre of the building, it had as solemn and impressive an atmosphere as if it stood alone. Softly tinted windows cast refulgence over everything.

Annizae's countenance was a study. She was confused by the magnitude of the dwelling. She began to understand why she and her child had been left in Cuba. Robert Percival had known that she would not be fitted to rule in such a place as this. She found herself wondering what the other woman from Cuba had felt when she had been led over the same ground. There had been the poison of loss to embitter everything for her, Annizae remembered. She rejoiced to feel that life here had not been all happiness for her beautiful rival. She was oppressed by the richness of the objects she looked upon. She thought with tenderness of the utter freedom of the forest life. Wickham's pale blue eye, with its trained stare, had appalled her more than anything that she yet had encountered. His friendliness for Zuñega had not extended to her. He had glanced her over from head to feet, and that glance had reduced her more in her own estimation than even the magnificence which followed.

On their way from the chapel to the library they passed down a long corridor, on one side of which there were great windows which overlooked the park. The opposite wall was hung with genealogical charts and a few portraits. It was to come into the corridor from that end that Mr. Milman and Mr. Lambert had planned the circuitous route which had been taken. To prevent any information being given save that which they desired to give themselves, they had chosen to dispense with the services of Wickham.

Suddenly Annizac gave a sharp cry.

All turned simultaneously to see what had brought it forth. Mr. Lambert and Mr. Milman looked at each other with significant glances that were full of satisfaction. Annizac had darted before the portrait of a most beautiful woman.

"Ah, I made you suffer—suffer!" she cried fiercely in Spanish. "I had my revenge! Is it not so? Did I not wring blood from your heart? You came here in my stead, but—had you ever a moment's joy?"

All of the evil passions of the mortal seemed warring in her face. She fairly was beside herself with the intoxication of revenge.

The interpreter repeated her words to the group. They observed her intently, while she appeared oblivious of any presence save her own and that which seemed to be in the unanswering picture. There was no gainsaying Annizac's recognition. She stood before it in the attitude of a judge administering sentence. Triumphantly she rehearsed the entire story of taking Zuñega from the ship and the subsequent flight into the mountains. She gave the details that filled the weeks immediately following the sailing of the vessel. She confessed frankly that, at first, she had little care whether the child died or lived. But by degrees her heart had grown tender toward him. After-thoughts brought her fear that they might not do for her own child any better than she did for theirs, so, with a vague idea of winning kindness for her deserted infant, she had vouchsafed better treatment to the one she had abducted. She related how they had drifted from one part of the island to the other. She had been in the tobacco fields of the Vuelta Abajo; she had picked coffee for planters; finally she had become a member of a nomadic band that plundered for subsistence; and later she had merged her fortunes with those of the notorious Gonzalo Alarcon, the terror of the country. She had grown proud of Zuñega with the passage of years. The memory of her hatred for his parents had faded somewhat. When she remembered, she joyed in the thought that of their heir she had succeeded in making a brigand, whose only retreat was the fastnesses of the forests. The solicitors had not dreamed of such an unrestricted outpouring. They had expected to drag the history from her by adroit questionings. This impassioned confession kept them silent. They did not even look at each other for fear that they might miss some of the life drama which was being told to the wonderful eyes which gazed forth from the frame on the wall. They were eyes that looked at one from whatever point of view. To the English lawyers they seemed to be appealing that punishment should be made to fall upon this offender who gloried so unrighteously in her crime. To Annizae they seemed to be suffering. To Zuñega they seemed to be peering deep into his heart with yearning love, and for the first time he understood what it was that he had been deprived of all these years during which he had been growing slowly to manhood. With his own face upturned to the tenderness which appeared to radiate from the exquisite one above, he presented a picture which quickly attracted the attention of the others. Annizae herself suddenly turned toward him.

"*Mira!*" she cried imperiously, pointing from the face of Lady Harberton to his features. "He has her eyes, her smile! I thought he might look like his father, but—it was my punishment never to be able to see anything but her expression." She shivered, then went on wildly: "Have I not hated him because of that? Sometimes, even now, I hate him. Think you I would have returned him had it not been for the hopes of this very moment, when I could speak these words that I speak which tear her soul even though she be in bliss? Yet now, after all, she seems to triumph over me! Her eyes are crying: 'He is not yours! You have had to give him back to me, Brown Annizae! You could no longer keep him in ignorance of what was his.' Ah, I was a fool! Had I not given him that ring, none ever would have learned my secret. He would have been ever what he was—an outlaw. But it was the judgment of God. It was meant that I should come to these walls to which *he* would not bring me. It is something to be here in spite of him and know that he cannot keep me away, for death is stronger than his hate !"

She moved on with a rapidity that had an object. She scanned the portraits as she passed. The others followed. She halted before the full-length picture of a man to whom

Zuñega was seen to bear a striking resemblance. Mr. Lambert pointed to it silently. It was the portrait which he had seen fit to mention in the office.

She laughed up into the English countenance tauntingly.

"Thou wouldst not have believed that Brown Annizae could have followed thee after all these years!" she exclaimed familiarly. "Thou didst little think that she would come to live in the home to which thou didst bring Zuñega's mother! Didst thou forget that Dios is just? Annizae was a fool when she believed that thou didst love her. She was no fool when she took thy child, thy ring, thy face!"

With a smile on her countenance, she extricated something hidden beneath her handkerchief. They watched her with absorbing interest. Her garb made her appear fantastic, but the expression of her eyes was tragic and gave her a dignity which all respected. She drew a reliquary from where it had been concealed. That it contained more than a bit of a padre's blessing her eager fingers suggested. Each pressed forward to ascertain what the object was.

Zuñega appeared the most surprised of any when she held up a small gold ornament, evidently a locket, heavy of design. On one side of it the Harberton crest was poorly engraved and was worn nearly smooth. So clumsy was the workmanship that it was easy to perceive at a glance that it was capable of being opened. Zuñega took it from her grasp and pried it apart with his thumbnail. Annizae made no objection. She simply looked down at what was revealed with an unreadable expression on her visage. The miniature which the locket contained was of the identical personage whose portrait hung above them. Exclamations that were not to be suppressed were the result of this discovery. This reticence of years thus brought to light provoked reluctant admiration. Zuñega studied earnestly the face that the ornament held. There was that in the candid, blue eyes that seemed to call for defence from the bitter words of this woman; yet Zuñega knew of no defence. His mind went with lightning rapidity over his own life. He saw two pictures compared: what he might have been—a landed proprietor to whom life held no great interest beyond the task of keeping all that he had accumulated; and what he was—a nomad at heart, throbbing with the thoughts of the massive undertak-

14

ing with which he had become identified and which was des.
tined to achieve a nation's freedom. He turned his gaze upon
Annizae.

"Was this my—mother's?" he demanded sternly.

Annizae nodded. She felt herself tremble. There was
that in his face now which made it difficult to acknowledge
her obliquity to him.

"Thou didst steal it?"

"I had nothing else;" she answered doggedly. "Was it not
little enough that I should try to keep his face, that I might
not forget my wrong?"

"Thou hast kept this a secret for long, long years—for love
or hatred, perhaps thou didst not know which," he said, looking into her eyes fixedly. "Thou still shalt keep it." He
laid the locket back in her brown hand.

Annizae's visage altered. She had expected other than this.

"It is thine," she faltered. "It was hers."

Zuñega was sorely tempted to take it again, but he refrained.

"Unwittingly thou gavest me much that compensates for
what thou didst rob me of; because of thee, I am a Cuban,
linked heart and soul to the island's hope."

"But you are as much an Englishman as a Cuban," expostulated Mr. Lambert, when he was told what Zuñega had
spoken.

"One thing I know," returned Zuñega, with his hand on the
head of the dog, which still lingered by his side; "I will make
a good Cuban revolutionist; I do not know if I shall make as
satisfactory an Englishman."

"We will strive to train you into one," declared the lawyer.
"Never has there been a Harberton who was not an enthusiastic lover of the land of his ancestors. We will have to
find some pretty English lassie to teach you fealty to England. Mr. Milman, do you not think that we may announce
that we consider him the rightful heir? He should be invested with the name of Robert Deene Percival and respond
to it until that day when publicly he is proclaimed to be
Lord Harberton and master of these wide lands and gray
walls."

Mr. Milman stepped at once in front of Zuñega and bowed
gravely.

"Robert Percival, permit us to say that we are glad to serve you as we served your father. To those who are here now I present you as the one whom we believe to be the lost son of the late Lord Harberton. May this house soon see you established within."

Zuñega glanced over his shoulder for Lithgow.

"I owe it all to you, my friend," he said softly.

Lithgow disclaimed all gratitude.

"Whatever you owe is to the Señorita Raquel," he said in a low tone. "She awakened you to a sense of true manhood and its possibilities. It was the obeying of your noble impulse that brought you to your own."

"The impulse was purely selfish," replied Zuñega honestly. "I returned her to the plantation because I could not see her the victim of Alarcon. I deserve no reward like this which has come."

CHAPTER XIX.

THINGS had transpired so much more quickly and satisfactorily than the most sanguine of lawyers could have anticipated that it almost seemed that the work of restoring Zuñega to his rights had been completed. Mr. Milman saw fit to treat Zuñega as if no delays or intricacies of law courts lay before them, and even addressed him occasionally by his title in order to accustom him to it, as he explained to his more conservative partner. Moreover, he insisted on showing the youth the entire *ménage*.

In obedience to orders received the day previous, Wickham had prepared a ceremonious luncheon, of which all partook in the breakfast room, which Mr. Lambert said had been the most cheery apartment of the whole house during the occupancy of Zuñega's father. It opened with great windows out on the rose garden, which, though bare and rather desolate at this time of year, revealed what a famous gardener the Towers possessed. This individual, a grumpy Scotchman, Zuñega encountered on a visit to the mews. The argumentative eyes peered out from under their bushy gray brows at the muscular form which kept pace with Mr. Milman on a tour of the premises. He had received no intimation of the coming of this troupe of sightseers; he had heard nothing of Wickham's convictions regarding Zuñega's identity.   In fact, few people ever had the temerity to inform old Grahame of anything, for he never had been known to admit ignorance or lack of perception on any subject.   This peculiarity was well known to Mr. Milman, and he sought to exhibit it for the benefit of the Americans who were accompanying him.

"Well, Grahame," he saluted, as they approached the gardener, who was partially concealed behind a group of leafless rhododendrons, from which point of vantage he studied the new comers.   "I've brought some strangers to see if they can discover your secret of making the roses of the Towers the finest in England."

"I sepad they are han' an' glove wi' the Almighty 'f they expect t' divine His works," responded Grahame calmly, going on with his labors.

"Perhaps you are better than they at the divining business," smiled the lawyer.   "I am going to ask you if you can tell who is this gentleman who comes to make your acquaintance."

Grahame lifted his head.   He looked at Zuñega squarely.

"There's sma' need o' me t' telt ye, Mr. Milman, 'at what I ken.   Spier the mon himsel'.   By his wy o' carryin' his heid, ye micht ken 'at the bluid o' the Harbertons runs in his veins."

"Bravo! Bravo!" cried the lawyer.   "I'll never doubt your powers again, Grahame.   I am converted forever.   Unless all signs fail, this man is the new master, son of Lord Harberton."

"I ken 'at too, or I ha' nae een," replied the gardener, humbling himself enough to pull his forelock of grizzled hair to the coming lord.   His sharp eyes summed Zuñega up with a satisfied conclusion which he uttered to himself after they had gone on:

"It's nae 'at richt seempl body as wull interfere wi' ma roses.   I can win' him 'roound ma feenger or ma name's no Sandy Grahame.   Be he lord or be he no, I wull grow ma roses as I like."

Out past the walls where were trained the pear and peach trees flat against the bricks like running vines; through the deserted walks that led down to the river where stood the old manor house, ivy-grown; around by the edge of the forest from which the soft eyes of deer shone forth timidly; back through the rustling, dead bracken into the park and the long avenue of limes, not yet shrouded with their spring-time fragrance, the solicitor led Zuñega and the two Americans.

Zuñega was silent. After the wanton luxuriance of tropical growth, this bare, bleak English country just escaping from the grasp of a severe winter seemed cheerless. The grandeur of the rambling house filled him with admiration and pride, but, he had no words of praise to bestow upon stark, ghostly trees that possessed no beauty for him.

The Americans, who knew what the scene would be when clothed with the verdure of summer, were loud in their expressions of pleasure.

Mr. Milman glanced often at Zuñega in wonderment. He was disappointed. He thought the Cuban very unappreciative.

Lithgow read the thought of both of them and endeavored to explain matters.

When Zuñega spoke, he asked:

"My mother,—was she happy here?"

"I fear not," responded Mr. Milman. "But you must remember that she mourned your loss."

Zuñega shivered. He looked down the row of great tree-trunks to where the dull sun was sinking, sending up a pyrotechnical display that was brilliant without appearing in any degree warm.

"She must have hungered for the greenness and the soft warmth of Cuba!" he sighed. "I wonder that your hearts do not freeze here. Annizac will die if she can not return to the island."

"She appears to be intending to take up her residence here," remarked Mr. Milman. "I am afraid that the county ladies would not care to accept the hospitality of Harberton Towers from her hands." He spoke half-jestingly. He knew that some other home than Harberton Towers must be hers. Where that home would be, time would determine. "If she desires to go back to Cuba, it might be the best thing, after everything is settled. Such affairs are generally slow in being arranged, though neither Mr. Lambert nor myself see why this should drag."

Zuñega was curious to learn how much ready money would become his, and what restrictions were placed upon his employing it, but, he restrained himself from questioning even Mr. Bertram.   As they went back to the house, he fell behind and walked with Lithgow.

"I feel as if this were a prison, *señor mio*," he whispered. "The fingers of these trees seem to shake themselves at me when the chill wind blows through them, and I hear them say: 'You are doomed to a life spent here among us. Never again shall you know the wonderful sweetness of southern breezes. You will be tied here to look after people who do not need you.' You must stay with me, my friend. I never will consent to be left alone in this land."

"Oh, you have become accustomed to nothing, as yet," re-assured the American. "When you can speak more English and have become acquainted at the clubs, life will wear a different aspect. You will not have to live here. You can make your home in London. After a week of initiation you will be surprised to discover how fascinating London can be. You will suffer no lack of attention, I can promise. Your pleasures will be provided for you, if you choose to accept them. You are homesick just as this moment. English landscape under a wintry sky is not cheerful, but you have no idea what the same scene is when spring has breathed upon it. You will see bud and blossom bursting forth, and you will feel a stirring within your own veins that will convince you that all of your Cuban fire has not been extinguished. All I fear is that you will become so intoxicated with the charms of the land of your father that you will forget Cuba and—" He did not complete the sentence.

Zuñega's sombre orbs blazed into sudden life.

He placed his fingers on Lithgow's arm and waited until the American looked at him.

"When I forget, *señor*, I shall be dead," he said solemnly.

On re-entering the hall, they found that Wickham had thrown open the apartments which had been occupied by Lord and Lady Harberton. There, in what was called the red drawing-room, Annizae sat, a picture of doleful triumph. Around her stood writing-tables bearing the stationery of the house; overflowing bookcases; luxurious chairs that tempted. Everywhere were signs of home-life. Wickham explained that the rooms had been left as they were at the time of the death of Lord Harberton. In looking about,

Lithgow discovered a work-basket from the recesses of which he extracted a bit of feminine fancy embroidery. He held it up before Mr. Lambert inquiringly.

"Lady Harberton had that in her hands when I last saw her," the solicitor said reverentially. "The late lord never would permit it to be touched. He kept it ever by his side. He was passionately devoted to his wife. I scarcely was surprised that he did not long survive her, yet he was a healthy man, judging from appearances. It grates upon me to see this woman, who brought them such pain, sitting here calmly amid their surroundings."

"Perhaps her son would like to take her and provide for her," suggested Lithgow, humorously seeking a solution of the problem as to what should be done with Annizae. "She is anxious to see him. I believe that she almost expected to find him here."

Mr. Lambert laughed heartily.

"I doubt if any argument could persuade Carlos Vaschez into assuming the care of any creature but himself," he returned, "but we will contrive to give her a sight of him. It must be done adroitly, for I have no idea of letting the fellow find out what claim he had on his benefactor. His demands then would be impossible to meet. I can summon him to the office and warn him against the fatal result of the life he insists on leading. Annizae could be present. If she wishes to know more of him,—but I hardly think that she will." He ended the subject with that abrupt decision.

Zuñega welcomed the hour of departure from Harberton.

He did not see how he ever could endure being an Englishman if it meant sojourning amid the placid atmosphere of rural England. He viewed the thousands of lights with distinct gladness as the train darted into the metropolis. He experienced a sense of pleasure in being a part of the stir of the city.

Lithgow made every effort to enter into the youth's frame of mind. For his own pleasure as much as for Zuñega's, he took him about from place to place during the week that followed upon their trip out to the Towers. The news had spread concerning Zuñega's expectations, and they were the cynosure of all knowing eyes wherever they went.

Zuñega added much to his education in various ways. He

even began to find it pleasant to be deferred to. Sometimes he caught himself wishing that Gonzalo Alarcon could see him amid these changed conditions. More often, it was Raquel of whom he thought. It was his desire to place himself on a par with her that made him so apt a pupil in all branches in which Lithgow chose to instruct him.

One morning, Mr. Lambert sent word to the hotel that he hoped that Annizae would be present in his office about two o'clock in the afternoon.

"She must not fail to come if she hopes to meet her son," read the message. "I have requested him to call on a matter of business, during the discussion of which Annizae can view him at her leisure, unknown herself."

It was with some trepidation, artfully concealed, that Annizae entered the carriage with Lithgow. Zuñega and Mr. Bertram had been at the office all the morning. When she passed through the antechamber, she recalled with shuddering the horrors which had beset her mind the day she had been obliged to remain there so long alone, under the curious eyes of the gloomy young man. Things had turned out so much better than her fears had suggested. Nothing but courtesy and deference had been shown her. She had begun to feel quite easy in her mind. She had not dreamed of dreading this meeting with her abandoned son until this moment when she was going to face him. A vague apprehension filled her soul.

Upon being seated within the sanctum of Mr. Lambert, she found that she was to be subjected to an examination that peered deep into the whole of her life. Neither Zuñega nor Lithgow were allowed to be present. A strange man acted as interpreter.

Page by page, her past was turned as persistently as though she had not revealed the greater part of it without pressure at the Towers. Word by word the story was taken down by a stenographer. When all this had been done satisfactorily, Zuñega and Lithgow were called in from where they sat in Mr. Milman's room with Lord Lestonbridge and another man of judicial appearance.

"I desire to show you, Lord Lestonbridge and Sir Crampton, the ring which led to the finding of Robert Percival," said Mr. Lambert when all were seated. "No doubt you have neard of the famous Harberton ring, and perhaps you also have heard something of its dangerous qualities—qualities which history claims that it possesses. The younger sons of the Harberton house are given rings like that which this young man wore when Mr. Lithgow met him. I mean now to compare it with the original, as a matter of curiosity, and relate the story which states that the ornament was found in Egypt, being picked up by a dead-and-gone Harberton during some excavations which brought to light an ancient tomb in which rested the mummified remains of an Egyptian princess, under whose head the ring was discovered, wrapped in many inscriptions. Since that time, it has descended to the one who is heir to the title."

He held both rings in his fingers and looked down at them as he spoke.

" The object is supposed to have been of Phœnician origin. That people were distinguished by the name of merchants; their colonies were found in all civilized countries; their ships plied all known seas. It is estimated that thus the ring found its way into the Nile country, which is believed never to have produced this style of workmanship. The stone of the copy is slightly dissimilar. When I look at the stone of the original, I always am reminded of that wonderful purple dye of the Phœnicians; and I marvel if they imprisoned the secret of the color in this jewel; no lapidary of to-day can find a companion to it. The world may almost be said to have been searched in vain.

" The history of the princess was traced in hieroglyphics on the wrapping of the ring. Like mortals of the present, she had loved, but beneath her station. Her passion was returned, but it also brought her hatred,—hatred of one of her own sex. What her quota of joys or sorrows may have been, fancy must supply. Her penalty alone remained to be engraved on the memory of those to whom her sad story became known; a bitter penalty it was for the bliss of loving, yet who could wish a sweeter death than hers? Her enemy was kind in her revenge. Jealous of the lover whose affections evidently had been taken from her; doubtless believing that, if the princess were dead, he the fickle-hearted would return to his first love; the neglected woman contrived to send to the daughter of the king this ornament and a message purporting to be from the lover, explaining that the ring had magic properties, for it had been touched by the lips of the god of slumber and into the deep purple heart of the stone had been breathed some of Morpheus' own strange gift. Not sleep alone was it said to bestow, but dreams as well.

"'Press thus upon the stone,' the message ran. 'Out from its hidden heart will steal a perfume soft and sweet as that which hangs above Karpasia. All of the spices and the scents known to the gods mingle in this: Breathe of it, sleep, and dream of him whom you love.'

"That she was a Pandora-like creature the sequel proved. She pressed upon the magic spring. Out from the purple well a glorious tide of sweetness flowed, lapping her in exquisite repose, stealing with its poison every sense until life itself swooned and vanished."

His voice had been subdued, impressive. Never had a narrator more intent audience. Lithgow translated it to Zuñega. Annizae alone was none the wiser for the tale.

"I am going to pass the two rings around now for you to inspect them," said Mr. Lambert, extending them to Lord Lestonbridge.

"I hope that it exhausted its soporific qualities on that day!" Lord Lestonbridge exclaimed, as he received them a trifle gingerly. "I have heard of this possession of the Harbertons. I am glad of an opportunity to look at it."

"You don't mean to say that you imagine that it ever did possess any such qualities as are credited to it, Lord Lestonbridge!" Sir Crampton relaxed his countenance sufficiently to say, as he leaned to peer a little over his neighbor's shoulder.

"Why not?" demanded Lord Lestonbridge sharply, disliking to have his judgment questioned in any way. "I presume that you are not ignorant of the perfection to which such instruments were brought in the time of the Medici. During the reign of Cæsar Borgia, rings were worn with a slide that could be slipped back by the wearer and poison be dropped undetected into the wine of a hated individual. Hollow points in the bezel, worked by an infinitesimal spring, communicated with the receptacle for the poison in such a way that, in giving a hearty grasp of the hand, one could inflict a mortal scratch that did its fatal work without getting its perpetrator into disrepute. There were no end of devices employed in those days, and so deadly and enduring was the poison that curio fanciers have been known to meet with sudden death by unwise handling of ancient jewelry and weapons."

Sir Crampton's curiosity was now thoroughly aroused. When the ring reached his hands, he attempted to make the stone move as it was claimed to have done. He desired to show Lord Lestonbridge that he had been right in ridiculing its power. He even tried to pry it with his nail.

"I advise you not to tamper with it," cautioned Lord Lestonbridge, thereby adding to the determination of the other to prove his fears at fault.

"Perhaps it was so hung that, on the emission of the poison, the jewel sunk deeper and never will move again," suggested Lithgow, who received it next.

"I will wager that it retains all of its old power," declared the old aristocrat with conviction. "Those objects were made to do duty more than once, believe me. The Harbertons have been wise to hold it in awe."

It went slowly around the group. Even Zuñega made an effort to manipulate the concealed spring. Mr. Milman passed it on to Annizae, noticing her eager eyes. He forgot that she had understood nothing of what they were discussing.

"I fancy that it had a poisoned needle which was thrust into the finger with the pressure upon the stone," he commented.

"Well, it certainly has lost its power of movement," said Sir Crampton.

"Possibly disuse has made it rusty," smiled Mr. Bertram.

Unnoticed, Annizae had slipped it upon her hand and was contemplating it with satisfaction. She supposed that it was the one which had been hers at first. She was determining not to give it up again. It had brought Zuñega good fortune; surely, he could not refuse to let her keep it, since he had permitted her to retain the locket.

"Buttons" swung open the door at that moment.

"Carlos Vaschez, sir," he announced.

According to previous arrangement, all but Annizae and the two lawyers disappeared into the adjoining office. Then Mr. Lambert ordered:

"Ask him to step in."

Annizae looked earnestly, apprehensively at the man who entered with an air of donned assurance.

His skin was as dark as her own, but the contour of his face was heavier, and he was thoroughly English in dress and manner. He glanced at her questioningly and seemed about to withdraw, believing that he had misunderstood the summons.

"I intrude," he murmured, with his eyes on Annizae's Cuban garb.

"Not at all, Mr. Vaschez," declared Mr. Lambert. "Please be seated. We have a communication to make to you."

Carlos Vaschez seated himself. He was aware that the eyes of the two lawyers were fixed on him in a way that was unusual. Their gaze went from him to the woman.

"We are dissatisfied with the style in which you dispose of the money which has been placed in our hands for you, Vaschez," Mr. Lambert went on gravely. "From reliable sources we learn that it immediately leaves your pocket; in fact, that it is squandered before you receive it. A year ago you were warned. We trouble to warn you again. If this sort of thing goes on, you will find some day that you can no longer look to us for a continuance of the allowance. It was ordered to be paid to you if you employed it in the manner first directed. You decline to comply with the condition; but one course is left open to us."

Carlos Vaschez' black eyes flashed ominously. He arose half-threateningly, then sat down again, as if he reflected that he could win nothing here by violence.

"Your benefactor desired that you should be made a worthy member of society," continued the solicitor, pushing his gray hair back from his forehead and deepening in impressiveness. "To that end, you were furnished with a college education. Every advantage has been afforded you. There is little—I think that I may safely say there is nothing that you could not do and be—if you would. But, instead of showing your appreciation, you exhibit the basest ingratitude. You consort entirely with fast men and women of low grade. The pounds which you have spent on cards, racing, and like pursuits would have been more than sufficient to build an immense home for London's poor. Your wild extravagance is beyond all patience. Your next allowance is the last unless you show signs of improvement. You soon will have an opportunity to see if you can turn an honest penny."

Carlos Vaschez rose to his feet again. He bowed acquiescence. Only his hot eyes and his hanging under-lip betrayed him.

"Tell my father—" he said with a sneer, "of course I understand that my benefactor is my father—tell him that had he thought it worth while to claim me, to give me a name—his name, I might have found it easier to conform to his wishes. But instead of aiding me, he has injured me. It has not taken me all these years to discover that I am educated above my station."

"Bosh and fiddlesticks!" exclaimed Mr. Lambert. "A man's station is what he makes it."

"Not in England, and especially not when the man is a—negro, and unnamed!"

He showed his white, even teeth in a smile devoid of merriment.

"Has any one ever called you a—negro?" inquired Mr. Milman, turning his glance away from Annizac, who was looking up at Vaschez with fascinated, anxious eyes, though she comprehended nothing of what they spoke.

"No person would dare call me that," Vaschez answered, drawing his figure up proudly. "But here,—to you who know who my father is and yet never tell me, to you I say that I know that I have negro, blood and I do not marvel that my father is afraid to let me learn his identity."

"Your father is dead," Mr. Lambert told him. "Your life has shown that you did not deserve so generous a parent."

The fellow's features softened a trifle. He hesitated.

"My mother," he asked finally, in an altered tone. "Where is *she?*"

On the impulse of the moment, Mr. Lambert arose, took Annizac by the arm, and drew her in front of Vaschez.

"This woman is your mother," he answered briefly.

There was intense silence for the moment.

The face of Vaschez worked convulsively.

Annizac had turned the gray hue which keen emotion gives to colored skin. In all her imaginings of her meeting with him, she never had dreamed of this—eyes like coals burning down into her own, until they seemed to scorch her very brain. She had fancied that he would thank her for the part she had played. She had hoped gratitude for the advantages which thus she had secured for him. It seemed to her that she reeled. She knew that her head spun like a top. To those observing her she appeared as bitter, as defiant, as emotionless as was her custom. And the man towering over her had the same bitterness and defiance in his face, added to which was a rage that, before they knew what he was about to do, caused him to seize her fiercely by the hands and push her back against the wall. Then he flung the back of his right hand against her face brutally.

"That is my gratitude for your giving me birth," he said savagely. "I would rather never have been born than be what I am."

Not a sound came from Annizae's lips, but her eyes glared like a wild beast's.

Carlos Vaschez walked out quietly and away before any one realized that he should be restrained from escaping.

Mr. Milman gave a cry of shocked surprise and leaped to his feet to wipe the blood from Annizae's face. Before he could reach her, she had slipped down beside the wall, but she was not unconscious.

"Dear me! dear me! I never thought of such a possible ending," Mr. Lambert lamented, calling the occupants of the other room. "He is a positive brute!"

"Perhaps he is not so much to be blamed, after all," suggested Mr. Milman, endeavoring to wipe away the blood from her stunned visage. "See the savagery in her own eyes! Blood will tell! A leopard can't change its spots. She is reaping what she sowed."

Lithgow and Zuñega rushed out with alarm. They had heard the words of Vaschez, but they had not known what accompanied them. Zuñega knelt down by the side of the woman and attempted to lift her up.

"Where can I get some water?" demanded Lithgow, stepping into the anteroom. "I think she is going to faint!"

The surprised "Buttons" flew to bring some, but Annizae had raised herself to a sitting posture with Zuñega's aid. She looked around upon their faces bewilderedly, then she struggled to get to her feet. Mr. Lambert took one of her hands awkwardly to assist her and, in so doing, perceived the ring on her hand.

"Bless me!" he cried with consternation. "I had completely forgotten it!" He sought to remove it and, to his amazement, found that he was unable to do so. "Look here, Milman!" he summoned. "What can this mean?"

At that instant, Annizae recovered herself sufficiently to comprehend what he was attempting. With a frenzy for which they were not prepared, she fought to retain it.

"She thinks it is the ring that was hers, *señor*," Zuñega explained, divining that she did not intend to let it slip from her grasp again. "I will take it from her."

He tried to elucidate matters, but Annizae only looked at him stupidly. It finally became clear that she understood nothing of his meaning. She leaned back in the leathern chair in which they had placed her. Her black eyes were fixed on Zuñega's features, but a strange film seemed to gather over her vision.

Take off the ring!" said Lord Lestonbridge suddenly. "Something serious is the matter with the woman! She has the appearance of one who is dying!"

Zuñega endeavored to drag the ornament off her finger. He could not move it. He called to Lithgow with fear in his voice:

"I can stir it not, *señor!* It is fast!"

Lithgow dropped to his knees beside Zuñega and attempted to wrench the circlet off. It was of no use. Lord Lestonbridge pushed his way through the wondering men that crowded around.

"Open a window!" he ordered, with the professional air of a physician. "Give the woman some air. It is that fatal ring! I knew it was dangerous! Sir Crampton should not have meddled with it!"

Sir Crampton made no reply. He was startled at this seeming proof that he instead of Lord Lestonbridge had been wrong. He hung over the chair anxiously as the lawyers did, waiting to see what Lord Lestonbridge intended to do.

A change, subtle but traceable, was passing over Annizae's face. The rage and hatred died out of the eyes. The bitter lines seemed swept away by soft fingers. A peace and a tenderness which might have been hers in youth shone forth through the countenance from which had been lifted the mask that years of nourished wrong had moulded. Her entire being had relaxed, as the physical does under the influence of an opiate. All the tension which had kept her nerves like iron gave way suddenly. Whether the shock of finding herself repudiated as a mother, or whether the secret power of the ring was accountable for this, they did not know. They watched her with curiosity that held fear. Mr. Milman had despatched "Buttons" for a doctor. Until that functionary should arrive, Lord Lestonbridge insisted on doing what he could.

With all the strength of his fat fingers, he tried to tear the ring from its position.

"It acts as if something pressed down into the finger," Lithgow said troubledly. "I think that the stone has sunk down."

There was no doubt of it as they inspected it closely.

Lord Lestonbridge took his pocket-knife and slipped a small blade between the ring and the finger. He found that he could not make the blade pass beneath the stone. Then, both he and Lithgow, with the points of their knives, attempted to push the stone upward.

Carefully but hurriedly they worked, glancing up once in a while at Annizae's face. She made no outcry. She appeared to be oblivious now of their efforts, yet her lids had not closed.

"It seems to be lifting a trifle," whispered Lithgow excitedly.

"I believe that it does move," murmured Lord Lestonbridge. "Push a little more to that side. There! Ah—at last!"

The stone had slipped back into position.

They drew the ring off. Beneath where the stone had lain was a tiny red point of blood.

Zuñega leant forward, but Mr. Bertram, suspecting his intention, pulled him backward.

"I can suck the poison out, *señor*," cried Zuñega, anxiously.

"Good heavens! Are you mad?" demanded Lord Lestonbridge. "Even should there be no question of danger to you, it is too late now. Look at her! That must have been a most powerful narcotic poison! She is swooning beneath its spell. Perhaps if we dragged her about the room—made her walk for hours as they do sometimes to keep people from the fatal sleep—we might save her from the effects of it, whatever the mysterious thing is!"

Acting on his suggestion, they endeavored to lift her to her feet. Her limbs bent beneath her. In no way could the members be made to support her. They resorted to extreme measures. They slapped her vigorously. They even pounded her. Annizae seemed unaware of the severe treatment. Her breath came less regularly. Her eyes took on the terrible, vacant stare that comes with the loss of intelligence.

When the physician appeared, the case was explained to him briefly.

He shook his head discouragingly. He pressed down her lids with his fingers.

"She does not see, even if they are open," he said. "They may as well be closed. I will do what I can by inserting a counterpoison into her veins. It may arrest the paralyzing power of the other; but, if the poisonous stuff reaches the action of the heart before what I employ has had time to accomplish its purpose, there is little or no hope. I know somewhat of the strange working of these old poisons, but whether I know anything of this particular one time alone will determine—not a very long time either."

Even while they watched him introduce a hypodermic injection at a point calculated to meet the on-creeping enemy, they could not but notice with apprehension that her breathing became shorter and shorter. Each respiration seemed fainter than the last.

Zuñega called her repeatedly by name in anguished tones. She was the only parent he had known. He could not endure to see her gliding out of life in this mystical manner. He chafed her hands. He stroked her hair, from which the turban had been torn. No response rewarded him, not even the flickering of an eyelash.

Before the physician had completed his experiment, Annizae's breath had ceased entirely. The beating of the heart became stilled. He looked around upon the different faces of the startled group with grave countenance.

"It was as I feared," he said. "The poison was of too insidious a nature to be baffled. The woman is dead!"

CHAPTER XX.

DURING this time the grinding had been going on as usual on the sugar plantation.

With the departure of the American, life had lapsed into the customary routine of uneventfulness for Gilbert Palgrave.

To Raquel, however, everything was changed. She loitered in the dreamy court as of yore, but she uttered no more speech to the palm.

Life was no longer rife with speculation. She knew what it held; and that made her silent. There were no questions to ask now. There was no wonderland ahead.

Her eyes grew quiet with that hopelessness which comes from pressing the entire future into one day and living it in fearful anticipation. She did not wait until misery actually became hers. She went out to meet it shudderingly. Thus she robbed of their joy these last days of her girlhood.

M. Theuriet lost no time in bringing over the letter which Lithgow had sent back to him by Diego.

"Zare ees a lectle word een eet for you," he told her as he placed it in her hands. He watched her while she read it. The flash of color which swept through her cheeks surprised him. He had observed nothing in the communication to arouse any suspicion in his mind, but her evident pleasure in the message gave him a slight pang of apprehension. Even though he knew that she was to be his, he did not relish having her thoughts occupied with the suggestions of another, however beneficial those suggestions might be. As she turned the pages of the book eagerly with a desire to find the marked sentences, he concluded that he would determine the nature of this volume which the American had left behind him.

"Will you not giv' me ze plaisir ov hearing you read ze passage he mentions, *ma chère?*" he requested. "Ze American was right. He knew well zat I hav' eenterest een all zat has eenterest for you."

Raquel looked up from the book in a startled way. It was the first hint she had received that she was accountable in any way to anybody. Her great eyes filled with rebellion. She arose and put the volume in his hands.

"You may read for yourself, Monsieur," she said, passing to the library shelves and picking up some poems.

M. Theuriet turned over the pages slowly, pausing here and there to read a line aloud. This he did not too comprehendingly. Metaphysical ideas evidently were not to his taste, judging from the critical expressions which moved across his features. Finally, he discovered the indicated sentence, read it to himself first, then read it aloud:

"'Ze action ov ze soul ees oftenair een zat which ees felt an' lef' unsaid zan een zat which ees said een any convairsation.' Um! *Ce n'est pas vrai!* Zink you, Raquel, zat we mortals are content wiz ze zings zat are lef' unsaid? *Non, non!* Par exampl', I nevair shall be satisfait to hear no word from you ov plaisir een ze years to come. My heart will show himself een ma actions, and ma devotion to you will crave some small return. Suppose zat I feel zese emotions for you but mak' no veeseebl' expression! Ah, zat would not be poseebl'! Lovin' you, I must shower proofs ov zat affection upon you. Ze action ov my soul so compels. Even now am I yearning so to do; but you repel me."

"I ask no gift,—I will accept none," Raquel answered, shutting her slender fingers closely into her palms. "I count it no gift, Monsieur, that you relieve my father from debt. That is the value you have placed upon me. It is no gift. I could not take it as such; but you must know once for all, Monsieur, that I do not love you. You must not ask it of me. I know that you will be kind, and I mean to be kind in return; but I cannot promise to make you a good wife. I am not submissive. I am insubordinate, that you well know. If you take me, you take me as I am, full of faults,—promising nothing."

"You will protect ma name?" he said with a shade of anxiety.

She regarded him with some wonderment.

"Will there ever be cause to have it assailed?" she exclaimed.

The Frenchman smiled. It gratified him to discover that she did not comprehend his transitory fear. How innocent she was! He felt that he would have to keep guard over her all the more vigilantly because of that innocence when they took up their residence in Havana. She would believe all that was said to her. She would have unlimited faith in the noble qualities of man. He caressed his upper lip with his under one in happy contemplation of initiating Raquel into the mysteries of the world. After some thought, he said gently:

"You will be much courted in Havana. Lov' will be made to you."

"Monsieur forgets that I shall be married," she corrected.

"Ah, I wish zat would mak' a difference," he sighed plaintively, "but eet will mak' you sought ze more."

Raquel regarded him with some mystification.

"But what good will it do?" she demanded.

"Leetle, save to please you," he answered, "and eet may bring unhappiness to me; but zat should not be, for ma joy must be found in makin' you happee, *ma chère*. I will zink only ov your plaisir. Your life has been gray and dull here. I mean to mak' it ov rose-color. I mean to place you where you will be appreciated. Here, zare ees none but your father and myselv to recognize your wonderful qualities."

Raquel looked out of the iron-barred windows, but she did not notice what she looked upon. Finally she asked slowly:

"How long will you permit me to remain here as I am, Monsieur?"

"Your desires are mine," he replied quickly. "My hopes —you need not considair."

He was not disappointed in the result of this speech. He could not have touched her in a more adroit way to turn her to his purpose.

She had not expected this unselfishness on his part. She had looked for urging and arguments, and had prepared herself to battle with them. This humble attitude of his, leaving it all subject unto her will, caused her to view the old man from another standpoint. He was more considerate than she had supposed he would be. She realized that the sooner she married him, the sooner would her father find himself strangely freed from the embarrassments which had troubled him for so long. She had intended to insist on a year of freedom, but this reflection concerning the benefit which would accrue to her father made her hesitate.

"What difference does six months, more or less, make in a lifetime?" she asked herself. "Six months may mean everything to papa's affairs. To me—? Well, shall I not be here, anyway? It is not as if I were to be taken to a far country. I do not lose him, nor does he lose me. He simply gains much by it without being aware that he does." She turned her face toward Theuriet with signs of determination written on it.

"Give me six months, Monsieur," she said. "I shall be a better wife for the waiting."

"As you will," he agreed, his French astuteness convincing him that to make a move in her direction would be to lose all the ground he had won. He did not stir from where he comfortably was stationed in the estrada. "Zat will be during ze coffee season, almost at ze beginning ov eet. You may defair ze marriage for nine months cef you prefair."

He could not fail to see the wave of relief that passed over the girl's countenance. This proof of her reluctance to assume the bond of matrimony did not seriously depress him. He reasoned that she was but a young romantic creature, who posssessed ideals which would never be realized. All women had them at first, he knew, and he had never observed that they were less happy when these impossible ideals were shattered, as they never fail to be upon contact with real life; but M. Theuriet's observations were not often more than skin-deep. He judged women by the visage they turned to the critical world. He dreamed nothing of the agony with which they bend over shattered shrines in the secret stillness of the heart.

"At ze close ov ze coffee-picking we can go directlee to Havana," he continued. "Zare will be operas, balls, dinners, a zousand and one dissipations which will entrance you. You shall spend what time you will zare. You shall deespense hospitalite. I mean zat ma beautiful young wife shall take ze city by storm."

There was no doubt that these words, picturing that even though she wore chains life would have a festive look which was new to her experience, lent a vague atmosphere of expectation to the future and rendered the contemplation of it less disagreeable. She had no premonition of the opportunities which would become hers for aiding the cause of Cuban liberty. Lithgow's letter from New York had not yet reached her father. She was ignorant that the volcano upon which the Spanish government is perched was smouldering and preparing for a terrific outburst, which was destined to topple an outrageous tyranny into the sea.

When that letter did arrive, it worked a transformation in her which astonished her father, even while it gratified him. It was not so much because she seemed to regain her old fever for action as it was that she sought methods of spending that imperative force. She emerged from the self-contemplation which her years of dreaming had fostered. She began to inquire into the particulars of his business. She was no longer content to be told that everything was coming out right and that she must not worry. She insisted on being allowed to accompany him on his matutinal rounds of the estate before the day was well on. She even attempted to master the intricacies of sugar-making.

Palgrave accepted the change with indulgent smiles at first. He was confident that her interest would wear off in two mornings, but as time crept on and she still persisted in familiarizing herself with matters that he always had thought were outside the province of woman, he commenced to wonder and his wonder grew. She no longer wasted temper and energy in despising Spain. She seldom mentioned the subject which had so often been her favorite topic. She seemed to have but one thought—to make her own every bit of information which she could find.

He questioned her curiously concerning this one morning as they rode on horseback slowly through the cart-paths that crossed the cane-fields.

"This constant companionship of yours is going to make me feel more lonely, *querida mia*, when you flit off to Havana," he mourned. "I never had so much—of your real self as I have had lately. I don't see how I can let M. Theuriet take you. What has given you this sudden interest in things concerning which you never thought before?"

"Something within me demands work," she answered. "Heretofore I have been content simply to yearn for it and yet make no effort to secure occupation. Now that I know other hearts as patriotic and more able than mine are linked to the cause of liberty, I cannot remain idle. I suddenly understand how ignorant I am. A son would have been your companion all these years. He would have made the particulars of the management of this great plantation familiar to his comprehension. He would not have swung in a hammock and eaten his heart out while he read of the great things which others have done. Because I must wear petticoats, must I be an ignoramus? May I not master the intricate workings of business? May I not be taught all that a boy would have been taught? Is it not this wide knowledge that makes men stronger and more able to cope with difficulties? I am not satisfied to be simply a woman. You long have known that. Now, I find that I can become posted on a subject which is of paramount interest to Spain; I mean to make the most of the opportunity too long neglected. I shall endeavor to learn what I can of M. Theuriet relative to coffee culture."

Gilbert Palgrave laughed heartily; then, for fear of paining her, desisted and queried:

"And what good—what particular thing do you expect to gain by it, *dulce mia?*"

"Spain derives her revenue almost entirely from planters like you and M. Theuriet, does she not?" she asked. "All that your life really amounts to is in procuring gold for Spain to send back in the form of oppression. You and the whole island of planters support tyranny. If it were not for what you raise, Spain could not maintain her government. In one way you tax-payers are responsible for Cuba's condition. As long as you are here to be wrung dry of every centavo, Spain will strain every nerve to retain possession. I wish to learn the exact resources of the plantations, what they are capable of, and what they now produce; then, one can estimate what tribute should be paid to the strong-hearted ones who have Cuba's liberation in view."

"But, you don't mean that we planters can furnish support to any revolutionists who may take it into their heads to come down here and make matters worse!" exclaimed her father. "That would mean confiscation by the government. Any attempt at a revolt should be checked. It only results disastrously to the planters. We are the only ones who have property to destroy; if we oppose the insurgents, they wreak vengeance upon us by burning our crops; if we help them, Spain takes not alone crops, but furnishes lifelong imprisonment. I would thank the men who are at the head of this intended uprising to let well enough alone. The country has not yet recovered from the ten-year war. Some plantations are lying waste yet."

"Because their owners are exiled or in Spanish prisons," returned Raquel. "What if the crops should be lost and we impoverished? The individual should not be considered when the welfare of the country is at stake!"

"Such opinions must not be voiced elsewhere. M. Theuriet will put a stop to it if he takes you to Havana. Neither his life nor mine would be worth a peso if you once were known to hold such views. You would be supposed to have derived them from one of us."

"But you surely feel as I do, papa," she cried.

"Men in Cuba dare not feel as you do; at least they never dare speak their feelings. I wish that letter of Mr. Hamilton's had never been written, if you are going to endanger property and lives by such lack of wisdom, urged on by the belief that Cuba can be torn from the grasp of Spain by a handful of patriots."

"It will be," she declared hopefully. "Even Zuñega will come back and fight for the island."

"Don't you believe it," said her father skeptically. "Cuba never will see him again. You have no idea of the life into which he will enter, providing that he is the heir. It is a pity that you could not have married him instead of M. Theuriet," he added jocularly. "He is nearer your age; and, I think I would like to see you at the head of an English home. 'Lady Harberton' would not be half bad as a title, would it?"

Raquel turned her eyes upon him with a look in their depths which he could not fathom. It was as if a thought had leaped into life with a force that its sudden birth did not warrant.

"I would be glad to have you out of Cuba, if there is to be any trouble with revolts. Promise me one thing, Raquel," Palgrave continued.

"I will promise anything," she said gently.

"Promise me that, if you go to Havana, you will guard your lips! Don't allow your sentiments to be even suspected. Feign to be loyal to Spain rather than avow your real feelings."

"I never could feign anything," she returned, "but I will do nothing to lead any one to doubt my loyalty. More than that you could not ask."

"When you have lived longer, you will see the wisdom of my caution," he explained.

"I see it now," she replied.

"But you are impulsive. You do not measure your speeches."

"I will," she said earnestly. "There is too much at stake to be brave in words. My silence shall attest my heroism."

And Gilbert Palgrave did not understand all that she meant.

That night she took from under her pillow the letter of Lithgow's relating to the society of Cubans in America. She re-read every word slowly, though she knew it by heart. Then she placed it before the tiny white crucifix and bowed her head upon it.

"Let him remember; dear, sweet mother of Jesu!" she prayed. "Let not his ears become dulled to the cries of his country!"

Three months after the death of Annizae, another letter came from Lithgow, with a tardy but graphic description of the occurrence. It told how she was, by the strangeness of fate, buried at the church of Harberton; and it gave the particulars of Zuñega's entrance into his rights, becoming invested with his title and proclaimed master of the Harberton possessions.

"This has just been consummated," the letter ran. "Affairs of this sort are notoriously tedious. Zuñega has become a great lion and is sought after until the poor lad is near dead with the wearisomeness of it all. He confesses that he craves the free life that he once knew, but society demands that he take possession of his properties and settle down into a right-minded landlord, wary enough to protect himself from the snares which already are being spread for his feet. It is easy to see that his heart turns ever to Cuba. He intends to take Annizae's remains back to the island. He says that he knows she never can sleep peacefully in this cold land. And when he returns to Cuba he will be what he swore he would be— one who will fight for two."

"What does that mean?" queried Gilbert Palgrave wonderingly.

Raquel indulged in a little smile of pleasant triumph.

"You prophesied that Cuba never would see him again," she reminded.

"Neither will it—unless a woman remains here for whom he will return."

"You malign your own sex," she cried indignantly. "Have men no lofty promptings of their own? Must it always be woman that urges them to noble deeds?"

"Nearly always," laughed he. "'As unto the bow the cord is.'"

The weeks and months wore on. It seemed to Raquel that they never had dragged so slowly, and yet she dreaded to see them creeping by.

Her old favorite books gave her not a tithe of the pleasure she once had derived from their pages. Their contents had been mystical while she stood on the verge of living; now that she had come some of woman's problems unto, a deeper meaning lay beneath the utterances she had read, re-read, and fancied that she understood. She began to comprehend with what sad, wide knowledge those truths had been exhumed from life's mines; she shrank from the discovery that life, as the earth understands it, is an unenviable possession in which joys are transitory and sorrow alone seems to endure. Even the optimistic teachings of the book that had been Beatrice's could not take her back to the land of yesterday, the country of dreams. It was true that she had fretted in that country, but it had been with an intangible pain. Now she closed her hands over her heart to still its aching lest her father should see her suffering in her face. The fact that the book had belonged to an American girl to whom it had been a source of strength and encouragement was of much comfort and urged her on to try to reach the full richness of its high teachings. Years were to reveal to her that the secret beauty of what now to her were hidden jewels of thought would be visible only as she reached a point of spiritual growth which would render her perception trenchant and keen enough to probe deep into her own consciousness.

One passage which Beatrice evidently had marked haunted her depressingly, yet she saw its truth: "The things we now esteem fixed shall, one by one, detach themselves like ripe fruit from our experience, and fall. The wind shall blow them none knows whither. The landscape, the figures, Boston, London, are facts as fugitive as any institution past, or any whiff of mist or smoke, and so is society, and so is the world. The soul looketh steadily forward, creating a world always before her, leaving worlds always behind her."

"It almost would seem that there is little use in trying to accomplish," she would muse. "We are scarcely more than butterflies, with the life of a day; and yet, ought not the very fact of the briefness of that day make us more anxious to fill it with a deed which may endure? I can give my whole life to secure comfort and freedom from worry for my father, yet that is not enough to satisfy me. I must do something for Cuba—when the hour comes."

M. Theuriet made no further efforts to peruse the volume which had excited his fears. He watched Raquel reading from it day after day, but he had become convinced once for all of its harmlessness. As the time drew near for the marriage, he spent much of his time at La Sacra Sonrisa. It was pleasant to his sight to see Raquel bent over fragments of needlework. He smiled when he saw how she detested it. She had not had the training of convent routine. A needle was her *bête noire.*

"You shall hav' zese zings done for you, *chérie,* when you are Madame Theuriet," he promised. "Worry not over zem. Havana can supply all ov your wishes. Parisian styles will be zare. You will not know yourselv when you are clad een French confections. You will rival Pepita de Urquiza."

"And she——?"

"Ees riche, beautiful, and a widow. She has broken more hearts zan any zree ozairs een Cuba. She has an immense estate near Villa Claro. She spends her time een many cities, abroad as well as at home. Eef she ees een Havana, we must mak' her your friend; zen all ozer women will adore you also, for ze Señora de Urquiza rules where she will."

And Pepita de Urquiza was the first woman with whom Raquel made acquaintance after her installation in the city as Madame Theuriet.

There was no doubt that the Señora de Urquiza came actuated somewhat by curiosity. All Havana was curious to see the young wife of M. Theuriet, who was well known. Despite his years, the Frenchman had been considered a good catch by wise mammas with a number of marriageable daughters. No one forgot the value of M. Theuriet's estimated fortune. He had been petted and cajoled unsuccessfully through many seasons; perhaps that consciousness made him regard Raquel's sacrifice as no sacrifice at all. He knew that there were those who would have been glad to marry him, and he expected that Raquel herself would discover this fact before the season in Havana was over.

At the first glance into the sad, girlish face, Pepita de Urquiza's trained eyes read much that Raquel fancied was concealed with skill. She knew also that Raquel had not married him for his money, though that report was afloat. Her heart went out to the young wife with an impetuosity that was one of her charms. Without a trace of the formality which Raquel had expected and dreaded, she took the wistful, fresh visage in her perfectly gloved hands and kissed it.

"I have been waiting for your coming, dear," she said smilingly.

Raquel was swayed by that friendly overture, though her well-set head was held with that inborn pride which was to serve her well during her initiation into Havanese circles. Without being aware of it, she could make herself very formidable even though her heart within was timid and shrinking. She was to discover that it is more disconcerting to meet the unfriendly, critical stare of her own sex than to face an army of disciplined soldiers, because the weapons of the former are subtle, unseen, consequently infinitely more dangerous.

"You have known—of my coming?" she questioned in surprise.

"Ah, indeed, have I not?" returned Pepita, lifting her beautifully arched brows. She seated herself with a most delightful rustling of silken skirts. Though gowned like a Parisian, her grace was the inimitable grace of the Cuban. Her voice was full of a caressing music; her smile won for her the adoration of all upon whom it fell. She leaned forward and took Raquel's soft fingers in her own gloved ones. "I must confess that, personally, I have known nothing of you, but your face, your eyes,—they are those for which I have been waiting for years. I puzzle you? I will make you understand. I will explain. Your eyes are full of truth, they are perfectly fearless, and in that they are uncommon. I have waited for the coming of such a one. I almost had despaired. Ah, you smile! But, it is true. I am a female Diogenes. Have you ever heard of Diogenes? *Sí?* Ah, that is well. You have read, then! When I behold you, you perceive how quickly I recognize your spirit! We are akin! We will be friends—no? It is not a small thing to have Pepita de Urquiza for a friend, is it, monsieur? Ah, you see I have conceit! But it is true that I make a good friend, and—it is possible that I make as good an enemy." She directed a shaft of light from her dark, dreamy eyes at M. Theuriet.

"You are eencapa-a-bl' ov proving an enemee, señora!" expostulated he. "Why should you be? Eees not ze whole world at your feet?"

"The masculine world, possibly," she agreed laughingly, "men are proverbially blind. They imagine charms and virtues where none exist. But the other half of the world—is made up of women! Win the love of the first half: lose the love of the second half. It is the law of compensation!"

"But ze women—zey obey your rule!" M. Theuriet murmured, mystified. "Do zey not copy——"

"*Mes robes?*" completed she, shrugging her incomparable shoulders. "And why? To please *me*, think you, monsieur? Ah, that proves again the blindness of you men! Believe me, I know well how unstable is my throne! I should be dragged from it by pitiless feminine hands were it not that masculine fealty is too strong to be combated; and I can depend on that fealty—why? Because I give no guerdons! She is wise who withholds gifts and delays rewards! They are prized most when not bestowed. I must teach all of these truths to your wife, monsieur. She will have great battles to wage. Her beautiful face will bring them to her. Do I terrify you, dear? They are unseen conflicts, and one has no weapon with which to protect one's self save the white mantle of purity and wisdom. I shall take you under my wing. The high position in which monsieur can place you will make you a target. But we will battle together. We will be successful, you and I, *Chita!*"

Thus was cemented the friendship which not only steered Raquel through a brilliant social triumph but brought to her the coveted opportunity to work secretly for the success of the uprising, suspicions of which even now were whispered cautiously about through the capital.

CHAPTER XXI.

ONE day, Raquel and the Señora de Urquiza were sitting together in the sala of the Señora Mendonez, chatting with that lady concerning the ball given the night previous at the Governor-General's palace, when the Señora Iriate was announced and came bringing the information, which she imparted excitedly, that an expedition had embarked from New York with the supposed intention of landing on Cuban soil and instigating another revolution.

Raquel's mobile face lighted with enthusiasm.

Pepita de Urquiza, seated opposite, caught the expression and understood at once where the girl's sympathies lay. She endeavored to give a warning glance, which Raquel did not perceive. Then, she hastened to say, with an excellent assumption of incredulity:

"And what then? What can a tiny handful of penniless Cuban exiles do when confronted with such soldiers as Spain gives us?"

"But those grasping Americans are said to be furnishing them support, Señora de Urquiza!" replied the Señora Iriate, unwilling to have her news discredited. She had received it, under promise of secrecy, the night before from her husband, and she had told it at every place at which she called.

"But there is an international law which will prevent their doing anything of the sort, you know," smiled Pepita de Urquiza calmly.

"I did not know. Is there a law against it?" queried the Señora Mendonez with a sigh of relief. "I am glad. I should hate to have our tobacco plantation devastated as it was before, during the ten-year war. How is it that you know all of these things, Doña Pepita?"

"I have travelled much, you know," reminded Pepita lightly. "Travel is a great educator. Actually, I scarcely knew anything when I first left Cuba to see other countries. Besides, you forget that you ladies have husbands to do your thinking. I am obliged to depend on myself, so I must not be ignorant of matters that ordinarily do not interest women."

"Ah, that is true," admitted the Señora Iriate. "but you might have a husband if you would, Señora!"

"I fear to find one less kind than the Señor de Urquiza," sighed Pepita.

"But he was old! Oh, pardon me, I beg!"

"Yes; he was old; much older than I," Pepita nodded sadly, "but he was kind, and he loved me. Young men love only themselves. Older men love their wives."

"That is right! That is right!" laughed the Señora Mendonez. "I believe that. Let us obtain the opinion of Madame Theuriet."

"It would be of small weight," replied Raquel. "Happy wives necessarily are poor judges of the world of men."

"Ah, any one can see that you are happy, by your sweet face," the Señora Iriate declared with conviction. "Not a wish goes ungratified. Is it not so? But if this shipload of wild exiles land and the blacks fly to their support, there is no telling,—we all may lose our riches!"

"Why do you try to cross the bridge before you reach it, Señora Iriate?" remonstrated Pepita. "When you stop to think, are you not disloyal in fancying even for a moment that Spain cannot cope with such a matter? It is so trivial and unfounded a rumor that I would not take the trouble to repeat it, were I you."

"But Señor Iriate had it from no other than Ruiz Alderete, and you know how near he is to the Governor-General!"

Pepita de Urquiza had achieved what she desired: she had discovered from whom had emanated the report. In spite of herself she felt that an expression of satisfaction stole over her countenance.

"Then believe me, Spain has received intimation of such proceedings," she urged. "We need not fear! Madame Theuriet, should we not be on our way to the home of Señora Galiano? What apology can we make to her for having been held thus fascinatedly by the Señora Mendonez? You must not make yourself so charming, Señora Mendonez."

When they were seated in the victoria and were being driven down the Prado at the customary pace, Pepita de Urquiza said warningly to Raquel:

"You must guard your features more carefully, if you wish to do no harm to yourself. Your eyes spoke more loudly than your tongue could have done when you heard the news of the embarkation."

Raquel turned her startled glance upon her friend.

"I read your heart aright, do I not?" questioned the older woman. "You would be glad to have the expedition land? You would be glad to see Cuba free?"

"Why think you so?" evaded Raquel.

"Because your eyes tell no untruths," answered Pepita. "They are the eyes of one who hates tyranny, who despises a power that will rule as infamously as Spain does. I read your nature, but I have not dared to ask you a question. I have no need to ask it. You revealed all that I longed to know. I may speak to you frankly now. You are a woman who knows the value of silence. I may trust you."

"You may trust me," replied Raquel. "Would *you* be glad to see the island liberated, Señora?"

"Glad? Do I not work for that one end?" cried Pepita under her breath. "Call me no more by formal names from this hour. I am your sister in the great common love which we bear our country. Call me 'Pepita.'"

Raquel caught the lavender-gloved hand with her own gloved fingers.

"What do you for Cuba?" she whispered eagerly. "Tell me! You must let me work too. There is nothing I would not do!"

Pepita looked at the patriotic fire which flamed in the bright eyes of M. Theuriet's young wife. She permitted a reflection of it to creep into her own, though even here in the open air of the Prado such a sign of the secret leaning of the heart was not advisable.

"You are not cautious enough," she refused. "You wear your heart on your sleeve. To work for Cuba, one must be able to play two parts; no, to play *one* part and live the other. Even though it grates upon your honesty of nature, even though it seems dishonorable, you must feign loyalty to Spain unless you wish to be immured in a dungeon. Wiser than the wise one must be! Only thus can you be of service to those dauntless souls who come to strike such a blow at Spanish rule as will shatter the hideous chains which eat into our flesh."

"I *will* be cautious. I can be wise!" declared Raquel fervently. "You do not know me yet! Listen! I have known of this expedition."

"You?" exclaimed Pepita with astonishment. "How learned you of it? This is the first breath that has been uttered of it. I have found now that the government has secured warning of it. I must notify at once those who can communicate with the ones at the head of the enterprise."

"I heard of the American Cuban organization and its hopes months ago," told Raquel. "I have waited anxiously to learn more."

"We are indeed akin!" cried Pepita. "But, how came you, on your quiet plantation, to be filled with such ideas? I thought little of them until I saw other lands and compared their government with my own."

"I know not," returned Raquel. "All my life I have yearned to do for Cuba that which a man should do. Were I a man, I would lead an insurrection, I would indeed."

"But who secured you the information concerning this intention of the Cubans in New York?" questioned Pepita wonderingly.

Raquel related the account which Lithgow had sent her.

"And to think that we have known each other for months now and, though holding the same hopes, never betrayed them to the other!" smiled Pepita. "I think there is no doubt but that matters of importance may be confided to you, if necessary. Yet you must gain control of your features. You must let indifference and incredulity take the place of joy until the fact is thoroughly established that we are—see, I was incautious then!—that the revolution has begun; then you must scoff at all news of victories for the revolutionists. You must be angered at them. You must feign fear for your estates. In short, you must play a part, no matter how it offends your sense of strict honor. Spain has violated every one of her promises to us. She won her victory at the close of the last war by promises which she never kept."

"But, may I do no more?" pleaded Raquel. "May I not do what you are doing?"

"Wait; we will see," said Pepita. "I am not accomplishing much now. Yet what we have heard to-day from the Señora Iriate is most valuable to those in that expedition. It will not do for them to come ashore where they expected to. If the

16

government has discovered one portion of the secret, it is safe to conclude that it has discovered all."

"But how is word to be sent to them?" queried Raquel anxiously.

"Little by little all these things will be revealed to you," smiled Pepita. "Be patient. Plans for communication are well laid. This uprising has been well planned. Some parts of it may miscarry; but it must succeed. We who imperil our liberty and lives for it will carry it on to a glorious termination. Spain's rule in the island is destined to end. With undying patriotism, our heroes have been working quietly but surely ever since the last war. Though seeming to slumber, the fire has burned unceasingly in Cuban veins. Even those whom you meet daily and believe to be identified wholly with Spanish interests are secretly with us. There is scarcely a soul in Cuba that dares to let its real sympathies become known, yet each stands ready to strike for freedom when the hour arrives. Munitions of war have been secreted for many months in different portions of the island. Brave José Marti, twice banished from Cuban soil because of his hatred of the Spanish tyranny and theft, will lead the sons of Cuba on to certain victory when he risks his life by stepping for the third time on territory which he means to wrest from its oppressors! He and General Gomez, who commanded the eastern wing in the revolution of '68, have left Santo Domingo. Their arrival is to be the signal for the uprising. Our watchwords will be *Viva Marti! Viva Cuba Libre!*"

"And are they with this expedition?"

"Hush, not so loudly," cautioned Pepita, though Raquel had spoken in the lowest tone possible. "It is difficult to tell. Marti expects to land on the south coast, having gone first to Vera Cruz to deceive the authorities. They may be here by this time. It is near the date. To-morrow is Sunday—no?"

"To-morrow is Sunday," nodded Raquel.

"That is the date," whispered Pepita. "From this time on you must be on your guard. Reports of battles will come in. You must have nerves of iron. I may not remain here in Havana. I may go, ostensibly, down to my plantation. It is in the vicinity of Villa Claro. One part of the revolution is to start there; another in Matanzas; a third at Guantanamo. Ah, Spain will think she has a hornet's nest about her ears!

She can buy peace with no more promises. She will send her soldiers over here by the thousands, but they will die. They cannot stand the climate. Those whom our heroes do not kill will die of the fever. Poor boys! They are none too ready to fight us. But, they must. Spain's will is a cruel one. But Cuba will break it! God help us!"

"And I, left here, can I do nothing?" demanded Raquel.

Pepita hesitated. She regarded Raquel's firm lips and steady eyes critically.

"Dare you?" she questioned.

"I dare anything," replied Raquel, with a strength in her face that even Pepita had not looked for.

"But M. Theuriet, would he permit it?"

"Need he know?"

"Not unless you betray it."

"Trust me," begged Raquel, forgetful that she had said to her father that she would maintain an infinite caution and imperil herself and the estates in no way.

"Well, if I leave Havana, it may be necessary to have one here whom I *can* trust," responded Pepita.

Raquel's hands were clasped tightly together. She was half wild with excitement.

"How strangely things move!" she thought. "Here, in the most unexpected way, my ambition is to be gratified! I shall be thankful to monsieur (she yet called him by no warmer title) all my days. I have helped papa, now I can aid Cuba in a small way. It is all that I have asked of life. If I should lose life in carrying out the things which are trusted to me,—what matter? I shall be satisfied. I wonder if Zuñega knows! He must, if he keeps up communication with the Cuban organization."

Two days later Madrid was discussing the proclamation which the Governor-General had issued to suppress armed bands of supposed brigands, which had appeared in the provinces of Matanzas and Puerto Principe. Havana was discussing the matter also. In another two days, it was reported in Madrid that the disturbances in Cuba were of a serious nature. The Spanish government, however, denied that it had received any report that twenty-four persons arrested in Cuba had been sentenced to death. Cuban sympathizers all over the world rejoiced at the news which was flashed over the wires that the revolution had commenced.

The report in Havana was that the rebels had met with the government troops at Santa Cecilia and that three were captured, while the rest had escaped to the woods. Only the most meagre news could be obtained. Official dispatches declared that the uprising, though simultaneous, had been subdued.

"You seem not so enthusiastic now zat ze rebels actually dare to take up arms against Spain," commented M. Theuriet to Raquel when he was relating what he had heard at the club. "I hav' plaisir een seeing zat you are wise, *chérie.* Eet ees only a few malcontents, at ze best."

"On the plantation I had nothing with which to occupy my thoughts," she answered. "Here it is different."

"Ah, eet gives me gratification to hear such words from you, *Quelita*," he exclaimed. "You are happee here?"

"Yes; I am happy here," she replied honestly, not deeming it necessary to tell him what made her so.

From that hour rumors of all sorts were repeated cautiously from mouth to mouth. All official reports that went out to the world proclaimed that the people of Cuba were unanimously against the insurrection. Yet the tide of righteous war crept steadily on. Martial law was declared. Spain began unloading on Cuba's shores all of the soldiers that she could muster. She negotiated for new war-ships. She bought her ammunition where she would. She patrolled the coast with gunboats. She had forty-two thousand troops in the island and was despatching seven thousand more with the greatest haste.

Raquel looked at Pepita with anxious inquiry when they met. There were days when they did not see each other, so cautious was Pepita. As yet nothing had occurred for Raquel to do. She only could listen with what indifference she could feign to the gossip that was carried from sala to sala. Coming from near headquarters as it did, this gossip was half truthful at least, she supposed, and the lack of success which appeared to attend the efforts of the rebels worried her. But suggestions were dropped from time to time that seemed to point to a suspicion that the utmost reliance could not be placed in the bulletins which Calleja allowed to be issued.

Society pursued its frivolities, though keen eyes could read that it was alert with suspense. Whenever fresh troops arrived, a monster demonstration was gotten up to convince the world that the inhabitants of Havana welcomed the speed with which Spain arrayed herself to put down an uprising which she declared already had been crushed.

As the days and weeks went on and it could not be kept entirely secret that the revolution was gaining headway, it was whispered about that many important arrests had been made. Some faces which Raquel had grown accustomed to see, she saw no more. It was stated that they had gone to their estates, which were in danger.

Raquel dared, innocently, to ask concerning one of these one day, and was silenced by the one she interrogated, who whispered with terror:

"Mention not his name! He has been suspected of being interested in a conspiracy which has been unearthed. Whether he is dead or within the dungeons of the Moro no one but Spanish officials ever will know. Even to mention his name now may place one also under suspicion. We must dine and dance and live as if there were no such thing as war. Spain declares there is none."

"Yet the harbor is full of war-ships!" said Raquel.

Señorita Zurita shrugged her shoulders and looked at Raquel sharply.

"I hear Maximo Gomez is, with three thousand followers, near Guantanamo," she said with an air of secrecy. "But the Governor-General claims they are isolated, surrounded by troops, and without arms. He claims, moreover, that not a single rebel is at liberty in the province of Matanzas. Manuel Garcia is said to have been killed."

Raquel divined that this mixed information was offered with the hopes of securing from her some expressions of her views. She had learned to be wary during even these brief days. Whether the woman was an insurgent herself at heart or one in favor of Spanish dominancy, Raquel could not determine. She looked her straight in the eyes. She could not have told what subtle intelligence passed between them, but the señorita arose and came close to her.

"My father was taken from his family during the other long war," she whispered. "We never have seen or heard from him since."

Raquel placed her hands over those of the girl and found them cold, as if she were under great excitement.

" Is he dead?" she questioned with quick sympathy.

" Ah, who knows?" sighed the other. " We have believed him to be in a Spanish dungeon. If these brave men only can burst open the hideous walls which have witnessed the sufferings of Spain's prisoners, God help them on to victory!"

" *Cuidado!*" cried Raquel. " You forget your own caution to me. Then you are for liberty?"

" With my whole soul! Since then, my mother has died of sorrow. I and my brother are the only ones left of the family, and he——"

" He?"

" He is determined to join Gomez.

" You would keep him from it?"

" I scarcely know! What shall *I* do if he goes? There are others—all the Cuban youths are wild to go; but dare they? If I only might go too! But, there is nothing we women can do save sell our jewels!"

" For what?" questioned Raquel breathlessly. There was no longer any reason for doubting this little Señorita Zurita. Incautiously but fervently, she was pouring out her heart.

" To help the cause! If they can secure gold, they can buy arms and ammunition. Thousands of Cubans will flock to the standard if there seems to be the least chance of success, but without arms, what can they accomplish? The machetes are powerful, but only in hand-to-hand conflicts. They must be supplied with arms as well as the Spaniards, if they are to conquer."

" Are there others who feel as you do?" Raquel asked anxiously.

" Every one who has true Cuban blood, yet few dare avow it."

" Know you any upon whom you can depend?"

The Señorita Zurita sighed.

" There are six that I dare speak to as I speak to you," she answered.

" And will they sacrifice their jewels?"

" Anything that they think they can give up without awakening suspicion."

" How can we dispose of jewels?" Raquel's mind was working rapidly. She thought of many ways, but none of them seemed practical.

"Ah, is not that the question?" grieved Señorita Zurita. "We must find some way! I will ask Ricardo. He is my brother."

"I have not many jewels," Raquel said thoughtfully. "M. Theuriet would miss them at once."

"And he would not approve?"

"I—am sure not."

"But he is not a Spaniard!"

"No; but, like many others, he thinks he has interests too great to imperil. If success becomes certain for the revolutionists, he might aid; but he has seen too much of Spain's treachery and her punishments to run any chance."

"It is that very fearfulness on the part of the planters that enabled Spain to win before!" the señorita said. "My father was one of the noble ones who supported the Cause. He said that it was cowardly to wait until the victory was won by the blood of others and then step in and enjoy the benefits. His blood is mine! If he is living, I will work to help those who will release him if they can. If he is dead, I will work to revenge him. You, Madame Theuriet, have no idea what a passion consumes those whose dear ones have lain in Spanish dungeons or been sentenced for life to African penal stations!"

With no premonition that these horrors of Spanish vengeance were to strike her as closely as they had Señorita Zurita, Raquel bent and kissed the anxious countenance of the distraught girl.

"Do not strive to hold Ricardo from joining Gomez," she urged. "You shall come and stay here with us."

Señorita Zurita shook her head.

"That would never do," she refused gently. "That would place you and M. Theuriet at once under suspicion. It will be known at once where Ricardo has gone. They will steal off in the night, he and those who are unable to hide their sympathies longer. I shall be under surveillance. I will not imperil *you*, no, no! But, we might intrust to him what we can obtain in the way of money or gold ornaments. He could turn them into ammunition, possibly."

"And if he should be taken prisoner with that jewelry upon him, it will be recognized." Raquel's argumentative mind saw all the difficulties and dangers of this undertaking.

"Yes," assented Señorita Zurita. "That is true; but if

nothing is ventured, nothing is won. When I hesitate, I re-member my father. Even if I can furnish only one gun, that will mean a few Spaniards less; a few steps nearer ascertaining my parent's fate. Can I sit still and do nothing? Could you?"

"I do not mean to," returned Raquel. "Come to me in a week. No one will comment on our growing friendship—even after Ricardo is gone—if our visits are infrequent. In the mean time, I may accomplish something."

"You have a way with you of inspiring people with great opinion of your ability or your strength, or something—I do not really know what it is," Señorita Zurita breathed gratefully. "I am so small, so infantile in manner that no one imagines that I could brave danger. I can plan, but I could not execute. I am not afraid of Spain herself. I have been drawn to you, Madame Theuriet, from the first, but you have awed me."

"I?" Raquel smiled unbelievingly.

"You do not know the proud expression that your eyes wear," went on the little woman. "You are one of those who are born to rule. If you were a man——"

"Ah, if I were a man," Raquel echoed wistfully, "I would be by the side of Gomez! No. I would lead my own men; I would supplement the great leader's efforts."

CHAPTER XXII.

THE government soon discovered that instead of burying Manuel Garcia, as the authorities supposed had been done, that individual was alive and fighting with unabated vigor, while Peppel Isleno, the acolyte, had been interred in his stead.

The following day the news could not be kept from the people that a Cuban victory had been won in the Vuelta Abajo district; the insurgents had captured the garrison of Vinales.

It was declared that Gomez had met a defeat and was on the point of surrender, but with the passage of days no confirmation came of this report.

One morning, Pepita de Urquiza sent a message for Raquel to come to her house. The envelope bore unmistakable signs of having been opened. Raquel's heart beat with apprehension as she glanced at the bearer. Had he read it himself, or had it been opened by one of the *guardia civile?* There was no use to remonstrate. Since the missive was sealed again, it would be claimed that it never had been opened and the question would be asked what the communication held that its contents should be guarded with such fear. But Pepita de Urquiza, if suspected, was not to be caught by such methods. She had written in apparent haste:

"DEAR MADAME THEURIET:

"I beg that you will pardon if I ask you to come and bid me good-by. I am too busy to afford time to make the calls I should. From information which the Governor-General has been kind enough to furnish me, I see the necessity of going at once to my estates. They are in danger. The country in that district appears to be over-run with prowling, predatory bands of brigands. The Governor-General assures me of protection. It is unfortunate for me that I must leave Havana now, but, since I am without a husband, I must not shrink from facing these perils that threaten my income. The insurgents have been surrounded and captured, Señor Calleja convinces me, and these brigands will meet the same fate, of course. Consequently it will not be long before I shall be among my friends again. I sail from Batabano to-morrow for Cienfuegos. Come and wish me 'God-speed!'

"PEPITA DE URQUIZA."

Raquel drew a breath of relief. She dismissed the messenger, wondering why Pepita had not sent one of her own servants. She did not understand until later that Pepita had chosen this very method of correspondence to convince whoever was interested in her movements that they were exactly what she had represented they would be. She was familiar with Spanish methods of maintaining surveillance over suspects, and she was cautiousness itself.

"There is more in this than eyes can read!" Raquel thought as she prepared to obey the summons. That her surmise was correct, a very few moments with Pepita revealed.

"Walls have ears here in Cuba!" Pepita murmured, making sure that they were completely alone. "We must talk of social matters in our ordinary tones. Now and then we can slip in a whisper."

"Can you not trust your own servants?" queried Raquel.

"Who knows?" Pepita lifted her brows. "But we waste precious moments. I have asked you to come that I might instruct you. You can be of material assistance. I will show you how. First, let me tell you that Maceo is at Fortune Island waiting for the schooner *Honora*, which will land him at Baracoa with a large party of men and vast stores of arms and ammunition. Strong leaders are scattered throughout the island. Centralization will follow. Few battles, such as the armies of the world term battles, are to be fought. It will be a waiting campaign, a harassing war that will keep the Spaniards guessing. If you hear that our brave men always 'run away,' be not discouraged. That will have to be their policy. The Spaniards will fancy that they are conquering when in fact they will be losing time and men. The rainy season will be in our favor. Spain will have to scatter her soldiers all over the island. Ignorant of the country, unaccustomed to the climate, they will stand small chance of success. The spirit of our valiant ancestors who shed their blood vainly for their beloved land is with those who fight now. This seeming lethargy of the Cuban people on which the Spaniards build such hopes is only feigned. Beneath that cloak of apparent indifference smoulders a flame that Spain herself has kindled through all the long years that she has piled wrong upon us."

"And you go—?" questioned Raquel, her eyes ablaze with the flame of which Pepita had spoken.

"To carry important messages from patriots here in this city."

"What if you should be seized and searched!" cried Raquel in a frightened whisper. "Your letter to me was opened!"

"Ah-h-h!" nodded Pepita with satisfaction. "As I thought! That was a scheme, child. I desired to ascertain if any suspicions were entertained against me."

"And now that you find that there are, what will you do?"

"Be more careful," smiled Pepita. "My opportunities for obtaining information of interest to our patriots have been almost unlimited, but I can do more good in another quarter now. I invariably spend some portion of the year in the little city nearest my plantation. I shall go there now. I can trust my home servants implicitly. I shall find no difficulty in maintaining a system of communication with the forces of the patriots."

"And I am to do what?" demanded Raquel.

"Dare you do what I have done? You are young and will not be imagined to take any keen interest in state affairs. Moreover, M. Theuriet's opinions, or those he professes to hold, are well known to the government. I hear that he speaks very bitterly of what he calls 'zese brigands' raids.'"

"It is true," assented Raquel. "He thinks that this is only one of the many futile attempts to free the island. He believes now that the trouble is ended."

"And the Governor-General will appreciate such unbounded confidence in his untruthful reports," Pepita declared. "You are the one to carry on this work here in the capital if you have the courage. Mind, I do not urge you to do this, Raquel. It is extremely dangerous. You have life before you. You have joy in living. Think well before you say that you accept the mission."

Raquel did not lift her lids now. She busied herself in arranging something about her gown as she answered:

"I should count the happiest life none too good to offer to Cuba."

Pepita de Urquiza knelt before the girl and pressed her face against the soft, creamy one with loving insistence.

"We will not talk about it, dear," she said, "but I understand. I do not know why you did it, of course, and that makes no difference. I am sure of one thing, you do not value the things that it has brought you. Your eyes are full of weariness—heart-weariness. Sometimes it has been all that I could do to keep from taking you in my arms. I have longed to comfort you as woman can comfort woman."

Raquel tried hard to keep the tears back, but Pepita's tenderness made a break in the wall of silent endurance with which she had shut herself in.

"I value this opportunity which has come to help the Cause," she protested.

"Oh, yes, but you wear your wealth, your gowns, your

jewels without the healthy pride that belongs to a Cuban nature," Pepita murmured. "Your soul is full of unsatisfied hunger. You are beginning to see the irrevocableness of it all. You faint at the sight of the years ahead. You would court death—an actual death rather than the torture of the daily death which is yours as the wife of a man whom you do not and cannot love."

Raquel pressed her hands against Pepita's lips.

"You must not say such things!" she whispered. "How did you know?"

"Because I went through it myself," sighed Pepita.

"But you said one day that the Señor de Urquiza was so kind that you feared you never would find one like him."

"Is not M. Theuriet kind also?" queried Pepita meaningly. "Does not his very kindness cut into your heart? Do you not shrink from it and then reproach yourself? Ah! You see that I have suffered too! I married to please my family. I knew nothing of life. I was not the thinker or reader that you have been; I am not yet. I was educated in a convent. I went from that into wifehood. I did not know what love is."

"Did you learn to love him?" asked Raquel hopefully, as if she thought that she might succeed if Pepita had done so.

"No: I learned to love another," confessed Pepita. "But I was true. That other does not know to this day that I love him. I do not think he ever will know."

Raquel placed her hands now at the sides of Pepita's face.

"Why do you not tell him?" she questioned.

Pepita shook her head. Tears were in her own eyes.

"What would his coming be worth to me if I had to ask him to come?" she said. "As long as he can live without me—I can wait!"

"Where is he? Here in the city?" Raquel ventured to ask softly.

"No: in the little town to which I am going; where I spend some portions of the year. Do you suppose that I would waste my time there if he were not near? Ah, we women! What fools we are!"

She rose to her feet and looked in a mirror.

"We show signs of emotion! Women must never indulge in emotion!" she exclaimed with a little hysterical laugh, pouring some rose-water on to a dainty handkerchief and bathing her eyelids, then performing the same operation on Raquel. "It is quite 'bad form,' I discovered while I was abroad."

"You have not yet told me the course I am to pursue," reminded Raquel anxiously.

"Is M. Theuriet jealous?" inquired Pepita irrelevantly.

"Why?" wondered Raquel.

"Because the young Señor Nicolas Valdes will attach himself to your train of admirers."

"Why, he is your most devoted follower!" exclaimed Raquel. "He will be disconsolate if you leave Havana. His adoration is the subject of many a jest."

"I know," nodded Pepita. "I must caution him not to let his change of allegiance be too sudden. You can trust him."

"You mean—?" frowned Raquel.

"He will salve his wounded heart by turning to you. Yes, yes, it is all arranged. He will play his part well. You must feign to endure him; you may laugh to your friends about his instability, but whenever you see him alone for an instant, you will receive some information from him or you must have some to impart. He will communicate it to me by a method known only to a few. He has performed this same office for me. He is cleverness itself. All Havana has supposed that the lad was consumed with love for me, when it is love for Cuba that actuates him. You must make a pretence of flirting with him — does that shock you? Staid señoras may glower a little, but they will forgive. Remember that it is for Cuba. Only thus can you keep track of what is going on, for the bulletins are not to be depended on. Cuban successes are never mentioned. Spanish losses are not told. Only thus can you repeat to me the little items that drop in your way and sometimes prove of the first importance. I think that you need anticipate little trouble unless M. Theuriet should object to Nicholas."

"I will run the risk," declared Raquel. "Of course he will not pretend to be madly in love with me as he is with you. He really must love you, Pepita."

"It is possible," shrugged Pepita. "It is a good thing if one can turn one's lovers to account. I flatter myself that love for me has made for Cuba some very fine soldiers out of what was indifferent metal. It is next best to fighting with one's own arm."

Raquel smiled. She found that her thoughts had flown to Zuñega. She was glad to think that, though love had not entered into the question, she had won at least one warrior for liberty's cause.

Not until Pepita had sailed from Batabano did Raquel recollect that, in the excitement of that last conference, she had forgotten to ask Pepita's advice about the jewel project.

The Señorita Zurita came on the day appointed. Her aunt, the Doña Izabel, remained out in the victoria.

"It is all decided," whispered the señorita eagerly. "There are fifteen who have poured their all into Cuba's lap. Ricardo is to take the gems. He may go to Key West with them and return with an expedition which will bring the ammunition and guns."

"When does he start?" asked Raquel, wondering which of her brooches she could part with without M. Theuriet discovering the fact.

"The night of the morrow."

"Does your aunt know?"

"Not an idea. She can keep no secret."

Raquel went into her chamber and brought forth a pin that held two diamonds and a ruby. She gave it to Señorita Zurita.

"I have but two," she said. "It would not do to let M. Theuriet dream of this action; so, I must retain one. Willingly I would offer both to the Cause. Tell your brother to be wise. All of our prayers will go with him. If he is in danger of capture, tell him to throw the jewels away. If they are found on him, Spanish officials will divine his intentions."

"*Cuba libre! Cuba libre!*" whispered the señorita into Raquel's ear as she concealed the brooch about her person. "How little my stupid Tio Izabel thinks that she is riding beside a conspirator! She would shriek with terror. She has none of our blood. She is only an aunt by marriage. She would be willing to let the Spaniards rule always if her skin could be safe and her mouth full of delicacies. *Adios*, Madame Theuriet, *Adios!*"

"God go with Ricardo!" murmured Raquel.

Days passed. Raquel heard nothing from either Pepita or the little daring señorita. She fulfilled her social obligations with a new realization of the folly of this gossipy existence. It was not in harmony with her nature. She wearied of the gayety. It wore on her to maintain a semblance of careless pleasure when her heart was in a far different sphere of action.

Despite the encouraging bulletins issued there were indubitable signs that the government was not so easy as it feigned to be. The month drew to a close.

One night, as she sat in a box at the opera, she saw Nicolas Valdes across the house. Intuitively, she felt that he intended to speak with her before the evening had passed. She was not disappointed. He verged nearer by degrees. Finally he appeared behind M. Theuriet.

"M. Theuriet, may I come in and talk with your wife?" the young Cuban asked, seating himself at the same time. "I have no one to worship now that the Señora de Urquiza has cast me off."

"You must not hav' ze audacity to worship my wife een ze same way you do ze Señora de Urquiza," smiled M. Theuriet, welcoming him. "And what ees ze latest news from ze seat of war?"

"Ah, M. Theuriet, you have admirable audacity in recognizing that there is a seat of war," replied the handsome Cuban. "The Governor-General recognizes nothing of the sort."

The old Frenchman shrugged his shoulders. "I zought ten days ago zat ze uprising was put down," he commented, "but advices still come. I shall go back to my coffee plantation soon cef zis continues! Zose robbers will devastate ze entire country!"

"Oh, this is only a matter of a few days, Calleja says," Nicolas Valdes returned easily. "Look at the number of Spanish soldiers that we have in the island. The government troops are said to be scouring through Manzanillo, and Colonel Santocildes has telegraphed as to what action shall be taken in case the rebels desire to surrender. You see he is quite confident."

On the stage the prima donna was singing: "*Oh, gioja che si senti.*" Raquel's attention appeared to be riveted on the music. M. Theuriet lifted his lorgnette again. Under cover of the melody rendered by the orchestra, Nicolas Valdes leaned toward Raquel and said quickly:

" A battle has been won at Jiguani.   Antonio Maceo landed three days ago at Baracoa.   Eight hundred soldiers who fought under him in the last rebellion have joined him."

Raquel could give no information in return, save that she had heard from the never silent tongue of the Señora Iriate that one hundred and fifty government soldiers had been sent from Guatanamo to prevent that very landing.

Nicolas Valdes laughed a little with satisfaction and caused M. Theuriet to look in his direction inquiringly, since the mad scene of " Lucia" scarcely seemed capable of affording amusement.

Within the next twenty days the Governor-General, deposed, sailed for Spain, and General Campos was planning out his campaign.   There was no use denying that the insurgents must have made some headway or Spain would not have deemed it necessary to take such measures.   What had been discussed as an improbability now assumed the appearance of a fact which no amount of argument in the clubs made less palpable.

The Havana hospitals were full of the wounded, who were brought in at the rate of twenty-five a day.   Three hundred injured had been sent by steamer from Santiago de Cuba because the hospitals were crowded there.   The dead were buried at night to hide as much as possible from the public.   General Campos had cabled to Spain for more troops.   Cuban taxes were increased five million dollars to provide war expenses.   M. Theuriet was furious alike at insurgents and Spaniards.

" Ees eet not as I hav' always spoken?" he said angrily to Raquel.   " Zese men who hav' no propairte to lose come here and rais' zis disturbance, burn plantations, terrify ze people, make Spain press us harder and harder.   We are ze ones always who suffair!   Ees eet not enough to bow now beneath ze last war debt which Spain placed upon us—two hundred million dollars?   Zese brigands will lose!   For all ze expense which Spain incurs, we planters will be held accountable, alzough we sympathize none wiz ze idiots!"

" Why do not you and your fellow-planters contribute toward freeing the island from such a monster then?" demanded Raquel, unable to contain herself longer.   She had met these querulous speeches with silence for two months.

It seemed cowardly not to say a word that might open his eyes to what his duty really was.

M. Theuriet regarded her with a startled expression as she went on passionately:

"It is only lack of funds and lack of arms that will prevent the accomplishment of Gomez's designs! Cubans are not allowed to buy munitions of war anywhere. Spain can buy where and what she will. She can borrow money of England and promise that we shall pay it when she has us conquered again. We can land arms and ammunition only secretly. We can secure no field pieces, while Spain has scores. We must fight from ambush. We must ask our heroes to use cane knives in lieu of guns. All the nations watch the uneven conflict and say: 'Demand nothing of us! We will not give it. We know that you have been robbed for years. We know that—unless you are more sharp than Spain believes you to be—you will be murdered by Spanish weapons of war now. We admire your courage; if you succeed, if you, with your poorly equipped handful of valiant men, conquer the hundred thousand trained soldiers which Spain will pour in upon you, we will be willing to recognize you as a people able to govern yourselves; but you must fight as never men fought before!' How can you expect Cuba's dauntless souls to win unless you give to them some support? You are the one who will profit. Through cowardice, you will go on paying taxes—increased taxes—to Spain so that her soldiers may be fed and paid while they shoot our men down. I hope that Gomez will burn every plantation that affords revenue to Spain. Only thus can he cut off her supplies. It is right. It is just. Spain has held you and my father in her merciless grasp for years; yet you dare not rise up against her now that thousands of patriotic Cubans are willing to do your fighting for you!"

"Hush! Raquel, dare not to speak anozair word, you wild, fearless creature!" cried her husband in a terrified whisper, as he rushed at her and endeavored to put his hand over her imprudent lips. "You wish to hav' me een ze Moro? Ah, pairhaps you wish to get me een troubl' zat you may talk more wiz zat dissolute Nicolas Valdes who comes here!"

Raquel pushed him away. She was an athlete beside him. She drew herself up proudly. Her eyes flashed angrily.

"You are ignoble to say such things to me!" she said in a

17

tense voice. "You need have no fear of the Moro. Spain knows your cowardice too well ever to accuse you of trying to help the land that gives you your gold."

M. Theuriet shrugged his shoulders.

"*Non;* I am too cautious," he smiled unpleasantly. "I hav' lived longer zan you. You believe een ze good intentions of zese men who are committing depredations? Ees eet poseebl' zat you hav' forgotten your Gonzalo Alarcon? Eet ees such unprincipled caballeros as he who are costing ze island so much. Pairhaps you had not heard zat Gonzalo Alarcon was among zose who were caught and hanged ze ozair day. When zat ees done to all ov zem, we may expect some peace. You are a child. Your enthusiasm runs away wiz you; but zis ees a time when prudence ees bettair zan enthusiasm. Eef you can hold silence no bettair, we return to La Buena Esperanza. I hav' received a lettair to-day from your papa."

"And you had not offered it to me!" exclaimed Raquel. "You know how I have been worrying because we have not heard for so long! Has he been ill? Does *he* tell about the fate of Alarcon?"

M. Theuriet sought for the communication and handed it to her, observing her narrowly. This outburst revealed to him that her indifference had been but feigned. He wondered that he had not suspected it before. He resolved to return to his plantation as soon as he could do so without exciting comment. There were several reasons why this seemed a wise course. Gilbert Palgrave's letter had contained the information that the work of the insurgents was not confined to one province. They appeared to be as great in number in the Santa Clara district as in Puerto Principe. This was news that surprised M. Theuriet. Moreover, he had discovered young Valdes in earnest conversation with Raquel several times during the last month, and she had worn every evidence of being extremely interested, being not the adept at concealment that Pepita de Urquiza was. Added to these arguments was the discovery he had just made.

"Ze soonair zat I get back to ze estate, ze bettair for all ov my affairs," he told himself, remembering Raquel's natural impetuosity. "She has no wisdom; she would say zese words to ze face ov General Campos. Eet ees ze courage ov ignorance. Zere ees no telling what she might do!" And, while he condemned, he admired her fearlessness, as age always, half jealously, admires youth. He was wise and diplomatic. He harassed her none with reproofs. He made no effort to argue her into his way of looking at the matter. He simply set about making arrangements for leaving the city.

Raquel read her father's letter with satisfaction. He had written fully of all incidents which had occurred at the sugar plantation, and he had related the reports which had reached him of the progress made by the insurgents. No mention was made of Gonzalo Alarcon. While she was thus engaged, the Señorita Zurita was announced. Her face was anguished and full of fear. She had been crying. Raquel went toward her swiftly, her mind full of apprehension.

"What has happened?" she cried.

"Ricardo has been captured!" wailed the sister in despair. "He is confined here in Havana. I have just heard it. He has been imprisoned for twelve days They have kept him in hopes that he would betray his confederates. I think—they have—tortured him!"

Raquel's heart gave one great bound, then seemed to stop. She put her strong arms about the girl and drew her closely.

"No, no, they would not do that, not in this age!" she declared reassuringly. "Campos would not permit that. He is clemency itself, they say."

"Ah, but the men under him may not be!" wept the girl unconsolably. "Nothing but torture would make Ricardo tell! Even torture will fail, I am sure."

Raquel's face was white. She understood what it meant if Ricardo Zurita were compelled by unbearable agony to reveal the names of those who had contributed to the rebel cause.

"Were the jewels found on him?" she asked.

"I know not," answered the señorita, swallowing the sobs that shook her frame. "I am going to General Campos and tell him I am the one who should be hung—for—oh, they will hang him!—I know it!"

Raquel tried to think. Her brain was awhirl. She still held the girl tightly.

"Do—have you told the others?" she questioned.

"No. I came here first of all. I am going now to the Palace. *I* will die for it. None of you shall suffer for it. It was my plan!"

"You shall not go one step to the Palace!" Raquel said authoritatively. "All would be lost then. We must take time to think. Perhaps something can be done."

"We shall be put in the Moro, or sent out of the country as exiles" cried the señorita. "There is but one thing to do! I must go to plead with General Campos. Perhaps he will let me be hung or shot in the stead of Ricardo. Ricardo could fight if he were free. There is nothing I can do for Cuba but this. I might just as well die this way as any."

The little woman's resolution was like iron. Raquel saw that it was not a matter in which one might act rashly. The secret which Ricardo Zurita held was one which threatened families to suspect which would be to shake Havana from one end to the other. Scores of arrests would follow. Estate after estate would be confiscated.

"Wait until to-morrow!" she begged. "There may be some awful mistake. One day will not make much difference after twelve days of imprisonment. Wait!"

Somewhat relieved by her tears and a trifle comforted, Señorita Zurita promised to do nothing rash before the morrow, and, returned to her home.

Raquel knew that there was to be a great demonstration that night in the city, owing to the arrival of more troops. She thought that, at the reception which was to be held in honor of the officers, she might be able to secure an opportunity to speak with Nicolas Valdes. He would be able to learn if there were any truth in the report. In her excitement she forgot entirely about M. Theuriet's remark in regard to the scarce perceptible attentions which the young Cuban had shown her. She was occupied now with but one idea—to learn if the jewels were found on the person of Ricardo Zurita. If so, the gravest of dangers threatened Havana's society leaders.

CHAPTER XXIII.

THE first individual with whom Raquel had any conversation that night at the reception to the newly arrived Spanish officers was Ruiz de Alvarez, a lieutenant. He gave her more information than he supposed he was divulging. He began by boasting that, owing to intelligence received from the Governor of Pinar del Rio, two suspicious-looking schooners had been prevented from landing near the Cayos de San Felipe.

"Do you know who commanded them?" questioned Raquel, endeavoring to keep the anxious note out of her voice.

"No, señora; but that is not necessary. "We shall discover, however, for they will be trapped when they make a second attempt. Troops have been dispatched there, and we will make it hot for the rascals. We will make it hot for the United States also, when we have wiped these insurgents out!"

"Why, *lugarteniente?*" Raquel murmured, exhibiting the charming ignorance which she knew was expected of her.

"Why, señora?" He lifted his black brows. "Do they not allow these filibustering expeditions to be fitted up on their shores? They claim that the revenue cutter *McLane* is patrolling Florida's coast, yet contraband goods are landed continually on Cuban shores."

"Is it possible that this is accomplished?" exclaimed Raquel in apparent alarm. "Then these terrible men under Gomez are gaining ground!"

"Not a bit!" declared the lieutenant, spreading his chest nobly. "We let them indulge in hopes while we discover their plans. By the way, I suppose you know that one of your citizens is to be shot in the morning for conveying tidings of our movements to the rebels. No? He seems to be known everywhere. I believe he was one of the most popular youths of the city. The matter has caused some comment. I have seen him—a fine, manly fellow. It is rather a pity! These Cubans are brave!"

"His name? Who is he?" asked Raquel, divining to whom he referred.

"One Ricardo Zurita, they tell me. He was taken with a large sum of money and papers of most incriminating nature upon him. It is said that he obtained the gold by disposing of family jewels, but no one can be found who will admit buying jewels of him. Rather daring, was it not?"

"I have seen the boy, and I know his sister—she is a little thing," said Raquel. "This is terrible! Can nothing be done to release him? He and his sister are orphans. What will she do?"

"You would not wish him released when it is certain that he is guilty!" exclaimed the Spaniard. "He would do the thing over again. There is only one method to pursue in such flagrant cases—administer death. That will teach others better than to follow in his tracks."

Raquel leaned back in her chair with a paralyzing sense of sickness numbing her heart.

Nicolas Valdes approached at that moment. Raquel looked up into his face with such an appealing expression that Valdes knew at once that, for safety's sake, it would be advisable to attract the Spaniard's attention in some other direction. Neither of them was aware or even suspected that Theuriet had stationed himself where he could observe Raquel without being seen by her.

"I heard Coronel Nuñez inquiring as to your whereabouts a few moments ago, *lugarteniente*," Valdes told the soldier. "He had the pretty Señorita Iriate on his arm. I think he wished to introduce you."

The lieutenant arose not too willingly.

Valdes and Raquel were left alone.

"Have you heard this awful fate that has befallen Ricardo Zurita?" she asked breathlessly.

"It is just beginning to creep out," he answered, seating himself in the chair the Spaniard had vacated. "I have not found out of what he is suspected. Perfectly harmless boy!"

"Harmless except to Spain," completed Raquel, repeating what the soldier had told her.

Valdes heard her troubledly.

"It is bad for Ricardo and threatening for those who may be implicated in the matter," he said anxiously. "He may be shot and he may not. That *lugarteniente* may have been sounding you as to your feeling on the subject. Did you think of that? These Spaniards are not always as innocent as they seem. Their system of espionage has been perfected during all these years that they have held the keys to Cuban households, as one might say. They have improved on the manners employed in the time of the inquisition."

"Is there no hope of freeing him?" asked Raquel, putting her fingers up to her throbbing temples.

"Was ever a man freed whom Spain suspected?" he answered meaningly. "There has been no way of knowing what becomes of those who are whisked from sight suddenly. Spain's method of silencing has proven very efficacious; but, please God, the dungeons of the Moro shall be thrown open to the vision of a shuddering world before the year is done! The horrible agonies of those fathers and brothers who were imprisoned during the war of twenty years ago may then be revealed."

"But to remain inactive while that poor boy suffers! How can we?" Raquel cried with a sob in her breath.

Valdes seemed struck by a sudden thought. He looked at her penetratingly. Did this indirectly threaten her, he wondered.

"It is for Cuba!" he whispered. "What more glorious death would you wish him?"

"His sister is determined to go and ask General Campos to let her be shot in Ricardo's stead," she went on. "I have begged her to wait until the morning."

"Ah, she has been to see you?" said he. "Then the soldier was not the first to tell you! This is more serious than it appeared. She must not go! Such an action would imperil not one life alone, but many—is it not so?"

"She believes that he might be freed and could fight again for Cuba."

"Ah, do Spain's victims not know her yet?" groaned Valdes. "The girl must not be allowed to go near Campos or any of his men. That is exactly what they want. From her little body they could drag all the information she possesses. No doubt she is under surveillance now. She must not come to see you, Madame Theuriet. There is too much at stake! Let them shoot Ricardo, if they will. It would be more merciful than imprisonment in Spanish jails; and—he will not shrink! He will be meeting only what he would stand in dan-

ger of meeting in the field. You may be certain of one thing
—all of the horses of the Spanish cavalry will never be able to
drag from him what secrets he may hold; he is a Cuban!"

Raquel drew a long breath and closed her fingers tightly
together.

"How cruel war is!" she murmured. "It is horrible to sit
day after day and week after week in inaction while the country calls. The little that I am able to do is so pitiably small!
I am not an adept at discovering state secrets as Pepita is!"

"Sh!" warned Valdes. "Here comes that gossiping Señora
Iriate!"

Those who noticed this absorbing conversation lifted their
brows and smiled knowingly, repeating the old adage:
"Hearts are caught in the rebound." Nicolas Valdes' swerving devotion was the subject of many a laughing comment.
M. Theuriet even was watched by gossipy eyes to discover if
he approved of this sudden friendship which had sprung up
between his wife and Pepita's admirer.

And M. Theuriet, from his post of vantage where he was
talking desultorily with a Spanish officer's wife, noted every
change of Raquel's features. A rage began to stir within him.
He had no thought but that Valdes was making violent love
to Raquel, and the appearances were that she was not dis-
couraging him.

"I learned one important thing from that officer," Raquel
was saying at that moment. "Spain has sent a detachment of
troops to prevent the landing of two schooners that were seen
hovering about the south coast."

Valdes smiled with satisfaction at this information.

M. Theuriet ground his teeth. "I wonder what she said to
him?" he stormed inwardly. "I will ask her! She shall tell
me!"

"That is a good place to keep the troops," Valdes replied
cautiously. "When they are there, they are not at more important spots. Collazo is sharp. He probably has landed
elsewhere by this time. I am glad you found that out. I
wonder if those were the troops that were sent off yesterday!"

"Oh, it was Collazo's expedition?"

"I think. It was expected at Bahia Honda, but the coast is
patrolled. A large expedition will put in soon at the Cayos
Cobos on the east coast."

"Who commands it?" she asked. "That will furnish arms for the Santa Clara district."

"Yes," responded Valdes, answering the last question first. "It is fitted out by a Cuban who has come into an English fortune. There is some satisfaction in feeling that as long as Spain borrows English money with which to obtain men-of-war, we can fight back with English gold that is given, not loaned. By the way, Carlos Cespedes is said to have contributed eighty thousand dollars to the revolutionist fund."

"Know you the name of the one who has the English fortune?" demanded Raquel, her face aglow, all things swept from her mind for the moment by this certainty that Zuñega was alert and acting.

Nicolas Valdes shook his head.

"Do you, madame?" he queried, noting the expression of gladness which banished the anxiety that had lain in her eyes.

"Yes," she smiled. "He is a friend. He has promised to fight not only for himself but for me as well. He knows my hunger to take up arms against——"

Valdes concealed the word she spoke by coughing, as that instant M. Theuriet suddenly appeared before them.

It was the first time that Raquel ever had seen her husband angry. She did not understand what was the matter, but she knew at a glance that something had gone wrong. She had an uneasy presentiment that this conversation of hers with Valdes had given M. Theuriet no pleasure. His words of the afternoon returned to her mind. She wondered that she had bestowed on them so little thought. It had been the entrance of the Señorita Zurita that had put them out of her memory.

"You are not looking well, monsieur," she exclaimed, rising. "Are you ill? Shall we go home?"

Theuriet bowed to Valdes and offered her his arm.

"Eef Señor Valdes will pardon me for depriving heem ov your societe," he murmured suavely.

"I fear that it will be a small deprivation," smiled Raquel. "*Adios*, Señor Valdes."

"Eet might be advisabl' to say a farewell to heem," Theuriet told her loud enough for Valdes to hear. "I hav' made arrangements to leav' Havana on ze morrow. We return to ze plantation. *Mes affaires* demand eet."

"Return to the plantation—now!" cried Raquel in consternation.

"Zat ees my eentention," replied the Frenchman. "I hav' learned eenformation zat mak' such a decision verra wise; for eenstance, eet is whispaired zat—but eet ees not senseebl' to repeat reports."

Raquel recovered herself quickly.

"You men hear news that does not reach feminine ears," she said. "I suppose that you fear for your coffee crop, monsieur."

"*Pas du tout*," he answered, shrugging his shoulders. "General Campos will hav' ze blind fellows all trapped before zey hav' time to creep up zrough Puerto Principe. I hav' fear for ozair mattairs which I will explain to you. *Adios*, Señor Valdes, *adios*."

"The old man has found out something," Nicolas Valdes thought uneasily, watching them making their adieus. "There was half a threat in his eye."

When they were within their own walls, Raquel demanded:

"Why do you take this sudden step?"

For reply, her husband asked meaningly: "Will you pairmit me to inspect your jewels, *ma chère?*"

She had not expected this. She knew that she exhibited surprise.

"You never have made such a request before. What is your reason?" she asked.

"I wish to place zem een safeety before we commence our journey," he answered. "Why should you hesitate?"

"I do not, monsieur," she replied indignantly, getting her jewelry without another word and placing it before him.

"One is missing," he observed; "ze *epingle* wiz ze ruby."

"Yes, one is missing," acknowledged Raquel, knowing of no other way than honesty by which to meet this trouble which was descending upon her.

M. Theuriet looked up at her proud, fearless face with a fright in his own.

"Where ees eet?" he demanded. Raquel shook her head. "I know not," she replied, reflecting that she did not know into whose hands it had fallen. "I have missed it for some time."

"Know you what your words lead me to suspect?" he questioned, his voice trembling a little with anger not unmixed with anxiety.

"That I have been careless?" she smiled. "I thought best not to tell you, monsieur."

"You have hoped to secure eet again?"

"No, I have held no such hope," she replied truthfully.

M. Theuriet faced her squarely.

"I will tell you why I hav' wished to see zese," he said. "I hav' zis night heard zat zare ees a whispair zat ze jewels of which Ricardo Zurita disposed were the propairte ov señoras here een Habana — women abov' suspicion who hav' done what zey could to help ze rebel cause. I hav' remembered your words ov zis afternoon. You would be one to do so fatal a zing. I ask for your jewels. I find one, ze most expensiv' one, gone. Zare ees but one zing to zink. I zink eet."

Raquel did not permit her eyes to quail before his. She herself might have been the accuser, so queenly did she look.

"I could not be a coward, monsieur, because you are one," she said quietly. "I will allow you to think what you please. You must ask me no questions. I shall answer none."

"You will need to answer zem to ozairs zan me," he cried angrily, "eef ze Señorita Zurita tells zat which the government zinks zat she knows! She ees kept undair guard, know you zat?"

"Since when?" demanded Raquel.

"I hav' not asked zat. I hav' leestened to zat which was told me. I hav' determined to fin' how far your lov' for Cuba has carried you eento danger. Now zat I fin', I shall waste no time een leaving Habana far behind. You hav' imperiled everyzing!"

"I have done nothing of the sort," Raquel told him calmly, though every nerve was quivering with the shock of what had befallen Ricardo's sister. "It is your own tongue and apparent suspicion that will get us into trouble. Who knows what ears may have heard your excited words?"

"You shall tell me eef zat beautiful *epingle* was offaired up to ze censane idea ov aiding zese scoundrels ov brigands."

"What matter since, if it *were* among those so offered, it fell into the hands of Spain?" queried Raquel, feeling as if she were turned into ice. "I will tell you nothing, because I know nothing of its whereabouts. If you prefer to believe that I gave it to the Cuban cause, you are at liberty to think so. You know where my heart is. Is it because of this that you leave for the plantation?"

"No. I had made my plans before I hav' learned zis. I go zat I may keep my honor."

"In what way is it threatened?" questioned Raquel. "*You* will never be suspected of affording aid to the insurgents."

"I go to prevent zat diablo ov a Nicolas Valdes from stealing away my wife," Theuriet said, rising to his feet and expecting to see her grow pale. Instead, the girl burst into laughter, hysterical laughter to be sure, but it disconcerted M. Theuriet none the less.

"Poor Valdes!" she cried, "No doubt he would be flattered to find that you deem him a rival, but he is languishing for Pepita."

"Men do not languish wiz such looks een zeir eyes as he gav' to you zis night!" Theuriet returned. "Zink you zat I hav' seen nozing? I hav' been where I could look at your face, Madame Theuriet. I hav' zis night watched you grow flushed and pale beneath his eyes. I hav' understood, at last. Now I say to myselv: 'You hav' been blind! Eet ees not only her patriotism zat you hav' to fear; you hav' also zis lovair, Nicolas Valdes.' You shall tell me what you hav' said to heem zat brought zat smile ov satisfaction to his face."

Raquel's eyes flamed into anger. She was on the point of denying indignantly his accusation, when she realized that to convince him of the utter falsity of his suppositions would be to awaken suspicions far more dangerous to the Cause.

"Why should you single out Valdes?" she inquired with an assumption of carelessness. "I talk much more with others."

"Eet ees posseebl', but you hav' not looked at ozairs as you hav' zis night looked at heem."

"Perhaps you have forgotten a conversation that we had at the sugar plantation before I became your wife," she said retrospectively. "You prophesied that love would be made to me, but that, such being the case, unhappiness should not come to you, for your joy would be found in making me happy. Now that you fancy that I am happy, you seek to put an end to it."

"I hoped to hav' made you lov' me, *myselv*, before zis, Raquel," he urged. "I am human. I cannot stand quiet and see you tak' plaisir een ze societe ov a man who transfers his attentions as quicklee as he has from the Señora de Urquiza to you.   I will not see myselv made ze jest ov ze eentire city! Zis, added to what I hav' discovaired about ze jewels, convinces me zat even anozair day een ze capital ees dangerous. How know we what ordairs may be issued?   What may not ze Señorita Zurita tell?"

"I have not admitted that the poor child can reveal anything that will endanger *me*," Raquel reminded him.   "Something must be done to help her!" she continued anxiously. "You need not expect that I will go from Havana and leave that little woman to whatever fate Spanish justice may decree.   I will go to General Campos myself and plead for her. He is fair-hearted.   He might listen."

"Not one step shall you' tak' from zese walls unteel we leave for ze steamer!" the old Frenchman shrieked as he freshly realized how impotent he really was to deal with this fearless spirit of young Cuba.   "Hav' you not imperilled enough?   Would you wish your papa and myselv locked in ze fortress?   I will mak' a prisoner ov you here!   I will watch ovair you!   You hav' no weesdom!   Ah, you will drive me crazy!   *Mon Dieu!*"

Raquel stood in the centre of the floor.   She looked like Medea.   There was that in her powerful eyes which told her husband how little she feared him.   His terror and anxiety showed her that, possibly, she was selfish in her desire to aid the Cause.   His safety, his property, and that of her father lay in her hands.   Had she any right to endanger them for the doubtful chance of benefiting the Señorita Zurita?   Were there other things she must consider besides her absorbing craving to help Cuba?

"If I am such a menace to all that is dear to me, lose no time in taking me from Havana," she said with emphasis, seeming to accept his government with a grace that her eyes belied.   "There will be other fields for action."

"*Dios* guard!" cried Theuriet.   "Not for you, Raquel!"

"Who knows?" she retorted.   "All Cuba will be swept by dauntless, tireless Cuban feet before this year is ended. Even now is not the entire island in commotion?   Spain calls the insurrection crushed, yet she is sending ten fresh battalions of infantry."

"How hear you zese zings, Raquel?" demanded M. Theuriet, aghast. "How dare you repeat zem?"

"They are repeated to me by wives whose husbands intrust them with encouraging news for the Spaniards. You are in favor of Spanish tyranny; why should not your wife be told all favorable reports for the Crown?"

"I hav' nevair said zat I am een sympathy wiz tyranny," protested M. Theuriet.

"But you do not say that you sympathize with the revolutionists," commented Raquel. "It is impossible to remain neutral in this matter."

"Eet ees posseebl' and I mean to do eet," declared the Frenchman. "I am not going to see my estate seized by Spain because ov incautious utterances. You call me a coward. Ze wise man ees zat one who knows when eet ees best to seem a coward. No man ees brave continuously. Bravery ees spasmodic, especiallee een Cuba. My words will be proven true when zese revolutionists geeve up zeir battle against Spain; for geeve eet up zey will! Zeir courage will wear out when eet faces starvation and defeat. General Campos will cornair zem. Zey will surrendair. Ah, zare hav' been ozair uprisings! I hav' lived longair zan you; you will see my wisdom."

"You malign your own nation, monsieur," Raquel returned. "What braver men has the world known than your countrymen? Bravery is not spasmodic. It is one with the fibre of the human heart. Danger allures man. He goes to meet it, and thrusts his defiance in its face. Neither starvation, torture, nor death will rob the Cubans of bravery. They fight for the future of their country, the freedom from galling chains."

All the evening M. Theuriet had spread the report that he was summoned back to his estates in the greatest haste. And, owing to his vigilance and the speed with which he transacted affairs, he succeeded in embarking from Havana without giving Raquel opportunity to exchange a word with any one save in his presence.

As the steamer passed the Moro, which has kept so well its ghastly secrets, Raquel's heart sunk within her. Her anxiety to learn Ricardo's fate made her every nerve tense. Probably no one ever would know more concerning him. If he had a burial-place, it would be only another one of those that Spain guards silently. She was depressed. Despite Pepita's instructions that she must not trust too much to the accuracy of government reports, she was weighed down by the information that M. Theuriet had given her. It was claimed that the rebels had sustained a severe loss that morning near Bayamo. That Jiguani ever had been captured by the insurgents was emphatically denied. No report was allowed to reach the people of Gomez's victory over the Spaniards at Jarajueta nor of the battle in Puerto Principe, where the Spanish loss was six hundred and ninety-two killed and wounded and three hundred prisoners.

The little steamer drowsed along on its course as though there were no such things as war or urgent business. It had for passengers, however, several naval officers whose destination was Sagua la Grande. These devoted themselves assiduously to Raquel's entertainment, and irritated her almost beyond the point of endurance by the confidence with which they asserted that another month would see the leaders of the revolution prisoners of the Crown.

When they had travelled as far inland as Taguayabon, M. Theuriet learned, to his consternation, that the remainder of the trip would have to be made by carriage, as the insurgents had destroyed the bridges and culverts.

"*Mon Dieu!* Ees eet possebl' zat zey hav' crept up zis far?" he exclaimed, looking at Raquel's gratified countenance.

"The whole province is honeycombed with them, señor," replied the official who had imparted the news concerning the impairing of the railroad. "You have come from Havana and know not this? Does Spain believe she is conquering these fellows? They are stronger than ever. The railway and telegraph lines are to be rebuilt and improved through Manzanillo, Bayamo, Puerto Principe, Santa Cruz, San Luis, and Soriano. Under Maceo, it is said, *señor mio*, that the insurgents derailed a train that carried a load of Spanish soldiers! What are we to expect? Spain must send us more soldiers! This coast is unprotected. Roloff is destroying railways everywhere."

Raquel turned upon her husband with a smile when they were *en route* for the plantations. She had dreaded this re-

turn to what threatened to be the old inaction. These accounts of the ceaseless activity of the rebel forces encouraged
her. She did not dream that she was going into an arena
compared with which her perilous work in the capital had
been child's play.

———

CHAPTER XXIV.

"I HAVE the Cuban revolutionary fever, Beatrice! I am
going down there with Zuñega to help strike the blow which
shall bring the island her freedom."

Lithgow stood in the centre of the studio and regarded her
with eyes that sought to read through the careless demeanor
she wore.

"I would go too, if I might," answered Beatrice, pinching
up a bit of clay between her thumb and forefinger thoughtfully. "Instead, I have done what I could. Shall I show you
what it is?"

Lithgow's face was full of questioning. He made no assent, for, without waiting for his reply, she had gone to the
great creation which had been the chief occupant of the studio
for many weeks. She began to unwrap the damp cloths
which swathed the clay production.

Lithgow drew close to her but she motioned him away.

"Stand at a distance please," she begged. "I want to see
the impression it makes on you. You need say nothing. I
shall be able to read your countenance."

Lithgow several times had essayed to obtain a glimpse of
this figure, but to all of his queries Beatrice had returned
evasive answers. Now that he was to be the first one to view
it, he waited its exhibition with eager impatience. It was the
largest work the young sculptor ever had attempted. and
with all his soul, Lithgow hoped that it would be something
which would add to the fame which she already had achieved
as a faithful worker whom it would be well to watch with interest. She had maintained such silence in regard to it that
his curiosity had been whetted. He was almost anxious, he
realized.

"I'll shut my eyes," he volunteered; "then, when you say
'Ready,' it shall burst upon me with all its magnificence."

Beatrice smiled slightly. She continued to unwind the wrappings. When finally the last one was laid aside she looked at the revealed work with a satisfaction that she could not conceal.

"Ready!" she said softly.

Lithgow opened his eyes to behold a life-sized figure of Zuñega standing erect with uplifted sword over the prostrate form of a beautiful creature, from whose wrists and ankles corroding chains had been wrenched away. The half-raised face of the maiden was filled with startled, incredulous wonder, as she appeared to realize that the bondage she had borne so long was a thing of the past. From the stern, dauntless visage of him who had freed her shone out the soul of liberty, progress, and light. All of the fire, the faith, the courage of the long-suffering sons of Cuba seemed merged into that countenance which Beatrice had moulded with inspired fingers. From the sad melancholy of the eyes an infinite pity looked forth yearningly, as if viewing the graves of the gallant Spanish youths whom Spain had offered up so heartlessly to feed her cruel ambition.

Lithgow was silent. He had no words. He was surprised out of speech.

Satisfied with his voiceless verdict, Beatrice began covering the work again.

"Don't—yet!" cried Lithgow with a break in his tone. "Let me view it longer. '*Cuba Libre!*' I never supposed that you would do such work as this, Bec! You will be famous."

"It will be owing to Zuñega, then," she said modestly. "It was all in his face."

"He must see it!" Lithgow exclaimed eagerly. "Let me go and get him."

Beatrice shook her head.

"Not now," she refused. "It would take too long. He may come to-morow. Perhaps he will not like it! I dared to take his face because it is that of a hero, such an one as we dream of heroes as possessing."

"I believe that you have fallen in love with him, Bec," declared Lithgow teasingly. "What else could enable you to interpret Zuñega's nature as you have? I always have seen it in him, but I could not express it."

"Neither could I—in words," answered the sculptor. "I

see that in his eyes which I hear in music—something that thrills me. It is something intangible. Have you never felt it when music throbbed about you?"

Lithgow's memory went back unbidden to that night of the contradanza. Softness and tenderness crept into his face. Even the thought of it moved him.

"You know how Jean Paul Richter voiced it," Beatrice continued. "'Thou speakest to me of things which in all my endless life I have not found and shall not find.' Those words come ever to me when I look into the eyes of Zuñega. There is a sadness in them as if they peered back through interminable years; there is a prophecy in them as if they looked forward endlessly. They entrance me with their mystery as music does."

Lithgow came back to the present. He listened to her dreamy words with intense surprise in which was mingled pain. He knew how completely Zuñega was bound up in the determination to merit the praise of the white-robed girl who had awakened him to life in the depths of the forest.

"You have lost your heart to him, Beatrice," he said gently. "Perhaps you are not aware of it; but nothing but love —unrecognized, if you will—could bring such words to your lips; nothing but love could read his heart and put into his face what you have put there. You have met your master, Beatrice—and it is not I!"

No smile came to Beatrice's lips; and no denial. There was no smile on Lithgow's. He was in deadly earnest. Did he not know what love was? Had he not battled with it with what strength he could ever since that night when he had touched Raquel's hand in the moonlight?

Beatrice stood still, looking into his eyes with a dawning realization in her own.

Suddenly she put both of her hands to her face and remained motionless, her head bent before him.

Lithgow was irresolute for a moment, during which something stung his eyeballs like fire. To see Beatrice, she the strong, the unyielding—to see her conquered like this! He told himself that he might have known that love would not come to her as it came to other, lesser women. He dared to go to her. He put his arms around her with the gentleness of a brother. He pressed her face against his shoulder and patted her hair with quick, nervous touch. She did not draw herself away. She appeared scarce conscious what he did. It was as if some shock had dazed her.

"It comes to all of us, dear," he whispered, "and it often comes in unappointed ways. It is something to be thankful for, something to thank God for. It is not the *being* loved that constitutes happiness, it is the fact of loving. All the devotion which I could have offered you would not have won you the deep, satisfying joy of discovering that you are capable of love yourself. It is something to be able to love in this age of the world, Beatrice! It is worth life—worth all the trouble of living—to find that the lofty spirit which has swayed the mighty in the past is just as powerful, just as mysterious to-day. You have not known what love is, Beatrice! It is not every nature that can feel it, though every individual is willing to swear that he does. The high name is dragged down to adorn baser affections. When love comes, it uplifts. Its fair face drives out the base. It resurrects the true; it destroys all that cannot bear its white light. You see I know what love is, Bee. Love has done this for me. I don't know what it will do for you, except place your fingers on the pulse of the world."

Beatrice lifted her face. There were tears on it. She did not wipe them away. She made no foolish effort to convince him that all his conjectures were wrong. She was lost in wonder concerning the truth of his words. Did she love this Cuban with the countenance of a conqueror? She knew well that he loved the señorita of the sugar plantation. She released herself from Lithgow's tender arm and went and sat down on the old settle.

"He must not know a word of this," she said with her usual directness. "I am aware that he loves the little Cuban girl whom you love. He must never dream that he has vanquished an American girl without even a shot in her direction."

Lithgow fell back a pace. She had taken him by storm.

"I never have told you that I loved any one—but you," he said.

"You did not need to tell me," she returned, glancing up at him with symptoms of her old reliant self. "I knew it without. I am sorry if—this has come—for—him. I—I—wanted to love *you!*"

Lithgow sat down beside her.

"Well, since you say that I love some one else—mind, I do not confess it—and I know that *you* love some one else, can we not start anew?"

She leaned toward him anxiously.

"Promise me that you never will tell him, Lithgow," she insisted.

"I promise," said Lithgow honestly. "I never will tell him; but you forget that the little Cuban girl of whom you speak is the wife of M. Theuriet. She cannot be Zuñega's."

"That makes no difference," Beatrice replied. "He loves her and he cannot help it. He revealed that to me. Such a love does no wrong; it is an honor to the woman who can inspire it. It is odd that she should have the love of both of you, yet—she married another."

"She does not know that Zuñega cares for her," answered Lithgow, "while I—there is nothing to prove that your suspicions are correct."

"Except your eyes," smiled Beatrice. "They tell no untruths."

She arose with a sigh and went to complete her task of placing the cloths about the clay again.

"I wish you had not told me, Lithgow," she said. "I was happier before."

"I wonder if the coming of love brings sorrow," he questioned. "There never are shadows until the sun bursts forth. Previous to that, all has been the darkness of night or the grayness of gloom. A landscape owes its beauty largely to shadows. A life may owe its grace and perfection to sorrow. Whether this love brings you happiness or not, Beatrice, there is one thing which it cannot fail to give you—the power to read others. To him who has known love, temptation, and sorrow, these lines are filled with meaning:

> "'Since I have walked with these immortal three,
>   There is naught written on my brother's brow
>   Nor in his heart but mine may understand.'

"To you, who have the gift of making inanimate clay speak, love will be a revelator. It is necessary to your work; otherwise you would be as many of your fellow-artists are, mechanical—lacking the understanding that clears your vision and lets you look deep into the human heart. All the tragedy of life is held in one soul. Depict that, and the world will recognize and worship."

Beatrice looked at him with quick comprehenson.

"Lithgow, I have underrated you," she said humbly. "You are nobler than I dreamed. You have thoughts that I did not know you entertained. I feel that I know you better in this last half-hour than ever before."

"Didn't you know that all humans go veiled?" queried Lithgow. "We hide behind our unreal selves all our lives. We peer forth as the Oriental women do from their yasmaks, and we smile to think that none of the other veiled figures know our dear, secret selves. We permit them to think we are consumed by the ambitions, the passions that move the rest of the mass; we rejoice to feel that they cannot read our mighty yearnings, our lofty aspirations, our outreaching soul cries. You know now that, for a moment, we have stood face to face. We never may again. You will be shrouded like your mummified creation there. I will be the jester that you so often call me. But we will not forget!"

An eager knock fell on the door.

Beatrice opened it to find Zuñega standing there, hat in hand.

"Señor Hamilton, I seek him," he said inquiringly. "I have good news!"

"Here I am!" cried Lithgow. "What is it?"

"There will be no trouble about the clearance papers. They can be made out for Bluefields. We are to start south to-night."

"*Viva Cuba! Cuba libre!*" shouted Lithgow, catching Zuñega's hat from his hand and giving it an enthusiastic toss into the air. "And the seven hundred of your countrymen, where do they join us?"

"It is all arranged. We pick them and the dynamite up on the Gulf Coast where it has been concealed for months. The schooner is loaded now with the rifles and ammunition, but we are supposed to sail with a load of lumber."

"Then we have not a moment to lose!" exclaimed Lithgow. "I have just confessed to Miss Warrington my intention of accompanying you. I supposed it would take days yet to get matters settled."

He moved about as if preparing to take his departure, then remembered the statue behind him. He turned suddenly and found that Zuñega had advanced and was gazing up at the work with wide eyes.

Beatrice had not uttered a word save to welcome Zuñega. Now she watched him with a hesitating expectancy in her face.

Lithgow remained silent. He also watched, while varying expressions crept swiftly over the youth's features, puzzlement, incredulity, recognition, delight.

"Ah, it is the face of Marti!" he cried. "See the look in his eyes, señor!"

"Bravo, Zuñega!" Lithgow said quickly. "Only a Cuban could wear that look! How well you recognize the yearning that shines from the eyes of those who love the island! This is 'Cuba Libre!' It is Miss Warrington's prophecy of what will crown the struggle into which we are going."

Zuñega turned his eloquent countenance toward her. It held astonishment and reverence. He bowed his head until the silky, black hair fell forward.

"In the name of my country, in the name of all Cubans, I thank you," he said in the soft, broken English he had learned to speak. "José Marti will be her savior. His name ever will be enshrined in the hearts of her people. God guard him!"

Beatrice was comparing the face of the clay figure with that of Zuñega. They were identical, line for line, feature for feature. The rapid work she had done in the short time she had had before they had gone to England had been splendid in its force. It had a strength that other work of hers lacked. She was surprised that Zuñega did not recognize himself. Never had she seen Marti. She was on the point of telling him so, when Lithgow silenced her with a meaning look that she did not understand, but obeyed. He had conceived a project that Zuñega's mistake made all the more possible of being carried to success. He meant to call the attention of the Cuban organizations to this production. Put into bronze, it would be a grand and a fitting statue for exiled Cubans to present to their freed land when its liberty was acknowledged by Spain—as it would be. But he knew that Zuñega, if he supposed that the figure of the liberator was his own, would give no support to the matter. Now that Zuñega had mentioned it, Lithgow could see that there was the same resemblance to Marti in the clay that he had noticed in Zuñega the first night at the Cuban meeting. Whether Marti or Zuñega, the figure represented Cuba's own son. It would be welcomed by all Cubans as a type of the courageous manhood that had shed its blood for the island it adored. Before he left for the scene of the conflict he resolved to apprise the prominent New York Cubans of this which had come from the fingers of a freedom-loving American girl. But Beatrice was to know nothing of it. If she received a commission to put the conception into bronze or marble, never should she know of the part he had played in bringing to her the recognition her labor deserved.

"While we are helping to win liberty for Cuba, Miss Warrington will be winning fame here," he said to Zuñega. "We have not much time and I have much to attend to, but we cannot leave the city without seeing the dear mother again. Who knows what may befall us? We may become prisoners of Spain. We may be among the fallen on a battlefield. We must take her blessing with us. I know of nothing so likely to shield one from harm"—he looked at Beatrice—"unless it be the love—that will pray for our success."

Beatrice bit her under-lip.

"What hour do you leave New York?" she inquired abruptly.

"Eleven-ten, I think," answered Lithgow. "You see we take control of the boat near Mobile. That was decided on three weeks ago. Zuñega, being an Englishman, encounters less obstacle and fewer inquiries than an American or a Cuban would. We have been fortunate. Our expedition will not have to be abandoned like the one off the Florida coast."

"We are to pick up some of the munitions that it carried," smiled Zuñega.

"Can you not come out home about eight o'clock?" asked Beatrice. "We will wish you 'God-speed,' and you can drive straight to the depot from there. I presume you will depart without any particular ostentation."

"Most assuredly," returned Lithgow. "Those who are to be of our number have been vanishing in the same quiet way for weeks. We will be with you near nine. I shall have my arrangements completed by that time. Until that hour, *au revoir.*"

He took Zuñega with him. Let alone, Beatrice finished her task of replacing the damp cloths about the clay figures. Then she locked the door and sat down on the old settle. Sparrows hopped about inquiringly on the window ledge and peered in at her. They never had seen her sit thus, with fingers closely locked in her lap and her golden, fluffy head bent forward.

The noise of the city drifted up to the north window. Faint suggestions of spring and bursting leaves came dreamily in through the opening. As if drawn irresistibly by that maddening longing which springs in the Northern heart when the sap stirs in the boughs, she arose with a deep, sad breath and went and looked out across the tops of the buildings to a far blue line of water. She held her hands tightly over her heart.

"I thought love meant gladness and ecstasy," she murmured softly. "It means pain—pain—pain! But the pain is sweet."

Zuñega expressed his admiration for Beatrice's work with eager speech as he and Lithgow went down the street. He could not find words enough to suit the need. The awe he first had felt for her had not diminished. This only added to it.

"She is what the Señorita Raquel might have been had she lived in any land but Cuba," he cried. "She is grand, noble—and the señorita is the same. But, in the island, women have tied hands. They must do nothing. They know not what liberty is as the American knows it. Even England knows it not. There is no land where woman is free like she is here in America. There is no land where she is revered so much. Ah, I have learned a few things since I have become Lord Harberton. We must make Cuba what America is; but Cuba must rule herself."

"Amen," said Lithgow. "I told you on the journey up from Cuba that you could give me your opinion of Miss Warrington after you had learned to know her. I never have asked for it. Now that you have given it, I will add that she is the most noble girl I know. She is beautiful, she will be famous—but she does not love *me.*"

Zuñega laid his hand sympathetically on the American's arm.

"Is it always so in life, señor?" he said wistfully. "One loves and the other does not?"

"Generally the right one does not," smiled Lithgow. "You, however, will be loved in return. You are sure to be."

Zuñega shook his head.

"The only one that I care to have love me—is another man's wife," he said with a sigh. "I must love unrequitedly always."

Beatrice was her old self that night.

"Since you have honored mamma and me with your last precious moment, we will have a little chafing-dish supper to celebrate your departure," she declared gayly. "I got a lobster on my way home from the studio and carried it myself. What do you think of that? If it does not prove my admiration for Cuba's heroes and my devotion to the cause of liberty, what does?"

Seated around the cosy table, with Mrs. Warrington plying Zuñega with questions concerning his plans, they watched Beatrice concoct one of the dainty suppers for which the Warrington house was noted among those who were admitted within its sacred precincts. Beatrice never had appeared to better advantage. Lithgow laughingly declared that, with her high-necked ruffled apron on, she looked as she had when she had won his heart in boyhood. None would have dreamed of what lay beneath the surface of her fair, sweet face. Even Lithgow, accustomed as he was to woman's power of concealment, was surprised to see how completely the Beatrice of the afternoon was put out of sight.

"She has her yasmak on again," he thought. "I may never see her minus it again."

When the moment came for taking leave, Mrs. Warrington impulsively pulled Zuñega's dark head down to her own.

"You have no mother to kiss you 'Good-by,' my boy," she said; "let me bid you the farewell that she would give you if she could."

Tears sprung into his eyes. He kissed her timidly, gratefully.

"You, señora, have taught me what a mother is," he whispered softly.

Lithgow looked at Beatrice with a gaze that recalled the afternoon.   A flush crept up through her cheeks.

"This is the last word either of you ever may hear me speak," he said in quiet farewell.   "I go without the protection of an American citizen when I enter Cuba's field.   If I am taken prisoner, I shall deserve no more consideration than if I were a Cuban.   Good-by, dear little mother!"   He placed his arms about her and kissed her tenderly.   "Be proud that you have two of your boys in Cuba's struggle.   Pray for the hope of the island."

To Beatrice he held out his hand.   Its pressure was firm and full of meaning.

When the carriage had whirled them away, Mrs. Warrington placed a loving hand upon her daughter's shoulder.

"I don't understand you, dear," she said gently.   "I used to think that you liked Lithgow.   I hoped—I may as well confess it—that some time you and he would marry.   He is all that your father was.   I would ask no better husband for you."

"I am never going to marry, mamma," Beatrice answered. "Art brooks no rival.   Lithgow asked me to be his wife when he went to Cuba.   I did not love him."

"But, you may—some day," murmured the mother, venturing to draw the girl into her embrace.   "His going into what may be death for him will teach you to know your heart."   She pushed back the sunshiny hair and touched the white forehead with tender lips.

Beatrice closed down her lids.   Tears started out from under her lashes.

"Isn't there pain in learning to know one's heart?" she said, with a sigh that endeavored to be a smile.

She watched the long hours of the darkness away with eyes that slept not.   When day broke, she turned on her pillows wearily.

"Why couldn't it have been Lithgow!" she whispered, burying her face.

Zuñega and Lithgow found the schooner ready for sailing when they reached the Gulf.   The utmost care had been exercised to keep the authorities from discovering the real nature of their cargo.   It had taken months of active work on the part of Zuñega and other patriots to get the expedition thus far along. Zuñega's capital had fitted it out. Zuñega's orders were to be obeyed. The captain was one to whom the eastern coast of the island was as familiar as a playground. He knew that he could wind his boat in and out among the little mangrove isles with perfect ease where a Spanish gunboat could not follow.

They cruised cautiously along the Gulf coast, taking on at different points the refugees who were now eager to go back to take part in the wresting of Cuba from the tyrant. The captain knew that American vessels were instructed to watch out for just such filibustering ventures as this, and he sheltered his craft in many harbors unknown to marine charts.

Owing to all this prudence, they finally put out from the southern coast one dark night a week after they were supposed to have embarked. Swiftly they cut through the waters of the Gulf and crept nearer and nearer the Cuban coast, moving down through the Canal de Nicolas. All one day the boat swung in the shelter of the islands off the coast of Santa Clara; then, under cover of the night, wound its tortuous way among the dangerous reefs with stealthy care. Its decks were crowded with silent, anxious men, who, armed for conflict, stood ready to step again on the soil from which they had been banished. And each knew that the land that he loved would be drenched with his life-blood before he ceased to struggle to tear Cuba from the grasp of Spain.

Zuñega and Lithgow stood apart. They were watching with field-glasses the fires which they could distinguish were being built on the coast. Anxiously they counted the number and position of the ignited piles.

"*Bueno!* The proper signal has been given!" exclaimed Zuñega. "Rafael Castro was to patrol this coast until we landed. Everything is well—unless the enemy have secured our plans and are luring us on to land our cargo."

"Let *us* put ashore," suggested Lithgow. "No risk should be taken. We can go in one of the small boats. Tell the captain that if three of the fires are extinguished after we land, he may know that the coast is safe."

"And if we should fall into the hands of the Spaniards?" smiled Zuñega. "Who knows what changes may have taken place since we got news? Castro may have been defeated and his papers been taken possession of. But the chances are that all is safe and sure. Twenty of us can row ashore. Say you so?"

A boat was lowered and manned. It shot out over the phosphorescent water. As it approached the land, its occupants could discern that none of Spain's soldiers were among the half-clad men who were feeding the flames with armfuls of dead forest branches.

"*Viva Cuba libre!*" Every throat in the band of rowing men gave out the cry. Every throat on shore took it up. The very heavens seemed to ring with the patriotic words.

"What is the latest news from the front?" was Zuñega's first inquiry when the boat was drawn up on the beach by eager hands.

There was sudden, complete silence. Each man looked at his neighbor. An ominous hush seemed to be breathed through the night air.

"*Por amor de Dios, speak!*" cried Zuñega. "Have we lost?"

Rafael Castro removed his head-covering. Each man did the same and turned his face upward to the mystery of the stars.

Zuñega felt a shiver of fear run over him. He looked around at those who accompanied him. They had bared their heads also. He followed their example and, with drawn, anxious brows, stood waiting for the words.

"*Marti is dead!*" said Rafael Castro sorrowfully.

Zuñega stepped backward as if he had been struck a blow.

"*Marti dead?*" he cried. "Why, this is *his revolution!*"

"His death will put no end to the struggle which he inspired," replied the voices of those who had watched for his coming. "For the love that we bear him and the land that he sought to urge onward to freedom, we will fight now as we had not fought before. José Marti's spirit is with us! He leads us still!"

Zuñega drew himself to his highest stature. He lifted high in the night his sword.

"I, because he was my friend and my hero, will fight not alone for myself. I will fight for three: José Marti, myself, and the woman I love!"

"There is not a Cuban arm but will fight for the same," cried the men with one voice. "Spain has to contend with three men in one when she meets a Cuban in this last war that Cuba means to have with her!"

Three of the fires were put out.

Obedient to the arrangement, the schooner slipped in shore, guided by a hand that knew every inch of the perilous way.

The seven hundred who stepped forth on the land with their personal arms were surrounded by the insurgent forces which had been keeping the coast clear.

The cargo which meant so much to the revolutionary cause was unloaded and carried into the mountains.

The craft which had performed such a service for liberty's sake crept away among the cayos again stealthily.

It had other work to do.

It would come again.

The fires were left to smoulder. The small army of men vanished into the mysterious aisles of the forest that covered the mountains behind them.

Zuñega threw back his head and inhaled rapturously the beloved scents given out by this crucible of the ages. He caught Lithgow by the arm.

"*Amigo mio*, you know how I have longed for this moment," he said softly. "Does not *your* blood course faster through your veins? Does not the odor of the forest thrill you? Listen! Hear you not the voices? I have heard them in my sleep calling,—calling—calling. They are the voices of the forest spirits."

CHAPTER XXV.

IT was a long, tedious journey that Raquel and M. Theuriet were compelled to make to reach the plantations. M. Theuriet consumed the time in impressing on Raquel's mind how imprudent she had been in Havana. After exhausting the subject, he would re-commence at the beginning.

Raquel, with weary eyes, sat in her corner of the conveyance and dreamed of the welcome which awaited her at La Sacra Sonrisa. She petitioned her husband to go directly there without pausing at the coffee estate. She wondered if her father yet had discovered that he owed no man anything.

M. Theuriet, unobtrusively, had settled all of those debts with the Catalans. She glanced at him out of the corners of her eyes.

"How kind he has been to me!" she told herself with a shade of reproach. "I suppose it is natural for a man of his age to be cautious. His blood does not stir with rage against oppression. He has bowed beneath it so long. It is true that I had no right to risk *his* possessions because I am willing to offer even my life to Cuba!"

As the road grew more familiar and they neared the sugar plantation, she scarcely could restrain her impatience. Her father knew nothing of their coming. How astonished he would be! And he would tell her how he had missed her. He had purposely refrained from speaking of it in his letters, she knew.

Their arrival was discovered before they reached the hacienda. Surprised blacks surrounded the volante, with joyful cries.

Gilbert Palgrave, summoned by the commotion, came from the court. Scarcely believing that his eyes did not deceive him, he rushed to welcome them with the words:

"Never was there so opportune a home-coming!"

The full significance of his exclamation was not made apparent until they were within the sala and the greetings all over; then he placed in the hands of M. Theuriet a letter which purported to be from the insurgents, demanding the sum of fifteen thousand dollars.

"*Parbleu!* What mean zis?" cried the Frenchman. "Zose scoundrels, do zey threaten us? You will defy zem, ov course."

"Is it wise to do so?" questioned Palgrave. "You have no idea what progress they have been making. Rumors reach me that this is no such uprising as we fancied. Would it not be best to keep them our friends, if possible? They understand how we are situated. They know well that if we openly express sympathy, Spain will confiscate every acre that belongs to us. They know also that we are the ones who will be benefited if their fighting is successful. I see no harm in contributing—or in being forced, seemingly, to contribute—if it does not reach Spain's ears; and how should it?"

"You are mad to zink ov such a zing!" cried M. Theuriet.

"Besides, where will you get your fifteen zousand? I will not lend cet to you!"

"You have done what is of equal value, my friend," said Palgrave, flushing deeply. He arose and went to Raquel, placing his arm about her and tipping her face up so that he could look down into her eyes.

"Did you know, dearie, that your husband not only extends the time on the debt I owe him, but has himself released me from the clutches of the Catalans; so that now he is the only man to whom I owe a centavo? He has done this because I am your father; I understand that, and I am grateful to him for the deed. What I must learn is this: did you know that he contemplated doing such a thing?"

Raquel nerved herself to utter the untruth which she knew was the crowning point of her sacrifice. To fail now meant that all that she had given to place her father right financially would be of no value. He would divine at once what had been the motive which had made her marry M. Theuriet. She did not permit her lids to fall. She looked full into his earnest, manly, blue eyes as she said with what surprise she could feign:

"Has he done this? He is noble, is he not? But you are my father—and his father, now. It was no more than right, yet I appreciate it."

"Answer me," commanded Palgrave. "Did you know that he was going to do it?"

Raquel heard M. Theuriet lean forward in his chair. She heard the start he could not repress when she answered:

"I knew nothing of it."

Gilbert Palgrave drew a long breath. He bent and kissed her.

"If you knew what a load this has been on my mind since I found it out!" he said with relief. "I would not write about it. I wanted to put the question to your face. Now that I know that M. Theuriet did it because of his friendship for me and his belief that I will be able to lift the debt, I feel a man again."

Theuriet's eyes followed Raquel as she moved about the room. He understood what devotion it was which had caused her to reply as she had. He realized something of the nature of this creature whom he called his wife. He knew well how distasteful to her was her marriage with him. He had given up all hopes of making her love him as he had hoped that she would. He was content now simply to possess her and to feel that in ways he was her master. When he had heard her call him noble, a warm glow had run through his heart. Indeed, he thought that he was nobler than she gave him credit for. He alone knew what it had cost his soul when he had carried out Raquel's wishes completely in the matter of setting her father free. He was ashamed to let her know how dear to him had been the gold with which he had satisfied the Catalans. But it seemed that Palgrave had not taken it that his debt to his neighbor was discharged; and M. Theuriet saw that it was best so. He would never demand payment, but it might be better for Palgrave to remain in ignorance of that.

"What propose you to do?" questioned he of the sugar planter.

"My inclination is to pay them what they demand," answered Palgrave. "Neither you nor I can shut our eyes to what this means for us if the fellows are successful."

"But zey will not be!" M. Theuriet shook his head. "Your fifteen zousand will go to fill zeir pockets."

"That is not true," Raquel spoke suddenly from where she stood inspecting her old books. "These men are not brigands, they are heroes."

M. Theuriet shrugged his shoulders.

"You and I do not agree upon zat, *chérie*," he returned. "You will see ze truth ov my words."

"But if I give not this money, they threaten, you see, to burn my cane before the time for grinding."

"*Mon Dieu!* Zink you zat General Campos will not be able to put zis uprising down before zat time? Not one rebel will be lef' on ze island."

"I cannot help feeling that you are mistaken," replied Palgrave.

"But, hav' I not just come from Havana?" cried the Frenchman, with irritation at finding his opinion was not given the weight he felt it deserved.

Raquel smiled. Her back was toward them.

"And you had not heard that the railroads were all demolished in Santiago de Cuba and Puerto Principe,'" she commented.

M. Theuriet looked at the back of her head and was silent.

"My answer is to be given to-night," said Palgrave with visible anxiety. "That is why I cried that never was an arrival so needed as yours. I wanted your advice."

"Yet you will tak' eet not!" said the Frenchman, with a gesture of displeasure. "How could you produce zat sum ov monnaie by zis time?"

"I can tell them when they can have it," returned Palgave. "I own that it may look odd to you, who are my large creditor, that I am ready to borrow this amount when you have just released me from debt; but fifteen thousand dollars is a small sum when compared with what my crop will be worth. If it insures the safety of my cane, then I will be in a position at the close of the year to repay you somewhat and pay the fifteen thousand as well to whomever I may borrow it of. From my point of view, it would be economy in the end."

"I would defy zem," M. Theuriet insisted.

"And what if they threaten your coffee crop?" queried Palgrave.

"I should lik' to see any one who could keep me from picking eet!" M. Theuriet responded, with an air as if he had an entire regiment to enforce his word. "I am not afraid ov zese rascals."

"Well, I am glad that you are not," sighed Gilbert Palgrave. "I know this; they have got to obtain support from us planters or else destroy our crops so that Spain will not reap the benefit. I mean to grind my sugar-cane this winter. How can I do it if it is burnt?"

"You will pairsist een believing zat zese insurgents are more powerful zan zey are," Theuriet replied comfortably. "I will call upon Spain for help cef zey attempt to keep me from picking my coffee."

"How long will it take soldiers to reach here?" questioned Raquel without turning around. "With railroads destroyed, you would be beyond reach of immediate help. I think papa is right. Contribute what they ask. It is cowardly not to. I knew all the time that papa's heart was where mine is, only he has deemed it best not to say so. Now has come the time for action."

M. Theuriet threw out his graceful fingers in a way that betokened that he declined to share any responsibility in the matter. "Eef you can sateesfy zem wiz promises, well and good," he said. "Before time to pay ze gold, zeir cause may be lost. Ees eet zis night zat zey come? How was ze message lef'?"

"Pinned to the door with a knife," answered Palgrave.

"Let us remain here until this is over?" Raquel said pleadingly to M. Theuriet. "No one at La Buena Esperanza knows that we have come. To-morrow will do as well for us to go home."

"It shall be as you wish, *ma chère*," answered M. Theuriet. "Your papa and I hav' faced ozair troubles togethair. I would not wish heem to meet zis alone. Eef zese men are as courteous as ze brigand, Gonzalo Alarcon—oh, by ze way, Palgrave, had you heard zat ze price which has been so long placed on ze head of Alarcon is won? No-o? Ah, ze word arreeved quicklee cen Havana! He was hung."

"By whom?" questioned the sugar planter. "It was a fate he deserved twice over."

"As I remembair, eet was ze insurgents zemselves who hav' hung heem," answered M. Theuriet slowly. "He offaired gold, which he had obtained by ransom and blackmail, to ze insurgent leader. Eet was refused and——"

"Ah, does that not prove to you the nature of these men who are fighting for the freedom of the island?" cried Raquel.

"I confess zat eet ees incredeebl'," Theuriet admitted, "but, to continue, his own men zen took heem and not only divided ze monnaie between zemselves but claimed ze reward offaired for his dead body."

Raquel sat down suddenly in the estrada and leaned her head back. The story sent a horrible sickness over her. She had known these men! The very ones who had peered at her that night, as she had sat with Zuñega at her feet watching the dance of Faquita, probably had participated in this act of treachery! From what a fearful life had not Zuñega and Faquita released her! Where was Faquita? Had *she* reaped the benefit of the reward?

She went up to the room in which she had slept through her girlhood. Not a thing had been changed in it. Tia Juana had seen that even the candle was burning before the little crucifix.

"How long ago it seems since I slept here last!" she sighed, touching the little white bed reverently.

She turned half-guiltily as she heard her father's voice behind her. He had followed her up in order to secure an instant alone with her, as a mother wistfully seeks to look into the face of her daughter who has gone out from the home nest. Raquel wondered if he would be able to peer beneath the surface which she endeavored to present to him.

He put his arms around her and drew her hungrily against him.

"I have missed you dreadfully, Raquel," he whispered with tears in his eyes. "When you had gone, I found that you were all that made the plantation a home to me. Time and again, I have been tempted to write and beg you to shorten your stay in Havana, but I conquered my selfishness. Now that you really are here, however, I may as well tell you."

"I longed to hear just such words," Raquel said against his cheek.

"Tell me, are you happy?" queried he troubledly. "There is something in your face that—was not there when you went away."

"I suppose—I have left—girlhood behind me, here in this dear room," she answered evasively. "One must change; I have seen something of the world."

"It is not that," Palgrave shook his head with conviction. "There is an expression of—indifference,—a sort of hopelessness in your eyes."

"Ah no, no! You do not read aright!" cried Raquel. "I tremble with anxiety concerning this venture of our patriots. You know how I yearn to do something myself. Oh, will you keep a secret? I have not told M. Theuriet, but I would like you to know."

"What is it?" questioned her father, visibly worried. "Have you been less wise that I advised you to be?"

"Possibly," admitted Raquel, "but it is not that. Zuñega *has* come back to fight! I told you that he would."

"How heard you so?"

"In Havana."

"How comes it to be known there? Spain will be making him a prisoner."

"There are many things known in Havana of which Spain

is not cognizant," she replied meaningly. "I am proud of
you, papa! You have laughed at my rage against Spain,
yet the same righteous indignation is in your English breast.
Tell those who come to-night that you wish them success in
their noble effort to give the island freedom. If Spain con-
fiscates what we have, we can go and fight against her. That
would be glorious! I could fight as well as these Spanish
boys who are sent over here to face a desperate nation. Poor
lads! It has been sad to see them land; for every Cuban
knows that they will return never to Spain. Fever will do
the work that Cuban rifles leave undone."

"You are more of an insurrectionist than ever," smiled her
father. "It is a wonder that you did not get both M. Theuriet and me into hot water while you were in the capital!"

And Raquel refrained from confessing how nearly she had
accomplished the very thing he feared.

Gilbert Palgrave, cautious ever, made preparations for
receiving his expected nocturnal callers. He called his large
force of men together and instructed them to supply themselves with whatever arms the plantation afforded; these, he
knew, were few and old; but each man possessed a machete
or cane-knife, formidable weapon enough in the strong hand
that knew how to wield it. One sweeping stroke of this keen
blade would be more than sufficient to cut a man's head clean
from his shoulders. That the insurgents themselves were
likely to be armed with these same instruments of Cuban
warfare he was aware; shut off from the markets of the
world, they had no recourse save to dig up the arms which
had been buried since the last war, or to employ the imple-
ments that gained them their livelihood.

M. Theuriet, not too confident of his neighbor's ability to
deal with characters supposed to be so desperate, sent a messenger commanding all of the available men on the coffee
estate to come to Palgrave's aid.

The astonishment which the servants of La Buena Esperanza experienced at learning of their master's unexpected return was lost in the more exciting news of the near approach
of the insurgents.

When they were all assembled and were being put through
a brief training, M. Theuriet said suddenly to the sugar
planter:

" Where ees Pepillo, ze mayoral?"

" He left suddenly at the first suggestion of war," replied Palgrave. "And to tell the truth, I was not sorry. I always was suspicious of that fellow. He was a Spaniard. I am convinced that he was a spy of the government sent here to determine if I was taxed to the fullest extent possible. My failure to render the full tribute demanded by the officials has placed me under suspicion, no doubt. You may be sure that he kept account of every pound of sugar raised on this plantation. It is a villainous espionage that Spain maintains over her subjects. I, for one, will be glad to see it over, and I do not mind contributing toward that end."

" I would rejoice as loudly as any eef Spanish taxes could be lifted, or, what would be bettair, eef ze Spaniards could be driven out ov ze island; but zat will nevair be done, so I remain on ze safe side."

" I am not certain which will be the safe side this time," returned the sugar planter. " Isn't there some old adage to the effect that it is not well to have all of your eggs in one basket?"

With the approach of darkness, the blacks were stationed all over the plantation with orders to resist any attempt to damage the mill or the crop. The air was full of suppressed excitement.

The house was secured against a possible attack. The iron-barred windows were fastened and guarded by men with machetes. Raquel, her father, and M. Theuriet remained in the sala, awaiting the arrival of the delegation. Palgrave was nervous and smoked two cigars to Theuriet's one. He knew in what danger he stood. The presence of the blacks at the various points of vantage reminded him of that fact and he could not remain seated. With hands in his pockets, he paced the floor hour after hour. Raquel's nerves also were strained to a high pitch, but she compelled herself to sit motionless. She had learned much self-control in the few months of her married life.

It was near midnight when, on the stillness of the air, the sound of horses' feet was borne to the ears of the watchers. Nearer, nearer, the tread came. Raquel shivered with apprehension. A terrible dread, that had not been hers before, paralyzed her. She gazed at her father in speechless anxiety. Noticing the look, he came and touched her hair with his lips.

"Thank God that you have some one to care for you—if anything happens to me," he whispered.

Raquel sprung up then and wound her arms around him passionately.

"Do you think—that—anything may happen?" she cried. "You shall not go out! Let me go! I will tell them——"

"Hush! They are knocking," he said, throwing up his head. "There is a God! He is with men in their hour of trouble!"

He went swiftly to the entrance and stepped out among the circle of men who stood there. Despite his express orders, Raquel followed him, taking the chains of the door from the unwilling hands of the man who was on guard. She heard the leader say in distinct tones:

"We come for the fifteen thousand which you are to contribute toward the liberation of Cuba. We know where your sympathies lie. We demand this expression of them."

"Where have I heard that voice before?" Raquel questioned puzzledly of herself. "It sounds almost as familiar as my own; yet I can not tell who is its possessor."

"It is true that my sympathies are with Cuba; whose are not?" Gilbert Palgrave said in reply, "but owing to Spain's exorbitant taxes I am not in a position to furnish you with the gold that you demand; but I am willing to promise that I will make every effort to borrow it, and, if I am successful, it shall be turned over to you. I know that I and my brother planters on the island are the ones who most will profit by this revolution if it wins the day. It is not fair that we support you not, yet you are perfectly aware of how Spain holds us. You know that at the first suggestion that we are favorable to the enterprise in which you are engaged, the government will take every possession from us and give us in return imprisonment or banishment. Therefore I ask you to be as generous as you can afford to be and permit me time enough to raise this sum without incurring suspicion from Spanish officials. If you will return a month from now, I will have it for you."

"That will not do, we must have it now," replied the leader.

"What further proof do we need?" cried a voice from the circle. "Has he not told us what he is? Are not Pepillo's words revealed to be true? He is a sympathizer with the revolutionists. Seize him."

"Pepillo?" thundered Palgrave. "Is that dog here? Ah, I understand this now! It is a plot to entrap me into making known my true sentiments. That devil of a Spaniard has betrayed me after being in my employ. I know not what he has heard me speak, but this I say to you, whoever you are: I now would put every dollar I possess into the hands of the men who are determined to teach Spain that her barbarisms have no place in the twentieth century. For nearly four hundred years Spanish cruelty has made this place a robbers' nest. Not content with deceiving the peaceful Caribs, she has deceived her own children. She has crushed and killed them! But their blood speaks again with a voice that Spain is destined to hear from the lips of the men of to-day. Seize me if you like. I am for Cuba and liberty! The flag of my country will protect me! I am an Englishman, and, if need be, I can die for the freedom of this land which I have made my home."

Raquel had darted without a cry from the shadow of the portal. She stood by his side. Her face was white. Her eyes were like stars.

"If you take him, you take me!" she said in ringing tones. "I am a Cuban and I defy the Spanish tyrant. You may kill me, but the patriotism that burns in my breast burns in that of every Cuban. You can never kill or imprison us all. Ever will there be a soul like Marti's left to lead us on to liberty."

"Seize him!" ordered the leader. "Leave the girl. There are other ways of dealing with her."

"My God!" cried the father. "Raquel, why have you exposed yourself!"

Raquel had given a cry that summoned every black within reach. The alarm was spread by two hundred throats. As Palgrave was made prisoner, an entire regiment of soldiers seemed to rise up from the shadows where they had lain in hiding. They came to the help of those who bound the struggling man.

But they found themselves surrounded by a mass of desperate, fighting blacks, at whose head was M. Theuriet, determined to rescue his neighbor even if the attempt landed him beside Palgrave amid the indescribable horrors of a Spanish prison.

There ensued a battle which for fierceness and desperation

had, as yet, had no parallel during the experience of the soldiers, who defended themselves from the furious strokes of the
frantic blacks urged onward by their love for their master and
by the voice of Raquel. Mauser rifles were of no avail in a
hand-to-hand scrimmage with crazed men who fought like
demons to preserve their master from the fate that threatened
him. Unknown to any of them, he had been borne away in
the thick of the struggle, and was now being taken rapidly
from the scene by mounted men.

Little by little, those who were able fought their path
through the army of cane-workers to where their horses were
standing. Swinging themselves into their saddles, they re-
treated from the machetes of the combined forces of both
plantations.

There in the darkness, Raquel stood in the midst of loss
and bloodshed. The groans of the wounded filled the air.
She was chilled through and through with horror. A scream
of terror rose from her heart, but it could not pass her stiff lips.

She feared that her father had been killed. Were he able
to speak, she knew that he would try to silence her fears by a
word that would tell her of his whereabouts.

The frightened women, headed by Tia Juana, obeyed her
order for candles. Soon, lights went flitting about over the
bodies that lay outstretched before the entrance.

Breathlessly, Raquel bent over the men, fearful of what
she might see. No thought entered her mind as yet concerning the fate of her husband. She had forgotten his existence.
Everything was swallowed up in her absorbing fear for her
father.

With gladness she noted that, thus far, those over whom
she flashed her light wore the uniform of Spanish soldiers.
Not a wounded black was to be seen. If any were dead, they
had been borne to the quarters.

One soldier groaned with agony as she passed him. She
halted an instant with the pity of woman.

"I will have your wounds attended to," she said. "I am
seeking my father."

"They have taken him away," the man told her, with another moan of pain that he could not repress. "He is a prisoner of Spain."

The candle dropped from Raquel's hands. She stood as if

turned into stone. Nothing so merciful as unconsciousness came to her. Before her mental vision passed in quick review all of the hideous cruelties which she ever had heard of being practised by the Spaniards.

Tia Juana, with a cry of alarm, darted toward her and extinguished the flame which had caught her gown from the fallen candle. In doing this, the woman made the discovery that the man beside whom Raquel thus stood frozen with fear was M. Theuriet.

Reaching up, she took Raquel by the arm and attracted her attention.

"M. Theuriet is wounded, *señorita mia*," she said tremblingly. "*Mira!* He moves not. He hears not."

Recalled to the things about her, Raquel dropped to her knees, remorseful that she had not thought of him sooner. She placed her fingers on his heart. It seemed to beat faintly.

"Call some one," she cried anxiously. "We must get him into the house!"

Awed by this terrible thing which had befallen the plantation, the men bore him into the sala carefully.

In the employment furnished by the effort to revive him to consciousness, Raquel, for a moment, lost sight of her greater trouble. When he opened his eyes, after she seemingly had exhausted every remedy known to Tia Juana, Raquel felt a wave of thankfulness sweep through her benumbed mind. She knelt beside him, stroking his hands.

"Ah, thank God!" she cried with relief.

Theuriet endeavored to raise his head. He looked about him in a dazed way; then, when recollection became his, he asked quickly:

"Palgrave,—where ees he?"

"They have taken him away!" moaned Raquel. "He is a prisoner of Spain. You and I must rescue him, monsieur."

The Frenchman fell back with a groan of despair.

"*Mon Dieu!* I zink I am dying," he whispered. "What will you do?"

"I will revenge both of you!" she cried, trying to gather him up in her strong young arms. "You are not dying! You have not been hurt seriously."

"I hav' received a sword-thrust from zat leader," murmured he feebly, putting his hand to his side. "I die—now!"

Frantically Raquel tore his clothing from the spot indicated.

It was true. How deep or how dangerous the wound was, she could not determine. She was surrounded by blacks more ignorant than herself. She watched the grayness of death creeping over his face and did not know what she looked upon. Even while she bent above him with wide, terror-filled eyes, there was a horrible struggle in his throat. Then he lay very still.

The minutes passed. She drew him closer in her arms. She smoothed the gray hair back from his forehead. Her fingers were wet with the dampness which stood on his brow. She observed his features anxiously. She waited for some further sign of recognition.

Suddenly Tia Juana gave a shriek and endeavored to take him from her.

"*See you not that he is dead, señorita mia?*"

With a tightening at her heart, Raquel put her face down to his.

"He has fainted again—with pain," she whispered, looking up at Tia Juana with startled countenance when she found that no breath came from his lips.

"*He is dead! Dios pity us!*" cried the woman. "*He is dead!*"

Raquel would not permit him to be taken from her.

She held him closer and glanced around the sala with a gaze that seemed to see nothing. The few candles scattered about afforded little light to dissipate the awful gloom of the waning darkness. The anxious eyes of the terrified servants who watched her did not read that she was taking a farewell of all she looked upon.

"Summon all that are of left of you," she said.

"Only Diego and Pedro are injured, señorita," old Pablo told her. "The Spaniards shot themselves, not us. Our machetes were powerful."

"They will need to be as powerful in the future," she said meaningly. "Call every member of the plantation here."

When they were assembled, awe-stricken and tearful, she looked up into their dark, faithful faces from that quiet one in her arms.

"I have no protector now but you," she said, hushing their

cries of woe authoritatively. "You have no masters now—but me. Are you prepared to obey me?"

"*Sí, sí, señorita,*" came from the dusky throats of her father's men, to whom, despite her marriage, she always would be the little señorita.

"*Sí, sí, señora,*" the voices of those from the coffee estate replied.

"Will you follow me wherever I may lead you?" she demanded.

"As long as we have life!"

"Spain's officials have robbed me of all that I hold dear," she said bitterly. "I will revenge the capture of my father, the death of my husband! I am Spain's avowed enemy! It will not be safe for me to remain here. I shall go to the mountains. I am a woman, but I can lead you against those whom Spain has sent over here to conquer us. As long as strength is mine, I will fight the power that has brought such desolation to my home, such ruin to our land. Have I the support of those who have lost their masters and their homes because of Spanish treachery?"

"We are yours, señorita. Our machetes are for Cuba!"

"There is no time to be lost." She seemed to have come into her own. Her voice was one of command. She was born to lead and she knew it at that moment. "The Spaniards will come back here after their dead. We must be away. This estate will become Spain's. What will be the fate of La Buena Esperanza I know not. We will do what we can for these wounded. Ay, it is the mercy of Jesu! We cannot leave them to suffer. Then to the forest! Spain has another band of insurgents now to harass her troops and lead them into ambush! We will do what we can to break Cuba's chains and throw open the doors of the prisons. And if death becomes ours in the struggle, we will welcome it—for the sake of our Cuba!"

The Spanish soldier to whom she had promised care lifted his head.

"*Viva Cuba! Cuba libre!*" he said under his breath. "Spain sends us over here to fight such a people as this! God give them freedom!"

CHAPTER XXVI.

RAQUEL remained beside the body of M. Theuriet while the women unwillingly attended to the wounds of those of the Spaniards who were not yet dead. With the break of day, the scene where the conflict had been presented an aspect that made the blacks full of shuddering terror.

Ten soldiers already were dead and three more slipped from life before the sun was an hour high. The machetes had done fatal work.

The soldier who had whispered " *Viva Cuba !*" requested that he might speak with Raquel. Tia Juana refused to call her. He caught the woman by the hand and drew her nearer to him.

"Call her!" he begged. "I can be of help to her. I heard what she told you. She intends to leave here. She must go quickly. Call her!"

Impressed by his earnestness, Tia Juana obeyed.

Raquel came. Her face was set and stern. She hated the sight of the Spanish uniform. The soldier lost no time in convincing her of his desire to aid her.

"Take the arms and ammunition from me and my companions," he told her. "I understand where you mean to go. It is wise. Pepillo Astucera will return here. You wish to do something for your island. I will tell you what her brave men will need. A hospital! You are prepared to give it them. Take your provisions, your remedies, your beds. Establish a place in the mountains where your wounded can be cared for. Cubans will bless you. If you will take me with you, I will lead your blacks on to whatever you desire. Ay, I am a Spaniard! But—God knows I am ashamed to be one! There are many of us who would join the insurgents if we dared. We knew not what we came to fight when Spain sent us over."

"I could trust no Spaniard!" Raquel returned slowly. His words showed her the necessity for action, but she could not see which way to turn. She knew beyond all hope of change that M. Theuriet was dead, yet she could not endure the thought of having him buried. To go and leave him was a thing impossible. To take him with them seemed as impossible. The soldier appeared to comprehend her trouble.

"Perhaps you are right," he sighed. "Since I came I have learned of things which Cuba has endured that Spain herself does not know, I think—the people of Spain, I mean. I did not know the nature of the work which we were to do here at your home. I was given to understand that your father was a dangerous conspirator against the government. We were ordered to accompany his accusers and enforce Spain's law. Let me atone what I can. Help me to join the cause for which you, a woman, are ready to fight. Leave your dead here until all else is safe; then, if there is time, return for them."

He was little more than a boy. His face was honest. His eyes, full of pain, looked into hers earnestly.

"I may be dead by that time," he added. "I suffer, but I do not know how badly I am hurt."

Raquel examined his wound with inexperienced eyes.

"I know not either," she told him troubledly.

"Give no thought to me," he urged her. "Summon your people. Take your animals and cart into the forest—all that you can carry."

"You are brave," Raquel said. "I will be as brave."

Even in less time than she had hoped there was little left within the walls to betoken a habitation. The blacks of both plantations worked as they never had in the busiest season. The carts, built for loading the cane to be brought to the mill, now served to convey the contents of the hacienda through the protected roads of the cane-fields to the river, which was easily forded though the rains had swollen it. From this point on there was more caution to be observed, but the transfer of the possessions of La Sacra Sonrisa went on uninterruptedly throughout the day.

Raquel found herself confronted by a fresh problem. What was she to do with the women of both plantations? They could not fight. It was true that some of them could act in the capacity of nurses, but there were too many to be thus employed or fed. She knew something of the difficulties of camp-life from her short experience in that of Alarcon. She finally decided to leave all that would remain at La Buena Esperanza and place, as guard and protection over them, one-third of M. Theuriet's own men. It soon would be time for the gathering of the coffee crop. It might be that Spain would permit that to be done. M. Theuriet was believed to have been most loyal to Spain. His estate might not be molested unless by the revolutionists.

To her consternation, she learned that none of them was willing to stay. They not only were afraid of Spain's soldiers, but they desired to accompany her on whatever expedition she chose to send them. After laying the case before them, however, she won the consent of thirty men, who agreed to remain with the women for two months at La Buena Esperanza and carry on the work as if their master still were in Havana, on the condition that, at the end of that time, their places should be taken by some of those who were to follow her.

The destination which Raquel had in her mind was the cave which Zuñega had revealed to her and Faquita. She remembered its location and believed that her men could find the way to it.

The children, mothers, and old women were removed to La Buena Esperanza. The dead Spanish soldiers had been buried. The only one that was alive was the boy, who watched all these things being accomplished.

"Are you going to leave me here, señora?" he asked wistfully. "I will prove no traitor to Cuba."

"We will take you with us," said Raquel. "They who suffer much can forgive much. You have tried to help me. I am grateful."

When the shadows were beginning to cast themselves far, M. Theuriet was placed in the rude coffin which Pablo had hastily constructed. The utter absence of a burial service made the scene no less impressive.

With her bowed head touched by the sunlight that sifted through the orange trees, Raquel stood looking down into the grave. She could shed no tears. She believed that never again would such relief ease the burning beneath her heavy lids. With what strange swiftness had come the end of her married life and her entrance into the arena where Cuba was fighting for her liberty with such desperation as the goaded bull exhibits beneath the tortures of the toreador!

"You have given your life to Cuba," she said softly as the

earth covered him from sight. "It shall not be in vain. The island will gain the strong hands and stout hearts of those who were your servants. They shall swell the mighty cry of '*Cuba libre!*'"

The wounded Spaniard was carried swung in a blanket between two horses.

Raquel led the way with M. Theuriet's Diego by her side. They pushed a short distance into the forest; then waited for the coming of another day, when they skirted the shoulder of the mountain over which Zuñega had led her. In spite of her belief that she could go directly to the spot, four long, wearisome days elapsed before they came to the river she sought. She had forgotten that Zuñega had said it was a subterranean stream, and much of that time they had crossed and recrossed where it was tunnelling its way unseen hundreds of feet beneath their tread.

Descending to where it rushed as fiercely as ever over its stony bed, the company took up its march to the destined cave. The finding of this Raquel had anticipated would be difficult, but, to her surprise, they had not gone far when they observed signs that others had been there recently. The dense tangle which she remembered, had been cut away. Following the cleared path with more speed, they reached a spot where she paused abruptly. She had forgotten how the place looked, yet, when she came to the spot where Zuñega had left the river, she recognized it instantly.

Apprehension seized her. She had not once thought of the possibility that the cave might have been taken possession of already. The indisputable evidence about her proved that such must be the case. As far as she could peer up the stream, the mass of green growth had been cut away sufficiently to allow easy passage.

"This is the cave," she said to Diego, who still was her body-guard, "but some one has been before us. The Spaniards have discovered it, or our patriots are using it. Keep the others back while I go and see."

Diego rushed to warn the long cavalcade which was following in the path Raquel had chosen. There were not lacking those who had found the journey an anxious one, and many had been the unuttered questions which had trembled on the lips of the men. But they were accustomed to obey, and Raquel

had shown them that she expected nothing less.   The soldier
had borne the tediousness of the slow forest travelling far better than any of them had expected.   His wound, a machete
cut, had yielded to the magic of the remedies which Tia Juana
had applied one after the other, and the inflammation had sub-
sided considerably.   He had raved over the beauties of this
plant world through which they cut their way, and he had
shivered when told that it abounded in vines the touch of
which was poisonous and deadly to those who, like himself,
were unacquainted with the remedies and unaccustomed to
the climate.

Raquel stole cautiously up through the green barricade
which nature had built before this retreat.   The huge boulder which had been there was pushed to one side, but the veil
of vines concealed the entrance sufficiently.   Trembling vio-
lently, Raquel thrust her fingers through the leaves and peered
in.   There were signs of recent occupancy.   She ventured to
creep in stealthily, not knowing what might be made manifest
by exploration.   Back among the shadows she stumbled over
a collection of rifles which evidently had been stored here,
together with what looked like boxes of ammunition.

She did not really grasp the nature of the discovery until
Diego had made his way to her.   Crazy with excitement, he
ran back and brought as many of the others as could follow
his fleet feet.

The Spaniard, hearing the commotion, demanded that he
should be carried into the cave.

" These are concealed by the insurgents!" he cried.   " No
Spanish soldier ever would penetrate thus far into a Cuban
forest.   He is not obliged to hide his war munitions.   Only
you Cubans must do that!"

The supposed ammunition he regarded with suspicion.

" They may contain ammunition and they may hold
dynamite," he told them.   " Roloff is blowing up bridge after
bridge with the deadly stuff.   Where he gets it, where he
keeps it concealed, we Spaniards have not been able to find.
This may be one of the hiding-places.   I am fearful of having
the boxes opened!"

" But what good are the guns without ammunition?" demanded Raquel.

" None," agreed he, " but I can tell you where to obtain

ammunition. Only there is no one to lead your men to it. They could capture it easily now."

"I can lead them!" Raquel said proudly.

The soldier looked at her, his surprise struggling with unbelief.

"Dare you, señora?" he asked quickly. "It will be perilous."

"Do you think I care for peril?" demanded she scornfully. "My life is worth only what it can win for Cuba. I shall count that every blow I can strike at Spain is that much toward the freedom of my father."

The Spaniard hesitated.

"You may deem me ignoble," he said finally. "I am going to betray to you my own country. I can fight for her no more. If I recover the use of my arm, I shall join the Cuban forces. That will be no worse than the action of those soldiers in Havana who continually dispose of ammunition to the friends of the insurgents. Spain's methods drive her own soldiers from the cause they are brought over to defend."

"It is only a noble soul that is courageous enough to refuse to support an unrighteous power," answered Raquel. "It is only a cowardly or a benighted mind that will war against Cuba when her deep wrongs are understood: cowardly, because afraid of Spanish vengeance; benighted, because not touched by the advancing spirit of civilization which demands the recognition of liberty and brotherhood!"

The soldier's eyes filled with honest admiration as he watched her slender, graceful figure draw itself up commandingly.

"Your soul is too large for your woman's body, señora," he sighed. "It is no wonder that we fail to vanquish a nation with such hearts as yours!"

"Where is the ammunition?" questioned Raquel curiously.

"Lieutenant Jaime Arco, with fifty soldiers, is detailed to guard a rude fort of logs in which is stored fifteen thousand rounds of ammunition, seventy-five Mauser rifles and some camp stores. You have ninety men with you, have you not?"

Raquel nodded assent. Her face was alight with daring.

"If they fight as they fought the other night, you can secure everything that the hut holds."

20

"Without guns?" asked Raquel, finding that the project was rather formidable when she came to contemplate it.

"Your men do not know how to use guns yet," reminded the soldier. "In their hands the machetes are twice as fatal. And in close conflict our rifles are of little avail. They carry too far."

"Tell me what to do," Raquel requested determinedly.

"I scarcely know where the place is," replied the Spaniard, "but it is called by name of Yaez. It consists only of a few houses and a dozen huts. The ammunition is being held there for our men, as they are expected to move backward through the country."

"I know where the spot is," Raquel said quickly, "but I do not know how to reach it from here."

"If I were able, I would lead your men to it," declared the soldier, "but I fear that I never will be in shape to do much for any cause again."

"Tia Juana has healed worse wounds than that, she says," Raquel encouraged him. "You yet will be so that you can follow Gomez."

"No; I will fight under you, señora," he swore, lifting his uninjured arm.

"I and my men may be Spain's victims by that time," she returned.

When the weary group of embryonic patriots had disposed itself to its satisfaction in and about the cave, the women prepared a meal, of which the half-famished men partook hungrily. The possibility of an immediate sortie filled them with delight. They fondled the weapons in the cave and obeyed the instructions of the weak voice of the soldier, who told them how to bring the rifles up into proper position. With the possession of the ammunition for which they were willing to go under Raquel's orders, they fancied that they would be in a position to work limitless damage to the men of Spain. They were so amenable that the soldier was delighted. With them to hear, he told Raquel what was the best course to pursue. He advised that the onslaught be made near night, when Arco might be drinking, as was his wont.

"I hate myself for being a traitor, but I find that I am a Cuban at heart even if I was born in Spain. I will be true to my inclinations. Kill none, if you can help it. Make them prisoners. Bring them here. If you capture them and return them to Spain, she will shoot them for being so remiss in duty as to permit themselves to be captured. Rather than return to be court-martialed, they will join the Cuban army. You will have a company of fighting men, señora."

"I will trust no Spaniard," she said.

"Yet you trust me," he reminded her.

"You are in my power," she returned.

Accustomed as she had been all of her life to care and luxury of home, Raquel found that she suffered from the fatigue of the travelling far more than she had anticipated. She disguised the fact as well as she could, and went among her men, encouraging them constantly by the sight of her sad, determined face. The truth was that they needed little encouragement. The prospect before them was exactly to their taste. They had all of the desire to see their land free, added to which was the negro desire for revenge for the wrongs which had been done Raquel and their masters.

The next morning, leaving the cave to be guarded by the women and the sick Spaniard, Raquel and the ninety blacks moved down the path which had been cleared through the dense foliage. They were watched out of sight by the fearful Tia Juana, who was apprehensive that the stalwart band never would return to the safety of this mountain stronghold.

Raquel may have had the same thought, but she did not voice it. She waved her hand backward with the cry:

"*Viva Cuba! Cuba libre!*"

She bore the gun which belonged to the Spaniard. Some of the blacks carried the others which had been taken from the dead soldiers.

Where this river trail would lead them she had no idea. She meant to follow it as long as the path was clear. She reasoned that a considerable force of men must have journeyed over this route, for there were signs that many machetes had been employed in devastating the underbrush. She wondered when they would come back again for their hidden stores. The novelty of this enterprise she had in mind, the certain danger into which she was going, combined to keep her from giving way to the grief which filled her heart with the memory of all that had happened since she had left Havana. She thought of Pepita de Urquiza and wondered what would be that person's comment on this action. She remembered that these were the paths through which Faquita even now might be moving. What had the girl done after the death of Alarcon? That had not been long ago. Had it not been for the knowledge that this forest was no longer the rendezvous of the brigands, she never would have dared to penetrate thus fearlessly into its depths.

The manner in which the foliage crossed and interlaced at the top of the gorge made it gloomy for those who crept along on the verge of the stream, ignorant of whether they were going deeper into the mountain fastnesses or coming out into the light of day.

Tirelessly Raquel led them on, resolving that she would not let the unfortunate fact that she was a woman keep her from achieving all that she had dreamed in those days when she had swung in the hammock of the quiet court.

Night overtook them. They slept by turns, watching over their mistress with eager, anxious care. Secretly they felt that they could do better without her, but they dared not tell her so. They were fearful of what might happen to her in the attempt to capture the store of ammunition. They failed to perceive what benefit a woman's brain would be to them in the battle that lay before them. They meant to fight desperately. What more was there to do?

But before the raid on the Spaniards was completed, they found that the calm judgment of the girl was to be depended on far more than the excited, varying opinions of ninety blacks.

They took up the march in the morning and were rewarded four hours later by coming out into the broad sunlight of a valley through which the river ran noiselessly, giving no hint of the tumultuous force with which it had dashed itself along through the mountain opening.

Here they discovered the hut of a *montero*, who not only made them welcome and provided them with as much of a breakfast as his meagre possessions allowed, but presented Raquel with his only horse when he learned the object they had in view.

"It is for Cuba, *señora mia*," he replied when she remonstrated. "It is all I have to give."

Knowing that she could return it to him or replace it

with another, she accepted it, seeing her mistake in not bringing those from the camp. The spirit within her had been so
mighty that she had not thought but what her body would be
able to obey all demands made upon it. To the blacks this
constant travelling was no more than they were accustomed to
the greater portion of the year. To her feminine frame it
was fatiguing beyond measure.

From the *montero* they derived the information that the
tiny hamlet which was their destination lay twelve miles
beyond. The road to it led through the manigua or thick
underbrush, which makes so excellent an ambush. He finally
offered to guide them there, and left his half-clad wife and not
clad children weeping.

Mounted, Raquel felt even more hopeful of success than
she had when creeping along the riverside. Her body became rested and promised to carry out the plan which she
was formulating in her mind. Everything seemed favorable
to them. There was no moon now. It would be a dark night.
The soldiers would anticipate little danger. They might be
off their guard. When two miles from the spot, the blacks
took to the manigua, lest they might be seen. She rode on
alone, but she could hear her men moving through the heavy
green growth. The knowledge of their nearness was not
without its value to her feminine mind.

On the verge of the diminutive town she halted, intending to wait for darkness. Diego stole nearer the collection of
dwellings and came back with the information that only five
soldiers appeared to be guarding the fort, the remainder of
them being occupied in watching a cock-fight in the court-yard
of the posada.

Ignorant of all war tactics, she divined nevertheless that
this was the moment for the master-stroke, and, with no warning, swept in upon the unsuspecting village with a swarm of
belligerent blacks at the heels of her horse. Before the soldiers at the mud-banked fort knew what had happened, they
were prisoners and the stores they had been guarding were in
the hands of this wild-eyed crowd of excited negroes, who
obeyed the orders given by a pale-faced girl.

With the swiftness of those who know that they yet have
much work to do, the muscular men conveyed every portion
of the ammunition to the manigua. They secreted there the

rifles also, relieving the bound soldiers of their arms as well. Not a shot had been fired. Not an alarm had been given. The five soldiers on guard had been playing dominoes at the time of the attack. Leaving four others beside Diego to guard these, Raquel led her men to the posada. She knew that horses and carts must be secured to carry the booty to the mountains. This could not be done until all of the soldiers were captured. The success at the fort had encouraged the men. They were ready for anything. As they rushed through the one street the inhabitants of the huts and few houses came out and followed in alarm to ascertain what meant this strange procession of blacks with a girl at their head.

Fascinated by the national game, the Spanish soldiers at the posada heard nothing of this outer disturbance. Not until a black with a murderous machete stood at the right of each of them did they comprehend that they were powerless to resist the capture which threatened them. Random shots were fired in the excitement that ensued. The keeper of the posada and six soldiers were thus disabled by the weapons of the Spaniards themselves.

The people of the hamlet made no effort to assist the soldiers. They gave their sole attention to the figure of the girl who presided like a general over this overthrow of the enemy. When each man had at last realized that he was a prisoner and that his personal arms had been taken possession of by his captor, Raquel stepped into their midst.

"You are my captives!" she told them with the tone and glance of a conqueror. "My men have seized your fort and taken your guns and stores. You Spaniards have made my father prisoner; you have killed my husband. This is the beginning of my revenge."

"*We* have not done this, señora," cried the lieutenant. "We know not of what you speak!"

"Spain's emissaries have done it, and you fight under the same flag," the retort rang out in her clear, fearless voice, "though how well you fight I have had no opportunity of observing!"

There was subdued laughter among the villagers, whose sympathies were all Cuban when it was possible to have them so safely.

She turned to them quickly.

"In the name of the country that affords us livelihood, I demand your carts, your horses, and all the provisions that you can gather together. The former will be returned to you when we see fit."

There was not a demur. Though not wholly awake to the need of their land, they were unanimous in the desire to afford this beautiful, masterful girl whatever she demanded of them. They laughed in the faces of the chagrined soldiers and went to obey her bidding.

Jaime Arco and his discomfited men knew what Spanish justice would accord them for the flagrant neglect of duty which had gotten them into this dilemma. Each looked into the other's troubled countenance questioningly. None of them relished the prospect of being shot in the Moro or, at the best, being transported.

In that moment of triumph Raquel thrilled with the joy of the victor. She felt as strong as if she had been a dozen men. Bound as they were, despoiled of arms, these bragging soldiers of Spain were like children in the hands of her men. They knew too well the power of the machete stroke to dare anything now, even were their limbs free. She smiled at their humiliation with the bitterness of a heart that found that even this triumph brought her no cessation of pain.

When the country people had brought out before the front of the posada all that they could spare, she sent ten of the men to load in the ammunition from where it was concealed in the manigua. As matters had turned out, that had been a quite unnecessary precaution.

She was glad that she had not made the mistake of waiting for night. All this had been consummated in much less time than she had expected, and they would be far on the road through the manigua before nightfall. She intended to take the prisoners along. She had decided what she would do.

Each one of her men now was well armed. The Spaniards were not aware of their inability to employ the rifles to advantage.

When ready to depart, the cavalcade assumed pretentious portions. Ahead rode Diego and old Pablo on two well-fed animals; immediately following them went the carts with the munitions of war and the provisions. Then marched the

Spaniards with a black beside each one, vigilant. On as many horses as were provided she mounted her remaining men, taking a fresh animal herself and returning the other to the *montero.*

As they passed out of the village, Diego lifted his sombrero and cried:

"*Viva Cuba libre!*"

The words passed from throat to throat in a continuous shout that was taken up by the villagers, who openly rejoiced at this defeat of the very men with whom they had been making merry a short time previous.

Mile after mile of this country road was traversed by the triumphant company. The blacks shot remarks at each other over the heads of their captives. They were enjoying every step of the way. They were ready to administer any manner of punishment that their mistress might devise.

The Spaniards marched gloomily. One and all had decided upon the course to pursue. They had no fear of the sentence of death from this band. They knew that in no case had a prisoner taken by the insurgents been shot. What they were afraid of was the judgment of Spain.

It was on the verge of the sudden darkness known to the tropics that Raquel gave the order which brought all the prisoners up before her in ten rows of five each. Surrounding them stood her men with drawn machetes.

Their faces blanched at the sight. What they had not expected seemed to have come upon them. They looked at the stern, white countenance of the girl leader with wonderment. Could she witness without flinching the sight which would follow the order which seemed to be on her lips?

In that hush of waiting, the lieutenant stepped forward as well as the stout cord which extended from one heel to the other would permit.

"*Señora mia,*" he pleaded, "we are ready to join the insurgent forces. Show mercy to us! Let us go with you. We will be loyal to your cause. We have learned your wrongs; we will be glad to fight with you. We dare not return to the Spanish army."

"I accept no one who has fought under the flag of Spain," she said in reply. "I understand what awaits you as soldiers. You deserve it. You were not faithful to the cause you espoused. I have no intention of offering you punishment. The law of Cuba is the law of mercy. In a moment my men will set you free. You will be at liberty to return to your empty fort or to find your way to the ranks of Cuba's revolutionists. I will have none of you."

At a significant motion from her, the waiting men cut the cord attached to the feet of the prisoners.

" You will have no difficulty in walking back to the hamlet," she told them. " The people there will be glad to release the thongs that bind your hands. The first man who attempts to follow us will be shot."

There was no mistaking her determination.

They understood that if they joined the Cuban army it would not be with her recommendation.

The lieutenant turned to his men and gave the order for attention. Then he faced the eyes of her who sat looking down upon them from her horse.

"We are men who are able to recognize nobility in an enemy," he said proudly. " You captured us fairly. We deserve no such consideration as you show us. As a woman, we revere your courage; as a Cuban, we respect you! You never may hear of us again, but—Cuba has won fifty soldiers! God save the island and her daughters! *Viva Cuba libre!*"

His men, obedient to their leader, echoed his speech with enthusiasm. The blacks, surprised, took up the Cuban cry.

Raquel's face flushed crimson with their tribute, then paled again.

The lieutenant gave quick orders. The Spaniards wheeled and marched down the rapidly darkening road.

Raquel and her men watched them out of sight silently. Then, leaving six to watch that no effort was made to follow them and learn their destination, the tiny army pursued its track back into the safety of the forest's edge.

CHAPTER XXVII.

THEY struggled on considerably farther into the crepuscu-lous gloom when the advance of day admitted, but they found that the carts would have to be abandoned and their

contents conveyed on the animals through the green-fringed
aisle.

This was an undertaking which promised to consume much
time. Here the blacks proved that their ingenuity and training was far in excess of that of their young leader. They cut
down the parasitic vines and ropes that had woven themselves
among the thick foliage. These they deftly manufactured
into panniers which would serve well their purpose. Elate
with their success in this their first raid against the enemy,
they made a vociferous medley with their excited voices, as
each related to each the struggle he had had with his soldier
before he had gotten the fellow bound and submissive. That
they felt at liberty to dilate somewhat on the extent of these
various victories was to be expected, and they improved the
privilege.

Raquel felt inclined to ride on alone to the cave and allay
the anxiety which she knew was reigning there in the breasts
of Tia Juana and the unprotected women. She was curious
to prove to the Spanish soldier that she had not over-rated
her ability to lead her men, but her fatigue was so great that
she was compelled to delay the satisfaction of this pride. She
sighed as she realized how ill-fitted she was in strength and
endurance to carry out the projects that formed themselves in
her mind.

"I shall have to become inured to hardship," she said to
herself as she lay, half-recumbent, among the soft green
things. "It will not be as difficult for me as it is for the poor
boys whom Spain sends over here to be seized with the fever
before they ever can fire a gun. I know the climate. I have
a will like iron. My body shall obey me! It never shall find
rest until my country and my father are free! God help!"

Her memory travelled back, by force of association, to that
other time when she had lain thus close by the water of this
very river that dashed so tirelessly on. How strangely Zuñega had looked at her on that day! And how far, far back
in the past it seemed! What unlooked-for things had the
future held for each of them! Where was he now? Was he
really to land the expedition of which Valdes had spoken?
Perhaps in this war his would be the fate which had befallen
her father or M. Theuriet! She shivered and laid her face
down against the soft leaves.

"Her ear, near the ground, caught the sound of horses' feet. She leaped upright and called to the negroes, but their voices had reached such a pitch that her cry of alarm was not distinguishable.

She rushed through the undergrowth with but one clear thought in view—to spring out in front of the horsemen, startling them with the unexpected sight of a woman. This, she calculated, would give her men time to get ready for action. But the riders were nearer than she had thought. She caught a glimpse of the face of the foremost one as his horse stole out of the wan twilight of the trees.

She halted, speechless, her lips apart. Her breath came quickly. Her heart beat with great, stifling throbs.

She heard the negroes give shouts of surprise and terror as they discovered the coming invaders, but she did not look toward them. She knew that they yelled to each other that the Spaniards had followed.

"We are no dogs of Spaniards!" she heard the first of the riders cry in a tone that had the command of a general. "We are for Cuba and *libertad*. Drop your machetes! What are you doing here?"

Like a wraith, Raquel slipped out from the shadowy veils of the festooned trees.

"They are my men!" she said, looking up into the face of the leader with gaze in which he read only unutterable woe. "They are for liberty also."

"*Raquel!—here!*"

With the fleetness of a swallow the man was out of his saddle and beside her. He caught both of her hands in his and stood looking down into her eyes, his own burning with an intensity that banished all of their melancholy.

"I have obeyed you," he said softly. "I have come back to fight for you!"

To Raquel, at that moment, all that ever had been in life seemed to be consumed by that fire in the face above hers. A marvellous sense of joy crept with the swiftness of light through her veins. Everything appeared possible and easy of accomplishment, even to the emancipation of Cuba and the freeing of her father, as she was held there with this youth of the forest absorbing her very life into his own with the look beneath his lids.

"I need you, Zuñega!" she answered, whether with her lips or her eyes, neither of them really knew.

"What has happened?" he cried. "What makes you a mountain refugee?"

"What but Spain!" was the bitter reply. "M. Theuriet has been killed! My father is a prisoner!"

Zuñega stepped backward with horror. He shuddered to think of what she had been called upon to pass through.

"Lithgow!" he called.

A figure which had sat motionless on his horse dismounted. He had seen it all—the revelation which had voiced itself from the girl's illumined face. He went forward with the smile in his blue-gray eyes that a man wears when he knows he is meeting the annihilation of a dream.

Through all the days of the journey toward Cuba, through all the hours of the wearisome tramping through the mountains, he and Zuñega had talked of Raquel and her probable gladness could she know that they were marching against the soldiers of Campos. And secretly each man had wondered what look her face would wear when she beheld him. This position at the Cave of Lost Spirits Zuñega had chosen because of its importance as the army of Gomez moved upward through the island; but both he and Lithgow knew that its proximity to the estates had not been without influence in the matter. They had stored a few arms and had gone back for another supply and to secure horses and provisions. It was during this absence that Raquel had taken possession.

Unconfessed, each had felt that, even though she was the wife of the Frenchman, she would be committing no crime if she allowed for an instant a glance of satisfaction to reward him for the effort he intended to make for the abolition of Spanish tyranny, and he had been anxious to obtain that glance. Now Lithgow knew that, however enthusiastic might be the look bestowed upon him by Raquel, it would lack that which, in his weak, selfish moments, he had hoped to see.

"What terrible thing has driven you to the mountains?" he cried, clasping anxiously the hands which she had withdrawn from Zuñega's grasp. "Has the plantation been burnt?"

"Oh, worse, worse," she answered, scarcely able to restrain the emotion which the sight of his familiar face awakened. "I am alone, trying to fight Spain with what strength I have.

I mean to rescue my father. He has been betrayed into the hands of enemies. He is dead or a prisoner! I—oh!—is your free country sending her gallant men down here to aid us?"

Lithgow shook his head. He was aghast at this which had befallen the genial planter. He knew of no words with which to express the pain and pity which surged up through his heart for this fearless, impassioned creature arraying herself and her forces as best she knew how against her country's enemy and the wrecker of her home.

"I come not as an American but as a man who will war against oppression wherever he finds it," he replied gently. "M. Theuriet—is—safe?" Her announcement that she was alone filled him with wonder.

"He is dead!" she told him with lips that trembled. "The Spaniards killed him. We have—buried him—on the plantation."

Lithgow looked at Zuñega with horrified eyes. Her anguish-drawn face, and grief-shadowed eyes told of what black terrors had assailed her.

"I have a thousand pairs of arms that will avenge you," Zuñega said solemnly.

"And I have ninety courageous men who have taken the Spanish fort at Yaez!" she said modestly.

Astounded, the two viewed the corroboration afforded her assertion by the collection of rifles and ammunition that the blacks were guarding, even though now they were convinced that the strangers were friends. Amazed, they exchanged incredulous glances and regarded her lithe form with masculine wonder. The entire company dismounted and surveyed the result of the raid, while Lithgow insisted on hearing a thorough account of the entire affair. Raquel gave the victory to the unmistakable valor of her men, and had it not been for Diego, who, despite her orders, obeyed Lithgow and related graphically the capture, the tale would have been a short one. But what Diego omitted the other men supplied, until the vanquishment of the fifty Spaniards was made known eventually with all its details to the listening men. When Diego repeated the speech of the lieutenant, . united shout went up from the throats of these Cuban sold.ers for the girl whose coolness, bravery, and finesse had wrought so unqualified a success from what might easily have been a disastrous failure.

They swept their sombreros low before her in one mighty tribute.

"The land that holds women who are as fearless and as patriotic as its men is not a land that will be crushed again by any force that Spain may send from her bankrupt soil!" cried one. "We will be led by a daughter of Cuba! *Viva libertad!*"

Zuñega looked around over his men with a light in his face that they read but did not wholly understand. The two noblest fires that ever burn in the human heart made his blood leap with godlike vigor through his veins. Before him, free, stood the woman whom he loved as men love once and once only. Around him rose the virgin forests of the country he would give his life to save.

"That is spoken like a Cuban," he said, with his grand head thrown back and a smile in his eyes. "In this war that we will wage against the barbarism of tyrant Spain there shall be committed no crimes at which our mothers and our sisters might blush! We fight for the women of Cuba and for our future homes! We will sweep over the island, but mercy, purity, and victory will be our watchwords! And the world shall know what manner of men it is who struggle for the land of their birth!"

He unsheathed his sword and extended it to Raquel, who had heard all this without comprehending its relation to her.

"My men have chosen you for their leader, I am under your command," he said, bowing.

Bewilderedly Raquel gazed into the enthusiastic countenances of the men who cheered the action.

"I am one of you," she finally said clearly; "I will fight side by side with you through every battle, if I may;—but led by your leader! This man who rides at your head is he who rescued me from the grasp of Gonzalo Alarcon, the bandit. He brought me through these very paths that lead to the Cave of Lost Spirits only a short year ago. He said then that when the hour came for the liberation of Cuba that he would follow the leader who might arise. That is José Marti!" She handed the sword back to Zuñega. She motioned her men nearer. "You are his followers now, not mine," she told them.

"Marti is dead!" Zuñega said sadly, "but we fight as if he

lived! I do not accept your men. They are subject to no orders but yours; yet, from this moment our bands will become united in one hope:—we will avenge the death of M. Theuriet; we will fight for the emancipation of our island; we will accomplish the liberation of your father."

The soldiers fell to work helping the blacks get the captured munition in shape to carry forward.

Lithgow occupied himself in winning from Raquel the history of all that had transpired since he had taken his departure with Annizae. He listened to what she had been able to do in Havana in affording information to the rebels of the movements in the official circles. He listened troubledly to the story of the disposition of the jewels. He commented on the strangeness of the fact that that danger had been almost providential in that it had brought her back to the plantation at the moment when of all others she most was needed. He was very tender and sympathetic. He read the meaning of the new lines which the bitter brush of experience had wrought into her face during the last year.

Despite the satisfying conviction that, in the matter of birth and fortune, he was now the equal of this woman who had stirred him from the lethargy of his forest-enclosed existence, Zuñega was conscious of the same timid, reverent feeling which had been his as an island outlaw. After the moment of surprise was over when he had allowed her name to leap from his lips as he spoke it religiously in the secret chambers of his soul, he was overcome afresh by the inexpressible adoration he bore her. He tried to shut his passion down beneath his lids, and he moved among his men, dwelling proudly on the enormous value of the stores she had made Cuban property. He scarcely saw the things he looked upon, however, so entrancing was the ecstasy which pervaded him. He had thrilled under the look which had come to her eyes when he had held her hands in his; every palpitating sense told him what he had read there, but he dared not drink from this chalice of hope. He rested his eager lips on its rim and peeped down wistfully into the magic draught. Was it for him to drain? A thousand and one little things had told him that the American loved her too. He glanced out of his dark eyes to where the two sat talking. He observed how completely they appeared to understand each other. He heard her tell Lithgow that she carried with her continually the book which he had given her. With the poignancy of torment he said to himself that he was no mate for her. What knew he of these books that had been her mind's food? He drew a long breath and looked up into the mass of florescence above his head. He had had no volume but Nature until *she* had come, and even that had been half-sealed to him until, with the lifting of her innocent lids, had been shown him the mysterious meaning of life.

He quivered with the remembrance that, in the days to come, he was to be near her. He marvelled over the fate that not only had made her a widow but had brought their paths together in this struggle which was to be the demolition of Spanish reign in the West Indies.

It was Lithgow who saw to it that Zuñega and not he rode before Raquel when the march was taken up toward the cave. He knew well what was in the heart of the youth; he thought he read what was struggling for recognition in the heart of the girl who spoke with him of the past while her eyes wandered unconsciously in the direction of Zuñega's steps. If to his own lips crept words that craved utterance, he smiled them back with grave control. He perceived that that clasp of fingers in the moonlight on the night of the contradanza had no such place in her memory now as it held in his.

As they moved on ahead of him through the intricacies of the green tangles which overhung the edge of the stream, he looked down at the sharp rocks which here and there jutted up out of the water fretted with the lacework of the foam, and he propounded to himself a problem that only the years ahead of him could solve: "What are Beatrice and I, who love those two souls ahead who love each other, to do with our lives and our love? Her heart and its comprehension will go into her art, and her work will live. It is only the unsatisfied heart that accomplishes and leaves its silent history written in its achievements. The happy human is content and stagnates! But what will I do with the half-century which probably is left to me? I can fight for Cuban independence, but after that——?"

He halted his horse and remained studying the waters until the long procession of horsemen came up with him.

Zuñega and Raquel passed on slowly out of sight.

There were a multitude of questions she might have asked him concerning the varied experiences which had been his since he had ridden away from La Sacra Sonrisa, but she thought of none of them.

He turned and looked at her now and then with his soul in his face.

And they did not know that they were silent.

A scarlet blossom dropped on her horse's mane, as if it had been flung by a laughing fairy's fingers. She caught it and pressed it to her lips. She was reproaching herself that she could feel the beauty of this ride when her father, hopeless, anguished, lay in the hideousness of some Spanish prison. But the sound of the horses' hoofs on the stones by the river kept time to something that beat in her blood, something new and wholly strange and indescribably sweet. And she asked not its name.

The green life which spread itself so luxuriantly about them seemed to understand far better than these evanescent humans did this sudden blossoming forth of joy. The dark leaves appeared to lean toward them yearningly as if to whisper. The secret stole like magic through the labyrinths. A murmur crept about them that they heard only when the time came that the path would allow no further progress on horseback.

Zuñega stood for a moment with his hand on the neck of her animal. He heard the sighing murmur. It seemed to him that it whispered that never again was to come such an instant as this out of life. His eyes drew hers irresistibly. The muscles of his arms quivered as he held them up to lift her down from the saddle.

"Have we not known this path before?" he said softly, as he placed her on her feet. "I loved you then, and knew it not. I love you now. I want you for my own, but—I will wait—I will wait! It is evil to speak while you have grief in your heart, but the words will not be smothered longer. They break their way up from where they have burned ever since I first saw you—that first moment when you faced Alarcon."

"Hush, do not speak!" begged Raquel. "Leave it all unsaid. I must not listen; I must forget your words."

"But you will not forget?" he pleaded. "I will speak them again never—unless you bid."

21

"Speak them again—when Cuba and my father are free," she said.

Lithgow, riding on with feigned laboriousness, rounded a curve and saw them through a misty veil of emerald lace as they stood thus, looking into each other's faces. He reined in his horse sharply, with a sick pain forcing itself upon his consciousness.

CHAPTER XXVIII.

ON reaching the camp they found that a great change had been wrought in the appearance of the place.

The Spaniard, wearying of complete inaction and to consume the long hours of the absence of Raquel and the men, had persuaded the women to follow his directions and prepare a cleared place which would serve the needs of the camp. Little by little they had made noticeable inroads upon the vegetation, and Zuñega was quick to perceive the value of the suggestion.

When all the explanations were over and the surprise and rejoicing had abated concerning the triumphant return of Raquel's band, he and Lithgow talked with the sick soldier, obtaining from him his account of the treachery employed to entrap the sugar planter. His praise for the girl who had borne herself so bravely through the disasters which had encompassed her won for him the friendship of the two men, who gave respectful attention to his ideas concerning the necessity of establishing in this safe retreat a mountain hospital.

"Here is running water, señors, and women to nurse the injured," he said, "while there still remains the plantation of the dead señor from which to draw supplies."

"But there have been few signs that the revolution is going to creep up into this province," Zuñega remarked significantly to him. "There may not be a battle big enough to furnish us with subjects for a hospital. José Marti is dead and the insurrection is believed to be ended."

The Spaniard looked the Cuban full in the eyes.

"You and I both know that this war never will be ended until Cuba is free," he returned. "Your leaders mean to make every district their own. You will lead the Spanish boys on weary marches that will net them nothing. They will die of the fever and despair. You know your island; we do not. But already we have learned one thing—you Cubans are magnificent enemies. Your Gomez compliments his prisoners on their valiant fighting, and, instead of shooting them, he returns to them their swords and sets them free! There is not one of us but would fight on your side if he dared. Your humanity wins you the admiration of the world. I am ashamed to be a Spaniard."

"Then we will count you one no longer," declared Zuñega. "When you are able to bear arms, if ever you are, you shall be one of us. Until then you shall be at the head of the hospital staff. You are right. We do mean to make every province our own. Puerto Principe will be in the hands of our men before the dry season sets in. If you have no other patients, you shall have Spaniards!"

And his words proved true—more than true.

Before the grinding season not only Puerto Principe but Santa Clara as well was in the hands of the revolutionists. Only the large cities remained unmolested. General Roloff continued calmly his plans of interfering with the transportation of troops and the transmission of telegraphic signals. General Gomez moved unhesitatingly up through the eastern portion of the island. Maceo carried on extensive operations in unison with other leaders. Pinar del Rio rose up with innumerable bands that kept the wearied Spanish soldiers constantly on the move. Spain no longer could keep the fact from the world that the entire island was in a state of revolt.

As the armies of the Cubans swept like magic from one spot to another, they were augmented by those who came out from the towns and joined their fortunes with the patriots. When the Spanish pursued, in hopes of forcing a battle, the revolutionists vanished, only to reappear at another place from which they obtained provisions, fresh animals, recruits. But when there was anything to gain, the Cubans themselves did the attacking, and the official reports—not given to the world —contained many dismal accounts of victories that placed the insurgents in possession of Spanish arms and ammunition. And, these reports more than once mentioned the fact that at the head of the dauntless column of men rode a beautiful girl, fully armed and conversant with the tactics of war.

Unscathed she went through many a conflict that Spanish correspondents spoke of slightingly, giving no suggestion of their brave dead that they left on the field to be borne away by the more humane insurgents. It was a strange thing which all the world commented on, that in no battle did the Spaniards lose, yet the revolutionists marched on undeterred and the Governor-General continually begged for more men from Spain.

The hospital in the mountain became filled to overflowing with the wounded, and the Castilian lad who, half crippled, watched anxiously over his patients under the direction of medical men who had slipped from the cities to the ranks of the patriots, saw to it that those who were Spaniards received no less care and comfort than did the impatient men of the island, who were anxious to be in the field again.

A satisfactory communication was carried on with the coffee estate. Local Spanish officials had not interfered with the picking of the crop. The deserted plantation of La Sacra Sonrisa had not been taken possession of by the enemy, and it even seemed to Raquel that it might have been well to have remained there, only she knew that she could not have endured the sight of the dear court and the absence of her father. In the rush and excitement of the scenes amid which she now found herself, she kept distinctly before her the thought that all this was for the freeing of him whom she loved. This terrible struggle, with its bloodshed at which her heart sickened and her head reeled, was to throw open the dungeons wherein had languished for years Spain's suspects. The horror of the life into which she had thrown herself became no less with the passage of time, but the knowledge that, though the forces of the Spanish were not annihilated, the situation was rapidly falling into the hands of the fighters for freedom, gave her strength to ride side by side with Zuñega or Lithgow. The soldiers declared that she won the battles. Her very presence seemed to dismay the foe. To merit her praise, the Cubans fought in a way that carried terror to the disheartened Spaniards, half fed, under-paid, if paid at all.

There came a time when she remained at the camp for some days, while plans were completed for the extended raid which was to carry them up through the Matanzas district. The Spanish at Havana were saying that the insurgents had become dissatisfied with their generals and were on the eve of a rupture; and while they thus deceived themselves, General Gomez was making the phenomenal march up through Puerto Principe into the district of Havana.

Tia Juana, half frantic at the hardships to which Raquel voluntarily was exposing herself, was in the middle of an eloquent remonstrance, to which the Spaniard lent support, when a messenger came from La Buena Esperanza with a supply of coffee and the intelligence that the sugar plantation was now in the hands of the mayor of the neighboring town, who declared that he would grind the cane in spite of all the insurgents in Cuba.

Raquel rose to her feet and put Tia Juana's retaining hands away gently.

"That mayor is one of the men who are responsible for the imprisonment of my father, I know," she said. "He is a Spaniard. Whether he or Spain is to derive the revenue from our sugar is a question I will not wait to have answered."

"Where go you, *señorita mia?*" cried Tia Juana, seizing her. "You go not back there!"

"Yes, and it is thou who wilt accompany me," answered Raquel determinedly. "There are no men here to do that which must be done; besides, I myself wish to see it. The plantation shall be fired!"

Unwilling, but not daring to disobey, Tia Juana mounted behind Raquel and they followed back through the forest the woman who had come.

"When the cane is burning," said Raquel to the woman, "you and those who are at La Buena Esperanza must load into the carts all of the coffee with which you safely can escape. They will take possession of that crop next—if they can."

"There is not much to seize, *señorita mia,*" laughed the woman. "We have been carrying it to the edge of the mountain and concealing it even as we picked it."

"*Bueno!* Who thought of so wise a thing?" exclaimed Raquel.

"The Spanish soldier, *señorita mia,*" explained Tia Juana, who never yet had been able to call her mistress by the matronly title she had acquired with marriage. "Thinks he not of everything—no?"

All the blood of the Palgraves flamed within Raquel when she came within sight of the walls of her lost home. Whether or not these were the men who were instrumental in the misfortune which had become hers, they were Spaniards and their tread desecrated sacred ground. Righteous rage was hers as she looked out once more over the wide-spreading fields.

"They shall lie blackened, the mill itself shall burn before one pound of sugar shall be made by those who still keep their heels on the necks of Cubans!" she vowed.

In the darkness she and Tia Juana made their way through the unguarded aisles of the cane estate. The fires were burning in the mill, but the number of men who could be procured to work were few and there was no grinding at night. With a hand that faltered not she touched the torch to the acres that Spain had confiscated. Here and there the flames began to spring up, slowly at first, then creeping with eager, lapping tongues on. When certain that no amount of fighting could save the sugar-cane, she and the tired, breathless negro woman rode out of the reach of danger and watched the conflagration sweep up grandly against the midnight sky. They could hear the cries of alarm which were given when the fire was discovered. They could see the figures of men, rushing back and forth excitedly, outlined against the lurid light.

It was a magnificent sight—that sea of flame! The two women watched it silently, while from the coffee plantation passed the remainder of the gathered crop, accompanied by those who now deserted the estate, fearing the brutality of the Spaniards.

The fire swept onward toward the mill resistlessly. Raquel laid her hand on Tia Juana's arm.

"It is all going to go," she whispered with a break in her voice. "From the works it will leap to the quarters and from there—through the orange grove to the house! It will cross the grave of M. Theuriet—but he will not know! I wonder if my father—wherever he may be—sees in a dream this awful crimson glow eating into the home where he brought my mother a bride!"

"Stop, *señorita mia!*" sobbed Tia Juana. "You break my heart! See! The quarters are catching! Oh, are you not sorry, *Chita?*"

"No!" answered Raquel; but tears filled her eyes and

rained down her face. It was the first time that actual relief in tears had come to her since that terrible night. All the scenes she had witnessed during the months she resolutely had followed Zuñega's leadership had not moved her as did this destruction of her home.

In spite of Tia Juana's pleadings, she stood watching until the red, ravishing blaze died into fitful up-leapings. And all the waving fields stretched wide and forlorn as if a plague had touched them.

Then, as the first pearly hues of dawn stole softly on the fringe of night's sable trappings, they hastened and joined the refugees from La Buena Esperanza, who were only too glad to have their guardianship of the property of the dead M. Theuriet brought to an end. One by one the men had slipped into the forest and had not come back. Fearful but obedient, the women had staid on alone, gathering the coffee berry and conveying it to places of safety, from which spots it readily could be obtained by the camp forces. As they pushed through the forest in a trail that now had grown familiar and friendly to them because of frequent travel over its soft mould, the women glanced pityingly at the traces of grief in the face of their young mistress. They hushed their speech and moved ahead of her, holding back the daring vines that constantly strove to twine their verdant strength across the path and obliterate the wreckage wrought by these trespassers.

Raquel followed them slowly, wearily.

The stupendousness of this task that faced the valorous Cubans had never seemed to oppress her as it did now, when the ashes of her home lay smouldering behind her.

"It is what must be done," she murmured sadly under her breath; "the plantations of Cuba must be sacrificed to the hope that is in our breasts. If the crops are destroyed, how can the planters pay taxes? And if they pay no taxes, Spain can no longer *with our gold* supply her soldiers with that which will enable them to conquer us! On the altar of liberty the Cubans will offer up their crops, their homes, if need be! And the light of the sacrificial fires will attract the attention of the world to our need."

The word spread through the insurgent camps, in that strange inexplicable way which baffled Spanish generals, that from the penal colonies of southern Spain a battalion of criminals had been sent and were now in active operation under the command of the officer who brutally had butchered the sick occupants of a rebel hospital camp, reserving only those who were Spanish soldiers, receiving care and medicine from the men against whom they had fought.

This act of hideous barbarism drove many into the ranks of the patriots who before had endeavored to remain neutral. If there was wanting anything to fan the Cuban fire into a universal conflagration, such uncalled-for inhumanity did the work.

By the same method of communication which kept the revolutionists in constant possession of every move of the Spanish army, Zuñega and the other bands in his vicinity were apprised that a government transport train of two hundred mules, carrying ammunition worth twenty thousand dollars, was hastening to the support of the anxious generals in Santa Clara.　It was understood that the same officer who had so richly won their hatred was commanding the expedition.

This was the time that both Zuñega and Lithgow begged Raquel not to accompany them.　They knew the peril for her far better than she did.

"What if you should be captured by these men who come from convict cells!" argued Lithgow.　"The fate which is your father's is nothing to what yours would be.　Remain in camp!　Every man among us will strike a blow for you.　You are our queen, but it is unwise to risk yourself in such a battle as this will prove to be."

"The accident of birth which made me a woman instead of a man shall not keep me from any struggle into which my company goes," she declared proudly.　"I am becoming strong and full of endurance.　No man would be allowed to shirk his duty because it promised to be disagreeable.　Neither must I."

She held her dark head with its riotous hair in the same manner in which she had carried it that day in the sala when she had told her father what she would do if she were a man. She looked the American in the face with eyes that showed the bravery of the spirit which would not be conquered by woman's fear.

"I have a queer presentiment, Raquel," he told her.　He called her by her name now.　She had said to him that it gave her a feeling of comfort to hear her name spoken as her father had spoken it. During this terrible time in which she had not faltered from her post, he had tried to take the place of father, brother, mother to her. In numberless ways he had contrived to make the privations of their life less. Resolutely he had buried every thought inimical to the love he bore Zuñega. So carefully had he sustained his part that the girl never dreamed of the gladness this self-contained Northerner found in being able to minister unto her.

"That I shall be killed?" she questioned with the calmness that comes from looking death in the face frequently.

"There are worse things than that," he replied, shaking his head. "I do not think you will meet with death in the field; bullets fly by you; your life seems charmed. But I feel that I am dreading something. What it is—I don't know. I wish you would not go into this engagement."

She smiled at him. He saw, with a sudden fresh realization, how all the youth was being taken out of her face. But the girlish softness of contour had given place to a wonderful character that told how her nature was chiselling itself into her features.

"Have you forgotten that in *our* book, yours, mine, and Beatrice's, there is something like this: 'If I have shrunk unequal from any contest, instantly the joy I find in all the rest becomes mean and cowardly'?" returned she. "When Cuba is free I could not bear to think that I had not struck every blow that was possible for me to strike."

And that was the feeling which bore her through the attack which was made on the Spanish detachment. Through the thick of the engagement she rode with her blacks obeying her orders. The sight of her seemed to demoralize the troops in the way that it often did. And this was the moment which was always taken advantage of by Zuñega's men. There were only six hundred soldiers to guard the ammunition and they quickly found themselves at the mercy of the enemy, but in the first mêlée there had been some desperate fighting done by the officer in charge, who knew that to lose this valuable store would mean for him disgrace and removal.

It was during this time that Raquel saw Lithgow pitch forward and fall from his horse. The blood left her heart. She reeled in her own saddle. Then she urged her men on wilder than ever.

When the entire transport train was theirs and the field lay strewn with the dead, Raquel crept with limbs that trembled under her to where she thought he lay. Those who had been in the rear had borne him to a place far from the hoofs of the horses. He was not unconscious. He tried to smile when she dropped on her knees beside him with her sorrow written in her eyes and trembling lips.

"My presentiment,—you know," he said faintly. "I am—so glad it was I,—not you."

"But you are not——"

"Yes," he whispered with an effort, "only just a few minutes more, dear. Will you write——"

"To Beatrice?" she asked, making no pretence of hiding her tears.

He assented by a pressure of her fingers which held his with that grasp which essays so vainly to restrain the flight of that which goes unseen.

. He studied her face, bent so near him, with eyes that were hungry and could no longer hide their hunger.

"Will you—kiss me?" he asked with growing weakness. "Once,—just once. I have loved—you—and you have not—known."

With a sob of inarticulate anguish she laid her face down against his.

"The contradan—za—you have—forgotten," he said softly. "I can—never——"

She placed her arms around him and held him thus while his eyes grew dim.

"I have not forgotten," she said. And the chords in her throat tightened and Cuba itself faded out of her mind. "But how could I know that you remembered?"

A fresh pulse of life became his for the moment. A joy pierced the mist creeping over his vision.

"If—" he sighed feebly. Then, with a thought, seemed to come a sense of necessity for action. He sought to lift himself, but fell back. "It is better so," he whispered with difficulty. "Marry Zuñega;—don't wait. You must not be alone here. Marry him—now. For me,—death is sweeter —than a life—without—you."

"But it is you whom I love!" Raquel cried wildly, her long-guarded secret breaking forth resistlessly. "You shall not go from me! I will not lose you!"

Frantically she tore at his blood-stained garment, suddenly realizing that precious moments had been spent.

"Zuñega,—Zuñega! He is—dying!" she moaned with frenzy, as she watched the light of love in his eyes give way to complete unconsciousness of his surroundings. "Save him,—save him! For I love him,—I love him!"

Called hurriedly from the far side of the field, Zuñega had galloped up madly and now flung himself from the saddle, in time for her passionate appeal to reach his ears. Its double import turned his face almost as gray as Lithgow's own. He sent one agonized glance into her anguished eyes and read there crushing confirmation of the avowal her grief had wrung from her.

Speechless with pain, he knelt beside Lithgow, aiding her trembling fingers in disclosing the wound. There was no time for expressions of woe. But his heart sickened within him as he suddenly grasped how deep, how immeasurable was the love he bore this American and how powerless was that love in a battle with Death.

"There is a chance,—one in a thousand," he told her encouragingly, as he endeavored to stanch the flow of blood. "But we must work rapidly."

All the surgical skill the camp afforded was brought into play. They labored breathlessly, their hearts failing them as he seemed to pass swiftly beyond all earthly succor. There came an awful moment of strange hush. Zuñega looked up at her blanched face with fear in his own.

"I myself would die to return him to you," he said brokenly, "but—it is too late!"

The last barrier of woman pride went down before that flood of sorrow. With a wail of sharp despair, Raquel pressed her quivering lips hungrily, entreatingly to Lithgow's, so chilled and unresponsive.

What startling telegraphy was that!

Back from the borderland of the vast Silence its quickening power summoned him. Through all his veins crept slow thrills of warming blood. There was faint pulsing of the heart once more.

The first stage in the fight with Death was won.

But it was destined to be a great struggle, in which nothing but sleepless, tireless love could prove victorious.

Days and nights of unwearied watching followed.

Not recognizing the identity of those who nursed him, Lithgow's fevered mind roamed back through the past. He

talked wistfully of his mother, long dead.   He called for
Beatrice.   He spoke familiarly of those whose paths his own
had crossed.

And Raquel endured pangs of acute jealousy amid her
sweet work of ministering to him.   Nevertheless, she wrote
to the northern girl, telling of his danger and the hope they
held of his recovery.   This letter was to be entrusted to
Zuñega, who, in turn, would give it into the charge of those
Cubans who formed means of communication with the coast.
To while away long hours, during which she sat by the side
of Lithgow, Raquel jotted down the events of the day together with Lithgow's symptoms and Zuñega's daring raids.
And the letter grew in size and became a sort of diary; and
it was long before it found its way to the one for whom it
was intended.

On one of the anxious nights when she and Zuñega kept
watch, the latter brought himself to whisper softly:

"When health comes again to him and he is able to be
conveyed, we will go to San Juan de las Yevas.   There the
padre will—marry you.   It should be so.   Always have I
known he loved you, but—I was selfish.   I am so no more.
My life belongs to my people.   His he has risked to battle
with us for our land; and—he has won a daughter of Cuba.
I myself will tell him it is so."

But the weeks were many and lapsed into months before
this magnanimous intention could be carried into effect.

Zuñega and the band were ordered to the support of the
leader of the insurgent forces, and, as there were several in
the camp too ill to be moved, Raquel and the women were
left in care of the hospital, with a few of the blacks to guard
and serve as messengers.   The young Spanish soldier had
recovered sufficiently to take the field, and he had gone with
joy to fill Lithgow's place.

Into the safety of the hospital retreat penetrated reports
that the tide of rebellion had swept through all the provinces
until, in despair, Spain had exchanged General Campos' civilized methods for the inhuman policy of his successor, who
speedily instigated the war of extermination of the helpless.
License, butchery, untold horrors boastfully were added to
the grievous burden of hideous wrongs the struggling Cubans
were giving their lives to avenge.

The pitiful cries of starving children, the moans of bereft
mothers, the sobs of outraged womanhood reached the ears
of those in the land to the north.   A thrill of sympathy swept

through its vast territory from coast to coast.   But the law
of nations stifled this expression; and a mighty people, afire
with righteous indignation, compelled itself to silence and
inaction.

And the men who fought for liberty fought also to secure
revenge for the murder and rapine wrought by the tyrants.
The tales told of the sufferings of the reconcentrados steeled
anew their sad hearts and added fuel to the deathless hope
burning within them.

And while all this transpired, Lithgow slowly tightened his
grasp upon the threads of life and began to weave again the
pattern of the fabric called his own.

There had been a dawn which brought a noticeable change
in his aspect.   Raquel had bent above him with a suffocating
leaping of her heart, which made her face white and strained.
She had felt herself a powerless witness to a struggle between
two opposing forces for the nerveless body of the man she
loved.   She had dropped to her knees in an agony of supplication and, at that instant, the lids which had been closed for
such a weary while had lifted slowly, questioningly, and his
eyes had looked into hers with answering intelligence.

"Raquel! Are both of us—dead?" he had whispered
wistfully.

Then he had slept the sleep of restfulness, knowing his
hand lay in hers.

CHAPTER XXIX.

THE old church on the road to the town of San Juan
basked in the tropical sunlight as it had done for a century.
Nothing disturbed it, not even the murmur of war's alarms.
But there came a day when its indolent padre was aroused
from his siesta by the loud clanging of the three bells.

He sprung to his feet with more alertness than was his
wont.   The reports that the rebels were near had not been
conducive to restful slumbers lately.   His fat legs shook
beneath him as he hurried to ascertain the cause of this
unusual commotion.

He found himself confronted by a circle of frowning
horsemen who commanded him to open the entrance to the
church.

"Sleeping?" demanded the leader, observing signs of
somnolency. "How can you dream while your country
bleeds?"

The padre made a conciliating attempt at conversation, noticing that the expressions their eyes wore suggested such a dire possibility as the poles on which the three bells hung being made to serve again their original purpose — a gallows.

"What would you, señor?" he questioned quakingly. "I can not fight. I am a priest, sworn to peace."

"So was Father Arteaga," returned the leader, "yet he fought in the ten-year war. But — it takes courage to fight; and you look as if you had but appetite. Open your church! You can marry, I suppose, even if you can not defend the land which provides you with a living."

Confused and fearful of what seemed to threaten him, the padre had failed to detect that one of the riders was a woman.

Regarding her curiously out of the corners of his heavy-lidded eyes, he swung the doors wide and summoned one to light the candles while he prepared himself for the ceremony.

As they moved up the nave to the martial music of the ringing of spurs, a cry of recognition broke from their lips at sight of the woman who appeared in response to the padre's call.

"Faquita!"

She dropped the candle she was lighting. With astonished gaze she faced those who advanced.

"What do you here?" cried Raquel excitedly.

"By day I serve the padre," she replied. "At night — I dance with whom I will." She laughed coquettishly at the group of Cubans.

"Do you not recognize me?" questioned Zuñega, stepping forward.

She shook her head, though she answered:

"You are of the great outside world; I can see that. Why have you come back?"

"For 'Cuba Libre,'" declared he boldly.

A swift look of fear crossed her features. She held up her hand warningly.

"Come with us," urged Raquel. "It is like a taste of the old life of which you were so fond."

Faquita shrugged her shoulders.

"There is life here," she returned carelessly. "The town is full of soldiers and there is gayety."

"Who is commandante?" asked Zuñega.

"One whom it would not be well for you to meet," was her answer. "He has sought you relentlessly since the day you stole the señorita from him."

"What mean you?" demanded Zuñega.

"I mean that Gonzalo Alarcon seeks to find you that he may have revenge because you returned his prize to the arms of her father." She glanced at Raquel and smiled.

"But you had a part in that, Faquita," reminded Raquel quickly.

"True," she admitted, "and proud am I of it."

"How comes it that he is commander here?" queried Lithgow.

"We heard he had met death by hanging," said Raquel, troubled at the discovery of the proximity of him who had brought to her so much of suffering.

"So it was announced," stated Faquita. "But to save his neck he swore to place at the service of the Spaniards all his knowledge of the forests and the plans of the insurgents."

"Traitor!" exclaimed Zuñega wrathfully. "He shall drink the cup of death at my hands. He always was a Spaniard at heart, as he is by birth."

"If Alarcon is at the head of the soldiers in yonder town, why are you here serving the padre, Faquita?" queried Lithgow curiously.

"What is that to you?" retorted she. "Perhaps I do penance."

"Penance because you also have turned traitor?" persisted the American.

Faquita flushed angrily.

"*Quien sabe?*" she said simply, controlling her tongue.

"Ah, who knows?" repeated Lithgow. "But I wish to know, Faquita. Let me tell you this: He who is true to Cuba is wise, for the hour approaches when America will aid Cuba to sweep from her shores both traitor and tyrant."

Faquita put out her hand impulsively. A joy shot into her eyes.

"Is it so?" she asked eagerly. "The señora will be glad."

Raquel leaned forward, struck by a sudden thought.

"Señora——?" she questioned.

Faquita exhibited annoyance at her apparent lapse of caution.

"The great lady of this province—is it she?" Raquel pressed the query with keen insistence.

The eyes of the two met and a swift interchange of

confidence took place, by what method neither could have told.

"And if it is——?" Faquita ventured.

"I shall ask you to bear her a message from me," said Raquel, to the complete mystification of the men. "You did me an inestimable service once. What can I offer you to serve me again?"

Faquita's ear caught the sound of the padre's steps and compelled silence with a gesture, but there was that in her manner which convinced Raquel that her appeal had not been in vain.

"Is she to be trusted?" whispered Lithgow anxiously.

"That is what we must discover," returned Zuñega troubledly.

Before the little altar in the bleak edifice which was destined to serve in the future as a hospital for wounded Spaniards, the wedding party knelt reverently, while Raquel and Lithgow solemnly took the vows which bound their lives as their hearts were bound—indissolubly.

It was wholly unlike the marriage in which, at times in his life, Lithgow dreamily had figured himself one of the chief actors. But his head whirled with ecstasy and his hand trembled when the priest placed Raquel's fingers within his and gave her the sacred name of wife. His mind shot back to the night of the contradanza. How their fingers clung together for that sweet stolen moment! The memory of it thrilled him yet. And he marveled at the strange fortunes of war which had awarded to him the very happiness against the striving for which he then had battled so valiantly.

Zuñega stood in the capacity of Raquel's guardian, his handsome face so successfully masking his emotions that Faquita studied·him curiously.

"I thought you it was who loved her!" she ventured in an undertone when the ceremony was over.

"So I do," was his calm reply, "too well to allow it to separate them. I have but one passion now—Cuba."

"Nor I," she whispered, glancing cautiously over her shoulder at the padre.

Zuñega sent a penetrating glance into the depths of her very soul and knew she spoke the truth.

"We need you," he said.

"I am needed more here," was her answer. 'You will comprehend when I deliver the message and bring her a reply. This will I do to-night if you camp within reach."

A hurried conversation ensued between the women, then

the cavalcade rode away as quietly as it had approached. The
padre turned over a glittering coin in his palm and secretly
debated the advisability of purchasing the fighting cock on
which, for months, he had had his eye.

Faquita returned to her interrupted duties. At dusk she
went cityward, as was her custom. She was bent on a dangerous mission. How well she executed it was evidenced
just before midnight, when, in company with another, she stole
out from the shadow of the city walls and sped toward the
dark forest mantling the hills.

Those within the rebel camp awaited impatiently her coming. When, at last, was heard the challenge of the sentry,
they leaped to their feet in keen excitement, prepared for
defense if it should prove they had been betrayed.

As two dark-robed figures were brought forward by the
guard, Raquel sprung toward them with a cry of strangely
mingled emotion.

"Pepita! How dared you come?" she sobbed gladly
against the face of Faquita's companion. "There is such
danger."

"The desire to see you was too great to be resisted," returned the Señora de Urquiza, clasping Raquel with the tenderness of a mother. "I am astonished, dear. Why are you
here? I have heard nothing since you left Havana."

Eager questions and sad replies followed. While the swift
hours flew, they rehearsed the thrilling events through which
each had passed; and anxiously they formulated plans which
Pepita de Urquiza believed she could carry into effect.

"And you say you have gained not one clew concerning
the fate of your father," she said pityingly. · "Did it ever
occur to you that this man, Gonzalo Alarcon, may have been
the instigator of that attack upon the plantation?"

Even Faquita started with surprise at this suggestion.

"I had not thought of it before," said Zuñega. "But it
would be like Alarcon. It was M. Theuriet he intended
should be abducted at the time Raquel was captured. He
had not abandoned the plan. In the attack he may have
hoped to secure Raquel once more after capturing or killing
her natural protectors. Years do not dull the edge of
Alarcon's revenge, as I will learn if I encounter him."

"Faquita should be able to unravel this mystery if——"
began Lithgow, regarding her closely by the illumination
afforded by the torches.

"I have known nothing of Alarcon since the day I returned

22

to camp after assisting the señorita to her home," answered Faquita bitterly.

"Oh, Faquita!" cried Raquel anxiously. "Was your kindness to me the cause of trouble? I feared it might be. I—what can I do to recompense you at this late day?"

"Speak not of it," begged Faquita. "It was meant to be!"

Noting that Lithgow and Zuñega appeared doubtful, Pepita de Urquiza said explanatorily:

"Alarcon accused her of spiriting Raquel away and, fearing for her life, she fled the camp and took refuge in the household of the padre. There I saw her one day. Gathering her history, I took her into my service because of the friend she had been to you, Raquel; and it seemed a strange freak of fate that across my path should come one who had been interwoven with the fortunes of yourself and your friends. Finding she could be trusted, I pressed her into secret work for Cuba and what she has accomplished has been of the first importance to the cause. When Alarcon was captured and sentenced to death her resentment vanished and, though a price had been set on his head for years, she longed to release him; but when he turned traitor to the island, he saved his neck at the expense of her love. She vowed then that she would labor to defeat him at every turn, and she has done well. Woman's wit when linked to hatred will devise schemes that man can not circumvent; and Alarcon's reign as commander in the town has not been a successful one, owing to her cleverness at unearthing all his plans."

"But does he not suspect her?" questioned Raquel curiously.

"He knows not of her proximity," replied Pepita smiling. "If he did, she would lie in the prison along with other unfortunates. She gains all information from the soldiers, none of whom relish having the notorious brigand placed above them, even though he be tireless in his attempts to exterminate the rebels. In fact, they condemn his energy which essays so many fruitless attacks upon the alert enemy that always seems to have been warned just in time to vanish. Under-fed and never paid, the Spanish soldier has little appetite for fighting and does not take readily to the guerrilla warfare Alarcon seeks to introduce."

"I would like nothing better than to make an assault upon that town and deal the fellow the desert he has escaped so long!" cried Lithgow. "I have heard it reported that he is a convict, one of the many Spain has seen fit to empty into the island."

"Mine must be the right to meet Alarcon with weapons," claimed Zuñega gravely. "He shall have his opportunity to secure revenge; and I—will make him reveal the fate of Raquel's father before I run my sword through his traitor heart."

He felt a touch on his arm and turned to see Faquita's hands held toward him appealingly.

"I wish not death for him," she said softly, "but punishment."

Zuñega hesitated.

"I saved the señorita," she reminded him wistfully.

"And—I will spare Alarcon," he promised slowly.

She bent her proud head and touched her lips to his hand.

"Señora," said Lithgow suddenly, "what was hidden in that suggestion that Alarcon may have prompted the attack on La Buena Esperanza? Were you wondering if——" He paused and she completed his sentence swiftly.

"Yes; I was wondering if Raquel's father might not be among those who crowd the prison at San Juan."

Raquel gave a cry. Pepita, with infinite pity, put her hand out and caressed the dark head of the bereft daughter.

"Do not hope too much," she cautioned. "Many have been brought to those bleak walls. Some have been—shot. Others have been taken to Havana. A few have been deported to Ceuta."

Raquel covered her face, shuddering with misery.

"There is a whisper abroad among the Spaniards," continued Pepita, "that America is wakening. They tremble with fear lest it be true. Ah, she has been deaf so long, so long! But now, if she comes to our aid, the doors of the prisons will be set wide and——"

"Within will lie the lifeless bodies of the prisoners," prophesied Zuñega. "That will be the last act of the Spaniard:—to murder those in chains."

"God grant you speak not the truth!" sighed Pepita sadly.

When she and Faquita stole like wraiths from the camp, wending their perilous way back to the church, every detail of necessary movements had been arranged as far as was possible. Zuñega was in possession of valuable information which he was to forward to other leaders, and he had been able to furnish Pepita de Urquiza news which would prove precious to her in her difficult rôle.

Faquita was to return with whatever discovery she succeeded in making. But she did not come on the second night; nor on the third.

Zuñega was confident that something wholly unexpected had occurred to make her thus fail in her promise. He knew her fearlessness of old and felt it had not deserted her at this juncture.

The camp was moved farther into the forest to guard against a surprise, and sentries were stationed to escort her through the labyrinth when she should appear.

On the fourth night there was a young moon; but its tender radiance had stolen softly down the west and deepest midnight was upon them before there was the slightest stir which alert sentinels could interpret as token of the approach of an intruder. Then, in reply to the demand for the watchword, Faquita's voice was audible; and she was led into the presence of the assembled camp members who noted that her manner indicated a message of portent.

Raquel caught her by the hand feverishly, questioning silently.

"It is as the Señora suspected," Faquita exclaimed breathlessly. "I have succeeded in learning that there is an old man confined in one of the dungeons who seems to be Gonzalo Alarcon's special victim. Other tenants of the prison have come and gone. Death by guns at sunrise has been meted to some; chained like criminals, others have been sent to the penal colonies; but the old man of whom the soldiers talk still occupies the dungeon. They say there have been times when, like a raving maniac, he has called for his daughter. After these seasons he lies for weeks uttering no word save when Alarcon visits him and taunts him thus: 'You crave to know of the señorita? Does it not comfort you to learn she is in my tender care? No? Why call me a devil? You sold her to the old Frenchman; I rescued her from him. For that should you not thank me instead of curse me? You owe me gratitude. Some day when we Spaniards have killed all these rebels, I will release you and let you see for yourself how happy I have made her. *Que?* You object to my caresses for her? *Bueño!* She shall have the love of others when I have wearied of her! Does that satisfy you?'"

"*Madre de Dios!*" sobbed Raquel. "Does not that torture drive him mad with pain? What frightful agony of mind has been his! There is no Spanish gun that can keep me from reaching and freeing him now that I know where he is! My proud father in chains—at the mercy of that—oh, come! come!" she implored them. "Let us go! How can I wait an instant? To think he has suffered thus while I have found—happiness!"

Lithgow placed his yearning arm about her tenderly, vainly trying to soothe her distress.

"Listen!" he whispered. "Faquita has not told all. She says it will be impossible for us to rescue him now, even though we know where to strike. The town is too well fortified. We must wait until we—what is that, Faquita?" he demanded, lifting his head with excitement as he caught her words.

"More soldiers have come in from Habana, señor," Faquita was relating, "and there has been the wildest rejoicing in the cities. They say an American battleship has been blown up by Spanish cleverness in Habana harbor."

"One of our battleships blown up?" echoed Lithgow, unwilling to credit his ears.

"Sí, señor; and the towns are all tumult, for the soldiers declare the 'Yankee pigs' will have to come and fight now or else prove themselves to be what the Spaniards always have called them—cowards. You should hear the fellows boast how they will attack America and teach its people a lesson."

"Let them try!" Zuñega cried contemptuously. "They who never saw a town larger than sleepy Cadiz would drop dead in their tracks at the sight of throbbing American cities."

"What was the name of the battleship?" demanded Lithgow anxiously.

"'The Maine', señor; and the soldiers drink to the death of the men who went down like rats in a trap," she told him.

"Devils!" he cried, his voice ringing with all the righteous rage evoked by an inhuman deed. "And they call that civilized warfare, as they call the starving of helpless reconcentrados! The throats that drink to the death of American sailors, brought to watery graves by Spanish treachery, shall plead for pity from the sword revenge!"

"The Señora de Urquiza bade me tell you that the hour for attack is not now," Faquita cautioned. "She has accurate information that America is rising in arms. War is to be declared! Cuba will be freed by American soldiers."

A wild shout went up from the insurgent camp.

"But my father must be rescued before that time," protested Raquel. "The Spaniards will put him to death before they will give him up to victors."

"Leave that to the Señora de Urquiza," advised Faquita. "At the present moment, we would meet with defeat. Everything we seek would be lost. Your father might be conveyed to another prison—possibly the Morro. Remember, it is said those dungeons connect with the sea. They will be flooded and all secrets washed away before Havana is captured."

"Faquita is right," decided the men. "Every plan must be perfectly made and magnificently carried into execution. It is not the hour for haste."

"The Señora de Urquiza is in communication with both sides, you know," continued Faquita. "She is endeavoring to secure the co-operation of our strongest forces, for the armory must be taken. They must be prevented from firing it. We need its contents. She is petitioning that Señor Heredia may be sent up from the south provinces to give you aid."

"Señor Heredia?" repeated Raquel with interest.

"Sí, Señor Heredia," replied Faquita. "He had vast interests in the asphaltum mines near here; but he left everything and joined Gomez."

"It is he whom Pepita has loved so long," murmured Raquel thoughtfully. "It is to be near and aid him that she shuts herself thus away in the interior—and he dreams it not."

"Manuel Heredia has a strong force," commented Zuñega gladly. "It is well equipped and absolutely fearless. It is said he drilled his employes for months in secret before they took to the field. He has been a powerful factor in this rebellion. I understand now the reason. He has had the quick wits of Pepita de Urquiza to supplement his own. With his aid I stand ready to meet any number of Spaniards. And —if the Americans come—long will live free Cuba!"

"Viva Cuba Libre!" rose the strong and faithful cry, piercing the heavy canopy of forest foliage which hid from them the magnificent constellations of the heavens. Through the night drifted the prayer of hope on the winds that blew from the Caribbean—"Viva Cuba Libre!"

And from coast to coast of the great land to the north that same prayer even then was thrilling, while yet the strong heart of the nation quivered beneath the shock which had come with the loss of the Maine and its men.

Unable to make even one struggle for life, two hundred

and sixty-six seamen on a peaceful mission sank to a horrible death in the night waters of Havana harbor !

And a nation of seventy millions leaped with desire to avenge its drowned dead, and worshiped them as heroes. Long-curbed sympathies slipped from leash. The incredible tales of Spain's uncivilized war methods had received overwhelming confirmation. Bugle calls rang clear throughout the Union. The blood of the busy North and the patriotic South stung with fever to follow the flag and fight side by side beneath it for the liberty it symbolized. An enormous army sprung into being and poured itself upon the historic battlefields of Virginia and Tennessee, ready to be sent to aid those who had fought a tyrant so long and so well.

And America voted millions for war and calmly pursued her wonted occupations, while through her streets sounded the inspiring music of the fife and drum and the tramp of marching feet eagerly rushing to the first war ever begun for unselfish love of humanity.

CHAPTER XXX.

BEATRICE read the war news as she took her morning coffee. She was heavy-eyed. There had been the sound of weeping through the city by night. Tears which had been bravely controlled when the gallant naval reserves responded to the call had had their bitter way when darkness came to hide them. The sons and brothers of many of Beatrice's friends had gone to the front and Beatrice had sorrowed with them.

"I smiled and cheered to the last," she told her mother, "but I could not keep back the tears. I knew that I looked for the last time into some of their faces. Teddy Simonds tore off his tie and thrust his arm from the car window to throw it to me with a shout of farewell. The little silk knot fell and was trampled under foot. See how crushed and soiled it is. But I rescued it and shall lay it away so tenderly."

"Dear boy! It seems wicked that he must go!" sighed Mrs. Warrington. "His mother is prostrated. He is all she has."

Both were silent for a time, then Beatrice added:

"I was wild to go with them. I told Teddy that I would

go and nurse him if anything happened. I don't see how you lived through the civil war, mother. The suspense we endure now seems awful ; but what must have been four years of it ?"

"Words never can picture what the women of the North and the South passed through during the war," said Mrs. Warrington slowly. "There are those among us who never can speak of that time save with hushed voice."

The maid brought in the early mail. At sight of one envelope Beatrice gave an exclamation of surprise.

"A letter from Jamaica—in a strange—no, it is directed in Lithgow's fashion ; but—so unlike his usual bold hand. Can he have been ill ?"

She tore open the missive nervously, scanning the closely written pages rapidly, seeking that which would explain.

"Lithgow has been wounded !" she cried. "He has been ill, very ill, for a long time. This is a sort of record which seems to have been kept by—the girl of whom they talked—Raquel. She has nursed him back to safety."

Mrs. Warrington leaned forward with anxiety on her sweet countenance.

"Lithgow wounded !" she echoed, watching her daughter narrowly. "We have much to thank the girl for if she has won him back to health."

Beatrice essayed to read aloud the disconnected diary, but at every mention of Zuñega's name she hesitated almost imperceptibly, seeming to dwell with intense interest on the portions relating to his achievements.

Suddenly she dropped the sheets and covered her face with her hands.

Mystified and filled with consternation at this exhibition of feeling, Mrs. Warrington sat motionless and undecided. Finally she arose and placed her arms about Beatrice with the tender, inquisitive touch of sympathetic motherhood.

"Tell me, dear, what is it ?" she whispered. "Can I help you ?"

"Oh, mother !" Beatrice answered, her whole form quivering with the stress of emotion. "They love each other. They have been married."

"Who have been married ?" demanded Mrs. Warrington puzzledly.

"Who? Raquel and—Lithgow !" explained Beatrice.

" My poor child ! " cried the mother pityingly.

Beatrice lifted her face with wonderment.

" Poor ? " she echoed. " Oh, you do not understand."

"Yes, I do," murmured Mrs. Warrington, shaking her head sadly. "But I must confess that you almost deserve it, Beatrice. You drove Lithgow from you; you treated him in careless fashion. I had hoped to—to see you his wife—sometime. Now, I can only be sorry for you."

Beatrice sprung away from the consoling embrace and regarded her mother with eyes into which all the illumination of love had leaped.

"No, you do not understand," she reiterated with a laugh in which was mingled a tinge of maidenly shame that she must make audible confession. "Do you fail to perceive that I rejoice? If Raquel is the wife of Lithgow—Zuñega must love elsewhere."

"Zuñega!" exclaimed Mrs. Warrington.

"Yes, Zuñega; for it is he whom I love!" declared Beatrice proudly. She drew herself up to her full height, and, with queenly daring, awaited the effect of her startling announcement.

"Beatrice! have you lost your womanliness?" fairly sobbed Mrs. Warrington. "How can you——"

"I have lost nothing," interrupted Beatrice softly. "I have discovered myself and a comprehension of my nature's needs. I know now that I loved him from the first. I did not know what strange thing it was which had come and nestled in my heart. Lithgow espied it and called it by name. He told me that I loved. Since then—I have suffered. When we heard that M. Theuriet was dead, I feared Zuñega would marry her; but I concealed my pain as women always must, though hearts break."

"Surely you do not mean to do any rash, unfeminine thing!" expostulated the mother.

"No, I could not," returned Beatrice comfortingly. "I am your daughter; that should be sufficient guarantee. I will wait. It is all that a woman can do."

"Whoever would dream this of you!" murmured Mrs. Warrington with incredulity in her tones. "You who have been so cold, so unimpressionable. You seem transformed."

"I am," asserted the girl with a deep breath. "I don't know why it does not seem unmaidenly to say it, but it does not. However, you alone will know. Even he shall not—ever. I turned the key for an instant, and let you look into the secret place of my soul. I now turn back the key, and—we will forget."

"No, we never will forget, dearest," replied her mother.

"You have suffered alone, but this glimpse of your struggle
has brought us very close. I—I saw in you, at that moment,
the exact semblance of your father. Not for the world would
I shut you from a happiness as great as was my own with
him."

"Then you will not oppose me if I wish to join Mrs.
Bucklain in her work of caring and providing for the
soldiers?" Beatrice pleaded, kneeling down impulsively at
her mother's feet. "She is on the point now of leaving for
Tampa. If the army moves into Cuba, she and her aids are
to go."

"I not only will not oppose you, but I will accompany
you," decided Mrs. Warrington. "You are not the sole
individual who yearns to be of service in this hour."

Calm, cool Beatrice threw her arms about her mother
enthusiastically.

"Three cheers for 'The Red, White, and Blue'!" she cried
delightedly. "We will go to the front! We will fight if
need be—and we will pray that those we love may be kept
safe from harm."

And those for whom she prayed were bending every
energy toward the rescue they had planned. But days and
weeks crept by before the hour arrived when they could
make the contemplated assault upon the city.

The rainy season begun. The American warships were
before Santiago. The hearts of the patriots beat high with
hope. That for which Cuba had fought and bled seemed
within reach at last.

The Cubans were closing in upon the southern stronghold to aid the American troops there landed. But Zuñega's
force and that of Manuel Heredia tarried in the vicinity of
San Juan to co-operate with the Americans who had come
in on the north coast escorting an expedition which had
been safely guided into the mountains to those most in need
of ammunition.

On a night when heavy clouds obscured the moon, the
attacking forces moved in upon the city from four points.
Manuel Heredia from the west with his trained blacks;
Zuñega from the east with Raquel by Lithgow's side riding
eagerly to the battle which was meant to give once more
to her father the sunshine of liberty. Up from the south
stole a stalwart band of Cubans, absenting themselves tem-
porarily from the siege against Santiago. And from the

north, a company of heroic men marching in order under the Stars and Stripes!

Soaked to the skin by the drenching rain which had been falling for hours, the American soldiers followed their guides with an ardor that did not diminish. They had brought to the men from the field fresh details of the victory at Manila and the departure of troops for the Philippines. And the wine of pure patriotism stung in their blood and made strong the cry: "Remember the Maine!"

Through the thick pall of the darkness shot vivid flames of venomous lightning. Forked tongues of fire appeared to run down the mountain slopes. Nature herself seemed desirous of protecting them; for they were able to creep stealthily upon the town under cover of constant cannon-ading of heaven's artillery. The furious storm had made the Spaniards less alert. Some had forsaken their posts. Meeting less resistance than they had expected, the Cubans and Americans burst in on the city like a West Indian tornado, traveling hand in hand with the phantom of Night.

Startled from sleep, San Juan leaped to defend itself. Its guns roared forth unavailingly. The foe already was within, warring hand to hand in an effort to capture the arsenal.

Wild and desperate was the battle in the dense gloom. The Spaniards, bewildered by the fierceness of what appeared to be a vast horde of demons rending the night air with unfamiliar war-cries, fought with what spirit was theirs; but it counted for little against the impetuous rush and daring of the men they encountered.

The first intimation that they were contending with men from the north came in a shout which rose above the din of battle: "Death to the Americanos!" It woke a savage fury that prolonged the conflict till day.

The gray tints of the dawn revealed that the streets were filled with the wounded and dead. The stones were red with blood. The Spanish had been overpowered by the united forces which sought to avenge not the heroes of the Maine so much as the thousands of starved babes and mothers whose lives were offered up for Cuba as certainly as if they had died with sword in hand.

Raquel had been in the thick of the fray, despite Lithgow's entreaties. The thought of her father urged her on through the frightful scene. She was seeking Gonzalo Alarcon. In the weird light of daybreak, she found herself face to face with him.

"Gonzalo Alarcon, you are my prisoner!" she shouted with triumph.

Under the accusing hatred of her beautiful eyes, the man of many crimes cowered for the first time in his daring life.

"You, señorita?" he exclaimed incredulously.

"Yes; it is I, come to avenge my father!" she answered, all the anguish of her heart breaking irresistibly through her voice. "Take him to the dungeon!" she ordered her men. "His own hands shall unlock the chains which bind Gilbert Palgrave."

Alarcon became dogged and defiant.

"You may kill me, but you never can make me free him," he swore savagely.

An unmistakable murmur of contempt arose from his own soldiers as well as from the victorious men. A bold fellow cried from among the ranks of prisoners :

"Señorita, if he who lies in the deep dungeon, chained to the south wall, be your father, I can tell you how to reach him. The key to his chains is in the possession of the commandante."

"Release him who has spoken!" ordered Zuñega.

The soldier stood forth, scornfully meeting Alarcon's venomous gaze.

"Though he has been appointed our superior, we bear him no love," declared the Spaniard fearlessly. "If you shoot him, let it be as he has shot our prisoners—at sunrise—in the back. If you chain him, I myself will come, if I may, and return to him the kicks he has given dying men, hoping thus to convince us of his fealty to the mother land. All of us are Spaniards, señorita, and are proud so to be, but not all of us are traitorous devils! And we have learned some lessons in this island:—its rebels die like heroes."

A tremendous cheer burst from the Cuban and American throats, and to this tribute from soldier to soldier the Spanish prisoners of war added their echo.

Quivering with hot but impotent rage, Alarcon stared fascinatedly at the imposing form of Zuñega. He recognized him, yet was unwilling to believe his eyes. Here, in the attitude of the conqueror, was the youth who nobly had robbed him of both ransom and Raquel. Awful had been the oaths he had taken in revenge ; now, not only was he powerless to fulfill them, but he found himself at the mercy of the man he had sworn to kill.

"*Buenos dias*, Alarcon," saluted Zuñega with mock deference. "Is not he a wise man who prefers death to dishonor? To be hung as a brigand is one death to avoid—if one can; to be hung as a traitor is a less desirable ending. Your fate I place in Faquita's hands. I have promised it her for the work she has done for the cause of Free Cuba."

"Faquita!" foamed Alarcon fiercely. I would——"

"Ah, you would have stabbed me in your anger," declared Faquita, as she stepped aggravatingly before him. "But all you have been able to do was to make plans that I joyfully defeated. When you became a traitor I became a patriot. In memory of other days, I petitioned Zuñega to save your life; but now—it has no value for me."

She turned on her heel with affected indifference, but Raquel saw that her eyes were full of bitter tears.

"Take him to the dungeon!" ordered Zuñega.

The heavily barred doors were swung wide that those who crouched within might come forth. But such action was beyond their powers. Strong arms would be needed to carry them to the light and the air of freedom.

The stench of the underground prison was so foul that the liberating party staggered back, choked by its poison.

There was a period during which strenuous efforts were made to keep Raquel from entering.

"Surely I can live for a moment where he has lived for months!" she cried passionately. "I will enter. Death could not deter me from reaching him now!"

But her face was white with grief, and her heart stood still.

"Papa! Papa!" she called through the fetid atmosphere. "It is I—Raquel. I have come to save you!"

A low moan of agony came through the gloom.

"Raquel!" it cried with unutterable pathos. "Is this his last stab? Tired of you, my poor darling, he brings you here to share this awful hole! If he would kill us both, it would be merciful."

Through the breast of every listener the wail of paternal grief penetrated like a knife. Each shivered in the presence of this frightful sorrow which Alarcon's heartlessness had caused.

"I have not come to share your dungeon, but to free you from its chains," triumphantly rang Raquel's tones. "The Americanos have landed in Cuba! We have taken the town; the Spaniards are our prisoners. Alarcon himself shall loosen your irons."

"Let not that—devil—come near me!" pleaded the plaintive voice of the captive.

"He shall not touch you!" declared Lithgow vehemently. "No hands but those of love shall give you liberty!"

With Lithgow at her left and the Spanish soldier acting as guide on the right, Raquel found her way through the indescribable horrors of the place to the side of her father.

Chained to the floor, he dazedly received the emancipation which came in the clasp of his daughter's arms, the tearful pressure of her face.

"Since the moment you were carried from me I have worked with this hope," she sobbed. "Alone I could never have accomplished it; but Lithgow and Zuñega have done what I could not."

"Lithgow and Zuñega?" he repeated. "Then—what Alarcon told me was—not true? Oh, thank God! I thought you were—in his power; and I have died a thousand deaths because of your unhappy fate."

"Alarcon has never seen me since the attack," she explained as she caressed him. "But I have fought in the field and have been under the protection of—my husband, Lithgow."

"Lithgow?" he questioned as, weak and trembling with excitement, he folded her in arms which vainly had ached for revenge. "I can not comprehend."

"But years lie ahead of us in which we will relate all that has happened," prophesied Lithgow hopefully. "Years during which Cuba will show the world she is capable of self-government."

Gonzalo Alarcon, in the grasp of his jailers, turned his head away as the emaciated form of his victim was borne past him in the American's pitying arms. All the remorse and physical agony to which he might be doomed could not equal the acute shame of that moment when he encountered Raquel's vengeful eyes for the last time.

Then, shorn of his uniform, he was dragged through the filth of the dungeon to the spot where the irons lay waiting.

The hands that locked them on him were Zuñega's.

"When Cuba is free, General Gomez himself shall decide the measure of your punishment," said the conqueror. "Until then—I will wear the key to your chains. A quick death would be too merciful; it shall be years in coming if I have my way."

Without the prison, Manuel Heredia stood before Pepita de Urquiza.

"It will be impossible for you to remain here, Señora,"

he was saying. "After conveying the ammunition from the arsenal into the hands of those who stand waiting, we mean to destroy the fortifications and return to our posts. Where go you next?"

"Toward Santiago; my work is finished here. They will need nurses in the field."

"You shall not venture there!" he declared. "You—I—I will not permit you to imperil yourself further. You have done so too long."

"But it is not your right to dictate," she said softly.

"Make it my right!" he cried daringly. "I have loved you for years—hopelessly, it seemed. Be kind to me now! Here—to-night—let the padre speak his blessing above us. Pepita, I love you! Be my wife?"

"But the wife of Manuel Heredia must work no less for Cuba," stipulated Pepita, after a time. "If my services as a spy are no longer required, I insist on being allowed to nurse our heroes. Let me go with you to Santiago."

"It shall be so," he agreed. "There will be American heroes to nurse as well as Cubans."

Pepita's eyes dimmed with quick sympathy.

"Ah, the mother hearts of America!" she sighed. "They are giving their dearest that we may gain liberty. Was ever such love shown!"

"It marks an era!" said Manuel Heredia solemnly. "Never before in the history of the world has there been so vicarious an offering on the altar of Freedom."

And the fierce battles which followed proved the verity of Heredia's words, as the Americans fought to establish peace and liberty in the war-scarred island.

After conveying the feeble frame of Gilbert Palgrave to a hospital retreat which would be safe from Spanish butchery, both the Cuban and American soldiers moved southward rapidly to reinforce the troops landing near Santiago de Cuba.

And they were none too soon.

The American marines at Guantanamo had defended valiantly the Stars and Stripes which they had planted; and the precious blood of heroes had made sacred to American hearts the soil of Cuba. To supplement the little invading party which had held its own so well, a vanguard of three thousand of General Shafter's army was put ashore at Baiquiri. These soldiers found themselves reinforced by a thousand Cubans who seemed to spring out of the ground at the proper moment to attack the Spaniards. Among these

Cubans were Zuñega, Lithgow, and Manuel Heredia, their knowledge of English being scarcely less valuable than their familiarity with the forest. Superb was the fervor with which their forces led the way, receiving the deadliest fire from the ambushed Spaniards. Cuban heroism won bitter reward, for over the dead and dying bodies of those who struggled for freedom, the American troops were forced to pass: as, maddened by this awful slaughter, they pushed forward steadily, relentlessly, in the face of a storm of bullets that mutilated like knives and mowed down as a blast from hell.

Suffocating with the terrible heat of the tropical sun, their flesh torn by the thorns of the dense underbrush, their tongues swollen and parched with thirst, the brave boys of the Northland rushed on. Those who fell wounded to the death urged with their last breath their comrades forward to achieve the lofty purpose for which they had been sent. And nothing but this—the righting of grievous wrongs—could have spurred men to win what they won that day.

When the Spanish had abandoned their position, retreating ignominiously before the advancing soldiers, who fought not with Apache methods but according to military rule, those able to do so immediately sought out the wounded and dead.

Almost the first face which Lithgow turned up compassionately was that of one of his own friends, a New Yorker, a millionaire youth whose movements had been of interest to two continents. Inexpressibly pained he staggered backward, but it was no moment for woe. He was destined to find many he knew among these gallant "rough riders" recruited from the first and wealthiest families of America. Pale and stern, he grew to rejoice that their blood had been shed in so noble a cause, and he thrilled with the thought that he looked upon the faces of those who would go down canonized in American history, but he sensed the horrible meaning of war as he had not been able to do before.

There were cases where his services were of value, but it seemed to him that where he loved most, hope was vain. All he could do was to cover them mercifully from the burning rays of the pitiless sun; and, later, to lay them sorrowfully to rest beneath Mother Earth.

It was when he was thus engaged that two soldiers approached with a wounded Cuban.

Lithgow uttered a cry of grief:

"Zuñega!"

But Zuñega heard no voice. He had been among those who first fell, and he had lain long in the scorching sun.

Trembling with fear lest it be too late, Lithgow summoned aid, and, as soon as was practicable, had him removed to the hospital ship, and from there the son of two nations was taken to Guantanamo, where the Red Cross Society had been established. That he was being sent into the hands of Beatrice Warrington, Lithgow little dreamed. But it was so.

And when the hour came that Zuñega looked out upon the world again and knew her, he tried to place his remaining hand over on her tender fingers which had nursed him back to life.

"Could you care for one—so changed?" he whispered.

And Beatrice adjusted the bandages on the torn right shoulder and answered softly:

"To me, you are not changed. You have gained, not lost. You are one of Cuba's heroes, and—though you never again can carry a gun or fight for her—she will need such as you to guide and govern her when she is free."

"And will you be—my right arm?" he asked wistfully.

And there was no need for reply.

Though her fair face flushed, Beatrice met his appealing eyes with love voiced in her own; then, she bent her golden head swiftly and touched her pure lips to his brow.

www.ingramcontent.com/pod-product-compliance
Lightning Source LLC
Chambersburg PA
CBHW032008120726
47902CB00014B/1429